The Play Maker

STEPHANIE ALVES

Editing: Wonder and Wander Editing Co.
Cover designer: Claudia Bonet

ISBN: 978-1-917180-17-7

This book contains detailed sexual content and graphic language.
You can see the full list of content warnings on my website here: stephaniealvesauthor.com

Happy Reading!

Also by Stephanie Alves

Standalone

Love Me or Hate Me
Holly's Jolly Christmas
Strictly Business

Campus Games Series

Never Have I Ever (Book #1)
Spin The Bottle (Book #2)
Would You Rather (Book #3)
Truth Or Dare (Book #4)
The Final Game (Book 4.5)

Colton U Playbook Series

The Rule Breaker (Book #1)

Playlist

- ▶ **The Risk**
  Gracie Abrams

- ▶ **Late Night Talking**
  Harry Styles

- ▶ **Close To You**
  Gracie Abrams

- ▶ **In Between**
  Gracie Abrams

- ▶ **Ceilings**
  Lizzy McAlpine

- ▶ **Out Of My League**
  Fitz And The Tantrums

- ▶ **Daylight**
  Taylor Swift

- ▶ **Oh Shit... Are We In Love?**
  Valley

- ▶ **The Blue**
  Gracie Abrams

- ▶ **Beautiful**
  Bazzi, Camila Cabello

- ▶ **Packing It Up**
  Gracie Abrams

- ▶ **Delicate**
  Taylor Swift

- ▶ **Feels Like**
  Gracie Abrams

- ▶ **You Are In Love**
  Taylor Swift

- ▶ **POV**
  Ariana Grande

- ▶ **The Only Exception**
  Paramore

For every big girl who's been told she's only a side character or belongs in the background—fuck that. You are the main character, and don't let anyone tell you otherwise.

ONE

Austin

I've made a lot of bad decisions in my life, but thinking I could wing this class might be the dumbest one yet.

"You gave me an F?"

Professor Carlisle peers up at me over his thick-rimmed glasses, one bushy brow already halfway to his hairline.

"You left the last three pages completely blank," he says, his brow climbing even higher. It freaks me out—looks like a baby caterpillar trying to crawl off his face. "You're lucky you even got a grade."

I scrub a hand down my face. "C'mon, sir. You know if I fail, I'll get benched."

He lets out a sigh, his fingers hovering over the keyboard for a second, before he starts typing again. "I'm sorry, Mr. Rhodes, but I don't give special treatment to anyone." He stops typing. Squints at me. "And that includes you and every other athlete on this campus."

My mind spins faster than my skates on the ice. Fuck. Fuck. *Fuck*. This can't be happening. If I get suspended from the team, my life is basically over. Hockey is the only thing I'm good at, the one thing that keeps my brain from spiraling into overthinking hell.

"Please," I beg, leaning over his desk, trying not to sound desperate, even though I totally am. "I'll do extra credit. I'll take the test again or—"

He removes his glasses, sets them down, and lets out another long sigh. "I told you already, Mr. Rhodes. No special treatment. You can't take the test again, though I'll be honest, I doubt it would make a difference."

He shakes his head, his disappointment practically radiating off him. Yeah, I'm disappointed in myself too… *trust me*.

"Look," he says, leaning back in his chair, arms folding over the worn tweed of his jacket. "The only thing you can do now is study. Actually study the material, and I have no doubt that you'll pass next time. But that's up to you and whether you're willing to put in the work or not."

Fuck. I run a hand through my hair, tugging at the strands in frustration. He doesn't fucking get it. I try. I try every single day to make sense of the stupid fucking words on the paper. And I can't. No matter what I do, it just doesn't click.

My jaw tightens. My body locks up. My chest feels like it's about to explode. Blood's pumping in my ears, making my head spin. I hate myself so much right now.

"So, there's nothing I can do?" I ask again, trying to stay calm, but the desperation creeps in my tone. I don't want special treatment. I just want… a chance. A shot to prove myself. To stay on the team. To keep my scholarship. To not blow the one thing I'm good at.

Professor Carlisle presses his lips together. "You could get a tutor," he suggests. "Maybe working with someone else will help you actually understand the material, instead of spending your weekends at the bar."

I slump. Yeah, he's right. I don't study nearly as much as I should. Instead, I party. Because studying is boring as hell, and my brain refuses to do anything that doesn't involve a puck or a shot of whiskey.

"A tutor?" I repeat.

He nods, keeping his eyes on his desk as he packs his stuff away. "Head down to the tutoring center and have a look. Maybe one of them will be able to help you." He finally glances up at me, pushing his glasses up his nose. "Though personally, I suggest Maisie Wilson. She's got a solid track record and happens to have a spot available."

He stands up, grabbing his bag and giving me a pointed look. "Now, if that's all, you can go. Class was dismissed ten minutes ago."

I blow out a breath, and turn around, heading up the stairs. I push the door open and step out into the hallway, feeling like I just got kicked in the nuts.

Great. Now I've got to track down this Maisie person. I've never heard of her, and I know a lot of women on campus.

Fuck, I hate asking for help. It's about as comfortable as walking naked into a lecture hall. It's humiliating. Embarrassing. It's—

I dig my phone out of my jeans and fire off a quick text.

Me: Confession. I fucking hate asking for help.

I hit send, leaning against the wall, my thumb hovering as I wait for the dots to pop up, though she might not answer right away. No clue what she's doing right now. Is she in bed? In class? Out with her friends? With a boyfriend?

I know next to nothing about her. Not her real name, not what school she goes to, not even what she looks like. And yet, somehow, we've been texting every day since that first message she sent me.

I scroll up, finding it easily.

Unknown: I'm going to kill someone.

I remember blinking at my screen like an idiot when I first read it.

Me: I'm scared to ask who this is.
Me: But also very curious.
Unknown: Bailey?
Me: Wrong number.

That should have been the end of it. A normal person would have said "oops, my bad" and moved on. But not her.

Unknown: Oh. I guess you won't help me hide the body then.
Me: Are you joking or should I be concerned right now?
Unknown: Relax. It's a hypothetical murder.
Me: Good. For a second I thought I was gonna have to turn you in.
Unknown: Right. Because if I were actually a murderer, I'd totally text a confession to a random number.

I snorted so hard I almost choked on my protein shake. And before I knew it, we were still texting an hour later.
Then the next day.
And the next.
And somehow, two weeks later, I was still texting her.

It wasn't just jokes anymore. We talked about real shit. Stupid childhood stories. Late-night confessions. Things we'd never admitted to anyone else.

But the one thing she refused to tell me? Her name.

I scroll down a little more, finding the texts.

Me: We've been talking for a whole week now and you still won't tell me your name?

Unknown: Nope.

Me: I feel like I deserve it at this point.

Unknown: You can call me Cherry.

Me: Cherry?

Cherry: Yep. That's the name I'm going with.

Me: Any particular reason?

Cherry: I like cherries.

Me: Solid reasoning. I feel like I should have a cool nickname too.

Cherry: You should.

Me: Alright. Call me Six.

Cherry: Six?

Me: Yep. That's the name I'm going with.

Cherry: Any particular reason?

Me: I like the number six.

Cherry: Wow. Solid reasoning.

I smirked at my phone, having way too much fun with a complete stranger.

Cherry: Okay, Six. Let's agree to keep this anonymous, okay? No real names. No details about our lives. No pictures. Just confessions.

I agreed at the time, thinking it was funny. Mysterious. Like something out of a cheesy chick-flick I loved watching every now and again—blame my thirteen-year-old sister for getting me hooked.

But now? Weeks later? I hate it.

I don't want anonymous. I want to know who the hell she is.

My phone vibrates and I glance down at the screen when I see her reply.

Cherry: Me too. It makes me feel like I'm a helpless child.

A grin tugs at my lips as I type out a reply.

I rewrite it three times before finally hitting send. Still looks wrong, though.

I hate texting. Always feel like I'm spelling shit wrong. I probably am. Which is why I use voice-to-text half the time whenever I text her. I don't want her to think I'm stupid like everyone else. So I spend extra time trying to get my words right, the punctuation and all that crap.

Me: Exactly. I just want to be able to do shit on my own. I don't want to embarrass myself in front of some stranger I barely know.

Cherry: Well, as a stranger you kinda know… I would have been more than happy to help you out with whatever it is you needed.

I exhale, rubbing the back of my neck. Because it always comes to this.

I want to meet her. I want to see her.

And she won't let me.

She thinks anonymity is what makes this work. That once we meet, it'll lose the charm of not knowing who the other is and we'll get bored, and eventually stop talking.

I don't agree.

Not knowing just makes me want to find her.

Me: Hate that you can't.

I pocket my phone and head toward the rink, spotting Ryan sucking face with Isabella outside the arena. I shake my head, laughing under my breath. Coach hates catching them making out, so they always get their fill before stepping inside.

The guy's an idiot for messing around with Coach's daughter, who also happens to be Nathan's sister. But I guess when it comes to her, he really doesn't give a fuck.

As soon as I step inside, the cold air hits me, and I take a deep breath. Smells like home. Like ice, sweat, and the faint, weirdly comforting scent of Zamboni fuel.

I glance toward the ice, watching some of the figure skaters still practicing. My eyes track a few of them, noticing their moves. It's kinda cool. They're like us in a way, skating in circles, pushing themselves, but they do it with way more grace. If a hockey player tried that shit, we'd faceplant in two seconds.

Except for me, of course. I'm awesome at tricks.

A hard slap lands on my shoulder, knocking me out of my thoughts.

"You good, buddy?" Nathan smirks down at me.

I groan, turning toward the locker room. "Not fucking good at all."

I push open the door, spotting the guys already inside gearing up and I put on my playlist, ready to get hyped for practice.

"What's wrong?" Nathan follows, narrowing his eyes. "Don't tell me you got someone pregnant."

"What?" I scoff. "Hell no. I wrap my shit up."

Ryan snorts from his locker. "Glad to hear it."

"So, what's the problem?" Nathan asks.

I drop onto the bench, kicking off my shoes and pulling on my pads. "Failed Anatomy."

The room goes dead silent.

I glance up. Every single one of them is staring at me like I just admitted to murder.

"You're fucking with us, right?" Ryan asks. "Please tell me this is one of your weird jokes I don't get."

"He's not kidding," Cole chimes in, popping his gum. "Look at his face."

I sigh. "Wish I was."

Nathan frowns. "Then why the hell are you getting into gear? No way Coach lets you play if he finds out."

"Yeah, yeah, don't put that bad energy out there." I wave my hands through the air, physically shooing away his negativity. "I passed the rest of my classes." *Barely*. "It's just one. One stupid class. All I need is a tutor, and Coach will never know."

They shake their heads, glancing away as they finish gearing up.

I drop onto the bench, pull on my skates, and lace them up tight.

"Alright you guys, I'm counting on you."

I kiss my fingers, then press them against my skates. The guys don't even blink. We're all superstitious as hell, and the first time I got a hat trick, I was nervous as fuck and randomly did this before the game. So yeah, now it's stuck.

If only it worked for school. Speaking of which—

I glance up, scanning the room. "Hey, anyone here know a Maisie Wilson?"

"Never heard of her," Nathan says, shaking his head.

"Me either," Ryan adds.

I groan, dragging a hand down my face, shutting my music off. "How the hell am I supposed to find this girl when no one knows who she is?"

Cole arches his brow as he steps past me, already fully geared up. "Better find her, or you're a dead man."

Logan sighs. "Hate to agree with him, but yeah, you're screwed, bud."

I turn to Nathan and Ryan, but their matching expressions don't exactly fill me with confidence.

I tip my head back, squeezing my eyes shut. "Fuck," I grit out.

Ryan stands, his helmet tucked under his arm. "See you out there."

"If he plays," Nathan adds as Ryan walks out.

My eyes snap to his, and I put on my best puppy dog face.

Nathan recoils. "The fuck are you doing? You look creepy as hell. Cut that shit out."

I drop the act with a sigh. "Can you talk to Coach? Daddy-son privileges and all that?"

Nathan makes a gagging sound. "First of all, never say "daddy-son" ever again. Second, that's not how it works. On the ice, I'm just another player. Not his son."

I grunt, yanking my jersey over my head and push open the door. "He won't know I failed if none of you fucking talk," I say, bumping Nathan's shoulder as we leave the locker room. "Just don't say anything, and it'll be fine."

Nathan shakes his head. "I hope you're right."

Fucking hell. I hope I'm right too. Hope the guys are all wrong, hope Coach doesn't find out, hope I can still play, hope—

"Rhodes," Coach's voice booms from across the rink. "Where the hell are you going?"

Both me and Nathan freeze at the sound of Coach's voice. He's standing there, arms crossed, eyes narrowed, and that godawful whistle of his dangling from his neck.

"Well, I was going to practice, but if you wanna go on a date, you need to ask first, Coach," I joke, throwing him a wink.

He does not appreciate it. At all.

Ah, well. Win some, lose some. As long as he lets me play, I'll cut the jokes out altogether… Alright, maybe not *altogether*, but I'll tone it down. I'll do whatever I have to do to get on the ice.

Coach doesn't say a word, just points behind him to the rink. "Nathan, get on the ice."

Fuck. *Not* a good sign.

Stay calm. Maybe he just wants to talk. Maybe he wants me to give him sex advice or something. His wife is hot as hell, and I doubt he's putting in the work to keep her satisfied.

"Good talk," I say, flashing a smile as I place my helmet on, tapping my head. "I'm ready to practice, Coach. Lemme just—"

"No."

The single word stops me cold.

"You're suspended."

My stomach plummets into my ass. No. No. No. This can't be fucking happening.

"Suspended?" I shake my head. "But—"

"I got the email from your professor. You failed, and that brought your grade average way down. You know the rules. You don't play if you don't pass your tests."

"What? Come *on*. Anatomy is fucking bullshit. I don't need to learn that to play."

"I'd disagree," he says with a shrug, his hard-ass face still perfectly in place. "And so would your professor. You're on the bench until you get your shit together."

"But—" I throw my hand toward the ice. "I'm the best center you've got. Who the hell is gonna replace me?"

"Jenkins," Coach barks, keeping his eyes on me. "On the ice."

The rookie freshman stands up, wide-eyed. "Me?" he asks, pointing to his chest like he's shocked someone knows his name.

Coach pinches the bridge of his nose and lets out an exasperated sigh. "Yes, you. Get on the ice. Now."

"Are you fucking kidding me?" I shout, throwing my arms up. "You're putting a rookie on instead of me? C'mon, Coach. You know I want this. I've been busting my ass for this team!"

He sighs, shakes his head, and for a split second, I swear there's a hint of sympathy in his eyes. But then it's gone. "Apparently not enough. Sorry, but you know the rules." He shoves a water bottle into my hands. "You want back on the ice? Chill out, hit the books, and you'll be back in no time."

With that, he turns and heads toward the rink, blowing that fuckass whistle I hear in my nightmares.

I exhale a heavy breath, rip off my helmet and skates, and toss them onto the ground. Sinking into a seat, I bury my face in my hands. God, I'm such a screw-up. I feel like a walking failure. A goddamn idiot. Dumb. Lazy. Selfish. Should've never skipped that lecture on muscles and bones or whatever shit Professor bushy brows was teaching.

"Dude, are you crying?"

I peek through my fingers to see Cole standing with his helmet under his arm.

"Get fucked."

He scoffs, raising an eyebrow. "We told you this would happen, genius."

I tilt my head, resisting the urge to throw something at him. "Yeah, I got it. Anything else you wanna rub in while you're at it?"

He pops his gum. "Better start getting comfy on the bleachers."

I narrow my eyes, grab my water bottle, and chuck it at him. Of course, the bastard dodges it, and it sails past him, slamming into the back of the bleachers.

"Ah!"

My eyes widen at the sound of a girl's voice crying out in pain.

"Oh, fuck," I mutter, quickly jumping to my feet and shoving Cole out of the way. I rush over to the girl who's holding her head, looking like she's about to pass out.

"Shit. I'm so fucking sorry," I say, kneeling next to her. "I didn't mean to hit you."

She groans, which… good sign, I guess. Means she's alive, and I didn't just take someone out with a damn water bottle. Silver linings.

"You okay?" I ask. *Stupid question, Austin*. Of course she's not okay. You nailed her in the head like an absolute dumbass.

Cole crosses his arms behind me. "Going on a violent streak, Rhodes?"

I groan. "Just—get Coach or something. She's not answering me, and I don't know if I gave her a concussion or blinded her or deafened her or… whatever the fuck else."

He sighs and heads off, and I hesitate before reaching out to touch her. Probably a bad idea. She might not appreciate the guy who knocked her out with a bottle trying to pat her on the head like a dog.

"Hey… can you hear me?" I try again. "Are you blind? Deaf? Did I break something? Jesus, I swear I didn't mean

to—"

"God, just… stop talking," she mutters, rubbing her head. "I'm fine."

My shoulders drop. "Alright. Can you move your hands, though? Just so I can see for myself?"

She lets out another groan but finally pulls them away, and I scan her head for bumps, bruises, or anything out of place. Her dark brown hair is still in a sleek bun, not a single strand loose, which is kinda impressive considering I hit her in the head. No blood. No giant lump. So far, so good.

And then she looks up. Blinks at me.

And holy shit.

I've seen blue eyes before. Plenty of them. But *hers*? They're something else. Not just blue. They're light, clear, the kind of blue that makes you forget what the hell you were just saying. The overhead lights catch them, turning them almost electric, like the damn sky cracked open just for me.

My brain completely short-circuits.

I definitely concussed myself in this whole process. No other explanation.

She winces, pressing her fingers to her forehead again, but my brain is still buffering, stuck on her eyes. Can't look away from them.

I snap myself out of it because, oh yeah, I *hit her in the head*.

"Are you sure you're okay?" I ask. "I can take you to the campus doctor. Or, like, pay for one myself. I don't mind. I just—"

"Can you—" She lifts a hand, stopping me mid-ramble. Then she looks at me again, and my chest fucking tightens. "Just… *shhhh*," she mutters, closing her eyes. "I just need a minute."

I shut up instantly, watching as she takes a deep breath.

Her lips part on a breath, and my gaze drags down, catching the way her pink jacket hugs every curve, her leggings stretched over thick thighs. One foot is still strapped into a scuffed white skate, the other bare, resting on the ground.

She must have been taking her skates off when I nailed her in the head.

The girl lifts her head with a sigh, and our eyes meet again. And *fuck me*. It should be illegal to have eyes that distracting. I don't know if it's the contrast against her dark brown hair or just some kind of witchcraft, but they're unreal. Siren-level hypnotic. The kind that could probably convince me to do something really fucking stupid.

Not that I need much help in that department.

"You can go now," she says, completely unimpressed.

My brows shoot up, but before I can respond, Coach's voice cuts through my soul like a goddamn executioner. "He's not going anywhere."

Jesus Christ. First, I fail my class, get benched, and now I've apparently decided to start assaulting innocent women with water bottles. Today is not my fucking day.

Coach stomps over, staring me down. "What the hell did you do to the girl, Rhodes?"

I lift my hands in surrender. "I didn't mean to. I was pissed at Cole, threw a water bottle, and——"

"Are you five years old?" He rubs his temples. "Christ. Did you at least apologize?"

"Yes," I say, nodding aggressively. "Multiple times. She told me to shut up."

Coach scoffs. "She did what all of us want to do." He faces her, his expression softening a fraction. "Are you okay? Do you need me to call a doctor?"

She shakes her head, glancing up at him. "I'm okay."

I narrow my eyes. "Are you sure? Do you remember your name? That's a sign of a concussion, you know. You might want to——"

"I *know* my name," she interrupts, those blue eyes cutting through me. "It's Maisie."

My shoulders relax. "Oh. Okay. Good."

Then the name actually registers, and I blink, a lightbulb practically flashing above my head. "Wait. *Maisie*?" I ask. "As in Maisie Wilson?"

She nods warily. "Yeah… how do you know that?"

I let out a bitter laugh, shaking my head. "The universe is fucking with me today, I swear." I glance down at her—the girl who can literally save my ass. "I've been looking for you."

Her brows furrow. "You have?" she asks, skeptical as hell.

"Yeah. Professor Carlisle said I needed a tutor. Suggested you. But I had no idea who you were, so I've been——"

"Typical," she scoffs, rolling her eyes.

I blink. "Anyway… will you tutor me?"

Maisie tilts her head, giving me a once-over before flicking her eyes away. She grabs her other skate and stands, and that's when I notice just how short she is—gotta be a whole foot under my 6'3. Still manages to level me with that unimpressed stare, though.

"My schedule is full," she says before she steps past me, heading down the hallway.

"Hey, wait up," I call out, jogging after her. "He said you had an opening."

"Not anymore," she says flatly, limping slightly as she walks, one skate still strapped to her foot, the other in her hand.

"C'mon," I groan. "Don't be like that. I apologized—a fuck ton—and you said you were fine."

"I am fine. Doesn't mean I want to tutor you."

"Why not?" I frown, genuinely confused.

She chuckles. It sounds bitter, but still a cute sound as she turns those way-too-blue eyes on me. *Jesus*. I don't think I'll ever get used to them. "I know who you are."

A grin spreads across my face. "Thank you."

"Wasn't a compliment," she replies dryly.

She turns, heading farther down the hall, and my grin falters.

"Wait. You're really not gonna tutor me?"

"Nope."

"Just because I hit you in the head by accident?"

"That has nothing to do with it. I just don't want to. That's the good thing about free will." She tosses me one last glance. "Are you going to follow me into the locker room, or can I get changed?"

I slow to a stop, watching as she pushes the door open and disappears inside.

Fuck. She was my one shot at getting back on the ice, and I fucking blew it—again.

With my tail tucked between my legs, I trudge back toward the rink, where Coach is watching me.

"She okay?" he asks.

I nod. "Yeah. She just went to get changed."

He grunts in acknowledgment, then blows his whistle, making the guys switch directions. I sigh, dragging myself to the bleachers, my gaze flicking toward where Maisie had been sitting.

That's when I spot something on the ground.

I frown, pushing up from my seat and walking over. Bending down, I pick up a small, familiar rectangle. An *iPod*.

Who the hell still uses an iPod?

Flipping it over, I see the back is covered in tiny stickers, mostly music-related, a few figure skating related ones and one that just says *fuck off* in pretty cursive. Huh. Seems fitting.

I clutch it in my hand, my lips tipping up into a smirk.

Guess I have a reason to talk to her again.

And convince her to tutor me.

TWO

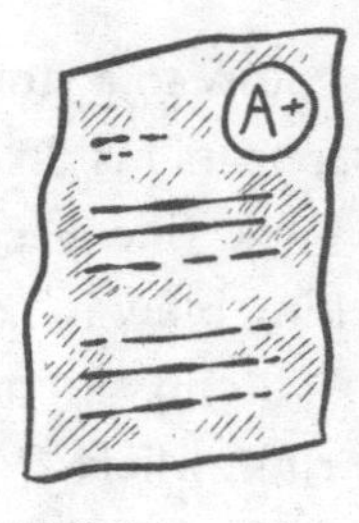

Maisie

I'm in love with someone who doesn't exist.

Alright, he does exist. I just don't know who he is.

And I guess I'm not in *love* with him. But I like him… a lot.

Which is kind of ridiculous, considering I don't even know what he looks like. I don't know his name, or if he even goes to the same school as me.

I guess I don't need to know in this little space we've created. There are no expectations, no awkward small talk, no pretending to be someone I'm not. Just endless conversations with someone who somehow always knows exactly what to say.

Maybe it's because he's one of the very, *very* few people I talk to. Or maybe it's because we spend every free second texting.

Which is why I almost trip on my way to my seat.

Too busy staring at my phone, waiting for his reply, I miss the step and twist my ankle like an idiot as I stumble forward.

A few girls giggle, whispering to each other, and I let out a sigh, gripping my phone as I sink into my usual spot—by the exit, at the top, where no one ever goes and no one ever bothers me.

Placing my bag on the ground, I pull out my laptop, and set it up before grabbing my phone and scrolling back to the text Six sent me.

Six: Burgers or pizza.
Six: Beware. I will judge you on your answer.

I let out a quiet laugh and type back.

Me: Burgers. Any day. And if you disagree, I think we can no longer be friends.

I check the time. Still ten minutes until class starts.
Out of habit, I send a quick text to Bailey.

Me: College sucks. I don't recommend it.

She probably won't see it. She's probably busy with her friends. But I still hit send, slip my phone into my pocket, and pull up my notes, determined to focus.

But then, of course, Austin Rhodes walks in.

Laughing, carefree with his friends, completely unaware of me—which is exactly how I want it.

But my stomach still twists at the memory of last week. My head still aches, and I swear there's a tiny bump where his stupid water bottle hit me. Not that I went to the doctor. Absolutely not.

They would've asked how it happened. I would've had to explain.

And I really don't want to see him again.

Which is why, when he walks into class, I try my absolute hardest to shrink into my seat and disappear. Not an easy task, considering I take up more space than the average girl.

Dipping my head only makes it worse, and sure enough, Austin's eyes land on me and widen in recognition.

"Maisie."

My name on his lips sends an involuntary shiver down my spine, and my stomach does this ridiculous little flutter thing that I immediately shut down.

I will *not* be one of those girls who blush and stare dreamily at Austin Rhodes. I refuse.

Rolling my eyes, I sit up straighter and glue my attention to my laptop, even though class hasn't even started yet. If I *look* busy, maybe he'll take the hint and—

Nope. A body drops into the seat beside me, the scent of a rich masculine cologne invading my space.

I chance a glance at him.

Of course, he's grinning at me.

"Nice to see you again," he says, leaning back in his chair.

"I can't say the same."

He chuckles, completely unbothered by my attempt to shut him down. "I didn't know you were in this class."

"Of course you didn't." I finally turn to face him, lifting a brow. *Why would he?* Austin Rhodes and I don't exactly run in the same circles. I've walked past him hundreds of times— practice, classes—and he's never noticed me before.

In his world, he's the golden boy of the hockey team, effortlessly cool, always surrounded by his usual type—girls who look like they walked off a magazine cover.

In mine, I sit alone at the top of the lecture hall, keeping to myself, headphones in, eyes down.

I don't exist in his world. And yet, here he is.

Austin presses his lips together and his gaze sharpens just a little. "Alright. You're still pissed about last week. Got it." He pulls something from his pocket, and my breath hitches.

My iPod.

The one I've been tearing my place apart in search of over the past few days—sitting there, casually, in his hand.

My mouth goes dry. I had seriously considered just accepting defeat and buying a new one. Turns out he's been walking around with it this whole time.

I sit up straighter, my pulse quickening as I stare at the iPod in his hands. "You… where did you—?"

"You left it at the rink," he says with a shrug. "Thought you might want it back." His fingers toy with the device. "I dig your playlists, by the way. I hope you don't mind, but I added a few songs of my own."

I blink, completely taken off guard. "I do mind," I say, irritation creeping into my voice. "I don't want you touching my stuff."

Austin just laughs, leaning back in his seat. "Well… too late for that, I'm afraid. You know what they say, right? Finders keepers, losers—"

"I won't be weeping," I snap, glaring at him. "What do you want an old iPod for anyway?"

He shrugs again, his lips twitching into a smirk. "Dunno. Gives me a reason to talk to you, I guess."

I scoff. "Seriously? You've resorted to flirting your way to an A?"

His cocky grin widens. "I mean, I'd be happy with a B, but I'll do what it takes to get it."

I roll my eyes, trying to mask the small flush creeping up my neck. I don't even want to play into whatever game he's trying to start. "Well, I'm not interested."

And neither is he. This flirting thing—whatever it is—has nothing to do with him actually liking me. It's all just part of his charm, the kind that works with everyone else. But I've been around the block enough to know that guys like Austin don't look twice at girls like me.

He's just using me. And I'm not going to let him.

"Ah, come on," he nudges my arm with his elbow, his cocky smile not budging. "Just a few tutoring sessions. I'm sure I'll get it down by then."

I take a deep breath, closing my laptop before turning fully toward him. "Listen, pretty boy. I know you're probably not used to being told 'no', so listen to me clearly. I am not interested in you or whatever this—" I wave my hand between us "—this flirting thing is. I'm not one of your puck bunnies, and I won't be drooling at the thought of spending time with you. So, I'm going to tell you this one last time. I do not want to tutor you. Goodbye."

When I'm done, I let out a harsh breath, noting his brows are slightly raised and his lips are parted in surprise. I don't really raise my voice, and maybe I was a little too harsh, but I wanted to make sure he understood that whatever he's trying to pull is not going to work on me.

But that shocked expression disappears almost instantly when he breaks into a smirk, revealing his perfect teeth. "You think I'm pretty?" he teases, his voice dripping with amusement.

I roll my eyes.

"And for the record," he says as he arches a brow, "I don't call them puck bunnies." He leans forward slightly. "I find it disrespectful and degrading. They're just women who are attracted to hockey players." He shrugs, flashing me a wink. "As are you, apparently."

I shoot him a glare. "Did you not hear me say I wasn't interested?"

He gives a slight nod, still smiling. "Loud and clear, blue eyes." He pauses, a mischievous gleam in his gaze. "I also heard you call me pretty, so that kind of cancels it out, doesn't it?"

I feel my skin heat, and I glare at him, biting back the urge to punch him in the arm. "Unbelievable," I mutter, shaking my head. "I'm not going to tutor you."

He points at me with a grin that only grows wider. "Yet?" he asks, his brows lifting in hope.

"Ever," I correct firmly, crushing that hope.

He shrugs. "Eh, I'm good at waiting."

"You'll be waiting a lifetime," I mutter under my breath, opening my laptop again, trying to focus on the lesson plan in front of me.

But I can still feel him next to me, his presence uncomfortably close. I let out an exasperated sigh before stealing a glance at him from the corner of my eye. "Are you going to stay here the whole lesson?"

He nods, his lips curling into a smile. "I like the view from here." He stretches his arm across the back of my seat. "Comfy," he adds, with a wink.

Dear god… Help me.

THREE

Austin

Tonight's already a shitshow, and I just walked through the door.

The place reeks of cheap beer and even cheaper cologne. Some guy's doing a keg stand in the kitchen, his face so red I half expect him to pass out. In the living room, a group of girls are playing beer pong against some frat guys.

Normally, this is my scene. The noise, the drunken fun, the dumbass decisions that'll be the highlight reel of practice on Monday. This is where I shine.

But tonight? Feels like I'm wading through wet cement.

Coach benched me. My grades are trash. My scholarship's hanging by a thread, all because I bombed a damn anatomy test. And now, instead of worrying about my next game, I get to spend next week in a meeting with my academic advisor, which is basically a formality before they slap me with academic probation. One more fuck-up, and my scholarship's gone. No hockey, no future, no nothing.

I shake it off. Not the time to think about it. Right now, I just need a drink.

"Austin!" Logan yells from across the room, already a few beers deep and standing on a chair—fuck knows why. "Look who finally decided to show up! Thought you were gonna flake, man."

I grab a beer and lift it in the air. "And miss this? This is my natural habitat."

Logan squints at me. "Yeah? Then why do you look like someone just kicked your dog?"

I smirk, letting out a laugh, even though it feels like someone just landed a slap shot straight to my gut. "Because my dog's named 'my hockey career,' and it's dying a slow, painful death. Thanks for asking."

Nathan slides up next to me. "You're being dramatic."

"Tell that to your dad. Pretty sure he's looking into getting "benchwarmer" stitched on the back of my jersey."

Logan snorts. "Maybe buy him some flowers—whisper sweet nothings about power plays in his ear."

I huff out a laugh, cracking open the beer. "Think he'd prefer red roses or a nice mixed bouquet?"

Nathan rolls his eyes. "You guys are idiots."

Maybe. But making jokes is easier than thinking about the fact that my entire hockey career is circling the drain.

I tip my head back, downing half the beer. It's warm and tastes like piss. Perfect. Nothing like a frat party to remind me that rock bottom has multiple levels.

"Austin!"

I barely have time to react before a girl steps into my space, glossy lips and a smirk that says she's here for a good time.

That's why I come to these things.

I shift gears, slipping into my usual role. Party guy. Fun guy. The guy who doesn't give a shit about anything other than the moment in front of him.

I flash her a grin and sling an arm around her shoulders. "Hey, babe."

She giggles, pressing a hand to my chest. "Didn't see you play this weekend." She pushes her lips into a pout. "Missed you out there."

And just like that, my stomach twists.

That's it, isn't it?

Hockey is the reason she's talking to me. It's always the reason.

Would she still be here, standing this close, looking at me like that, if I wasn't Austin Rhodes, hockey player? If I was just some random guy on campus, would I even exist to her?

Doubt it.

I force a smirk. "Yeah, well, Coach said I should focus on my classes." I roll my eyes, letting out a scoff. "Which is ridiculous, obviously. I'm basically the team's backbone. They're lost without me."

I sell the joke like I always do—cocky smirk, playful shrug—but my stomach twists as I say it. Because the team looked fine out there this weekend. More than fine. And I wasn't on the ice.

Do they even need me?

Does anyone?

She hums, tilting her head. "I don't know if I buy it." She steps closer, her sickly-sweet perfume flooding my nose. "Maybe you should prove it to me sometime... privately."

That should snap me out of this funk. Should boost my ego. Should remind me that, hockey or not, I've still got it.

Instead, my phone buzzes.

And suddenly, I don't care about the girl in front of me anymore.

I pull it out, glancing at the notification.

Cherry: Confession: I hate parties.

A slow grin tugs at my lips.

"I'll catch you later, yeah?" I say, already stepping back. She blinks, surprised, but I don't wait for a response. I'm already ducking into the hallway, leaning against the wall as I open our texts.

Me: Confession: I officially think you're crazy.
Cherry: So dramatic.
Me: How can you not like parties?

Also, does this mean she's at a party right now?

My phone stays in my hand, the beer in my other forgotten. Someone shoves past me, nearly knocking it out of my grip, but I barely notice, keeping my eyes on the screen as she starts typing.

Cherry: What's there to like? The music is deafeningly loud, and the people are all fake. Everyone's acting like they're having the time of their life, but it's all just a show.

The words jump around on the screen for a few seconds before settling into something I can actually read.

I let out a short laugh, shaking my head as I glance around. She's kinda got a point.

The guy in the corner is taking body shots off a girl he'll probably never talk to again. The group of sorority girls squealing like they're best friends when I know for a fact two of them hate each other.

It's all a performance.

Me: Okay, you might be right. So, what do you like then, if not parties?

I take a swig of my beer, grimacing when I remember it's warm, and toss it into the trash, taking a seat on the stairs.

I should be having fun. I'm supposed to be the guy who thrives in places like this, the life of the party, always laughing, always moving, always keeping the energy up.

But right now, I'm sitting on the stairs, staring at my phone, waiting for a reply from a girl I don't even know.

Cherry: We agreed. No specific details.

I groan under my breath, dragging a hand through my hair.

Me: Come on. One tiny clue. You're killing me here.

Someone calls my name from the kitchen, but I don't answer. I don't care. Not when her text comes through a few seconds later.

Cherry: I like baking.

My lips twitch before I can stop them.
Baking.
I don't know what I expected her to say, but it wasn't that. I try to picture her, some faceless girl standing in a kitchen, messy hair, a smear of flour on her cheek, maybe humming to herself as she pulls something out of the oven.

Me: Baking? That's all you're giving me?

Cherry: Well, you only asked one thing. I did love baking when I was a kid, but dorm life makes it pretty much impossible now.

I can't help but grin. That's another little clue she's thrown out without realizing it. She lives in a dorm.

Me: Is that where the name Cherry comes from?
Cherry: Maybe.

Maybe.

God, she's annoying. And frustrating. And somehow the most interesting person I've talked to in forever.

She might like the mystery, but I don't. I've never liked surprises. I'm the guy who looks up movie spoilers before watching. So yeah, this whole anonymous thing? It's killing me.

Me: Anything else you can tell me?

I run a hand through my hair, exhaling as I glance around. Ryan and Isabella are across the room, laughing, her hands on his chest, his on her hips. Then he cups her face and kisses her.

I remember when those two were sneaking around for months. They thought they were so slick. They weren't. I clocked Ryan's dumbass heart eyes the first time he looked at her. See? I'm not dumb all the time.

My phone buzzes in my hand, pulling me back.

Cherry: Doesn't seem fair that you get to know two things about me, and I don't know anything about you.

I chuckle, typing out a reply.

She doesn't realize it, but she already knows more than most people do. Everyone else gets the jokes, the cocky grins, the life-of-the-party guy who never shuts up. But her? I kinda want her to know more. To know the thoughts in my head that I don't tell anyone else.

Me: You can ask me anything you want, Cherry.

Cherry: What's one thing you can't live without?

Easy. Hockey. No doubt about it.

My thumbs hover over the keyboard. It's my first instinct. But I can't say that. We agreed to no specific details. And if I tell her, that's all she'll see. That's all everyone ever sees. The hockey guy. The athlete. The guy who's only worth something when he's scoring goals.

But she doesn't look at me like that. She doesn't even *know* me like that. And I like that she likes *me*.

I pause for a second before typing the real answer.

Me: My family. I don't know what I would do without them.

I set the phone down for a second, my mind drifting to Scarlett and Mom.

Scarlett's probably at home, messing with Mom just for fun. She's a little shit sometimes, but she's got the biggest heart. I remember the first time I taught her how to skate, how stiff she was, arms flailing, like Bambi on ice.

God, I miss them like crazy. The smell of coffee in the morning, Mom in the kitchen, half-dressed for work, always in a rush but never too busy to give me a hug before she left. Even when she was dead on her feet, she still made time for us. She always did.

My phone buzzes, breaking me out of my thoughts.

Cherry: Damn, I thought you were gonna say me. I'm offended now.

I let out a laugh, shaking my head. She might be joking, but she's not wrong. I don't know what I'd do without these texts. It's only been a couple of weeks, but she's already a constant in my life, something I look forward to every day.

And apparently, I've been too busy smiling at my phone like an idiot, because next thing I know, someone smacks the back of my head.

"Are you seriously on your phone right now?"

I turn to see Logan and Nathan standing beside me with matching grins on their faces.

"Leave me alone, I'm in a committed relationship," I say, locking my screen.

"With your phone?" Logan snorts.

"Yep. My phone and I are in love. You wouldn't understand."

Nathan claps a hand on my shoulder. "We're losing him, man."

I roll my eyes as they walk off, but the second they're gone, my attention is right back on my screen.

I have no idea who this girl is. Is she blonde? Brunette? Does she have pink hair? No clue. Blue eyes? Brown? Green? Couldn't tell you. She might walk past me every day, sit next to me in class, brush shoulders with me on the quad.

Hell, she could be in this room right now.

The thought makes my head snap up. I scan the party, my gaze drifting over every girl in sight. What if I've already met her? What if the girl standing ten feet away, twirling her hair and giggling at some guy's bad joke, is *my* Cherry?

The thought makes something pull tight in my chest.

Me: If you were at a party tonight, what would you be wearing?

It's a long shot. She might not even be here. She might not even answer.

But damn, I want to know.

What if she's here?

What if I find her tonight?

Cherry: Is that your way of asking if I'm at a party?

Me: Is that a yes?

Cherry: We said we wouldn't look for each other.

Me: That was your rule, and it was a terrible one. I demand a recount.

Cherry: Since there are only two of us in this conversation… Motion denied.

Me: Damn. I really thought I had a chance there.

Cherry: It's good to have dreams.

I huff out a laugh, shaking my head.

God, I have way too much fun talking to her. And all I know about her is that she likes baking, lives in a dorm, hates fake people, and somehow, in a way I can't explain, she gets me.

Me: So, if one day we were in the same place… would you want to meet me?

Cherry: And ruin the fun of this mystery? Not a chance.

I exhale, smiling to myself.

Fine. I'll play her game.

Tucking my phone into my pocket, I glance around, scanning faces like an idiot, knowing it's pointless. She could be anywhere. She could be someone I've never met. And somehow, that just makes me want to know her more.

FOUR

Maisie

I like the quiet.

I like having my own space. I like when the world slows down and no one expects me to talk or smile.

But tonight, of course, the loud, obnoxious frat party down the street is trying its best to ruin that. I can hear the music thumping through the walls, the occasional drunken shout cutting through the air. I just roll my eyes and burrow deeper under my blanket.

It's late, but I'm not tired. Or maybe I am, but my brain's too wired to shut off. Not when Six messages me back.

A grin tugs at my lips. Honestly, I don't know how we ended up here. One wrong number, and now I'm lying in bed in the middle of the night, having an actual conversation with a guy I've never met.

But the weird thing is… it doesn't feel weird.

Maybe because it's easier this way. Maybe because talking through a screen makes me braver than I really am.

Six: So tell me. What are you doing tonight if you're not at a party?

I snort softly, adjusting my pillow.

Me: How do you know I'm not? I could have just come back from a rager. Shots, dancing, got into a fight, ran from the cops.

Six: Sounds fake but please continue. I'm intrigued.

I let out a laugh.

Me: Fine, you caught me. I actually spent the night in bed, eating Oreos and peanut butter.

Six: What a weird combination.

Me: Don't knock it until you try it.

Six: Okay, okay. So, what I'm hearing is, if I ever want to impress you, all I have to do is show up with Oreos and peanut butter?

Me: The real stuff, though. The off-brand versions never taste the same.

Six: Cherries and Oreos? I'm one step closer to cracking the mystery of who you are.

Me: How would that even work? Are you going to go to every store in the country and ask for their customer lists?

Six: If that's what it takes.

I find myself smiling a little, imagining what he must look like when he says that. I can almost hear the teasing tone in his voice.

Me: A dessert for a dessert. What's your go-to snack?

Six: Oh, Cherry baby. You just opened the floodgates. Where do I even start? Brownies, gummies, cookies… Basically anything that's loaded with sugar.

Me: So, you're a child at heart. Got it.

Six: I'm not ashamed. Sweets are a basic necessity of life.

Me: Is there anything you don't like?

The dots appear and disappear for what feels like forever until the text comes through, making my chest tighten.

Six: Not knowing who you are.

I read his text over and over, my eyes tracing the words. He thinks that only because he doesn't know me. What if we meet and it's awkward? What if I'm not as funny or interesting as the girl he's imagined? What if he thinks *she's not what I thought she'd be?*

My stomach churns at the thought, and I can't shake the feeling that I'd disappoint him.

Me: If you knew, you'd be bored with me in a second.

I type it without thinking, but it's true. It's easy to hide behind a screen, to be someone else, or at least a version of myself that feels braver than the girl in real life.

Six: Not possible. I'm literally at a party, and all I want to do is leave so I can spend all night talking to you.

I'm pulled from my thoughts when something hits the door with a heavy thud, followed by muffled giggles. Frowning, I get out of bed and open the door.

One of the girls from down the hall is sprawled out in front of me, her head clearly taking the brunt of the fall against the door. She blinks up at me, eyes a little dazed from the impact.

"Oh my God," one of her friends chuckles from behind her, rushing over to help. "Sorry, Mary."

I blink. "It's Maisie," I say, quieter than I meant to.

Her face scrunches in confusion. "Huh?"

"My name," I add, a little louder. "It's Maisie."

The girl laughs again. "Oh shit, sorry. Did we wake you?"

"No, it's okay," I say with a small smile. "I was still awake."

The girl who fell manages to sit up, rubbing the back of her head. "I'm fine," she slurs, her words slow and fuzzy, clearly drunk out of her mind.

One of the others snickers. "Sorry again," she says, flashing me a nervous, sheepish smile as they shuffle away.

They're already moving on, giggling as they disappear down the hall. I watch them go, a hollow ache settling in my chest.

I don't know why it stings. It's not like I expected them to talk to me, or suddenly make me part of their world. I don't even know them.

But for a moment, I imagined what it'd be like to have a group of friends like that. Not to spend every night alone, tucked away in my room, talking to someone I've never met.

Maybe I only like the quiet because I'm used to being alone.

It's always been this way. In elementary school, I played by myself during recess. In middle school, I learned that blending in was safer than trying to fit in. I stopped raising my hand in class, stopped speaking unless someone spoke to me first.

By the time high school rolled around, I'd perfected the art of staying invisible.

But it didn't matter. They still found reasons to make fun of me. My body, my voice, the way I took up space that wasn't meant for someone like me.

I shake my head, snapping myself out of it. No point in dwelling on the past.

I close the door and sink back into bed, my phone buzzing in my hand a few seconds later.

Six: Did I lose you? Sorry. I should let you go to sleep.

My thumb lingers over the screen before I finally type back.

Me: No. I'm still here.

I don't tell him what just happened. I don't tell him how, for a second, I wished I could be more like them—loud, carefree, a part of something. Instead, I swallow the lump in my throat and focus on the one connection I have, even if it's just through a screen.

Because maybe this is all I get.

FIVE

Austin

Showing up late is kind of my thing.

Not on purpose. Not really. But if I walk in after everyone's settled and halfway tuned out? Well, that's just good timing.

I shoulder the door open, and the low hum of the lecture falters just enough for a few heads to turn.

A couple of girls glance back. One of them is in the middle row—blonde, in a tight tank top, glossy lips parting slightly. She's practically preening in her seat, her notebook open but untouched.

And, yeah, I know that look. She doesn't smile with her mouth, just with her eyes and the slightest curve at the corner of her lips. She shifts her bag off the seat next to her and lets it drop to the floor.

An invitation.

My mouth quirks up, just a little.

I take a step. Then another.

But just as I take the next step, my eyes drift to the side.

Back row. Five seats from the left.

Maisie.

I freeze for a second.

She's in this class, too?

How the hell have I never noticed her before?

I mean, okay, this class is huge. And yeah, I'm not exactly memorizing faces while I'm rolling in ten minutes late. But… she's at the rink, she's in my classes. She's always around.

And somehow, I've missed her all this time?

She's hunched over her laptop, staring at the screen. Her soft, faded pink cardigan slips past her wrists, and her messy bun is barely holding itself together. A few strands keep falling into her face, and she pushes one away without looking up. Then she pauses, reaches into her bag, and pulls out a tube of Chapstick. She smooths it on, caps it again, and goes right back to typing.

My eyes drift to the sticker on her laptop—a cartoon frog in glasses, reading a book.

It's dumb. And kind of weird.

But I can't stop looking at it.

She's completely alone. No one within a three-chair radius.

And for some reason, I stop walking.

Blonde girl is still looking at me. Still waiting. That half-smile flickers when she realizes I'm not moving toward her. She shifts in her seat, and glances away.

I drag my feet up the stairs without really thinking about it, like my body's decided before my brain can catch up.

Straight past the empty seats. Past the perfume, perfect hair, and easy flirtation.

Right toward the one girl who hasn't looked up once.

I slide into the empty seat beside her, making sure to keep my movements quiet. The lecture's already started, and I'm not about to be the guy who interrupts, so I lean in close, my voice low enough that only she can hear.

"Hey."

She doesn't look up. Not even a flicker of acknowledgment.

I grin anyway. "You always this friendly, or am I just getting the VIP treatment?"

Still nothing. Her fingers are flying across the keyboard like I don't exist, like my presence doesn't even register.

I lean in a little closer, enough that her scent hits me—vanilla. Warm, sweet, and stupidly distracting. Like she showered in a bakery this morning.

"Not even a glance? That hurts, Maisie."

That gets her. Barely. Her fingers pause just long enough for her to turn her head and hit me with a single raised brow. Her eyes are glacier blue and sharp as hell, knocking me in the chest and making me forget what I just said.

"What are you doing here?" she grits out.

I shrug, throwing her my best grin. "Saw you sitting all alone. Thought I'd keep you company."

Not even a twitch of a smile. No eye roll, no smirk. Nothing.

"Lucky me," she mutters, already turning back to her screen like I'm not even here.

I chuckle under my breath, settling into the chair and leaning back. "There's the warm welcome I was hoping for."

She keeps typing, her focus locked in on whatever's on her screen.

Honestly, it's kind of impressive.

Most people fake a little interest. A laugh, a compliment, *something*. But Maisie? She's not faking a damn thing.

I rest my chin on my hand and watch her fingers move. There's something hypnotic about the way she types, like her fingers are dancing over the keys.

I glance at her screen with no clue what I'm actually looking at. Whatever it is, it looks like a foreign language. I let my eyes drift to the weird-ass frog sticker on her laptop instead.

I huff a laugh under my breath. "What's with the frog?" I whisper.

She doesn't answer.

Of course she doesn't.

I don't even know why I'm still trying. She's clearly not in the mood for conversation.

But there's something about how focused she is. Like the rest of the world's background noise and she's just tuned it all out.

She's different. Definitely not like anyone else I've met.

"You know…" I murmur, leaning in a bit closer, just to test her limits, "you're really quiet."

Her fingers hover above the keys for half a second. Then she turns, lifts one perfectly arched brow at me.

"You should try it sometime."

I can't help but laugh. "What, being quiet?"

"No. Being tolerable."

A grin tugs at the corner of my mouth. "Damn, Maisie. You got jokes."

Her eyes snap to the professor, who starts speaking again.

I try to follow her lead and focus on the lesson. Really, I do.

But the second I glance at the board, the words start doing somersaults. Swirling together, twisting into a blur of shapes and symbols that don't mean a damn thing. My brain taps out instantly.

I blink hard, shift in my seat with a sigh and let my gaze drift right back to her.

Maisie's still completely absorbed, her face lit by the soft glow of the laptop screen, highlighting the curve of her cheekbones and the faint pink of her lips. They're parted just slightly as she reads, her brows pinched with concentration, that tiny crease between them practically begging to be smoothed out with my thumb.

I catch myself smiling before I even realize I'm doing it.

She's cute.

Like, stupidly cute.

I lean over again, dropping my voice to a whisper. "Psst. You got a pen?"

Her fingers don't pause. "No," she grits out.

"But I need one."

"Then go get your own."

"You really won't share?"

She turns slowly, her eyes narrowed, sharp, and still so unfairly gorgeous.

"You really won't shut up?"

I shake my head, tutting. "Afraid not. Not how I roll."

She stares at me for a second, like she's trying to decide if I'm worth the energy. Then she exhales, drops her hands from the keyboard, and finally turns to face me head-on.

"What do you want?" she asks.

I blink. "A pen?"

"No." Her voice is flat, but her eyes never leave mine. "I mean, from me. Why are you here? What do you want from me?"

Her words throw me off balance, and I lean back in my seat. "I want you to tutor me."

Her eyebrows shoot up. She lets out a breathy, humorless laugh and shakes her head. "Seriously? You didn't even know who I was five days ago."

I scratch the back of my neck, glancing down at my notebook. Still blank. "In my defense, I'm around a lot of people. Doesn't mean I remember all of them."

She gives me the slowest blink I've ever seen, then turns back to her laptop like she's officially done with me.

"Amazing. You're not only unprepared, you're also self-centered."

I lean in again, trying to close the distance between us just a little. "Come on. Help me out. I'll owe you. Name your price."

Maisie doesn't flinch. Doesn't even look up. She's locked into that screen like I'm just another annoying buzz she's trying to ignore.

I ease back in my seat, letting the silence hang for a moment. I don't really know her, but one thing's clear. She's not the type to jump at an offer. Definitely not the type to make it easy.

"Alright," I say, watching her from the corner of my eye. "You want something in return. That's how this works, right?"

Finally, she pauses. Her fingers hover above the keyboard for a beat, then she turns her head toward me. Not all the way. Just enough to make it clear I've got exactly ten seconds of her attention before she decides I'm not worth the effort.

I tap my fingers on the desk, thinking it through.

"Okay. You want my lecture notes? Wait, no, I don't have those." I sigh. "How about I carry your books to class?"

She blinks once, no change in her expression.

I nod to myself. "Noted. Too cliché."

She shifts in her seat, adjusting her cardigan slightly, but she's still watching, still waiting for me to come up with something that might catch her attention.

"Free coffee every morning?" I offer, watching for any flicker of interest.

Her brows lift a fraction, still not impressed.

I blow out a harsh breath. "Tough crowd," I mutter.

She turns her focus back to the screen, and I curse under my breath. I've lost her.

"Silence?" I continue. "I can give you, like, five minutes of that. Max."

She turns her head slightly, like she's considering it, but that unimpressed look never quite leaves her face. Zero for three.

"Okay, an hour," I say, leaning in a little. "No talking, no jokes. What do you say?"

I can tell by the puff of air she lets out through her nose that it's also a no.

I squint at her, smirking. "You're hard to read, you know that?"

Maisie just raises an eyebrow, still not giving me an inch. I sigh, glancing around the lecture hell. The professor is still rambling on about God-knows-what, and some dude is tapping his pen on his desk two rows down. The noise starts to fade as I turn my attention back to Maisie.

"Okay, then." I pause, studying her profile. The way the light hits the slope of her nose, the small freckles scattered across her cheeks. Tiny details I didn't notice before but can't seem to look away from now. "Is there a guy you like?"

Her fingers freeze. Just for a split second. Barely noticeable. But I catch it.

Bingo.

I grin. "You do."

She stiffens, just a fraction, but then—bam—she's back to typing, like her life depends on it.

"No way," I tease, leaning in a little. "You've got a crush."

"I don't," she snaps, way too quickly.

I chuckle. "Lie to me all you want, Freckles. But I can see it clear as day."

Her gaze flicks to mine at the nickname that slips out, but she quickly shakes her head, trying to dismiss it by diving back into her screen.

"You want me to help with that?" I ask her.

Her eyes lock with mine, a crease forming between her brows. "I didn't say that."

"But you didn't *not* say it," I counter, shooting her a grin. "Come on. Let me help you."

Her lips press into a tight line, and she looks away. "I'm not talking about this with you."

"Why not?" I smirk. "I'm a guy. I know how guys think. I could be a valuable resource."

Maisie exhales sharply, an annoyed puff of air, then glances sideways at me. "You're the last person I'd go to for advice."

"Exactly why you should reconsider." I tilt my head, studying her reaction. "No one would expect it."

She doesn't answer right away, just stares at me for what feels like forever. "You're exhausting," she mutters.

"Yeah, but in a charming way," I say with a grin.

She lets out a sigh and her eyes flick down to her screen again, but she doesn't start typing. "I don't have time to babysit you," she mutters under her breath.

I shrug one shoulder. "Don't need a babysitter. Just someone to help me understand this shit so I can pass my classes."

She frowns, probably weighing the pros and cons of punching me in the face. Can't blame her.

I brace myself, blinking a couple of times, my shoulders slumping in defeat, bracing myself for the inevitable rejection. But then she sighs, and my eyes flick to hers.

"Fine," she says, with a sharp exhale. "I'll tutor you."

I blink. "Wait. Really?"

Maisie holds my gaze for a long moment, like she's double-checking that she's not about to make the biggest mistake of her life. "I'm not doing it for you."

I raise an eyebrow. "Oh?"

She glares at me. "I just can't listen to you annoy me for another lecture."

I can't help but grin. "So… this is a mercy mission."

"No," she says flatly. "It's damage control."

I chuckle, leaning in just a little, trying to keep the mood light. "Knew you'd fold eventually, Freckles."

Maisie rolls her eyes. "I'm already regretting this." She shoots me a deadpan look. "Say one more word about crushes and I'm out."

A grin tugs at my lips before I can stop it. I sling my arm over the back of her seat. "No promises."

She shakes her head, but just before she turns away, I catch the tiniest twitch at the corner of her mouth.

Yeah. Game on.

SIX

Maisie

The first time Austin Rhodes asked me to tutor him, I assumed he was joking.

Not because he's the kind of guy who makes jokes like that—at least I don't *think* he does—but because I didn't think someone like him would ever think of asking someone like me for help.

There are at least five other tutors in our program who would leap at the chance to spend an hour alone with Austin Rhodes. And I'm not one of them.

He's a cocky hockey player. Loud, always surrounded by people, the kind of guy who walks into a room like he owns it. Girls orbit him like he's the sun, and he never seems particularly fazed by any of it. I doubt he even notices. That easy kind of popularity only comes to people who were born into it.

I, on the other hand, was not.

So, no, I didn't understand why he asked me. He'd never spoken to me before. I sit in the back row, take detailed notes, color-code my planner. He shows up ten minutes late and spends most of the lecture half-listening and half-whispering to his friends.

We exist in different academic ecosystems.

Still, he asked. And I said yes.

Because… well, he wouldn't shut up unless I agreed. But also, I am good at this. Smart. Organized. Straight A's since high school. I know how to explain things clearly, how to break down information into manageable pieces.

And helping Austin—no matter how often he flashes me that pearly white smile of his—will be no different.

Still, I'd be lying if I said my heart wasn't hammering when I packed my books after class the other day, because my brain doesn't know how to not catastrophize.

My brain doesn't know how to leave things alone. It picks at every word, replays every look, and spins a hundred possible outcomes.

Overthinking is my default. I have entire conversations in my head before I even manage to get a word out.

It's exhausting.

I push open the rink doors, and immediately feel that familiar chill settle in my bones. But what hits me as soon as I walk in, is the unmistakable sound of hockey skates cutting through ice. The guys should've been off the rink ten minutes ago. But, of course, they're still out there, taking their sweet ass time like they own the place.

Unbelievable.

I roll my eyes. This is why I can't stand hockey players. They're entitled, strutting around with that smug look, like they run the entire school. And now, thanks to them, the ice is a mess, turned to snow, which means we'll have to wait for the Zamboni to come out and refresh it.

"Are you kidding me?" Coach Nikki appears beside us, her arms folded, gaze fixed on the rink. "They're cutting into our practice time."

A few of the girls standing nearby groan in response.

"They do this every time," one says, rolling her eyes.

"Ugh, I know," another adds with a small laugh. "But honestly, they're so hot to look at, I almost don't care."

Coach raises an eyebrow, then shakes her head. "Go on in and get changed. I'll see if I can get this sped up."

The girls head toward the locker room in a group, talking to each other. I follow a few steps behind, my duffel bag bouncing lightly against my hip.

Everyone starts getting changed, pulling off their coats and sweaters, chatting without much thought. I see a few girls shimmy out of their jeans with no hesitation as they strip down to bras and thongs.

Me? I head straight to the showers, ducking into a stall with my bag like it's second nature. I've done this every practice since I was twelve. I never undress in front of the other girls. Not because I'm ashamed of my body exactly, but because I'm aware of it. Of how different it looks from theirs.

I step into a stall and lock the door behind me before I start tugging my clothes off.

I pull on my black leggings, then the soft pink zip-up jacket I always wear, over a white t-shirt. I adjust the hem and pull on my pale pink ankle warmers, and twist my hair up into a bun.

When I step back out, the girls are still changing, chatting about some guy on the football team. I sit down at the end of the bench and focus on pulling my ankle warmers into place.

Then I reach for my phone, my eyes lighting up and my chest pounding when I see a new text from Six.

"Hey."

I blink, a little startled as I glance up. Savannah is standing in front of me, her blonde curls tucked into a headband and earbuds slung around her neck. It takes me a second to realize she's talking to me.

My voice catches in my throat before I manage a low, "Hey."

She gestures vaguely downward. "You're sitting on my jacket."

Right. Of course I am.

"Oh," I scramble to my feet so fast my water bottle tips over and clatters to the floor with a hollow thunk. "Sorry. I didn't realize."

She doesn't say anything else. Just bends down, grabs her jacket, and walks off.

I sink back onto the bench, my face burning as I pick up my water bottle and glance back at my phone, the screen still open to Six's message.

I exhale slowly, my thumbs hovering over the screen as I read his message.

Six: Confession: I once faked a phone call to get out of a class. I think I said my dog had food poisoning. I don't even have a dog.

A smile tugs at my lips before I can stop it. I shift back against the locker and type out a reply.

Me: Cruel. Poor imaginary dog.

Six: He made a full recovery. Real fighter, that one. Pulled through against all odds.

I bite back a laugh. This is the easiest part of my day. With Six, I don't have to think about how I look, or how I sound, or whether my leggings are rolling down weirdly in the back. He doesn't know me. I don't know him. Somehow, that makes it better.

Me: Confession. I hate phone calls.

Six: Anything worth saying could be sent in an email.

Me: Exactly.

Three dots appear on the screen, and disappear a couple of times before his reply comes in.

Six: So, does that mean there's no chance of you ever picking up if I called? Even just once?

My heart hammers in my chest. My fingers pause over the keys. Because the truth is, I *do* want to hear his voice. I want to know if he sounds like I imagine. If he laughs the way I read his texts.

But I'm scared, too.

Calls feel risky. Like it'd break the spell. Strip the mystery.

He might hear my voice and *know*.

Or worse. *I* might know *him*.

And I'm not ready for that.

Right now, it's perfect. Safe. Secret. Just two anonymous people telling each other their confessions.

My fingers hover over the screen for a few seconds before I type out my answer.

Me: Too risky.

Six: Uh oh. You think you'll fall in love with my voice?

I roll my eyes, smiling like a total idiot. I feel all warm and fuzzy and… happy. I always do when I talk to him.

Me: You wish.

Six: I do, actually.

And now I'm blushing. Because what the hell do I even say to that?

Six: So, what else don't I know about you?

I pause. There's a list. A long one. Too many things I've never said out loud, and way too many I wouldn't say to a stranger—even one I like talking to more than most real people.

I settle on a small confession, not wanting to dull the mood.

Me: I hate orange-flavored candy.

Six: Damn. That's rough. I was gonna propose with a bag of orange Skittles.

Me: Glad I dodged that disaster. They taste like cleaning supplies.

Six: Okay, that's fair. Cherry reigns supreme anyway.

I pause, staring at his last message. It's just a throwaway comment. But my stomach still flips, like it means more than it should.

I glance up, watching the other girls move around me like I'm not there. And weirdly, I don't mind it as much right now. Not when I have someone to talk to who actually wants to hear what I have to say, even if I don't know his name.

I swallow hard, and tighten my laces before heading out of the locker room. I'm used to being invisible. Especially with the girls here. I kinda thought it'd be different once I started college and was skating with a bunch of other girls. But nothing's changed.

The only person I don't feel invisible with is my little sister, Lottie. She's sixteen, way cooler than I've ever been, and has more friends than I'll probably have in my entire life. She's also the only person I tell everything to. Which is… sad, I guess. But she never makes me feel like I'm too much. Or not enough. She listens whenever I want to rant about anything and everything, and I wouldn't trade her for the world.

I just… I wish I had someone that wasn't my sister to talk to. Someone that I could hang out with and go out with and just—

I let out a sigh as I step onto the ice, and the rambling thoughts in my head quiets. I push forward, each stroke carving into the surface with a satisfying scratch.

The surface is smooth and fresh as I circle the rink, slowly at first, letting myself sink into the rhythm. My body knows this choreography like the back of my hand. This is the only place I ever feel fully like myself.

Strong. Graceful. Beautiful, even—though I'd never say that out loud.

I've spent enough time trying to fold myself smaller in every room I walk into to know that I'm not lean or long-limbed like the girls who land triples like it's nothing. I jiggle when I jump. My thighs press together even when I'm standing straight. I am soft where they are sculpted, round where they are lean. And still, I am here. And I deserve to be here.

The other girls are spread across the ice, practicing their spirals and chatting between runs. I glance at them, swishing as they glide like they were born with skates on their feet.

One girl executes a flawless double toe loop, and I watch the way the others nod, impressed.

I rip my gaze away and do a few warm-up laps, shaking out the nerves. My body knows what to do. Muscle memory takes over, and I fall into the rhythm.

I transition into a catch-foot spin, keeping my arms extended, then slowly pulling one leg up behind me, grabbing the blade and holding tight. The stretch burns through my shoulder and thigh, but the spin feels centered. Controlled.

"Elbow up," Coach calls from the boards. "Hold the line through the exit."

I nod, dropping my foot back onto the ice. She's right, the exit was sloppy. Still, not bad. Better than last week.

I push off again, coasting around to gain momentum for the jump I've been working on for months. The double axel— forward outside edge takeoff, two and a half rotations in the air, land on the opposite foot.

I've landed it in drills, in slow practice runs.

But never at speed.

Today, maybe.

I gather speed along the boards, my arms tight against my body, keeping my breath even, and push into the rotation, but my toe pick clips the ice, and I go down hard.

My breath punches out of me as I slide to a stop.

I lie there for a second. Not because I'm hurt. Just… stunned. And tired. And maybe a little humiliated.

Coach's voice cuts across the rink. "Maisie, get that right hip up! Think about getting your butt through the jump. You're sitting back too early."

I wince, nod, and push up from the ice.

"Nice one, Carly," Coach calls out to one of the other girls. "Way to hold the landing!"

I stand, and try again.

Skating is a ton of repetition. You fail, you try again. You fall, you fix your edges, your timing, your damn hips, and you go again.

On the next attempt, I over-rotate. The landing is too wide. My blade wobbles, and I have to put a hand down to stop the fall.

I circle back into position. Breathe. Focus. Try again.

On the third attempt, I drive through the takeoff, push my hips forward, and remember Coach's words. My arms lock in, core pulled tight. I spin once, twice, then half again and land clean.

I glide out, my pulse hammering, heart in my throat.

Holy shit… I did it. I actually landed it.

"Better," Coach says, nodding once in my direction.

I blow out a breath, unable to keep the smile off my face.

I want to tell someone. I want to text Six and say, *You won't believe what I just did.*

But I can't. I can't tell him I skate. That's the rule. No names. No real details.

Just secrets. Just confessions.

And this? This is a piece of me he's not allowed to know.

But still.

Maybe I don't look like I belong here.

But I do. Even if I have to say it a hundred times to believe it—I belong here.

And I just proved it.

SEVEN

Austin

Some days, I swear the world is out to wring me dry.

By the time I get home, I'm fried. Physically, mentally—whatever other kind of "-ly" there is. Classes, gym, and then practice on top of it. My head's still spinning when I push open the door and step inside.

"Tell me someone brought food," I groan, dragging myself onto the couch and kicking my shoes off.

Ryan doesn't look up from his phone. "You've got two legs and a wallet. Figure it out."

I grab a throw pillow and place it behind my head. "I'm emotionally fragile. The least you could do is feed me."

Nathan glances up from his phone, arching a brow my way. "You're suspended, not starved."

"There's a kitchen right there," Ryan adds, nodding toward it.

I give it a quick glance, then scowl. "You know I can't cook. That's why God invented takeout."

Logan kicks back on the couch, one arm slung over the backrest. "You guys down to check out that new bar near campus tonight?"

I glance at Nathan. He gives a shrug.

Ryan doesn't miss a beat. "Can't. I've got plans."

I grin. "Lemme guess. Hot date with your PS5?"

He shoots me a smug look. "Hotter," he says with a smirk. "Isabella."

Nathan groans and drops his head back against the cushion. "For the love of God. Can you not?"

Ryan grabs a chip from the bowl and flicks it at him. "Can you be less dramatic?"

"She's my *sister*, man."

Can't even blame him. The idea of my little sister dating a hockey player makes me want to crawl into a hole and stay there. We're the worst.

Ryan just shrugs and a smug-ass smirk pulls at his lips. "And she loves me."

Nathan scoffs. "She also used to eat glue and thought *High School Musical* was peak cinema. Her judgment's always been questionable."

Ryan chuckles. "You've got to get over this, man. She picked me."

Nathan shoves his shoulder. "She likes making bad decisions, clearly."

"Must run in the family," Ryan shoots back with a smirk.

Logan barks out a laugh. "Hey, how long before we start calling Ryan your brother-in-law?"

Nathan's face goes flat. "Don't."

"I'm picturing the wedding already," I say, stretching out my hands behind my head. "Matching tuxes. You crying in the background."

"I will light myself on fire," Nathan mutters.

"Better get used to me," Ryan says with a wink. "Family dinners, holidays, matching Christmas pajamas—"

Nathan grabs the nearest pillow and clocks him in the side of the head. "Shut the hell up."

Ryan laughs like he lives for this. And honestly, maybe he does.

This is the best part of the day. Sitting around, talking shit, no pressure. Just the guys being dumb. For a minute, I can pretend I'm not drowning in stress over the essay I didn't finish or the scholarship I'm barely holding onto. Pretend I'm not one bad grade away from losing everything.

Right now?

I just breathe.

I stretch out on the couch. "It's inspiring to witness true love bloom while I slowly flunk out of college."

Ryan downs some water and wipes his mouth with the back of his hand. "Thought you had a tutor?"

"Working on it," I mutter. Technically true. I've agreed to let someone help—someone who barely looks at me and might ghost any minute.

Ryan raises a brow. "You gonna be ready by playoffs?"

"Planning on it." I prop my feet up on the coffee table.

It's been rough. Showing up to practice, knowing I won't see a single shift. Just standing behind the bench, setting up drills, taping sticks—whatever needs doing. I joke around, stay loud in the locker room, act like I'm still part of the team.

But fuck, I miss skating.

I miss the feel of the rink under my blades, the sound of my stick cutting through a pass. The adrenaline, the noise, the rush. I miss the *game*.

And if I don't get my shit together soon, I'm terrified I'll lose it for good.

Nathan glances up from his phone. "Don't forget you've got a midterm in two weeks."

"Awesome," I deadpan. "Can't wait to bomb that too."

They laugh. I laugh, too. Or at least, I pretend to.

I'm good at making people laugh, at being the dumb one who they chuckle at and shake their heads—so I do just that. Keep the jokes coming, keep the noise up. If I play my role right, nobody notices the cracks.

But underneath… It stings.

I make jokes about dropping out like it's some kind of punchline. Like I'm not waking up every day with that fear curled tight in my chest.

Because it's not funny. It's fucking terrifying.

I'm not here because my parents made a generous alumni donation. I don't have a safety net or a plan B. Hockey *is* the plan. My full ride is the only reason I'm here at all. If I screw this up—if I don't get drafted—then my mom keeps scrubbing floors at that fancy prep school for rich kids who never have to worry about their futures. And Scarlett? She'll start to believe college is just a dream for kids with better dads and deeper pockets.

So yeah, I joke. It's easier than saying I'm scared shitless I'll never be enough.

Because if I blow this—if I don't turn it around—I'm not just letting myself down.

I'm letting them down. My mom. Scarlett. Everyone who's ever believed I could make it.

And I don't know how many more chances I get before that belief runs out.

"I'm heading up," I say, pushing off the couch with a grunt.

Ryan eyes me. "Got a hot date with your pillow?"

Logan lets out a scoff, scarfing down chips. "With his right hand, more like."

I grin, tossing him a look. "Hey, at least my right hand never bails on me."

They chuckle behind me as I head up the stairs.

I push the door open and let it slam shut behind me. I toss my backpack on the floor and reach under the bed for my guitar.

I flop down onto my bed, running my hands over it. It's beat-up, the wood worn smooth in spots, strings a little dull, but it's still the best thing I own.

I tune it by ear, my fingers moving on instinct, until the sound feels right.

I don't play for anyone. Not at parties. Not for the guys. Definitely not online.

I start picking through a melody I half-wrote weeks ago. There's something in it I still haven't figured out.

I don't write songs for attention. I write 'cause it's the only place I don't have to fake being okay or funny or loud.

I strum softer and let the sound fill the room.

Then my phone buzzes.

I glance down, seeing Scarlett's name flashing on the screen.

I place the pick in my mouth and swipe to answer the call. "What's up, Shrimp?"

"Why do you sound like you got run over by a truck?"

I chuckle, shaking my head, and take the pick out of my mouth. "Hello to you too, Scar," I reply.

"Are you okay?" she asks.

I flop back onto the bed, my eyes flicking to the ceiling. "Yeah. Just tired. Long day. How's school?"

"Boring. You?"

"Also boring. Except mine's stupid expensive and might ruin my life."

She laughs. I miss that laugh. I miss tickling her and annoying the shit out of her. "You're so dramatic. Did you play anything new?"

"Maybe." I sit up, resting my back against the headboard. I strum a few soft chords, not really sure if they sound right. "This one doesn't suck."

She chuckles. "You say that every time."

I smirk. "Maybe I'm just humble. And consistent."

There's a pause on the other end. "Or maybe you're scared people might actually like it."

I stop playing for a second, fingers frozen above the strings. Damn, maybe she's got a point. "You sound like my therapist."

"I am your therapist. And my rates are going up."

I laugh and pick up the rhythm again. "You wanna hear it or not?"

"You know I do."

I settle the guitar and start messing with the strings. My fingers move on autopilot, like they always do when I'm trying to unwind. It's not a song yet, just a few chords I can't seem to get out of my mind. It's still a little rough around the edges, but that's fine.

"It's really good," she says after a while. "You should post it."

"Nah." I set the guitar down. "I'm good with just you hearing it."

She sighs, knowing I won't ever post it, no matter how many times she tells me to. "When are you coming home?"

"Soon," I assure her, running a hand through my hair. "Maybe during winter break."

"You better. I miss you or whatever."

I chuckle. "Miss you too, Shrimp."

Most people are glad to be away from their family, but Scar and my mom are the most important people to me.

I still remember when I taught her how to skate. Mom was working late, and I needed to practice. Dad wasn't around, so I always had to be. I'd push Scarlett around on the rink, her tiny hands clinging to a traffic cone like it was her lifeline. She'd shriek every time she thought she might fall through the ice.

She hated it. Not a fan of skating, which honestly, I don't get. Skating's one of the best things in the world. But she always loved watching me play. She used to sit in the stands, her feet swinging, a bag of Skittles in her lap. She made signs for my games, and I kept every single one tucked in my closet.

We talk for a few more minutes. She complains about math, I threaten to call her teacher. She makes fun of my taste in music, I tell her she has none. It's easy, fun. I love this kid.

After we hang up, I peel off my clothes and step into the shower. When I'm done, I wrap a towel around my waist and I wipe the fog off the glass, staring at my reflection for a few seconds.

Still the same mess.

Still pretending like I've got my shit figured out when I have no clue what I'm doing.

I pull on some sweatpants and flop back onto my bed, grabbing my phone. I check for any new messages from the one girl who's been occupying my head every damn day.

I don't even know her real name, but every time my phone lights up, I hope it's her.

I check my phone. No new messages from Cherry.

Instead, I end up scrolling mindlessly through social media until something makes me stop.

Maisie Wilson followed you.

I click on her profile immediately. It's pretty minimal, with only a handful of pictures, but my gaze catches on a pinned video, and I click on it.

I hit play, not really expecting much, just out of curiosity, I guess. But the second the video starts, I'm frozen.

She's gliding on the ice so gracefully, I blink in shock. How is this the same stubborn girl who barely glanced at me the other day? Her leg lifts as she leans forward, moving around the rink like she owns it.

And then she starts spinning. Fast. Like, crazy fast. She lifts her arms above her head as she rotates, and a few seconds later, she launches into a jump, spinning in the air. She lands it perfectly, gliding backwards with her arms stretched out.

I blink. Rewind five seconds. Watch it again.

Jesus.

I knew she skated. But this? This is another level. She's not just good, she's incredible. Sharp and focused and so fucking graceful it kind of makes my brain short-circuit.

I blink. Scroll to another one.

This one's set to some old Adele song—definitely not my usual vibe—but shit, it fits.

She dips into a turn, her leg sweeping behind her, and it's so fucking beautiful, I can't stop staring. She moves like the ice is an extension of her.

I didn't know she could move like this.

Didn't know anyone could.

I double-tap without thinking.

Then, because I can't help myself, I send her a message.

Me: u stalking me freckles?

She unfollows me.

Immediately.

I bark out a laugh. Ballsy move.

Before I can even decide whether to message her again, my phone buzzes and my lips tip into a grin when I see it's a reply from her.

Maisie: I wasn't stalking. It was for research.

Me: oh yeah? what were you researching?

Maisie: Whether your ego is as big as everyone says it is.

Me: and…

Maisie: Inconclusive. Too many shirtless pictures.

Me: so, ur saying u were distracted?

Maisie: Disgusted more like.

Me: since ur clearly fascinated by me…

Maisie: I'm not.

I can almost picture her rolling those bright blue eyes of hers.

I chuckle to myself, shaking my head. She's so fucking stubborn.

Me: and obvs in denial. how about I get a second chance to redeem myself and we set up a tutoring sesh?

I tap my foot against the floor, waiting for her reply. My fingers curl around the edge of my phone, anxiety prickling under my skin. What if she tells me to shove it? Honestly, wouldn't blame her, but she's the only thing standing between me and my dream.

I'm ripped out of my thoughts when my phone buzzes in my hands, and I glance down at the screen.

Maisie: Wednesday. Four PM. Library. I'll bring notes. You bring a functioning brain.
Me: that's asking a lot.
Maisie: I'm aware.
Me: it's a date.
Maisie: It's tutoring.
Me: why can't it be both?

She doesn't reply, and I set my phone down, still smiling.

EIGHT

Maisie

The library's mostly empty when I get there.

I head straight for the back table. It's tucked in the corner, quiet, with a good overhead light and two outlets. I drop my bag onto the chair beside me and start unpacking. Textbook, lecture slides, flashcards, notebook, pens. Everything's already organized, but I double-check anyway. Color-coded notes. Diagrams. Flashcards grouped by chapter.

I don't half-ass tutoring sessions. Especially not when the guy I'm helping is already hanging on by a thread in this class.

Five minutes go by.

Then ten.

I tap my pen against the side of my notebook, flipping to the next page even though I'm not reading. The library's so quiet I can hear the hum of the overhead lights and the faint tick of the old clock by the front desk.

Still no sign of him.

I check my phone. No texts. No missed calls.

Where the hell is he?

I very clearly said 4 p.m. Not 'around four', not 'sometime tonight'. Four.

I let out a breath and sit back in my chair, crossing my arms. Maybe I should just leave. I've got an exam of my own next week. I didn't clear my schedule so he could flake.

I'm reaching for my pencil case when I hear footsteps echoing across the floor.

I glance up just in time to see Austin Rhodes walking in like he's got all the time in the world. His hoodie is unzipped over a tight gray shirt, his backpack dangling from one shoulder.

He spots me and heads over. He doesn't rush, even though he's ten minutes late. Just strolls right up, drops into the chair across from me, and slouches down so low he might slide off entirely.

His backpack hits the table with a loud thud.

"Sorry I'm late," he says, dragging a hand through his hair. He pulls a crumpled bag of chips from his hoodie pocket and holds it up. "Vending machine robbed me. I retaliated." He flashes me a lazy grin, then reaches into the bag and pops a Cheeto into his mouth.

I blink at him. Is this guy for real?

"Congrats on your win," I say dryly. "Can we get started now? We're already behind."

I pick up my highlighter and go back to marking the notes in front of me.

He's quiet for a beat. I can feel him watching me, but I keep my eyes down, even when his chair creaks as he shifts forward.

"Want one?" he asks, holding the bag of chips in my face.

I shake my head without glancing up.

"So…" he says, placing the Cheetos back into his backpack. "What's the game plan?"

"You read," I say, pushing a piece of paper toward him. "I help."

"Oof," he says, his brows lifting into his hairline. "You're strict."

I sigh and finally meet his eyes. "Austin. You're failing. This isn't the time for jokes."

He blinks, like I've caught him off guard. His eyes meet mine and hold. Just for a second. Long enough to make me wonder if I've got something on my face. Then he shakes his head and that slow, crooked grin slides into place.

"There's always time for jokes."

I roll my eyes and slide the packet across the table and tap the first paragraph with the end of my highlighter. "Start reading."

Austin groans. "Do I have to?"

"Yes."

He drapes himself across the table, his chin hitting the wood with a soft thunk. "Can't you just explain it to me?" he asks, his eyes flicking to mine. "You've got that student-teacher thing going for you." He breaks out into a cocky smirk. "Very sexy, by the way."

I narrow my eyes at him. "Read."

He lets out another groan as he grabs the packet and opens up the worksheet. At first, he's loud. Making jokes, trying to distract me. But when he starts reading, he slows down. Words trip him up. He stumbles over a sentence and mutters something under his breath.

Another line. Another pause. He scratches the back of his neck, sighs, and starts over.

He stares at the next sentence a beat too long before starting. "The… mar…ginal… u…tility… of… consump…tion…"

"Keep going," I encourage him.

He does, but it's halting. Uneven. And the longer it goes on, the more tense he gets. His knee starts bouncing under the table.

He rubs the back of his neck, then leans forward like getting closer to the page will help.

Then, finally, he exhales and drops the packet on the table. "This font is, like, aggressively small."

I glance at the packet. It's literally standard twelve-point Times New Roman.

I don't say anything. Just wait.

He messes with the hem of his hoodie, twisting the fabric in his hands. "Okay, look. I'm trying, alright? This just isn't…" He makes a frustrated sound and doesn't finish the sentence.

"Do you always struggle to read like that?" I ask, even though I already kind of know the answer.

He hesitates, eyes flicking away like he's trying to disappear into the chair. Then he shrugs, like it's no big deal. "Yeah."

I nod slowly, noticing how he avoids my gaze. "Have you ever been tested for dyslexia?"

He looks up at me sharply, his brows knitting together. "Yeah. When I was a kid." He blinks, a little surprised. "You could tell?"

I lift my shoulder. "You read 'vertebrae' as 'vegetable.' Twice."

The tight line of his mouth softens, and a quiet laugh escapes him. His smile spreads slow, dimples popping on both sides, and his eyes crinkle just enough that I have to look away for a second. I know without a doubt he gets away with so much just by showing off those dimples.

"Most people just think I'm an idiot," he says after a beat. "Or lazy. Or both."

I lift my eyes to his, seeing the vulnerability flashing in them.

"You're not," I assure him. "You just learn differently." I pause, tilting my head. "Did you ever get help for it?"

He lets out a dry chuckle, but it doesn't reach his eyes. "Nah. I've just gotten good at winging it."

I lean back, folding my arms. "Winging it only gets you so far. You're stuck now, aren't you?"

His smile slips for a moment, like he wasn't expecting that.

"Look, I get it. Asking for help can feel like admitting defeat. But it's not humiliating. You just need a little extra time to let the words sink in."

He meets my gaze, a flicker of something flashing in them. "Yeah? You think you can help with that?"

I nod and lean forward, resting my elbows on the table between us, closing the distance. "We're going to slow this down. You don't have to tackle everything at once. We'll break it up. I'll read some, you read some. Deal?"

He blinks, eyes narrowing for a split second. "You're not gonna give up on me?"

Sometimes I think I've got him figured out. The cocky hockey player, used to getting away with murder and flashing a grin while he does it. But then he says something like that, and it hits me again how little I actually know about him.

"Not a chance," I say, shaking my head.

His shoulders relax, and that smile of his comes back, slow and a little crooked.

I try to ignore the fluttering in my stomach when he does. But when it's clear it isn't going away, I let out a sigh. Screw it. I'm only human. And his smile is really freaking pretty.

No denying that.

We work for almost an hour.

I show him how to use the colored overlays I brought, just in case—blue seems to help him the most.

He jokes between every other line with dramatic sighs, terrible accents, asking if this counts as foreplay.

I don't dignify that with a response.

But the thing is, I'm starting to realize it's not because he doesn't want the help. It's the opposite. He's just not used to getting it like this. Without strings. Without judgment. Without someone rolling their eyes or giving up on him before he even starts.

We make it through two whole paragraphs. It's rough. He loses his place constantly. Misreads half the vocabulary.

But there are moments—quick ones—where it clicks. Where I see the flicker of something shift across his face. A line he reads without stumbling. A word he nails on the first try. There are no jokes, no flirting. He's really trying.

And for a second, I start to think that maybe there's more to him than the cocky guy I pegged him for.

But then he ruins it.

"Is it weird that your voice makes this stuff sound kinda sexy?" he asks, wagging his brows at me.

I narrow my eyes. "Do you want to learn, or get slapped?"

He laughs, leaning back in his chair. "You're good at this."

My eyes flick up. "Tutoring?"

"Yeah. But also…" He shrugs, eyes falling to the page. "Like, not being annoying about it. You don't try to rush me. Or make me feel like I'm stupid. It's kinda nice."

I blink, caught off guard by the fact that he actually means it. Normally he flirts to mess around. Deflect. Keep things light. But this isn't that. This is genuine.

He's watching me, and it's not the usual look he gives me. There's no smirk, no teasing glint in his eye. Just curiosity.

"So," he says. "What's your deal?"

I raise an eyebrow. "My deal?"

"Yeah." He nods, his arms folded across his chest. "You figure skate, right? I saw your videos."

I freeze.

My stomach drops, just for a second. "You… saw them?"

He shrugs. "You followed me the other day. I clicked on your profile. Sue me."

Heat crawls up the back of my neck. Great. Austin Rhodes, king of hockey, professional flirt, has now seen me twirling on the ice. Fantastic.

I brace myself for the smirk, the joke, some sarcastic jab about glitter or twinkle toes. Because of course, that's what a hockey player would do.

Instead, he smiles. "You're good," he says. "Like… really good."

And I don't know what to do with that.

My skating life has always been separate from everything else. A world I keep walled off from people who wouldn't get it. It's not that I'm ashamed of it. I love it, but I'm used to being able to decide when and how people see that part of me.

With him, I didn't get that choice.

"You're blushing," he adds with a grin, those damn dimples making an appearance again.

"I'm not."

"You totally are. It's adorable."

I narrow my eyes at him. "Do you ever stop talking?"

"Nope," he says, unapologetically. "It's part of my charm."

I roll my eyes, but I'm smiling before I can stop myself. Damn him.

He shifts in his chair, and I pretend like I'm not ridiculously aware of the way his knee just barely bumps mine under the table.

"What made you start skating?" he asks.

I blink. "My mom put me in ballet lessons when I was six. She always thought it was beautiful, and I... loved it too," I admit. "But I fell in love with figure skating. It was like ballet, but on ice. I liked that it wasn't about being the loudest person in the room. You could just... move. Be quiet. And still say something."

He tilts his head. "That's kind of cool."

There's something in his voice, almost like interest and respect. It disorients me. Guys don't usually listen to me like this. Especially not him.

"What about you?" I ask him. "Why hockey?"

His gaze drops to the table as he spins his pen between his fingers.

"Started playing at six too. My mom works as a cleaner at this rich-kid prep school. They had a rink, let staff kids join their programs. She said I had too much energy and needed an outlet."

He shrugs, still looking down. "It was always the one thing I was good at. When school sucked. When... everything sucked, actually."

I shift slightly, my arms folding in front of me. His tone is different now. The jokes are gone. His voice is quieter. I've never heard him be this quiet before.

"I used to feel like a screw-up every time I came home with a bad grade. But hockey?" He pauses, glancing up at me. "I could show up, skate fast, hit hard, and for a couple hours… it felt like I wasn't failing everything."

Something twists in my chest.

I don't know what I expected when I agreed to tutor him. Probably eye rolls and frustration and me doing 90% of the work while he scrolled on his phone. I didn't expect this. I didn't expect him to be… a person.

"But now I'm suspended from playing," he says, letting out a laugh, but there's no humor in it. "So… yeah. I kinda need to pass this class." He wipes a hand down his face and mutters under his breath, "God, I hope this works."

And suddenly, I get it. The jokes. The charm. The flirty deflections. They're armor.

He's scared. And he's trying really hard not to look it.

"You're suspended from hockey?" I ask.

Austin exhales. "Temporarily," he says, dragging a hand through his hair. His eyes meet mine when it falls to the table again. "Coach still makes me show up to practice and help. Tape sticks. Run drills." He sighs. "It fucking sucks."

His fingers tap a slow rhythm against the edge of his notebook. "I miss skating," he says. "That's the worst part. I miss the burn in my legs. The cold. The noise. I miss being tired because I worked hard, not because I stared at a screen for three hours trying to understand words."

He groans and leans back like the words sting more than he wants to admit. But it's there in his voice, the kind of honesty you don't throw around unless you think someone might actually understand.

And maybe I do.

Not the hockey part. But the need to escape. The part where you know who you are when you're doing something that means everything, and how everything falls apart when it's gone.

"I'm going to help you pass," I tell him.

He glances at me again.

"We'll get you back on the ice."

It sounds simple. But it isn't. I know that. He knows that. Still, I mean it.

Austin holds my gaze, like he's searching for the lie. "You really think that's possible?" he asks.

I nod. "Yeah. I do."

He nudges my foot under the table. It's barely a touch—more like a soft kick—but it makes me glance up.

"You know," he says, with a smirk, "you're way nicer than you pretend to be."

I smirk. "And you're a lot smarter than you pretend to be."

He lets out a laugh, and wags his brows at me. "You're hot when you compliment me."

And we're back to the jokes.

I shoot him a flat look. "I'm not above stabbing you with a highlighter."

He grins, unabashed. "Knew there was a little violence in you, Freckles."

By the time we wrap up, Austin's head is tilted back, eyes heavy-lidded like he's half-asleep. His jokes have slowed, and the sarcasm that's usually on a ten is down to a sleepy three.

"That was… less painful than expected."

I lift a brow. "High praise."

"You make it fun." He smiles, a lazy, lopsided one. "I actually get this now. Like, a little."

"Don't get too cocky," I say as I start gathering my notes. "You've still got a long way to go."

He stands, stretching his arms above his head until his hoodie lifts just enough to show the waistband of his boxers. I force myself to look back at my bag. *Jesus, Maisie. Get a grip.* It's just abs. Abs from a guy you have no interest in.

He yawns. "I'll keep that in mind," he says, rubbing the back of his neck. "Thanks. Seriously. Dunno what I would do without you."

I slide my notes into my folder and zip my bag. "Same time next week?" I ask, lifting out of the chair.

He nods. "Same time. I'll even be on time. Probably."

I narrow my eyes. "You won't."

"True." He grins, flashing me his perfect teeth. "Thanks, though, for not treating me like a lost cause."

I pause, my fingers still curled around my bag strap. For a second, I don't know what to say.

Because he isn't a lost cause. Not even close.

I glance at him, squinting slightly. "Don't make me regret it."

His smile widens and he winks. "No promises. See you, Freckles."

He turns around, tucking his hands in his pockets, and strolls out of the library.

I watch him go, my lips twitching into a small smile despite myself.

Austin Rhodes is a pain in the ass.

But damn, he's good at making it hard to hate him.

NINE

Austin

There are few things more humiliating than being benched. Actually, scratch that. There's *nothing* worse than chasing loose pucks across the ice while my teammates fire off slap shots and chirp me like I'm their personal assistant.

"Rhodes!" Coach Hayes shouts. "You're on cones!"

I look down at the stack of bright orange triangles. Sick. Cone duty. My favorite.

I skate over to the corner and start setting them out, resisting the urge to just launch one across the rink. Not worth the extra laps I'd probably get slapped with.

This is my life now. Skate around, set stuff up, get yelled at. Repeat.

It's a cruel punishment. Like dangling a plate of wings in front of a starving man and telling him he can sniff them but not eat.

I've been playing hockey since I was six. I've broken bones for this sport. Bled on this ice. Missed vacations, parties, everything. And now I'm out because of *Anatomy*. A class I didn't want to take and still don't understand.

"Move your ass, Rhodes," Coach calls again.

I glance over my shoulder. "I am moving. This is premium ass movement."

"Less sass, more hustle."

I mutter under my breath and keep skating, setting up the rest of the cones while the guys start warming up. I try not to look at them, but it's hard not to feel it. They're flying through drills, calling out to each other, laughing. Meanwhile, I'm the team's cone boy.

"You guys better be grateful," I say under my breath. "I didn't sign up to be team equipment manager."

Logan skates past and taps the top of my helmet with his glove. "Lookin' good, water boy."

I shoot him a glare. "Blow me."

"Tempting," he calls over his shoulder with a grin before he skates off like the little shit he is.

Cole follows behind him, chewing gum, of course. "You missed a puck."

"Thanks, sunshine." I blow him a kiss. He doesn't even blink. Figures. Cole's got the emotional range of a brick wall. You could light the bench on fire and he'd just sit there.

Although, lately, there's been one person who actually gets a reaction out of him. I don't know what went down there, but it's weirdly entertaining. And yeah, I've thought about asking, but I'd probably get a shoulder check for even bringing it up.

I skate over and start dropping cones, one by one. It's cold. My fingers are stiff. My back's starting to ache. I know no one's gonna thank me for doing this, but whatever.

I finish the setup and drop to the side of the rink, leaning on the boards. Coach blows his whistle, the guys explode into the first drill, and I just stand there, arms crossed, freezing my ass off.

This sucks.

I miss being on the ice. I miss the noise, the pressure, the rush. I even miss the dumb stuff. Coach yelling, the gear digging into my shoulders, sweat dripping into my eyes. I'd take all of it over this.

And yeah, I screwed up. I know that. I should've paid more attention in class, turned my work in and whatever else. But it's not like I was partying all the time. I just… suck at school. Always have.

I lift my head when I spot Isabella making her way over, clutching her clipboard to her chest. She slides down onto the bench beside me without a word and gives me a sideways look.

"Hey, baby Hayes," I say with a forced smile.

"You alright?" she asks, narrowing her eyes a little.

I shrug, staring back at the ice. "Peachy."

She lets out a soft hum and watches the guys tearing through drills.

"You miss it?" she asks, nodding toward the ice.

Hell yeah. I want to say it out loud, but it sounds pathetic even to myself.

Instead, a bitter laugh slips out. "It's the only place I belong," I admit.

She gives me a quick smile. "You'll be back soon," she says.

I raise an eyebrow. "You sure about that?"

Isabella's nice. Too nice for someone dating Ryan Reed, but hey, love's blind and all that. Still, she didn't see the look of disappointment on her dad's face when I got suspended.

"Don't think that's happening anytime soon," I tell her, my eyes flicking back to the ice. Nathan's glove snatches a puck midair. I swallow the knot in my gut.

"Ryan said you got a tutor."

I nod, slowly, glancing at Isabella. "Yeah. Her name's Maisie. And she's… she's actually pretty great at it," I admit.

I catch myself smiling just thinking about Maisie. The way she organizes her pens by color, how she uses every shade of highlighter known to man.

I wasn't expecting to like tutoring. Wasn't expecting her, really.

I breathe out a laugh. "She hates me most of the time."

She rolls her eyes like it's a full-time job. Doesn't laugh at my dumb jokes. Huffs at everything I say. But for some reason, I keep pushing her buttons anyway.

It's fun. Teasing her. Watching her get flustered and then act like it doesn't bother her.

"Most of the time?" Isabella teases, raising an eyebrow.

I grin. "Well, obviously, she secretly loves me. I'm Austin Rhodes."

She shoots me a look. "And humble, too."

I laugh, rubbing the back of my neck. "She's smart," I continue, her face flashing in my mind. "Weirdly patient, and doesn't take my shit, which is kind of refreshing." I pause, my eyes tracing the players moving through drills. "It's actually fun. More fun than I thought it would be."

The whistle blows again and the guys reset for the next drill.

I swallow hard. "Fuck, I want to be out there so bad."

Isabella bumps me lightly with her elbow. "Then don't screw things up with your tutor."

I thought I didn't need a tutor, that asking for help would make me seem weak.

But maybe I need her more than I want to admit.

Because if I want to get back on that ice, I need to pass. And if I want to pass, I need her.

"Yeah," I say, blowing out a harsh breath. "I'll try not to."

She stands up and heads back to her spot beside her dad. She watches the guys on the ice, jotting stuff down every once in a while.

I pull off my gloves with a long sigh. My hands shake just a little from the chill as I reach for my phone in my pocket.

I know I shouldn't, but I'm weak, and I need a hit of serotonin. So, I swipe my phone open, and the second I see her name pop up, my lips twitch into a smile.

Just seeing her message there makes the freeze in my chest thaw a little.

It's a stupid little thing, really, but right now it's exactly what I need.

Cherry: Confession: I waved at someone who wasn't waving at me and now I can never walk past the science building again.

Her text pops up, and I blink, trying to make sense of the jumble of letters.

I bite down a laugh before typing back.

Me: Confession: I think I'd still wave back at you. Even if it wasn't meant for me.

Cherry: Flirting with me already?

Me: I work quick. I dunno who's gonna snap you up. I don't want to lose my shot.

Cherry: You're so dramatic.

Me: You love it.

Cherry: I tolerate it. Barely.

Me: You wound me, Cherry. I thought we had something special.

Cherry: We do. It's built entirely on sarcasm, insults, and the fact that you don't know my name.

I rub my hand over my face, grinning like an idiot.

Me: I don't need your name. Texting you is the most fun I've had in, honestly, ever.

The second I hit send, I regret it a little.

I like this girl. I might not know her, but I've never had this much fun with someone before. But still, saying it out loud feels like a line crossed.

But the thing is, I can't remember the last time I looked forward to something the way I do with her messages. Can't remember the last time someone made me laugh this much without even trying.

Cherry: Please tell me you're having a better day than I am.

I pause, staring at the screen, noting how she changed subject. My fingers hover over the keyboard.

I want to tell her about today. How much it sucked watching from the sidelines. How I'd give anything to be back out there. But that means telling her *why*. Which means telling her *who* I am. And I don't want to do that. Not with her.

I like that she doesn't see me as "the hockey guy." She doesn't talk to me like I'm someone who always screws up or can't get his shit together. She just… talks to me.

Me: Sorry. Today sucked.

There's a pause. I picture her reading it, frowning. Maybe sitting in class or curled up in bed somewhere.

Cherry: Wanna elaborate or keep it cryptic?

Me: You're the one who said no details, remember?

Cherry: Right. My bad. Well I'm sorry about whatever happened that you can't tell me about.

I lean back against the boards, reading it again. And again. Wishing I could tell her. Wishing I could call her, or see her or just… fuck. Anything.

Me: You're the only thing keeping me from losing my mind today.

Cherry: In that case, do you want to hear another confession?

God, yes. Anything. Anything she'll give me. I want to know absolutely any shred of information she can tell me.

Me: Uh oh. Another public humiliation? Don't think I can survive the secondhand embarrassment.

It takes a few minutes for her to reply. I wonder what she's doing, who she's with, where she is. But then her message comes through.

Cherry: I like talking to you.

My chest does that weird tight thing again. I try to ignore it. Can't, though. It always happens when I talk to her, or think about her, or picture her, not that I can, but still.

Coach's whistle pierces the air.

"Rhodes!" he shouts. "Phone away. Now."

Fuck. Busted.

I quickly lock my screen, slipping it into my hoodie pocket, pretending like I wasn't just flirting with my anonymous pen pal in the middle of practice. Not that Cherry and I are *flirting*, really. We're just… talking. A lot. Constantly. Every night. Most mornings. And sometimes when I'm supposed to be focusing on practice.

"C'mon, Coach. Let me on the ice," I groan, pleading with him.

Coach doesn't even look at me. Just points to the stack of pucks.

I lift my ass off the bench and do the work. With a lot of heavy sighs and theatrical grunts for good measure. But I do it. Because deep down, as much as I hate every second of this, I want back in. I want to play. I miss the adrenaline, the rush, the sound of my name being shouted from the stands.

And if shoveling pucks and setting up cones is what it takes to get there again?

Fine.

But I'm still complaining about it the whole damn way.

TEN

Maisie

Austin has been staring at the same anatomy diagram for fifteen minutes.

Not labeling it. Not even pretending to try. Just sitting there with his pencil hovering midair, brow furrowed like he's waiting for the drawing to whisper the answers straight into his brain.

Honestly? It's impressive. The sheer commitment to doing absolutely nothing while looking like he might be working.

I cap my pen and lean back in my chair. "You know staring at it harder won't make the labels appear, right?"

He lets out a sigh and drops his pencil, flopping back in his chair. "There's got to be an easier way to learn this crap."

"There *was*," I say, flipping to the labeled diagram in my notes. "It's called going over it again until it sticks."

He groans, dragging a hand down his face. "You make it sound so easy."

"It's not easy," I say, leaning in a little. "It's repetition. And focus."

He shifts in his chair, glancing at the page. "My brain doesn't want to focus. It wants to set this paper on fire."

I smile. "Unfortunately, setting it on fire won't help you pass."

"Are we sure?" he asks, arching a brow. "Feels like a solid option."

"Hate to break it to you, but you're stuck with me."

His lips twitch into a smirk. "Well when you put it like that, it doesn't sound too bad."

God, he makes it impossible not to get distracted when he says things like that. I swear, tutoring Austin Rhodes is less about actually teaching him and more about surviving his constant flirting.

He blows out a breath, swiveling in his chair to face me. "What if I circle back to the bribery thing?"

I look up, catching that cocky grin spreading across his face. "You already tried bribing me," I say, flipping to the next page. "With candy, *and* that mirror selfie from the gym."

His smile deepens. "Didn't hear any complaints about the abs."

I shoot him a flat look. "That's because I was too busy praying for temporary blindness."

Which is a lie. Kind of.

I mean, the flexing was ridiculous and totally uncalled for.

But also... the guy has perfectly sculpted abs. Which I'm only aware of because he insists on parading them around at every possible opportunity.

Austin clutches his chest. "Freckles, you wound me."

He calls me that all the time now. Freckles. I don't even have that many—just a faint dusting across my nose, the kind you can only see when the sun hits just right. But he latched onto them weeks ago and hasn't let go since.

I reach into my bag and grab my Chapstick, twisting the cap off with one hand and smoothing it across my lips, more out of habit than anything else.

"Cherry?"

My eyes widen when I look up at him. "What?"

He tilts his chin toward the cherry Chapstick on the table. "Your Chapstick."

"Oh." My shoulders drop. "Yeah."

There's a pause, then his chair creaks as he leans forward with a smirk on his lips. "I knew you'd taste sweet."

That makes me freeze for half a second. I glance up slowly, narrowing my eyes. I jab my pen toward the worksheet. "Three questions left. Focus."

He groans and slumps lower in his chair. "Three? That's, like… two too many."

"Poor baby," I mutter, placing my Chapstick back into my bag. "Do you want a gold star?"

Austin doesn't answer right away. When I glance up, he's not even looking at the worksheet. He's squinting at my bag, which is half-slouched against the leg of the table.

"I want to know what the frog's about."

I blink. "What?"

He points. "The little guy. With the crown."

I follow his gaze. It takes me a second to realize he means the enamel pin clipped to the front pocket—a tiny green frog with googly eyes and a lopsided gold crown. I've had it forever. Didn't think anyone noticed it, let alone *him*.

"I've seen it every time we study," he adds. "I need answers."

I glance at the frog. He stares back, vaguely unbothered.

"It's just a pin."

Austin raises an eyebrow. "That's your whole explanation?"

"I like frogs."

"That's it?"

"Yup."

He tilts his head, unconvinced. "You've got the same guy on your laptop too, don't you?"

I glance at the sticker on the back of my laptop case. Sure enough, same frog. Just slightly bigger.

"It's not a thing," I say, flipping the page. "I just like frogs."

Austin doesn't buy it. "You definitely have a reason."

"Maybe I just think he looks funny."

"Come on." He leans forward, forearms braced on the table.

I let out a breath, pressing my pen to the corner of the worksheet. "Why do you care?"

"Because," he says, with a shrug, "I want to know more about you."

I hesitate. Not because I don't know what to say, more because I didn't think anyone would ask.

"It's dumb."

He smiles, his lips slowly lifting into a smile that makes my belly warm. "Try me."

I follow his gaze to the frog pin. "My dad gave me this when I was a kid."

He raises an eyebrow. "A frog?"

I shrug, a little smile tugging at my lips. "Yeah. He said frogs are survivors. No matter how many times they get knocked down, they keep hopping back up."

His expression softens. "Sounds like he's a pretty smart guy."

"Yeah. He was." I glance down at the pin, my fingers brushing over it. "He's been gone for a while now, but I still like to keep it with me, as a reminder."

Austin doesn't say anything, but he's still watching me.

I clear my throat and shake my head. "Told you it was dumb."

He shakes his head slowly, a quiet smile spreading across his lips that makes his whole face soften. "No. It's pretty cool." His eyes meet mine. "I like learning things about you."

The words catch me off guard. I want to laugh it off, but the honest way he says it makes me pause.

I tuck a stray lock of hair behind my ear, my fingers trembling just a little. "Well… don't get used to it."

He chuckles. "Too late for that. I'm a quick learner when it comes to you."

He leans back in his chair and stretches, long arms hooking behind his head. His hoodie rides up just enough to reveal smooth, tanned skin—a flat stomach riddled with abs that dips low, where a thin line of dark hair trails teasingly beneath the waistband of his pants.

I definitely do not stare.

Maybe just for half a second.

Okay, fine, maybe a second and a half. *Max.*

I rip my eyes away and look back down at the worksheet, but I can't ignore the way my chest is thumping. I hate how easily he gets under my skin. Or maybe I don't hate it as much as I think I'm supposed to.

I clear my throat and peek up at him. "I told you about the frog. Now you owe me the last three questions."

"Maisie," Austin groans, dragging out the word, rubbing the back of his neck. "Come on, we've been at this for over an hour."

I flick a glance at my watch. "Forty-five minutes."

He shoots me a look that's half annoyed, half pleading. "I'm starving."

I raise an eyebrow. "You had a protein bar like fifteen minutes ago."

"That was a snack," he says, arching a brow at me. "I need real food. You know, something with sauce. That fills me up. I'm a growing boy. I need sustenance."

I roll my eyes but can't hide the corner of my mouth twitching. "You're dramatic when it comes to food."

He leans forward, that familiar cocky smirk tugging at his lips. "Come on," he says, packing up his notebook. "You're coming with me."

I hesitate, swallowing a little. Saying no feels easier. I've got reading to finish, a quiz coming up, and honestly, eating around people isn't really my thing. Not that I'm about to admit that out loud.

"I'm good," I say quickly, hoping that's the end of it.

Austin sits up straighter, brow furrowed. "No, you're not. You haven't eaten either. And I'm excellent company, I promise. Five stars on Yelp."

I bite the inside of my cheek, trying to stay firm, but he's not letting up.

"Fine," I sigh, snapping my notebook shut. "But if you show me one more shirtless gym selfie, I'm walking straight into traffic."

He raises his hands, shooting me a grin. "Shirt stays firmly on," he says, then that grin slides into a teasing smirk. "Unless you want it off."

I try not to smile, but the corners of my mouth twitch anyway.

We start packing up. Austin's already halfway done, but I take my time, organizing my pens and notebooks before sliding out of my chair, pulling my top over the curve of my stomach without even thinking. Habit.

Halfway to the door, two girls step in, blocking the way. One plants herself right in front of Austin, the other closes in from the side. I step back, not wanting to get caught in the middle.

"Austin," the first girl says, voice light and sweet. "Didn't expect to see you here."

He shifts, like a switch flips. His back straightens, that easy grin settling in.

"Yeah," he says, rubbing the back of his neck, knowing full well how that flexes his bicep. "Just studying."

The second girl laughs. "Smart and cute. Dangerous combo."

They keep chatting, Austin still smiling. I catch myself glancing at the girls again. A sharp ache twists low in my stomach and I don't bother pushing it away.

Because I know the truth.

I'll never be like them. I'm not the girl who holds a guy's attention like that. I'm not the one you search for in a crowd. I'm no one's first choice.

For a second—just a flicker—I think about Six. About all those late-night messages that made me believe maybe someone could see me like that. That maybe, when we finally meet, he'll look at me like every rom-com hero looks at the girl.

But I know that couldn't be further from the truth.

Austin's still grinning as he turns back to me. "Ready?" he asks.

I nod, forcing a smile. "Sure."

♥

Austin orders like he hasn't eaten in three days: burger, fries, milkshake—

"And a side of onion rings," he adds, flashing a wink at the waitress, who turns her attention to me next.

"I'm good," I say quickly.

He frowns, just a little. "You're not eating?"

"Not hungry," I lie, swallowing the knot tightening in my throat.

He doesn't push, just glances down at the menu.

No matter what I eat, I can feel their eyes on me. Like every bite is being judged. Too much, too little, too fast, too greedy. If it's healthy, I'm pretending. If it's not, well… no wonder I look like this. There's no winning.

So I stopped eating around people altogether, because every bite feels like it's under a microscope, like everyone's just waiting for me to mess up.

Aside from the sad little yogurt cup I had this morning, I haven't had a chance to eat anything. But the thought of eating in front of him, of shoving fries into my mouth while he sits across from me looking like a damn Calvin Klein ad… nope. No thanks.

Of course, that's the exact moment my stomach betrays me with an embarrassing growl.

Austin raises a brow and turns back to the waitress. "Add an order of mozzarella sticks, too."

The waitress nods, and leaves.

My head snaps up. "Austin, you didn't—"

"They're for me," he says, cutting me off before I can finish. "I'm starving. You're not gonna judge me, are you?"

I breathe out a laugh. "No," I say, shaking my head. "Just… impressed."

He chuckles, running a hand through his messy hair. "Appetite of a hockey player," he says with a shrug. "I work out a lot, so it kinda cancels out. Clears my head also. Though, I haven't exactly been going to the gym since the whole suspension thing."

I shake my head, my eyes falling down the length of his torso. "Well, you can't tell."

I blink. *Shit.*

His grin spreads, slow and smug, and he lets out a low laugh, shaking his head. "Maisie *Freckles* Wilson… have you been checking me out?"

"Not my name," I mutter, narrowing my eyes. "And no, I wasn't checking anything out. Just making an observation."

"That I'm attractive," he says, the teasing obvious in his voice and in the way his eyes are actually *sparkling*. Who the hell has sparkling eyes in a dim diner?

"Hate to break it to you," I deadpan, "but I don't think that." *Oh look, I'm lying again.*

He laughs again, leans back in his chair with ease. "No?"

"No," I say, crossing my arms and dragging my gaze away from his annoyingly perfect face. "I mean, yeah, objectively, sure. You're attractive. Every single girl on this planet seems to crawl at your feet. But you're not my type."

His brow lifts as he reaches for his milkshake. He takes a slow sip, tilting his head, eyes still locked on mine. "And what *is* your type?" he asks.

My mouth opens, then closes.

Because I don't have an answer. Not a real one. I don't think I have a type. Not physically, anyway. I just want someone who's kind. Someone who listens. Someone who doesn't make me feel like I have to shrink myself to be worthy of attention.

But if I *did* have a type? It would probably look a hell of a lot like Austin. Messy light brown hair, hazel eyes that somehow always look lit from the inside. Broad shoulders. That stupid smile that makes it hard to breathe if I stare too long.

But I am not telling him that.

Because as much as he drives me crazy—and he does, constantly—he's also been… kind. He doesn't make me feel like an obligation. He doesn't act weird about being seen with me, or talk over me, or look through me like some of the other guys I tutor.

But if I admit I might have the *tiniest* crush on him?

Everything would shift.

He'd stop looking at me the way he does. Stop flirting and teasing and calling me *Freckles*. He'd say that I'm a nice girl, but he doesn't want to lead me on. That I'm not his type.

And that would be worse than lying.

He leans forward, his arms braced on the table. "So… no type?"

"Not really," I say, with a shrug. "I like people who are… decent. Who aren't full of themselves."

He gasps, hand over his chest. "Are you calling me full of myself?"

"If the shoe fits."

I glance at him, and of course, he's already looking at me, smirking like he knows exactly what he's doing to my pulse. And maybe he does.

God, he's annoyingly attractive. And worse, he knows it.

"I just think it's funny," he says after a second. "You claim I'm not your type, but you can't stop looking at me."

"I'm looking because you keep talking," I shoot back. "If you'd shut up, maybe I wouldn't have to."

He grins, a low chuckle leaving his lips. "Are you flirting with me, Wilson?"

I shake my head, but I can't stop the heat creeping up my neck. "I think you're confusing bullying with flirting," I mutter.

"Nah," he says, still watching me. "I just think you're a lot more into me than you let on."

"You're exhausting."

"And you're a little liar," he teases.

Luckily, the waitress comes back before he can say anything else, placing the copious plates of food down on the table.

God, it smells like heaven.

Austin digs into his burger, groaning when he takes a bite. "Holy fuck, that's good."

Without saying a word, he pushes the plate of mozzarella sticks toward me.

My eyes flick up, confused.

"You like these, right?" he asks, arching his brow a second later. "If you don't then there's something seriously wrong with you."

I let out a laugh and nod slowly.

"Then have one." He shrugs, the corner of his mouth lifting into a smile. "I won't quit until you do."

I blink. My hands are still in my lap, curled into fists under the table.

I reach out, trying not to overthink it as I grab one and take a bite.

The mozzarella stretches on the first bite, and he looks up again, his lips stretching out into a smile. For the first time in a long time, I don't feel like everyone's watching. Just him. And somehow, I don't mind it.

"So," Austin says, wiping his mouth with a napkin, keeping his eyes locked on me, "tell me about the guy."

I almost choke on my mozzarella stick and have to swallow hard. "What guy?"

He raises one eyebrow, grinning like he's got the answer before I even say anything. "The one you like."

My chest tightens, and I fight the flush creeping up my neck. "There's no guy."

"Aw, Freckles." He leans forward, a smug smile tugging at his lips. "You really think you can lie to me? I see right through your flushed cheeks."

I swallow again, hoping he'll drop it. "I don't wanna talk about it."

He takes a slow sip of his milkshake. "Come on. Spill."

But I can't. Because the guy I like is anonymous. Just a faceless guy I've been texting and have no idea who he is.

I don't know his hair color or his eye color or what his laugh sounds like. I don't know if he's tall or short or if he wears glasses or has a crooked smile. I don't know what music he listens to, or if he'd look at me the way I've always wanted someone to.

Austin shifts in his seat. "I can help you out," he says, breaking me out of my spiral. "Tit for tat and all that."

I arch a brow. "Help me how?"

He shrugs, that cocky smile creeping back. "Make him jealous. Or help you find someone better. Dealer's choice."

My eyes narrow at him. "I'm not looking for help."

He grins, completely unbothered. "Seriously though. Who is he?" He leans in closer, his voice dropping to a whisper. "Is he in here right now?"

I roll my eyes, heat prickling behind my ears. "You're ridiculous."

"But you like it." He winks. "Come on, he goes to our school, right?"

I don't answer. Because honestly… I don't know.

"Then he'll probably be at the party tomorrow night," Austin finishes when I don't answer. "Perfect opportunity to get your man."

I shoot him a glare. "First of all, never say that again. And second, I'm not going."

"You are now."

"Austin—"

"Maisie," he says as he slides his plate closer and steals the last mozzarella stick, "don't make me beg."

He leans back in the booth, one arm slung casually over the seat, the other bringing the mozzarella stick to his mouth. That slow, amused smile curves his lips—the one that makes it way too hard to look at him for too long without forgetting how to speak.

"You need to let loose sometimes, Mais. You can't spend all your time wrapped up in your head."

A weird feeling swirls in my stomach, and I bite back the urge to argue.

Because he's not wrong. I do live up there in my head, spinning circles and chewing thoughts until they're paper-thin.

His smile softens. The teasing fades from his voice. "You helped me out a shit ton with classes," he says quietly. "Let me do this for you. I'm a good wingman—I promise."

I open my mouth, then close it again.

Because, as much as I hate the idea of being in a crowded room with sweaty bodies full of people I don't know, I also don't want to spend another night alone in my bedroom, staring at a screen, wondering if I'm ever going to feel anything real.

So I exhale slowly. "Fine."

His grin widens. "I knew you'd cave."

I roll my eyes, but the smile that tugs at my lips feels inevitable whenever I'm around him.

He takes a massive bite of his burger, chews, swallows, then turns back to me. "It'll be fun. I promise," he says, his mouth quirking into a boyish grin. "I'm going to help you get your guy."

And even though I know the odds of Six being there are next to nothing, I can't help the way my chest flutters at the thought of spending more time with Austin.

Because when I'm with him… I don't feel like hiding.

ELEVEN

Austin

"**Y**ou're gonna break your teeth clenching your jaw like that," I tell Nathan, grinning as I nudge his shoulder with mine.

He doesn't look at me, just glares across the room.

Jeez. What a mood kill. Parties are supposed to be fun, and to let loose, but I don't think Nathan has ever heard that word in his life. Which is ironic, since everyone loves him. He has the girls in a chokehold, not that he ever pays any attention to any of them.

I follow his gaze across the living room, and there's Ryan, with one arm wrapped around Isabella's waist, whispering something into her ear. She laughs, leaning into him like they're the only two people in the room.

It's kind of adorable.

Nathan, however, doesn't seem to think so as he takes a slow, furious sip of his drink.

I let out a laugh. "Want me to go shove him into the fridge or something?"

He shrugs, his eyes still fixed on them. "If it's not too much trouble."

I pat his back. "What are teammates for?"

Before I can make good on that fake promise, Logan slides in at my side, with a red solo cup in hand.

"What's wrong?" he asks. "Ryan licking Isabella's ear again?"

"No one is licking anyone," Nathan snaps.

"Yet," I add.

Logan snorts into his drink.

"I hate both of you," Nathan mutters, shooting us a glare sharp enough to cut glass.

Logan just winks. "You love us. Besides, it could be worse. She could be dating Cole."

We all look around until we spot him—Cole—leaning against the back door, half hidden in shadow, hood up, hands shoved deep in his pockets, eyes burning a hole through the room.

Logan raises a brow. "Why does he look like he's planning a murder?"

"Because he probably is," I say. "Just a question of who gets it first."

I follow Cole's gaze and spot Aurora standing in the corner—tight dress, killer heels, swaying seductively to a slow R&B song.

"I've got a pretty good guess," I say with a low laugh.

Logan lets out a whistle. "Oh boy. We're all screwed."

Those two hate each other's guts. They can't be in the same room without going at each other, which I don't really mind. It's entertaining as fuck watching them.

Logan downs the last of his drink in one long gulp. "Be right back," he says, already slipping away.

I squint after him. "Where you going?"

He jerks his chin toward the kitchen, where some blonde in a denim mini skirt is flipping her hair and giving him the look.

I let out a laugh. For a rookie, he's got game—more than I have tonight, honestly. It should make me nervous. I don't want to lose to a rookie, but whatever. Let him have it.

"Need a wingman?" I offer.

Logan scoffs, shaking his head. "Nah. You'd drag me down."

My jaw snaps open as he starts to walk away. "Your fucking loss," I yell. "I'm a fucking *phenomenal* wingman."

He doesn't look back.

Pfft. Drag him down? Lucky for him I'm not interested in that girl, or I'd swoop in just to prove a point. Rookie wouldn't stand a chance.

I glance over and see Nathan still hasn't moved, his drink gripped tight in his hands.

Only now he's not watching Ryan anymore.

He's watching Logan.

Jaw tight, eyes narrowed—the exact same look he had before. Except now it's aimed somewhere completely different.

I nudge him. "What? You think Logan's gonna murder someone too?"

Nathan finally blinks, like he forgot I was there. "What? No. I just…"

He trails off, lifts his bottle, and takes a long sip.

Weird.

But I'm not about to pry, not with half a keg left and a living room full of distractions waiting for me.

I lean back against the counter, letting the noise of the party wash over me—sweaty bodies pressed close, shitty lighting flickering, music pounding. This is what weekends are made for. No assignments. No coach breathing down my neck. No pressure. Just noise, beer, and the sweet relief of forgetting for a few hours that I've tanked half my semester.

The music shifts, a faster hip-hop beat thumping through the walls. More people flood in from the backyard, and the heat in the house spikes another ten degrees. I catch sight of some guy doing a keg stand in the hallway, and someone next to me starts chanting.

It's sweaty. It's dumb.

And I fucking love it.

I should dive in, join the chant, refill my drink, lose myself. But instead, my eyes scan the crowd, and my stomach drops.

I'm doing it again.

Looking for her.

I don't even know if she's coming. She said she would, but maybe she changed her mind.

"What are you looking at?" Nathan's voice pulls me back.

I blink, tearing my gaze from the door, seeing his brows knitted together. "Nothing. Just… invited Maisie."

He raises a brow. "Maisie?"

Right. Forgot the guys don't really know her. Which is kind of nice. I like having her all to myself.

"My tutor," I add.

He arches a judgmental brow at me. What is it with everyone having very expressive eyebrows lately? "You think it's smart getting involved with your tutor?"

I shoot him a look. "It's not like that, okay? I can keep my dick in my pants. She's just always working and stressed, and I thought she needed a night to chill." I shrug. "Let loose."

Nathan takes a slow sip of his drink, shaking his head like he's already written me off. "Hope you know what you're doing."

"I do," I say, maybe a little too fast. But Nathan's wrong. Yeah, it's fun to flirt with her, but I'm not about to fuck up this tutoring thing. She's my only shot at getting back on the team.

Besides, she's into someone else. Apparently, I'm not her type—which is bullshit, because I'm a catch. But whatever.

She might not come. Probably won't. But damn, I hope she does.

I just want to see her. Out of the library, out of her hoodie, smiling—preferably at me.

I sneak another glance toward the door for what feels like the hundredth time tonight, and I forget how to breathe.

Holy shit.

For a second, I don't think it's real. My eyes are betraying me. They have to be.

Because Maisie Wilson—the girl who rolls her eyes and grumbles through every study session—is standing there in a tiny denim skirt that shows way more leg than I've ever seen on her, and a strappy pink top that hugs every curve, showing off collarbones and shoulders and all the things I didn't even realize I was obsessed with until this very moment.

Her hair is loose, shiny, bouncing as she laughs at something someone said, and I swear to God, my chest actually fucking hurts.

What the hell is wrong with me?

She's Maisie. My tutor. The girl who hands me worksheets and calls me out when I use the wrong *your*.

I shouldn't be looking at her like this.

And yet...

I can't stop. Can't tear my eyes away no matter how hard I try. Fuck, she looks beautiful. I always thought she was cute as hell from the moment I first saw those siren eyes, but this? This is different.

I need to stop staring.

I force myself to look away and slam back the last of my beer, hoping the buzz will dull the weird tightness buzzing in my chest. But then I hear her laugh.

Light. Soft.

And it's aimed at some guy in the crowd who's clearly got her full attention.

My blood runs cold.

It's just a laugh. Just a guy talking to her. But something about it feels so fucking wrong.

My eyes snap back, locking on her.

She's standing way too close to whoever the fuck that is, laughing like they're sharing some private joke. And that's when it hits me.

Holy shit. I don't like this. At fucking all.

My jaw clenches.

I can't see his face—just the back of his head—but something inside me bristles.

Who the hell is that?

A weird, hot pressure builds in my chest, and before I even think about what I'm doing, I'm moving straight toward her.

She doesn't notice me at first. She's still smiling up at him, oblivious to the fact that I'm spiraling over here like a goddamn idiot.

I slide in next to her, closer than I probably should, and let my arm curve around her waist like it belongs there.

It doesn't. I know it.

But the guy next to her glances up at me, gives me a weird look and that's good enough for me.

Maisie startles, her whole body jerking under my touch as she spins toward me.

"Austin?" she breathes, eyes wide, looking up at me.

Fuck.

I've seen her a hundred times—across the library table, her sleeves pushed up, biting her lip in concentration, hair falling messily over her face as she tries not to laugh at my dumb jokes—but I've never seen her like this.

Her eyes are impossibly bright—an unreal kind of blue, like something straight off a beach postcard or through a perfect lens filter. Except there's no filter here. Just her. Staring up at me, wide-eyed and blinking, full of surprise.

And then there's her face.

Her round cheeks are flushed pink. A scatter of freckles dust her nose and cheekbones like some perfect little constellation. I wonder how many she's got. Too many to count, probably. But damn, I kinda wanna sit and count every single one.

I feel the warmth of her body under my hand, soft and full in all the ways that make my brain glitch. My fingers spread slightly, instinctive, like my body's trying to memorize the curve of her. There's something about the way she fits against me that makes me grip tighter instead of letting go.

She smells so fucking sweet, like peaches or candy or some other thing I can't quite place. Can't think straight right now, not when she's still looking at me like that.

Without even realizing it, my head dips a little closer, inhaling the sweet scent of her shampoo.

No clue what the hell I'm doing, but fuck it, I'm doing it anyway.

"Hey," I say, voice low and rougher than it should be. Her breath catches. "There you are."

She blinks fast. Her cheeks are flushed and so fucking pink it's almost unfair.

"What are you—" she starts.

But before she can finish, I shift closer, brushing my hand along her side as I glance up at the guy she was with.

Huh.

Shorter than me by a good few inches. Blond. Dressed like he's about to present a PowerPoint—pressed button-down shirt, stiff as hell.

Is this her type?

Pfft.

I'm better looking than that. And I don't wear beige slacks to house parties.

Maisie glances awkwardly between us, then offers the guy a tight smile.

"Sorry, I'll uh… I'll catch up with you later."

The guy doesn't even look mad that I just stole her away.

I guide her off before she can rethink it, my hand still curved around her waist, my thumb brushing the soft cotton of her shirt.

She doesn't pull away. Doesn't say a word.

She just walks with me, quiet and slightly breathless, like she's still trying to figure out what the hell just happened.

It's not until we're out of the room and into the quieter hallway that she finally turns to me, her eyebrows scrunched in disbelief.

"What was that?" she demands.

Good question.

Because now that I'm here, feeling my heart slam against my ribs like it's about to bust out… I have no clue.

"Was that him?" I blurt before I can stop myself.

"What?" She blinks up at me in confusion.

"The guy you like," I clarify.

She makes a face. "What? No. He's just someone I tutor."

I squint, shaking my head. "No."

"No?" she echoes, a little laugh slipping out.

"I'm your only student."

Her laugh spills out again, and my god, I want to bottle that sound forever.

"You're acting ridiculous," she says, shaking her head.

She's right. Dunno what the hell is going on with me, or what the fuck I'm feeling.

"Come on," I say, slipping my arm back around her waist. "I wanna introduce you to some people."

She raises an eyebrow. "Are you always this touchy?"

"Only with you, Freckles." I grin and shoot her a wink.

Her mouth opens like she's about to argue, then closes again as she looks away, her cheeks flaring pink.

I don't miss it.

God, she's fucking gorgeous when she's flustered.

We weave through the crowd, and I keep my hand low on her waist, partly to guide her, mostly because I don't want to let go.

I lead her to the corner of the living room where the guys are clustered, half-drunk and arguing about whatever the fuck else.

"Hey," I call out. "Play nice. I brought someone."

They all look up.

Maisie hesitates beside me, a flicker of tension in her.

"This is Maisie," I say. "She's my tutor."

Her face flushes a deeper shade of pink as she tucks a loose strand behind her ear. Shy isn't a word I'd ever used to describe her before, not like this. Sure, she's quiet at times, but she's always been cutthroat and stubborn and had no problem calling me out on my shit.

"She's the one trying to keep me from failing out," I add.

Nathan nods. "Thanks for your service."

Maisie laughs, glancing up at me. "It's an uphill battle."

I grin. That's my girl.

"She's cute," Aurora says, sliding in from the side, a drink in her hand. "Why haven't you brought her around before?"

"I don't know," I admit. "Felt like keeping her to myself."

Maisie goes quiet. Her eyes flick to mine, and I feel that spark in my chest again, something I don't quite get, but I *really* fucking like.

Aurora eyes her for a beat, then nods toward the butterfly clip nestled in Maisie's dark hair. "Cute hair clip."

Maisie fingers it self-consciously. "Oh, um… thank you."

I glance down, catching that soft pop of pink against her hair, and my lips curl into a stupid smile.

Before anyone can say more, some random dude strolls over, eyeballing Aurora like she's the only girl in the room—which, to him, maybe she is.

"Hey, you're hot as fuck," he starts, running a hand through his hair, flashing her a smile, coming off way too strong. I huff out a laugh. Rookie move. "Can I buy you a drink or something?"

Before Aurora can shut him down—given that she has a boyfriend—Cole jumps in. "She's a venomous snake, man. I'd stay the hell away."

Aurora doesn't even blink. Her eyes narrow sharp enough to slice his throat, and honestly, I don't doubt she wants to.

"Don't worry. I wouldn't touch your tiny dick even if you paid me."

Logan chokes on his drink. My eyes widen, an amused smirk tugging at my lips. But Cole's jaw locks tight, the muscle ticking.

"My dick's nowhere near small, Viper," he replies. "Too bad you'll never find out."

Aurora cocks her head, rolling her eyes. "Spare me the bullshit, Reaper. I bet you couldn't find a woman's clit with a map and a compass."

The poor dude mutters something and scrams, disappearing into the crowd.

"Jesus," Ryan mutters. "You two, cut it the fuck out before you scare Maisie off."

Maisie's standing there, mouth slightly open, shocked.

I lean in close, chuckling against her ear. "Don't worry, they're always like this."

She smiles up at me. *Christ*. She has got to stop looking at me. Or like... do it forever. I don't know which I want right now. My brain is muddled.

I shake my head, trying to steady myself. "Fuck, every time you smile at me, I forget what I was about to say."

Her lips part just a little, and I swear I catch a blush rising in her cheeks.

"Oh wait," Isabella says, perched on Ryan's lap. "I've seen you before. You skate, right?"

Maisie's gaze snaps to her, and she nods, surprised. "Yeah. I'm on the team."

"You're really good," Isabella says with a warm smile. "I watch you skate sometimes when I'm waiting for the guys to get geared up."

Maisie blinks, clearly not expecting that. "Thank you."

And something about the way she says it, quiet and sweet, does something to me. And I realize this is probably the first time I've ever seen her really interact with other girls.

Maisie's always alone, always quiet. Even when I pass her on campus, she's off to the side, like she doesn't quite belong anywhere.

I don't know why that bothers me.

Maybe it's because I like seeing her with my friends. Because she fits in here—with us.

When she laughs at something Isabella says, something in my chest eases.

I want her to laugh like that again.

I want her to be friends with my friends.

I want her to keep looking at me like I'm something other than the pain-in-the-ass student she's been stuck tutoring.

Because now?

I'm not just *looking* at her.

I'm *seeing* her.

And I don't think I can stop.

TWELVE

Maisie

There's something sacred about the rink when it's empty.

No teammates shouting, no squeaky whistle from Coach. Just the soft hum of overhead lights and the low whir of the cooling system.

It's quiet here. Like the whole world slows down, and for a little while, the ice belongs only to me.

I glide out to center ice, my blades slicing clean lines into the surface beneath me.

There's comfort in the quiet. In being alone out here, with no one here to watch me screw up.

My thighs burn as I push harder, building speed along the curve of the rink. I can feel every muscle in my legs screaming, my breath catching sharp in my throat, but I don't ease up. I can't.

The double loop is coming.

I prep the turn, wind up for the takeoff. My arms cross tight at my chest, everything in me coiled like a spring.

Then I launch.

And immediately I know it's wrong.

I barely get the rotation before my blade hits the ice too early, and when I come down, my left blade clips the ice at the wrong angle.

And I go down.

Fast and hard.

Pain slices through my leg on impact as I slam into the ice, landing on my side. The cold seeps straight through my leggings, biting into skin.

"Shit," I mutter, one hand pressing to my knee as I wince.

I stay there for a second, trying to catch my breath.

The fall wasn't too bad, but it stings. My knee's gonna bruise for sure.

I glance at the clock above the scoreboard. I've been here for almost an hour, and I still can't land that jump cleanly.

I *should've* landed it. I *have* landed it.

Regionals are next month.

Four weeks until the lights go up and the music starts. Four weeks until I have exactly three minutes to land every jump, hit every spin, and prove I deserve to be out here at all.

I wipe the back of my hand across my face and let out a long, shaky breath.

Skating used to feel like magic when I was a kid. Back when Mom used to care. When she used to brush my hair into tight buns before competitions, pack my gear bag with homemade protein muffins and handwritten notes.

But after my dad died, things shifted.

She had two younger kids to take care of. A house to keep running. A full-time job.

I get it. I really do.

I was the oldest. The calm one. The easy one. So, I learned to take care of myself.

I braided my own hair, packed my own bags, took the bus to the rink.

Mom stopped coming to competitions, and eventually stopped asking about practices. Not because she didn't care, I don't think. She just didn't have anything left to give.

And yeah, I understand. But it still hurt. Because I never stopped caring.

I never stopped trying to be better and better, hoping that one day she could come to one of my competitions, watch me skate, and I'd make her proud.

Sometimes I think… if I'd fallen apart a little more, she might've noticed. But I didn't. I held it together, because that's what everyone needed.

And maybe that's why I can't celebrate my achievements, because, in my mind, it's my obligation to achieve them.

I blow out a breath and shake out my arms, pushing the thoughts aside.

I roll back into motion, building speed as I loop around the far end of the rink. I bend my knees, square my shoulders, and zone out everything else.

Loop. Step. Takeoff. Rotate.

I go for the double toe loop.

The takeoff's solid. Rotation clean. My blade connects with the ice in a sharp snap and I hold it.

I glide out of it, heart racing. My breath clouds in the air, and for a second, I let myself feel the relief pounding in my chest. Maybe I'm not as hopeless as I felt five minutes ago.

And that's when I hear someone clapping.

I slam to a stop, my blades kicking up a rough spray of ice shavings.

What the hell—

I spin around, my breath catching in my throat, and of course… it's him.

Austin Rhodes. Standing just beyond the boards with his skates slung over his shoulder and that stupidly pretty smirk on his face.

"Jesus," I mutter, my hand flying to my chest. "You scared me."

He steps out from the tunnel in sweatpants and a backwards cap, a grin spreading across his face. "Sorry. Didn't want to interrupt you."

I blink at him, still trying to catch up. "How long have you been here?"

He shrugs. "Since the wipeout."

A flush climbs up my neck. Of course. Because the universe really loves to humiliate me "Great. Hope you enjoyed the show."

"You made up for it," he says, nodding toward the ice. "That landing was… damn."

I narrow my eyes. "Are you being sincere right now or sarcastic?"

Austin lifts a hand, placing it over his heart. "Swear. It was hot," he says with a smirk. "And also very impressive, but mostly hot."

My stomach drops and flutters at the same time, which should not be physically possible. I glare, my face instantly going hot. "What are you doing here?"

He starts walking toward the gate. "I could ask you the same thing," he says, tilting his head.

His hoodie sleeves are shoved up to his elbows, his forearms flexing as he shifts his stick into his other hand. His sweatpants hang low on his hips, like he just rolled out of bed looking annoyingly perfect.

I fold my arms, lifting my shoulders into a shrug. "I prefer practicing at night."

He raises a brow as he drops down onto the bench and starts untying his sneakers. "Because you're secretly a vampire or…?"

I wipe my forehead with the sleeve of my hoodie, avoiding his eyes. "Because I don't like being in anyone's way."

He stills mid-lace, his head lifting slowly, and when his eyes find mine, his whole expression hardens. "Has anyone said anything to you to make you feel like you're in the way?"

"What? No," I murmur, too quickly. It's technically true. No one ever had to say it out loud. I've always just… known.

He watches me for a beat, like he's reading between every line I didn't say. Then his jaw tightens, his eyes darkening just slightly. "If anyone ever makes you feel that way," he says, voice rough, "you come to me. I don't care who it is. I'll make sure they never do it again."

I stare at him, caught completely off guard, my chest going tight.

"What *are* you doing here?" I ask him.

He finishes lacing his skates up, then stands, taps the gate open with his stick, and hops over the boards. "Couldn't sleep," he says, skating a slow lap around me, tipping his head back to look at the rafters. "And I miss the ice like crazy. I figured I'd come sneak a few laps before Coach drags us into another 6 a.m. hell practice where I have to set up fucking cones again."

I track him as he glides on the ice. He's not even trying, and he still moves like the ice was made for him.

I let out a breath. "Well. Sorry. You'll have to share."

He grins, turning back toward me. "Oh, I don't mind sharing," he says, with a smile that makes me feel warm, even though I'm on the ice. "Especially not with you."

Austin flirts like it's his native language. It's so baked into his personality that I don't think he even knows when he's doing it. And normally, I'd dismiss guys like him. Cocky athletes with pretty faces and permanent smirks don't usually earn space in my brain.

But then he had to go and be my tutoring assignment. And now he's not just an annoying jock, he's thoughtful and has dimples and a way of looking at me like I'm not invisible.

And it's messing with me.

He circles around again, then slows to a stop in front of me.

"Alright," he says, tapping the end of his stick against my skate. "Teach me some moves."

I raise a brow. "You'll break your tailbone."

He shrugs. "I've had worse."

He's watching me too closely now, and his attention on me makes my skin buzz and my brain glitch.

I glance toward the other end of the rink. I was planning to try the jump again. Just one more go before I called it for the night.

"Fine. But don't sue me when you dislocate something."

He skates closer. Close enough that I have to look up to keep my eyes on his.

"I'd never sue you," he says, voice dipping low. "Might make you kiss it better, though."

I groan, pushing at his shoulder. "Gross."

He chuckles, but waits for me to show him some moves. And maybe I should tell him to stop looking at me like that, to go skate his laps and leave me be.

But instead, I roll my eyes and skate backward into position. My blades bite into the ice, and I keep my arms tight to my sides as I launch into a simple waltz, landing clean and smooth, coming to a soft glide.

When I straighten and blow out a breath, I sneak a glance toward Austin, who's watching me carefully.

He skates a slow, thoughtful circle, his brow furrowed.

"Okay," he says, lips pursed as he drops his stick onto the ice. "I got this."

He skates in a circle to gain momentum, and then pushes off the ice, his arms spreading out as he attempts a spin. His knees lock at the wrong time, his arms flail in opposite directions, and by the time he finishes his sad little turn, I'm doubled over, clutching my ribs.

"Okay, no, stop." I can barely breathe. "You look like a baby giraffe learning to walk."

"I'm insulted," he says, placing his hand on his chest.

"You should be," I say, unable to stop the smile from creeping onto my face.

His eyes narrow. "Alright. Round two."

"Austin—"

Too late. He tries again, this time aiming for the jump. Or a version of it. There's a moment where I think he might pull it off since he gets a surprising amount of lift, but then he over-rotates, loses control, and lands flat on his ass with a loud, echoing thud.

"Jesus—" he groans.

I skate over, still laughing, and crouch beside him, the ice biting into my knees.

"You're terrible," I say, poking his shoulder.

He groans, placing his hand on his chest. "You wound me, Maisie." He sits up, brushing ice shavings off his hoodie. "I should've warmed up first," he mutters, rubbing his back.

"Or not attempted a jump with zero figure skating experience," I say.

He grins. "Fair. Wanna trade? Want me to teach you how to handle a puck."

I raise a brow. "What makes you think I don't know how?"

"Please." He snorts. "You glide around like a ballerina. Bet you've never even body-checked someone."

"Correct. I've also never tried to impress someone with a waltz and nearly broken my tailbone."

He smirks and pushes to his feet, stick in hand. "C'mon. Let me make a hockey girl out of you."

I pause for half a second before gliding over to the edge of the rink, where his gear bag sits unzipped. He pulls out a puck and drops it onto the ice.

I come to a stop a few feet from him, eyeing the stick in his hand. "You're gonna have to show me what to do," I say. "I've never even held a stick before."

His mouth quirks, and a low laugh escapes him.

I narrow my eyes as the innuendo hits me. "Don't say it."

He holds the stick out to me, a grin still tugging at his lips. "Didn't say anything."

I snatch it from him with a sigh, trying to ignore the heat climbing up my neck.

It's heavier than I expected. I shift my grip awkwardly. It feels like I'm holding it wrong—which, judging by the way he immediately laughs, I am.

"Alright," he says, skating around behind me, wrapping his arms around mine. His chest brushes my back, and it takes everything in me not to lean into him. "Top hand here." He adjusts my left hand. "Bottom hand here." His fingers brush my right hand, lingering just a second too long. "That's your power hand. Like this."

I can't breathe.

"You good?" he asks, his low rumbly voice making my skin break out in shivers.

I nod. *Definitely not good. Probably never been worse.*

He nudges a puck toward us with the blade of the stick, then skates around to face me. "Alright. Try moving it. Just little taps."

I shift my weight forward and tap the puck. It skitters across the ice in a straight line.

"Okay," he says slowly. "Not terrible."

I skate after the puck, clumsily steering it back toward him. It bumps off my skate and drifts off-course.

Austin chuckles. "You're treating it like it's fragile."

"I don't want to break it."

"It's a puck. It's literally a hardened rubber disk designed to be smacked around at sixty miles an hour."

I blow out a breath. "I don't think I'm very good at this."

He skates closer, tilting his head. "Aw, come on. Don't give up just yet. If you can land a double toe loop, you can definitely figure out how to hit a puck."

I glance at him, surprised. "You know what that is?"

He shrugs. "I googled some stuff."

That makes something flutter weirdly in my chest. "Why?"

He shrugs again, rubbing the back of his neck. Oh god… is he… blushing? "Couldn't stop thinking about the videos on your profile."

Heat rushes to my cheeks. I glance away, hoping he doesn't notice the way my face is definitely on fire.

He slides closer, positioning himself behind me again. "Alright, let's try it again." He adjusts my grip again, this time slower, his fingers wrapping over mine, big and rough. Not that I've noticed. Obviously.

I can feel his breath fanning against my cheek, the solid heat of him behind me, and I'm suddenly very aware of the fact that no one else is here.

He wraps his hands tighter over mine and gently swings the stick forward, hitting the puck so it glides cleanly across the ice. It's easy. Way easier than when I tried.

I glance up at him. "Okay… that was cool."

"You're a natural," he murmurs, but he doesn't step back.

And I don't move either.

"I didn't do anything," I reply, my breath thick, and my heart beating against my chest.

How is it possible that someone like him exists? Like, truly, his proportions are… unfair. If I weren't actively trying not to notice, I'd be thinking about his biceps under that hoodie. About the veins on his forearms when he holds his stick.

He catches me looking and flashes that grin again.

I swallow harshly. "What?" I ask.

He chuckles as he grabs the stick from my hands, his hand flying to my hips as he spins me around until we're facing each other, my hands instinctively flying to his chest. "You're cute when you're flustered."

I narrow my eyes. "I hate you."

He laughs again. I can feel the rise and fall of his chest underneath my palms, and all I can think about is how wide it is, how solid he feels under my fingers.

"No you don't," he says with a smirk. "You love me."

I arch a brow at him. "You think everyone loves you."

"They usually do." He says it like it's a fact. Like gravity.

And he's not wrong. Girls love him. Boys love him. Professors—even the ones whose classes he never shows up to—somehow love him.

"Don't expect me to," I say, attempting to breathe.

He pulls me into him, one arm sliding around my waist. "Never. I prefer when you roll your eyes at me," he says, his lips tugging into a smirk.

I glance at them, full and perfect, and I don't know when I started thinking about what it might feel like to kiss him.

But the thought is there now. Buzzing behind my ribs. Settling in the hollow of my throat.

God, how is this real?

How is this me?

Because if you'd asked me a year ago—or even a month ago—I would've said no way. No way a guy like Austin Rhodes would ever look twice at me. No way I'd ever let myself want someone who flirted with every breathing girl on campus.

But he's looking at me now.

And no one ever looks at me.

His eyes search mine, quiet and unreadable.

And then he glances down.

At my mouth.

My pulse spikes so fast I feel dizzy.

We're so close.

I can feel the space between us pulling tighter. My lips part. My brain short-circuits.

"Hey!"

We jolt apart, eyes wide.

Austin's grip slips from my waist and he whips around. "Shit."

The janitor is standing at the edge of the rink, squinting at us under the fluorescent lights.

"Fuck," Austin hisses as he grabs my hand. "Run."

We take off, our blades scraping across the ice, stumbling as we hit the edge and fumble to pull the rubber guards onto our skates.

We bolt through the hallway, ducking into a supply closet.

Austin slams the door behind us, and as soon as we're swallowed by darkness, I let out a breathless chuckle.

"Shh," he says, chuckling as he covers my mouth with his hand. "You're going to get us caught."

I lift my eyes to his and I'm suddenly very aware that his body is pressed against mine in this dark, cramped space.

I should be freaking out.

But all I can feel is him.

His presence is like a gravitational force, pulling my focus to the shape of his jaw, the heat of his skin through his sweatshirt. I shift slightly and his hand drops from my mouth.

He doesn't move away.

Neither do I.

I can feel him looking at me, even in the dark.

I want to say something—I don't know what.

I want to ask what we're doing. What this is.

But then the janitor's footsteps echo down the hall and a door slams. And the moment breaks.

Austin lets out a hard exhale and takes a step back. "Come on," he says, turning around. "Let's go before they bust us."

He opens the door, peeking into the hallway before slipping out of the closet. I follow quietly, stepping into the dim hallway behind him.

I pretend not to notice the distance he's put between us. I don't say anything, just keep my eyes on the floor, trying really hard not to feel disappointed.

And I hate that I do.

Because for a second, I thought maybe... maybe he was looking at me differently. That maybe he was going to kiss me. That maybe all the flirting wasn't just him being him.

But I forgot who I'm dealing with.

Austin Rhodes flirts with everyone. One look, in a dark closet, doesn't mean anything.

And I need to remember that.

THIRTEEN

Austin

Six weeks.

Six whole weeks without sex.

Honestly, I'm starting to wonder if there's a secret monastery somewhere in this city I accidentally signed up for.

I shift, feeling the worn-out fabric of the couch underneath me, the faint smell of spilled beer and old pizza lingering in the air. Ryan's sprawled out on the armchair across from me, scrolling on his phone, slowly sipping his beer, Nathan's pacing near the window, and Logan is leaning back in a chair, half-smiling at something on his phone.

"Hey," I say, sitting up and flicking a peanut at Ryan's head. "Quick question."

He looks up, blinking. "What's up?"

"How did you deal with blue balls?"

Ryan almost chokes on his drink, sputtering as he coughs. "Are you serious?" he asks, shaking his head.

"Come on." I sit up. "Last year before Isabella, when you were all moody and grumpy like this one," I nod at Nathan, who shoots me a glare, "how did you deal with it?"

Logan laughs. "Having a dry spell, bud? What's it been, two, three days?"

"Six weeks."

The room goes quiet instantly, like I just dropped a bombshell.

"Fuck," Logan breathes out, his eyes widened.

I groan, rubbing my face. "Yeah, I know."

Nathan frowns. "What's going on? In the two years I've known you, I've never seen you have any problems getting a girl."

I shrug again. "Just haven't felt like it," I tell them honestly.

"Uh oh," Ryan says with a teasing smirk. "This is about a girl."

"No." *Yes*.

I don't even know if I did it on purpose, but ever since Cherry started texting me, I haven't even *thought* about hooking up with anyone.

It's dumb. I've never met this girl, I don't even know who she really is, don't even know if she's near me or if she lives halfway across the world. But this girl has hooked me like no one else.

Well, maybe one girl has—

No. Fuck.

Stop thinking about her.

Yeah, too fucking late. My mind flashes to Maisie, to her eyes. Those drop-dead gorgeous eyes that I swear have me under a spell. I think back to the way she laughed at me on the ice the other night, like she forgot that I'm the annoying jock she has to tutor—just for a second. The way she looked up at me when I pulled her close during our fake hockey practice, and her breath caught in her throat like maybe I wasn't the only one feeling whatever the fuck was happening between us. How I almost kissed her, how bad I wanted to.

Fuck.

I scrub a hand through my hair, hard.

I need to get these thoughts out of my head.

Maisie is… She's just Maisie. My tutor. The no-nonsense, zero-bullshit, too-smart-for-me girl who rolls her eyes every time I call her Freckles. She doesn't even like me.

But the way she looked at the party. And the way she was looking at me…

And now I can't stop thinking about her lips. Those soft, pink lips. Wondering if they would feel soft against mine. If she'd push me away, or kiss me back, or—

"You're blushing."

Logan's teasing voice drags me back. I blink, finding him grinning at me.

I flip him off, which makes him laugh harder.

Nathan shakes his head with a smirk. "I think it's nice you're falling for someone."

I roll my eyes. "I'm not falling for anyone. I'm just trying to figure out how to deal with these blue balls before they turn purple."

Ryan runs a hand through his hair and blows out a breath. "Fuck, I can't believe I'm saying this but…" He looks at me dead serious. "I jerked off."

I blink. "Yeah, no shit, Ryan."

"No, I mean a lot," he adds quickly. "Like, more than usual. It was brutal."

I arch a brow, smirking. "Little too much info there, buddy."

His eyes narrow. "You asked."

I laugh and give him a grateful nod. "I did. Thanks for sharing, I guess."

My phone buzzes, and I glance down, my heart skipping when I see it's Cherry.

My lips curl into a smile and I pocket my phone. "Gotta go study."

Nathan scoffs. "You've never studied in your life."

"I study now," I say with a shrug.

"Bullshit," Logan says. "You're texting a girl."

I sigh, already standing up. "I'm going to my room."

"Tell her we say hi!" Logan calls after me.

"Tell her she can do better!" Ryan adds.

"Tell her to run," Nathan says dryly.

I take the stairs two at a time until I reach my room. Pushing the door open, I kick my hockey bag out of the way. I drop onto the bed, my leg slung up over the comforter, and pull out my phone.

Cherry: Confession. I hate malls.

I'm already smiling. Can't help it. Every time I see her name flash across my screen, my heart thuds in my chest and I get this weird feeling swirling in my stomach. I hate it. And love it. And don't understand what the hell it is.

I hit the voice-to-text button.

Me: What's so dangerous about a mall?

Cherry: The fitting rooms. The lighting. The trauma.

Me: You say that like it's a war zone.

Cherry: Honestly, I'd take a battlefield over trying on clothes.

I let out a chuckle, rubbing a hand over my jaw, before replying.

Me: Show me.

Cherry: Excuse me?

A smirk curls my lips.

Me: C'mon, Cherry. I feel left out here. Just one picture. It doesn't have to be of your face, just... something.

I stare at my phone, watching those bubbles appear and disappear, and then... nothing. I blow out a breath, lifting my head, squeezing my eyes closed, wondering if I went too far. But then my phone buzzes and I snap them open, glancing down at the picture.

"Oh fuck."

I lift a hand, wiping it across my mouth. Because on my phone is my first ever picture of Cherry.

It's not of her face, or... anything really. Just a sliver of her legs in the mirror, wearing a flowy white dress.

But my brain still short-circuits.

Because now I have legs to imagine.

Legs.

Bare. Warm. Wrapped around—

Focus, man.

Me: Fuck, Cherry. You look incredible.

The silence stretches, but I'm not ready to put my phone down. I tap my fingers on my thigh, nerves fluttering like butterflies.

Cherry: You can't even see my face.

Me: Don't need to. I bet your eyes wreck people. And your smile is probably criminal, too.

Cherry: You always say the exact thing I wish someone would.

My eyes close for a second, and I lean back, the headboard rough against my shoulder blades.

Why the hell does she do this to me?

I've had hookups. Casual flings. One night stands. And every single girl I could ever want. But somehow, one text from her feels better than all of it combined.

Me: Fuck. I want to see that on you so bad.

Me: Actually, I just want to see you.

Cherry: If we met in real life, it wouldn't be the same.

Me: How do you know?

Cherry: Because in real life, people get disappointed.

Me: You think I'd be disappointed?

Cherry: Wouldn't you?

I stare at the screen, heart thudding.

No.

Not even a little.

I want to tell her she's wrong.

That I wouldn't hurt her. That I wouldn't be disappointed, because I know her.

Maybe I don't know her height or what color her eyes are. Maybe I've never seen the way her hair falls around her face. But I know *her*.

I love the way her mind works, the way she says things that stick with me hours later. She feels like home in a world that rarely makes sense.

And God, I want to tell her that.

That if she were here, I'd hold her face in my hands and kiss her until every memory of the assholes who made her feel like she wasn't enough faded into nothing.

Because to me, she's more than enough. She always has been.

I want to ask her to meet me.

But I already know what she'd say.

It would ruin the magic.

And I can't risk ruining anything between us.

Not when she feels like the only real thing I've got.

I look down at my phone again, scanning her messages.

But if she asked me to meet her right now, I'd go. I'd book a flight to wherever she is and run.

And that scares the shit out of me.

Because I don't run for anyone.

Not since I was eight years old, standing at the edge of the driveway in my socks, running after my dad as he drove off for the last time, with tears falling down my face.

My mom didn't cry in front of me. She comforted me and my sister, held us as we cried in her arms. But later that night, when she was in her room and thought we were asleep, I heard her sobs.

I saw the light go out of her eyes every time another guy left. Like she was learning to expect less and less every time. That's what love did to her. And I swore I'd never let it do that to me. Or make anyone feel like that.

So yeah, I flirt, I hook up, but I don't do relationships.

I don't risk hurting someone, or being hurt by someone. I don't want someone seeing me for real, then deciding I'm not enough.

Until now.
Until this.
Until her.
I blow out a breath and fall back on my bed, staring up at the ceiling. What the hell is happening to me?

FOURTEEN

Maisie

I should be asleep.

My eyelids ache, heavy from a full day of classes, tutoring, and skating, but instead I'm curled up in bed, wrapped in my fleece blanket, watching the phone screen light up every few seconds.

No new notifications.

I should be used to it by now. I've never really been the first person anyone texts when plans pop up. Never been the one people lean on or want around. I've never been the best friend or the person people call first.

But with Six... I don't know. I kind of thought our friendship mattered to him like it does to me.

My mind keeps slipping away, no matter how hard I try to concentrate. I should be outlining my psychology paper. Or reviewing Austin's latest stat sheet for our next session. Or honestly, just sleeping. But none of it sticks in my brain right now. Not when I'm waiting for a text that probably won't show up.

My thumb hovers over the screen and I tap again. Still nothing. I let out a breath and drop the phone on my chest, staring up at the ceiling.

My legs burn from practicing the double lutz over and over. I only have three weeks until regionals, which means the extra practice is necessary—which is why I have been going to the rink late at night every night.

Austin hasn't been back since that one time. Not that I expect him to—I don't—I just… I can't stop thinking about it.

And I hate that.

Because every time I think about him—and that night—I remember that this ridiculous crush I have on him is just that. Ridiculous. I promised myself I wouldn't be one of those girls that fluttered my lashes and beamed at him, but the guy makes it impossible not to notice him.

And now, my heart thuds in my chest every time I think about him, or have to tutor him, or see him in class or in the rink. And I only have myself to blame.

My phone buzzes beside me and I roll onto my side, swiping open the text.

Six: Hey. You still up?

I smile, the corner of my mouth twitching as I tug the blanket tighter around my shoulders.

Me: Am I ever not?
Six: I'm glad you are. You're kind of my safe place.
My heart does this slow roll in my chest.
Me: Yeah?

The typing bubbles flicker, disappear, come back. I tuck my feet under the blanket, the cold crawling up my skin.

Six: You know you are, Cherry.

I imagine what it would be like to see my name instead of the stupid nickname I gave him on the screen. If it would make my chest flutter this much, or even more?

I roll onto my back, typing out a reply.

Me: It's kind of weird you didn't start with a confession.

His reply comes back a few seconds later.

Six: Alright.
Six: Confession: I hate being alone.

I stare at the screen for a second too long, my heart aching for him.

Me: I never would've guessed that about you.
Six: I guess I'm good at hiding it. But I don't want to hide from you.
Me: You don't have to. You can say whatever you want to me. That's the best thing about the anonymity.

It takes him a while to reply back, but I keep my eyes locked on the screen until his message pops up.

Six: I can walk into a room, say all the right things, make people laugh. But the second I'm alone, it feels like no one really sees me.

I pin my bottom lip between my teeth. It's been just me for so long now, that I've gotten used to the quiet. I've gotten used to not being needed by anyone, or invited anywhere or thought of when making plans.

Me: Here's my confession. I think I've gotten too good at being alone. It's practically muscle memory.

I hit send, and blow out a breath, squeezing my eyes closed. The whole reason we started sending each other these confessions was to be able to tell each other things no one else could. But this is different. It feels like letting him into my mind.

Six: That makes me so sad. I hate the thought of you being alone.

My nose burns as I start to feel moisture building in my eyes, but I quickly shake it off, typing out a reply.

Me: I don't feel it as much when I'm texting you.

I curl further into my blankets and let out a long, slow breath.

Six: I wish I was there for real. You'd never be alone again.

My chest pulls tight. I wish that could happen so bad. I wish I was brave enough to tell him who I am, and to meet up with him, and take this… friendship—or whatever it is we have— out of the texts.

Me: What would you do? If you were here.

The second I send it, my stomach flips. Regret blooms in my chest, but it's too late, because he replies almost instantly.

Six: Right now?
Me: Right now.

I watch the screen intently as the bubbles appear, my heart thudding in my chest once I finally read his reply.

Six: I'd sit next to you, let you lean on me. Maybe hold your hand, if you wanted, give you my hoodie. Fuck, you'd look so good in it.

I let out a chuckle.

Me: Giving me your hoodie implies we're close enough for you to be hoodie-less around me.
Six: Cherry, baby. I'd one thousand percent be hoodie-less around you, because my body would be burning up over how good you look.
Me: You can't just say stuff like that and expect me to stay normal.
Six: Falling for me, already, Cherry? You don't even know what I look like. I could have buck teeth and glasses and wear a burlap sack.

I chuckle, shaking my head, picturing what six would look like. I imagine a quiet broody guy with curly hair, even though I know he likes parties, which could probably mean he's more social than quiet and broody. I don't even care.

Me: You don't know what I look like either.
Six: Don't need to. I already know you're gorgeous.

My chest flutters, but doubt creeps in anyway. He says that because he's never actually met me, but what if that changed and he didn't like what he saw?

Me: You're kind of ruining other people for me, you know.

Six: Good. I want to be the only one who gets this part of you.

My smile stretches so wide it physically aches.

Six: Be honest. Would you ever want to meet?

The smile slips from my face as soon as the message comes through.

It's not the first time he's asked, but every time it sends my stomach into a slow, spiraling freefall. And every time, my answer is the same.

Me: I don't think that's a good idea.

Six: Why not?

I stare at the message so long the words start to blur. My thumb hovers over the keyboard, frozen, thinking all of the reasons why it would be the worst idea ever.

Because... I'm scared.

Because if we meet, you'll see me. You'll see the soft curve of my stomach, the way my thighs touch, the roundness of my face, and I'll see it happen—the moment your face changes. The flicker of disappointment. The moment you realize that the girl you built in your head doesn't match the one standing in front of you.

Because I'm more than just my body, but no one ever seems to look past it.

And I don't want you to be one of those people.

Me: It's just better like this.

Six: Better for who, Cherry?

I don't know what to say to that. Not without telling him the truth. That it's easier to be invisible than to be seen and rejected.

I drop my phone onto my nightstand and drag my laptop across the blanket, flipping it open before I queue up a rom-com I've seen more times than I can count. The opening credits start to roll, and I let out a content sigh.

I love love.

I always have. Even when it feels like I'll never get to experience it myself.

I tuck my hands under my cheek as I watch the movie, wondering if anyone will ever look at me the way those guys look at the girls in movies? Will anyone look at me and think 'Wow. She's beautiful.'? Will anyone ever hold my hand in public, or press their forehead to mine like they can't believe I'm real?

It's the cruelest kind of irony. I hate men. But I still want one. I want to be seen. Held. Chosen. Just once. Just to see what it feels like.

My phone buzzes again, and I sneak a glance at the screen, but this time it's not a text from Six.

Austin: hey ur in hawthorn hall right?

I blink at the screen, watching his profile picture light up beside the new message. He always types like he's in a rush. No punctuation, no capital letters. Sometimes words are wrong. But they sound like him. I like knowing he put effort into texting me when he probably hates it.

Me: Yes?

Austin: whats ur room number?

Me: Why?

Austin: just tell me. please.

I freeze for a second, staring at the message. Why the hell is Austin Rhodes asking for my room number? My mind starts racing, running through every possible reason. Maybe he's messing with me, maybe he's had a few drinks, or maybe he's here for some girl in my building.

Against my better judgment, I type it out anyway.

And five minutes later, there's a knock at my door.

My stomach twists as I shove my laptop aside and stand up, tugging at my pajama sleeves.

I open the door and blink as Austin stands in my dorm hallway, his hair wild and messy as usual, and a half-empty Gatorade in one hand. He lifts his chin in greeting like it's the most normal thing in the world, which is definitely not how I'm feeling right now.

"Hey."

I blink. "Uh… hey."

He exhales, lifting his chin to peek past me into the room, then back at me. "Mind if I come in?"

"Uh… yeah. I guess." I step aside before my brain can catch up.

He steps inside, and I close the door behind him, leaning against it, wondering what the hell Austin Rhodes is doing in my dorm room.

He takes his time, his eyes roaming over the room—my unmade bed, the messy stack of books on my desk, the half-empty bag of chips next to my laptop, and the plushies scattered all over my room.

His gaze settles on a stuffed penguin perched on the edge of my bed.

"Wow," he says, stepping closer, his fingers brushing the plush fabric. "You really like stuffed toys, huh?" He lifts the penguin, turning to face me with a teasing grin. "They've got names, don't they?"

I feel the heat rush to my cheeks and cross my arms defensively. "Are you judging me?"

He shakes his head, a quiet laugh slipping out that sends a warm pulse through me. "Not at all. I think they're cute," he says, his eyes on me. "Like you."

My ears burn. "Very funny."

He grins wider. "Come on, don't tell me this guy doesn't have a name."

He jiggles the penguin a little in his hand, and I reach out to snatch it back, but he takes a quick step back, laughing.

"What is it?" he teases. "Mr. Waddlington? Sir Flapsalot? I need to know."

I roll my eyes, fighting a smile as I grab a pillow off my bed and throw it at him. "You're an idiot."

He breathes out a low laugh, running a hand through his hair. "I think we established that already, hence why I asked you to tutor me."

The smile slips off my face, and I feel guilt curl in my stomach. "I didn't—"

"It's fine," he says with a shrug and a lopsided smile that doesn't look quite right. "I know I'm not the smartest guy around."

"Austin." He glances up at me, I hate the saddened look on his face. "Just because you learn a little differently doesn't make you dumb." He swallows, his Adam's apple bobbing. "You know I didn't mean you're an *idiot*, right?"

He holds eye contact, swallows once more then nods, breaking out into a grin. "I know. You meant that you love me."

I roll my eyes, and he chuckles as he flops down onto the edge of my bed, my stuffed penguin still tucked under one arm. He glances around my room again.

"Waddles," I say before I can stop myself.

He snaps his eyes to mine, blinking. "Huh?"

"His name," I clarify, my cheeks warming as I nod toward the penguin in his hands. "It's Waddles."

Austin looks down at the penguin, then back up at me, the corner of his mouth twitching. "Of course it is."

He sets Waddles gently on the bed, then leans back on his palms with a low breath. "I like your room," he says after a beat. "Feels like you."

I raise an eyebrow. "What does that mean?"

He shrugs, his eyes finding mine again. "It's warm. Adorable. Kind of makes me feel like I can actually breathe."

Something shifts in my chest. Does he really see me that way? As a place he can breathe? I don't know what to say to that, so I just cross to the other side of the bed and sit, tugging absently at the hem of my sleep shorts.

"What are you doing here?" I ask him.

"The guys are at the away game," he explains. "I'm suspended, remember?"

My brows knit together. "You didn't want to go with them?"

He shakes his head immediately. "Sitting in the stands would be torture," he admits, dragging a hand through his hair.

"Being at home alone was fucking agony, though." His eyes meet mine and he smiles, tilting his head slightly. "I needed company."

I laugh quietly. "And no other girls were free to keep you company?" I ask him. "You're scraping the bottom of the barrel, huh?"

His eyes narrow slightly, his lips tugged into a frown. "You were my first choice."

My breath catches.

"There might've been other people who I could call over," he adds with a shrug. "I don't know. I didn't check. I wanted to hang out with you."

The room feels warmer. Too warm. The thin pajama shorts feel like I'm wearing a parka right now, because every inch of my skin flushes with each second his eyes are on me.

I shift back on the bed, lifting my shoulder in a shrug. "Well, I'm sorry to disappoint, but I might not be as fun as they would've been," I add with a small chuckle.

He shakes his head, his lips lifting in a smile. "You're more fun than any girl I've ever met."

God, how can he say these things? How can he be here, look at me like that, and expect me not to feel the fluttering in my stomach?

His gaze flicks to the laptop. "Wait, is this—" He grins, turning his body to face the screen where He's Just Not That Into You is playing. "I love this movie."

My eyebrows lift, surprised. "You do?"

He meets my eyes and shrugs. "My mom and sister are obsessed with this movie," he says a little sheepishly. "They used to have romcom nights. I always ended up watching with them."

My heart melts a little. "That's actually really cute."

"Don't spread it around, Freckles. You'll ruin my street cred," he teases, bumping my shoulder. "Scooch over."

I shift over without thinking. He climbs in beside me, his long legs stretching out, arm brushing mine as we settle. He's warm and smells so good.

He looks over at me with that half-smile. "Bet you're not used to having a hockey player crash your movie night, huh?"

I bite my lip, twisting the blanket in my hands. "I'm not really used to having anyone over."

He blinks, like he didn't expect that. "What do you mean?"

I look down at my hands, twisting a loose thread on the blanket. "I don't… really have any friends, I guess."

His brow lifts, surprised, but he stays quiet.

I let out a laugh that feels hollow and my chest tightens. "Maybe there's something wrong with me, I don't know." I shake my head. "I mean there must be, if no one ever wants to be around me."

"Maisie." I look up and catch the frown on his face, his hazel eyes narrowing on mine. "There's absolutely nothing wrong with you. I could punch the people who made you feel like you weren't enough. If I didn't want to be around you, I wouldn't have come here. When I was alone in my room all I could think about was you."

My throat tightens, and I swallow hard.

"The only person I wanted to see tonight, was you."

I don't say anything. I don't even know what I'd say to that. He doesn't say anything either. Just watches me, his expression softening, like he's waiting for me to catch up.

I rip my gaze away from him and pull the blanket tighter around my legs, shifting the laptop between us, trying not to think about how close he is—or what he just said.

His arm brushes mine when he shifts slightly, close enough that I can smell the faint hint of whatever cologne he wears—clean, a little woodsy. It's distracting.

He's right there, just a couple of inches away, and it feels weird and kind of nice all at once. I want to look at him, but I don't want to mess up whatever this is between us right now.

"I've watched this so many times," I say, my eyes still on the screen, "and I still don't get it."

Austin shifts slightly beside me. "Get what?"

"How you're supposed to know if a guy actually likes you," I murmur, my fingers tugging at a loose thread in the blanket. "Not just… stringing you along."

He pauses for a moment. "This about your guy?"

I finally glance at him and catch his hazel eyes slightly narrowed. "My guy?"

He nods, but his usual smile's long gone. "Yeah." I notice a muscle in his jaw tick. God, even his jaw is perfectly chiseled. "The guy you're into."

I drop my gaze. I shouldn't be thinking about Six right now—not with Austin right here, on my bed, with his body angled toward mine like it's the most natural thing in the world.

"Maybe," I mutter.

He doesn't smile. Instead, his jaw tightens ever so slightly, and then turns his attention back to the screen. "I don't know who your guy is or if he's leading you on or not, but… this movie does get one thing right."

"What's that?" I ask, glancing at the movie playing.

He nods toward the screen. "If a guy likes you, he'll find excuses to be near you. He'll touch you when he doesn't need to. Look at you more than he should."

My eyes flick to his, and he's already watching me.

My brain races through everything that's happened between us.

That night on the rink, when he skated circles around me, trying to pull off a move.

The day he showed me how to hold a hockey stick, his hands steadying mine. How close he leaned in. How he knocked on my dorm room door tonight. How he's sitting here now, his arm brushing against mine.

Is this… something?

Or is he just like this with everyone? Am I reading into it more than I should?

I swallow, looking away.

He shifts beside me, running a hand through his hair. "My mom used to watch this movie a lot. Especially when a guy broke up with her," he continues. "She'd put it on and grab a glass of wine and a bowl of ice cream."

"Was it just you guys growing up?" I ask.

He nods. "My mom, me, and my sister. Our dad left when I was eight. Walked out and never really came back," he says with a shrug. "It's just been the three of us since then."

I nod slowly, letting the silence hang for a moment before I speak. "After my dad died, it was just me, my mom, my sister, and my brother. We kinda had to be everything for each other."

He looks at me, letting me go on.

"I didn't really have a friend group like you growing up. Or a best friend. Or… anyone, really," I admit with a laugh. "My sister was, and still is, my only friend, pretty much," I admit, pressing my lips into a thin line.

Austin turns to me, his brow furrowed. "That's not true," he says.

"What isn't?"

"That she's your only friend," he clarifies. "You have me now."

I blink. I guess I do.

He's still watching me as he lifts one hand to brush the back of his hair, his hoodie riding up just a bit, revealing the waistband of his sweats and a sliver of tan skin beneath.

I quickly avert my eyes, trying to focus on the screen. I shouldn't be thinking of him like this, or looking at him, but god, he's pretty to look at.

"So… the midterms are in two weeks," I say, trying to change the subject before I do something dumb like stare at him again. "Are you ready?"

Austin huffs out a short laugh. "I mean… with you tutoring me, I hope so. It's making more sense than it did before."

I smile a little. "That's because you're not stupid, despite what you say, or think. You just have your own way of doing things, and that's fine. You're getting it, Austin. I can see it."

He shakes his head, exhaling as he sits up straight. "I just… I need to pass. It's not optional."

My brows pull together. "I know. But you're—"

"No. You don't get it," he cuts me off. His jaw tightens, and his throat moves like he's swallowing a lump. "I *need* to pass. I'm on a scholarship, and if I don't—" he cuts himself off, shaking his head. "Hockey's my whole life. It's all I've got."

His knee bounces. He swipes his palm over his face, like he's trying to push the thoughts away but they're crawling under his skin anyway.

He swallows again, hard, then his breathing quickens, shallow. "If I lose it…" His voice cracks.

He stops talking, jerking onto his feet so fast I flinch. "Austin?"

He won't look at me. His steps are quick and uneven as he paces across my dorm, rubbing his chest.

"I think I—I need to go to the nurse or something. I can't— my chest—"

His voice is strained, shaky. *Panicking*, I realize.

I swing my legs over the bed, already crossing the room to him. "Hey. Austin."

He backs up, hand to his chest, his breath shallow.

"Austin." I grab his hands. They're clammy. Shaking. I step closer until we're chest to chest, until I'm right in front of him and he can't look away. "Hey. Look at me."

He blinks, his eyes glossy and unfocused, like he's slipping away somewhere just beyond reach.

"It's okay," I whisper. "You're okay. Just breathe with me."

I press one hand gently to his chest, right over his heart, and lift the other to cradle his jaw, nudging his gaze back to mine.

"In," I say, drawing in a slow breath. "Out."

His breath catches, then stumbles out, then comes again, slower this time.

"That's it," I murmur. "Just like that. In. Out."

I feel the rise and fall of his chest beneath my palm, the steady thump of his heartbeat, the tight tension in his shoulders starting to loosen, bit by bit, with each exhale.

"Focus on me," I tell him. "Focus on your breathing."

His breathing eases a little. His hands find my waist, gripping like he needs the anchor. I let him, even as my own heart kicks into overdrive.

"You're okay," I tell him, tracing the rough scrape of stubble under my fingers. "I promise."

His hand tightens around my waist, his eyes locked on mine as his breath steadies.

"Thank you," he exhales.

I smile, dropping my hands from his face and chest. "You don't have to thank me."

"No, seriously." He pulls his hand away from my waist and runs it through his hair, his fingers tangling in the messy strands. "Thank you."

"That's what friends are for, right?" I say, a small smile tugging at my lips. Never in a million years did I think I'd call Austin my friend—yet here we are.

He lets out a tired laugh, shaking his head. "I'm so glad I met you, Maisie. You have no idea."

I shrug, flashing him a smile. "Anyone would've helped you, Austin."

He holds my gaze for what feels like forever, swallows, then shakes his head. "That's not the reason why."

My heart stutters, and I want to say something, but I'm frozen. Waiting.

For what? I don't know. But I can't seem to move.

After a few minutes, we both settle back down on my bed, and this time, his arm swings around my shoulder. I stiffen for a second, before letting myself lean into him.

The movie keeps playing, but I barely register what's happening onscreen. Every few minutes, I sneak a glance at him. Just to see if he's still here. Just to make sure this isn't in my head.

His knee nudges mine, and he doesn't move away.

I don't either.

FIFTEEN

Austin

I'm early.

Which is ridiculous, because I'm never early. Especially not to practice, where I now do nothing but watch my teammates on the ice. Yet here I am, parked on the bench at the side of the rink, my water bottle in hand.

Really, I'm just waiting.

The skating team still has a few minutes left, and I know—because I definitely, totally checked the group schedule—that Maisie's practice runs right up against ours today.

I stretch my legs out in front of me, roll my shoulders, and try to play it cool even though all I want to do is just watch her.

She's not even doing anything fancy. Just gliding, her arms stretched out for balance, her head tilted slightly to one side. But it's still… captivating. Still enough to make me stop and watch her.

A month ago, I didn't even know her name. Now it's like my eyes search for her without asking me first. She's just… there, in my brain.

She's a part of my day now. My week. My everything, kind of. And I'm not sure how it happened, only that I don't want it to stop.

The guys clatter in behind me, loud as always. Ryan's the first one through the rink doors. Logan and Nathan trail him, mid-argument about whatever it is they're arguing about today. Cole's quiet, as usual. Dude needs to lighten up. I wonder if his face hurts from constantly frowning.

"Hey, look who's already here," Logan says, grinning as he drops his gym bag onto the bench with a loud thud. "Is that Austin freaking Rhodes, early to practice? Alert the media."

Ryan arches a brow at me. "You trying to win points with Coach or just waiting for your girlfriend?"

I scowl. "She's not my—" I pause. Start over. "I'm not waiting for her."

He scoffs. "Right. You just like hanging out at figure skating practice now."

The sound of a skate landing on the ice reaches me, and I don't even try to be subtle as I glance up.

Maisie has her arms stretched out as she lands a jump, and my eyes drift to her cropped top that shows the tiniest sliver of her stomach when she moves.

"You're literally drooling," Ryan whispers beside me.

I elbow him hard enough he grunts. "Shut up."

He chuckles and heads into the lockers when the figure skating coach blows her whistle, signaling for the girls to get off the ice.

Maisie doesn't see me at first. The other girls start trickling off the ice, heading for the locker room. She heads over to the bench and bends over, pulling out the rubber skate guards from her bag, snapping them over the blades. That's when she looks up, and sees me.

Her eyes widen just a little, then she smiles. It hits me straight in the chest. Those eyes. Those freckles. I swear it does something to my ribcage. Like my heart expands just a little too fast for the room it's in.

"Hey," she says, a little breathless, her cheeks flushed pink in the most adorable way.

"Hey." I grin and lean back against the bench, like I haven't just been staring at her like a creep for ten straight minutes. "Didn't know I'd get a pre-practice performance."

She rolls her eyes but she's still smiling. "That was just practice," she replies with a shrug. "Nothing special."

"Well," I say, blowing out a breath, "ten out of ten. Judges are floored."

Maisie chuckles as she bends to adjust her skate guard, her top riding up slightly, revealing the waistband of her leggings and a peek of her lower back.

I try—really try—not to be obvious about how I look at her. But I just... can't look away from her. The curve of her waist, the way her leggings hug her hips and thighs and don't hide a damn thing.

As she straightens up, the sound of voices echoes through the tunnel as the guys saunter out of the locker room in gear.

Logan gives me a mock-sympathetic pat on the shoulder as he passes. "Let us know if you need us to tape your ankles. Wouldn't want you straining anything from all that sitting."

Ryan chuckles, shaking his head, and even Cole arches a brow at me, his face tinged with amusement.

I flip them all off as they step onto the ice. "You bitches wish you looked this good doing nothing."

Maisie scoffs beside me, and I glance down at her, arching a brow.

"Oh, you think that's funny, huh?"

That gets a smile out of her. "A little," she says, scrunching her nose in the cutest fucking way.

"Rhodes!" Coach's voice rings out across the rink as he appears from the staff hallway, his whistle swinging around his neck. "Stop flirting and get back to the bench."

Christ. Busted by the ball buster himself. "I'm not flirting, Coach," I lie—because I was definitely flirting—and gesture toward Maisie. "She's my tutor."

Coach squints at her, probably remembering how I almost knocked her out with my water bottle.

Maisie flushes. "Hi."

He grunts. "Hope you're good, sweetheart. You'll need divine intervention to pull this one through midterms."

"I'm trying my best," she says with a small shrug and a polite smile.

Coach eyes me. "Good. Because if Rhodes doesn't pass, he's not skating. And if he's not skating, I've got to watch Logan try to run power plays, and I'd rather eat a jockstrap."

"Hey!" Logan calls out. "I heard that!"

Coach waves him off. "Get on the ice."

"Hi." I turn my head, seeing Isabella, with her clipboard in hand, smiling at Maisie. "Maisie, right?"

Maisie blushes instantly. "Um… yes. And you're Isabella."

"That's right," Isabella says, flashing her a smile, her curls tucked into a messy bun today. "You were really good out there."

Maisie's voice softens. "Thanks."

I watch her tuck a strand of hair behind her ear, blushing. I don't think she gets compliments like that often, but she should. She's so—God, I don't even know. I have no fucking words for what this girl is. I suck at words, suck at saying what I think. But I swear, if I had a single poetic bone in my body, I'd write a whole damn sonnet about her.

"If you ever get bored with Austin, you can always come and hang out with me," Isabella teases, flashing her a smile.

I give her a dry look. "No one ever gets bored with me."

Maisie twists her lips. "That's debatable."

I lift my brows, glancing down at her, seeing that adorable teasing smile on her face. "You love my company, Freckles. Don't lie."

She chuckles. I love the sound of her laugh. Her whole face lights up when she smiles and it makes me feel like I'm looking at sunshine. And maybe that sounds cheesy, but whatever. I'm standing here getting knocked flat by a damn smile.

"I should get going," Isabella says, placing a hand on Maisie's arm. "But it was nice to see you again."

Maisie smiles. "You too."

Isabella heads off, standing beside her dad, and Maisie shifts, her eyes flicking toward the locker room.

"I should go change," she says.

"Yeah," I say, rubbing the back of my neck. "I'll see you Friday?"

She nods. "Friday." She takes a few steps, then glances back. "Don't be late."

"Wouldn't dream of it," I reply with a grin.

She rolls her eyes, before she turns around, and I watch her go, the soft bounce of her ponytail, the way her skates click on the rubber mat. She disappears into the hallway, and I sit back on the bench, letting out a breath.

The guys are already skating drills, sticks clacking, shouts echoing off the walls.

I should be out there.

But I can't play until I pass.

And to pass, I need her.

But if I'm being honest?

Even if I didn't need her—like, even if my shitty grades were magically wiped off the face of the earth—I'd still want to be around her.

I'd still want her smile, her sarcasm, the way she looks at me.

Maisie Wilson is my tutor.

But she's also becoming something else entirely.

And I don't think I'm ready for what that means.

But I want to be.

God, I want to be.

SIXTEEN

Austin

Midway through the second period, I'm ready to crawl out of my skin.

The crowd is on their feet, buzzing with energy. Music thumps through the speakers, echoing off the rink walls, and I swear I can feel it in my teeth.

Our boys are lined up. Logan at left wing, Cole on the right, Ryan holding down defense, and Nathan crouched in net.

And me?

I'm sitting behind the fucking line like a fucking mascot.

Suspended. Benched. Irrelevant.

Logan steals the puck, slices down the left, jukes a defenseman. I lean forward, my jaw tight as I track his moves. If he passes right now, they've got a clean shot. But he doesn't. He cuts in, tries for the corner, and the goalie blocks it with his chest.

I know every inch of this rink. I've played on it more times than I can count. I know the way the puck bounces off the boards in that back corner, the dead zone where the sound dies for a beat when you pass through it, the exact amount of pressure to apply on a wrist shot from the left circle.

And I know—I *know*—I could have made that play.

Ryan missed the opening. I'd seen it a full second before he did, but he hesitated. Passed instead of taking the shot. And just like that, a perfect scoring opportunity vanished.

It feels like I'm watching my life slip out of my hands in real time.

My fists clench, thumb twitching against my palm.

I don't belong on the bench.

I belong out there.

Fixing that. Driving the play.

But instead, I'm stuck here. Powerless.

My leg bounces restlessly. I run a hand over my face, and close my eyes. Just for a second. I try to block out the cheers. The whistles. The crash of skates against the boards, but none of it works.

They need me.

But I let them down.

I let *myself* down.

I exhale through my nose, drag my hand down my face.

Screw it.

I pull my phone out of my hoodie pocket, notifications lighting up my screen, but I swipe past all of it and tap on Maisie's name.

Her profile picture pops up, then our thread. I scroll, rereading our last few messages like I don't already have them memorized.

I wanna text her. Just see what she's doing. Hear her voice in my head when she types something sarcastic.

Mostly, I just wanna feel like I'm not completely fucking drowning. And for whatever reason, being near her quiets the noise.

But my thumbs hover. Frozen.

Because last time she saw me spiraling like this she looked at me like I was about to shatter. Like I was fragile.

And I don't want her thinking that. Not again.

I let out a sigh, and exit out of her profile, pulling up my text thread with Cherry instead.

Me: You busy?

Cherry: Wouldn't you like to know.

My lips twitch.

Me: I would. Tell me.

Cherry: Maybe I'm out living my best life without you.

I shake my head, leaning back in my seat as the scoreboard flashes—end of second period. We're up by two.

I lower my eyes back to my screen, typing out a reply.

Me: Not possible. I'm great company.

Me: Are you out shopping again? Clubbing? Secret underground chess tournament?

Cherry: None of the above. I'm at a hockey game.

My brows pull together.

Me: Wait, what?

Cherry: You seem so surprised.

Surprised that Cherry is at a fucking hockey game? Yeah, I am.

Me: I just didn't know you liked hockey.

Cherry: I'm still deciding if I do. I kind of hate how aggressive it is.

I glance back at the ice just in time to see Cole take a monster hit near the boards. He bounces off like a pinball, his shoulder crumpling slightly as he skates it off. The whole crowd lets out that collective *oooh.*

My nose scrunches, practically feeling the pain. That was a hard hit.

Cherry: For example, a guy just got slammed into the boards. How is that fun to watch?

My heartbeat stutters.
I sit up straighter, my thoughts running wild.
It… can't be… right?

Me: Hold on. Which game?

Cherry: Why?

Me: Because I'm literally at a game right now.

There's a long pause before she replies. Feels like it takes for fucking ever, until I feel my phone vibrate and her text comes through.

Cherry: Oh.

I blink down at my phone. Could she be watching *this* game?

Me: What game are you at?

I watch the dots come and go, my stomach twisted in this weird knot.

Cherry: We said no details. Remember?
Me: Cherry. Are you at Colton U?

More dots. Longer this time.

Cherry: Please don't come find me.

That makes my pulse spike.

Holy shit.

She's *here*.

My head jerks up, eyes snapping to the crowd like I'll spot her among thousands of fans packed into the stands, bundled in team jerseys and face paint, swinging foam fingers and waving cardboard signs.

I shift in my seat, trying to get a better view of the bleachers across from the bench. The lights catch on a dozen ponytails. Girls in beanies, flannels, fleece vests. That girl two rows down with popcorn in her lap and her eyes glued to her phone—could be her. Or maybe the one in the oversized hoodie near the railing, tapping something out with her thumbs and smirking at the screen.

Is she alone? With friends?

Is she someone I know?

The thought knocks something loose in my chest. My stomach flips, too full of nerves and questions.

I lean forward, my elbows digging into my knees as I scan the crowd again, searching for something—anything—that might make it click. Like I'll just *know*. Like my heart will recognize her before my brain does.

But it doesn't.

I don't know what I'm looking for. I don't even know what she *looks* like.

This is insane.

I suck in a breath and push to my feet, muttering a quick sorry as I shimmy past someone's dad holding a tray of nachos. A girl glares at me when I bump her elbow, but I barely register it. My mind's somewhere else entirely.

I hit the concrete concourse behind the bleachers, the cooler air hitting my face. I pace a few steps, then stop, my thumb hovering over our text thread. I could message her again. Ask where she's sitting. What she's wearing. Who she's with.

But what would I even say?

Hey, are you the girl with the puffer jacket and peanut M&Ms?

Yeah. No.

I exhale hard and let my head fall back against the cinderblock wall behind me. My heart's still pounding. This whole thing is stupid. She told me not to look for her. I should respect that.

But I can't stop thinking about it.

I can't stop thinking about *her*.

I don't know who she is.

But I want to.

Badly.

My fingers tighten around my phone. My thoughts are a mess, spinning too fast, colliding into each other. I lean my head back against the wall, eyes closing for half a second, just trying to *breathe*.

But then I hear footsteps and I glance up, freezing when I see Maisie.

She's walking toward the exit, head tilted down slightly, one hand curled around the strap of her bag.

I push off the wall without thinking.

"Maisie?"

She startles slightly, her head lifting. She stops walking when her eyes lock on mine and blinks. "Oh. Hey."

My brows knit as I step toward her. "What are you doing here?"

She shrugs. "I don't know," she says with a shake of her head. "I don't even like hockey."

I press a hand to my chest, mock wounded. "I kinda like you, so I'm gonna pretend you didn't say that."

She rolls her eyes, her lips twitching at the corners.

"But seriously," I ask, taking a few steps closer, "if you hate it… why are you here?"

Maisie's mouth parts. Her gaze drops to her feet as her fingers twist the sleeve of her jacket. "I just… I wanted to support you."

Something inside me stutters.

She looks up again. "I can only imagine how hard this must be for you. Watching them play and not being able to. I figured… maybe you'd need someone."

I swallow hard. My chest does something weird. It tightens and lifts all at once.

Because she's here.

For me.

She didn't have to do this. She could've stayed home, stayed in her warm bed with Waddles by her side. But she came anyway. She just sat in that crowd because she thought I might need someone.

"You came to a game for me?" I ask, unable to stop the smile that tugs at my lips.

Maisie shoots me a dry look. "Don't make it a thing."

"I'm definitely making it a thing."

She lets out a little huff, tucking her hair behind her ear.

I sit down on the edge of the old wooden bench near the ticket booth. I nod toward the open spot beside me without saying anything.

Maisie pauses. She shifts her bag higher on her shoulder, glances back down the hallway like she might bail. But then her shoulders sag, and with a quiet sigh, she lowers herself beside me.

The game noise is faint now, just a dull hum behind the concrete walls. I lean forward, propping my elbows on my knees.

We don't talk at first.

And for once, I don't feel like I have to fill the silence.

Maisie just sits there, her hands resting on her thighs, her fingers picking at the edge of her sleeve.

I stare at the scuffed floor between my sneakers and mutter, "It fucking sucks."

She looks over, but doesn't speak.

I shake my head, trying to swallow down the knot in my throat. "Not playing. Sitting there, knowing I let everyone down. My team. Coach. Myself." I pause. "My mom."

Maisie doesn't say anything, but I can feel her listening.

"She works at a private school," I continue, voice low. "She's a janitor there. Been doing it since I was a kid."

My leg bounces. I press my hand down on my thigh to stop it.

"She used to come home with bleach stains on her pants and holes in her sneakers, but still found a way to buy me skates. Ice time. Weekend camps. She said if I loved hockey, she'd make it happen. Even when we could barely afford groceries, she made sure I had new laces before a tournament."

Maisie's hand shifts slightly on the bench, close to mine. She doesn't touch me, not quite. But I can feel the space between us shrink.

I let out a breath, staring straight ahead. "I owe her. I owe her to make it. Get drafted. Go pro. Buy her a house. A car. Something. Anything that says thank you for working yourself into the ground for me."

There's a long pause before she finally speaks. "That's not on you, Austin."

I drag a hand through my hair, breathing out a harsh breath. "Feels like it is," I say. "Like every time I fuck up, I push that dream further away. Like I'm wasting everything she gave up for me."

My voice cracks at the end. I hate that. I bite the inside of my cheek to shut it down, my jaw clenching so hard it aches.

Maisie shifts beside me. Her knee brushes mine.

And then her hand slowly rests gently on top of mine.

The contact makes my throat close up in a different way.

We sit like that for a while.

Maisie shifts beside me on the bench, her hand still resting lightly on mine before she slowly pulls it back, folding it in her lap.

She glances over. "You ready for the midterm?"

A groan escapes me before I can stop it, and I drop my head. "Don't remind me."

She nudges her knee against mine. "As your tutor, that's literally my job."

I lift my head enough to shoot her a look, raising one brow. "Is that all you are?"

Her expression stutters for half a second. "What else would I be?"

The question hangs in the air. Open. Waiting.

I could lie. I could say something dumb and flirty, play it off like I always do.

But my brain goes somewhere else entirely.

The girl I look forward to seeing every Friday.

The only person I've let see the scared, messed-up parts of me.

Someone I want to kiss.

I swallow it down, force a smirk. "My best friend, of course."

Maisie rolls her eyes, but there's a smile there, tugging at the corners of her mouth before she tries to hide it.

I watch her for a beat too long. The way her lashes brush her cheeks when she looks down. The soft pink tinting her face. The little curve of her lips like she's fighting the urge to grin.

I tip my head back against the concrete wall, closing my eyes for half a second. "I'm terrified," I admit, swallowing harshly.

Maisie looks over again.

"I want this," I say. "Hockey. School. All of it. I want to be better. But I'm scared I'll screw it up anyway." I blow out a breath, squinting at her. "I'm afraid you'll think you wasted your time on a lost cause."

Her eyes soften as she shifts a little closer. "You're not a lost cause, Austin."

The way she says my name hits somewhere low in my chest.

Her eyes search mine, steady and warm, and the urge to lean in and press my forehead to hers is almost unbearable.

She shifts a little closer. Our knees bump again, and this time, neither of us moves away.

"Plus," she adds, "Tutoring you has kinda been fun."

That pulls a grin from me. "Oh yeah?"

She narrows her eyes. "Don't let it go to your head."

Too late.

It's already there. In my chest, in my throat. In every breath I take around her.

I study her face. Her eyes. The way the corner of her lip curls up when she's trying not to smile.

I think about that night in her room. How she didn't flinch when I fell apart. How she stayed. Just stayed, like it was the easiest thing in the world.

And something shifts inside me.

I like her.

I really fucking like her.

And I don't even know what to do with that.

I haven't liked a girl in—God, maybe ever.

Because I've spent years keeping girls at arm's length. Hookups. Flings. Nothing serious. Nothing that could get close enough to break something. I suck at this shit. Feelings. Being real. Not just… hooking up and pretending none of it matters.

But this? Sitting here with her, heart pounding like it's trying to tell me something I'm not ready to hear?

I can't remember the last time I wanted something like this.

I glance down at my phone again.

Cherry's last message is still sitting there. Waiting for me to say something. Waiting for me to figure it out.

But I can't.

Not when Maisie's sitting right here beside me, close enough to feel the warmth of her arm. Close enough that I catch a whiff of her shampoo every time she shifts.

I came out here looking for Cherry.

And now all I can think about is Maisie.

The girl sitting beside me. The one who came to a game she didn't even like just to be there for me.

Before I can say anything else, a buzzer blares from inside the rink. The crowd erupts into cheers, stomping feet, the unmistakable thud of excitement echoing through the concrete.

Game's over. I don't even know who won, but I don't want to move.

I let out a sigh. "Thanks for keeping me company."

Maisie stands, brushing off the front of her jeans with her palms. "Well," she says, adjusting the strap of her bag, "don't get used to this. It won't happen again."

A smile tugs at my mouth. "Not even when I get back on the ice?"

Maisie pauses, twisting her lips. "I'll think about it."

I nudge her shoulder gently, grinning. "We both know you'll say yes."

She doesn't answer. Just rolls her eyes and starts walking. That little smile playing on her lips says everything her mouth doesn't.

I stay seated, watching her go.

And I just sit there.

My heart pounding.

My mind spinning.

All I know is that somewhere in that crowd is a girl I've only ever known through a screen.

And walking away from me is a girl who's changing everything I thought I wanted.

And I don't know which one I'm supposed to be chasing.

SEVENTEEN

Austin

Cherry goes to my school.

That sentence hasn't stopped echoing in my skull for days.

It's almost midnight, and I'm still lying here in the dark, one arm flung across my pillow, the other holding my phone above my face as I reread our messages for the hundredth time.

She goes to my school.

She's not some mystery girl in another state I'll never meet. She's here. *Right fucking here*. Walking the same sidewalks. Sitting in the same lecture halls. Probably stood behind her at the café without even realizing it.

It's driving me insane.

I let my thumb hover over the screen for a second before typing.

Me: Confession. I can't stop thinking about you. It's actually messing with my head. You're so close to me and I still don't know who you are.

I press send before I can overthink it.

Cherry: I think about you too. More than I probably should. But please don't come looking for me. Please, Six. I'm not ready.

The words punch through my chest.

She's not ready.

I get it. I do. I respect it. But it doesn't stop the restless, gnawing feeling in my ribs. The ache of wanting to know who she is—to finally *see* her. Talk to her. Look her in the eye and say, It's you. You're the one who's been inside my head all this time.

I rake a hand through my hair and drop the phone onto my chest, staring at the ceiling for a minute.

I flip open my laptop and scroll, trying to distract myself with something—*anything*—else. I click on a movie without thinking, and it takes about five minutes for the memory of watching He's Just Not That Into You with Maisie that night in her dorm to crash in.

How she quoted every line toward the end. How she snuggled up against me. How I didn't want it to end. Didn't want to leave.

Before I know it, I'm reaching for my phone again.

Me: hey u awake?

It's a long shot. She's probably asleep, with Waddles tucked under her arm. But I can't sleep. And I want to talk to her.

The second my phone lights up, my chest gives this stupid, involuntary squeeze.

Maisie: Yep. Can't sleep.

A smile creeps across my face before I can stop it.

Me: me neither. what are you doing right now?

Maisie: Watching a movie.

Me: me too. which one?

Maisie: Crazy, Stupid, Love.

I sit up, resting against my headboard. I search it quickly, hit play, then FaceTime her. She answers with a small surprised smile. She's curled up in her bed in soft pink pajamas with hearts all over them, clutching the penguin to her chest—called it by the way.

God, she looks so fucking adorable. I kinda want to head over there right now.

"Hey," she says, voice soft and sleepy as she blinks at me.

"Hey. I'm syncing up with you. What part are you at?"

"Right after the scene where Ryan Gosling tells Steve Carell he's lost his manhood."

I scrub a hand over my jaw and find the scene. "Okay, synced. Ready."

Maisie shifts, getting comfy again, and props her phone up against something. The screen wobbles and steadies. She's close now, her face filling most of the frame.

Have I mentioned her face?

That warm, freckled skin. Those tired, pretty eyes. The way her nose wrinkles when she smirks. Every damn time I see her, it gets worse.

"Have you watched this one before?" she asks, chin tucked into her penguin.

I let out a scoff. "Of course. This is a classic."

Maisie raises her brows, a smile tugging at her mouth.

"You seem shocked," I say, tilting my head at the screen.

She shifts on the bed, hugging that penguin tighter. "No, just… a little surprising the hotshot hockey guy would be watching a rom com with his tutor this late at night."

The grin on my face widens. "You think I'm hot?"

She rolls her eyes. "I said hotshot. Get over yourself."

"Too late," I reply with a shameless grin.

She chuckles, shaking her head. "What's your favorite rom-com?" she asks, settling back against her pillows.

I blow out a breath. "God, that's hard. How the hell do you expect me to just choose one?"

She lets out a quiet laugh—makes my heart race.

"I think it has to be 10 Things I Hate About You," I say. "That poem scene? Paintball date? Iconic."

She grins, her cheek resting on her penguin's head. "Mine's You've Got Mail."

I blink. "Oh yeah?"

She nods. "I like the idea of falling in love with someone through words—without ever seeing them."

I glance at her, her words resonating with me more than she knows.

"I've always thought of opening a bookstore one day. Like she did in the movie," she continues. "With a little café in the back. Tables by the windows, fresh flowers everywhere. Maybe a community board where people can leave poems or Polaroids or stuff they want someone else to find."

I watch her eyes drift away like she's imagining it all.

She bites her lip, then shrugs. "Who knows if it'll ever happen. But it's what I think about when everything else sucks."

I sit there for a second, watching her fingers brush over the frayed edge of her blanket.

"That's probably why I like watching rom coms," she adds, her eyes flicking down. "Because it gives me hope. Like maybe someday I'll find someone who looks at me like that."

I shift a little, propping the laptop against my knee. "Why do you say it like it won't?"

She shrugs again. "I just… I don't think I'm the kind of girl a guy would run through an airport for. Or fall in love with, for that matter."

She says it with a little laugh, like she's joking. But it doesn't feel like a joke.

"Sometimes I feel like a side character in my own life," she continues. "I don't mind being single, but I just wish someone looked at me and thought, *that's the one*. I wish I was loved like that."

I swallow hard. I look at her, and all I see is someone I can't imagine not being in my life. Smart and sharp and funny, and so fucking beautiful. Her fingers are still curled tight around that penguin, and I want to reach through the screen and *hold her*.

I shift closer to the screen. "Maisie—"

She looks up.

I open my mouth to say something— though I've got no clue what—but my phone buzzes and lights up with a call.

Mom.

"One sec," I mutter toward her, reaching for my phone.

I mute the FaceTime and answer. "Hey, what's up?"

"Hi sweetheart," my mom says, her face filling my screen. "I just got home and wanted to check in. Did you eat yet?" she asks, narrowing her eyes. "And don't roll your eyes."

I let out a laugh. "I wasn't going to."

"You always do," she replies with an arched brow.

In the background, I hear my sister's voice. "Wait. Let me talk to him!"

There's some shuffling, and then Scarlett's face fills the screen. "Hi, loser!"

"Hey, shrimp." I smile. "Shouldn't you be sleeping?"

"Shouldn't you be studying?" she fires back.

"Brutal." I laugh, shaking my head. "I don't know where you get it from."

"Who's *that*?" my mom asks, squinting at something behind me.

"What?" I glance over my shoulder, realizing the camera's angled straight at my laptop, where Maisie's face fills the screen.

I shake my head. "No one. Just a friend."

"A friend?" she says, drawing the word out.

I groan. "Mom."

"She's pretty," she says with a smile.

I look back at the screen. Maisie's zoned in on the movie, totally unaware.

Yeah, she is.

"Is she your girlfriend?" Scarlett shouts in the background.

I let out a laugh, dragging a hand down my face. "Alright, you two have officially butted into my life enough tonight. I gotta go."

"I can see that," my mom says, with a teasing look. "Remember. Use protection. I'm too young to be a grandmother."

"Jesus, mom," I groan.

She laughs, blowing me a kiss, and I end the call before they can embarrass me more. I roll back onto the bed, grab my laptop, and unmute the FaceTime.

"Sorry about that. My mom just got home," I tell her. "She always calls to check in."

Maisie's head lifts a little from her pillow. "That's okay." She sinks further into her blankets and glances back at the screen. "So when's our next study session? Or are you hoping this counts?"

I let out a low laugh. "Hey, this was extremely educational."

She arches a brow. "Oh yeah?"

"Definitely. I learned you like to sleep with Waddles. Very important intel."

She chuckles. "That's not anatomy, Austin."

"Sure it is," I say with a shrug. "I'm studying your brain."

She gives me a look. "God help me."

I let out a laugh and sit up a little. "Seriously though, I do need to actually study if I wanna get back on the ice."

"What time are you free next week?" she asks.

I scratch at my jaw, grabbing my phone to check my calendar. "Monday's out, I've got team lifts and a meeting with Coach. Wednesday I'm free after practice."

She hums. "Wednesday works. We can do the library again if it's not packed."

I pause. The thought of her curled up beside me again, brushing against me every time she leans over my notes—it's dangerous. Especially now, when I don't know what the hell I'm feeling anymore.

I clear my throat. "You could come to my place instead. Fewer distractions."

She lifts a brow. "Right. No distractions at all in a house full of hockey guys."

"They won't be there," I say. "The guys have a banquet thing for alumni donors. Coach is making them go. I got out of it since I'm suspended and, quote, 'not a good look for the program right now.'"

Maisie scrunches her nose. "Ouch."

"Yeah, well. I'll take the quiet house." I meet her eyes again. "Come by around seven?"

She bites her lip, like she's thinking it over.

"I'll even make sure my room's semi-clean," I add.

She chuckles. "Okay."

Her voice is soft, kind of sleepy. Like maybe she's starting to drift.

"You tired?" I ask, sitting up. "I can go if you want to sleep."

She shakes her head quickly. "No. I wanna stay here with you."

A warm feeling nestles deep in my stomach and I breathe out a laugh, my eyes glued on those pink cheeks scattered with freckles, and those eyes I can't stop thinking about.

"Yeah," I breathe out. "Me too."

Her smile stretches, and she snuggles deeper in bed.

We watch the rest of the movie together like that. Talking. Laughing. Just being here with each other. I don't want the movie to end. I don't want to say goodnight, or hang up.

I want more of this. Of her.

I want all of it.

EIGHTEEN

Maisie

The moment I step onto the porch, I know something's off. A few people are out here smoking, someone laughing too loud over the thud of music bleeding through the open door. The bass rattles the floorboards under my feet, even all the way out here.

There's no way Austin threw a rager and forgot to mention it. Right?

I pull out my phone and check it again, just to make sure I didn't misread the message he sent.

Austin: still good for 8 tonight?

That was hours ago. And he's the one who said studying at his place would be better. Quieter. Less distracting.

Right.

My tote bag feels heavy on my shoulder, stuffed with notes, flashcards, and a granola bar—because I knew he'd get hungry. He always does.

But this? This doesn't look like a guy ready to study anatomy.

I shift my weight from one foot to the other, hovering on the porch. There's yelling from inside, and the smell of weed drifting through the open window. Someone's singing off-key, horribly.

This is so not my scene.

It never has been.

Still, I came here for a reason.

I came for him.

So I hitch my bag higher on my shoulder, suck in a breath, and push open the front door.

It's warm inside. Uncomfortably so.

The second I step in, my sneakers stick to something suspiciously tacky on the hardwood. I wince and try to keep moving, hugging my tote close, eyes scanning for any sign of him.

I try to weave through without brushing against too many people, but it's impossible. My shoulder gets bumped. A guy I've never seen before gives me a slow, curious once-over. I duck my head immediately, mumbling sorry under my breath, heat crawling up my neck.

I clutch the strap of my bag tighter, pushing past a couple making out so aggressively against the wall I have to physically sidestep them.

This was a mistake.

I should just go, text him later, say I swung by but he was clearly busy. I'm halfway to turning around when I see him.

He's in the middle of the living room, his shirt untucked, hair a mess, and a stupidly bright smile as he laughs at something one of his teammates says.

Then his eyes find me, and his smile widens. "There she is," he slurs a little, "the only person I wanted to find tonight."

He walks toward me with his arms stretched out wide, and I barely have time to brace before he's wrapping one of them around my shoulders, pulling me into his side "You came!"

"I…" My voice gets swallowed by the music. "Yeah, I—"

I try not to stiffen. But I'm not used to being touched like this. Especially not guys like Austin. Not in front of this many people.

"We were supposed to study," I say, tilting my face up toward him, trying to keep my voice level.

His eyes widen slightly, then squint as he tilts his head down at me. "Shit. Were we?"

I give him a flat look. "Austin."

"Maisie," he says, mimicking my tone and giving me a dopey grin. "You're so pretty when you're mad."

My stomach flips, and I hate that it does. He's leaning on me more than standing next to me, and I should tell him to get off, but for some reason, I don't. His arm is still heavy around me, but oddly comforting.

"I'm sorry," he says, the words slightly slurred. "I completely spaced." He grins, his dimples deep, and his eyes crinkled. "But you're here now! Wanna dance?"

I blink up at him, caught off guard. "What?"

"I said"—he does a weird half-sway to the music— "dance with me."

I take a step back, folding my arms across my chest as my nose scrunches. "I'm not dancing."

"Oh, come on. Just one song. You owe me."

"I owe you anatomy flashcards and a serious talk about scheduling."

He laughs, causing a few people to glance over. His teammates are scattered across the room, all of them with drinks in hand. I catch Ryan elbow Nathan and nod in our direction. Nathan follows his gaze, and he shakes his head when he sees me.

"Sorry about this," Nathan says, weaving through the crowd until he's in front of us. "I told him he was forgetting something."

Austin waves him off. "I remembered. She's here." He turns back to me, beaming. "See? Maisie's here."

Nathan gives me a helpless smile. "Coach is out of town, so there's no practice tomorrow. So obviously," he gestures around us, "this turned into a thing." He lowers his voice slightly. "He's been drinking since six."

Of course he has.

I sigh and ease out from under his arm. "Come on. Let's get you to bed before you do something stupid."

He frowns. "But I was having fun."

I arch a brow. "You can have fun horizontally."

His eyebrows shoot up. "Maisie. You can't just say stuff like that to me."

Heat crawls up my neck. "I meant sleeping. Alone. In your bed."

There's a burst of snickering from somewhere behind us. Of course his teammates heard that.

Austin grins. "Fine," he says with an exaggerated sigh. "Only because you're hot when you're bossy."

Before I can say anything else, his hand slides around my waist, his fingers curling into the curve of my hip like it's second nature. He falls into step behind me, his warm breath grazing the back of my neck.

My heart kicks against my ribs as we head toward the stairs.

"Mmm. You smell good," he murmurs, voice low and a little too close to my ear.

A shiver runs straight down my spine.

I force myself to breathe evenly, like this is fine. Normal. Like I don't feel every inch of him behind me.

His hands stay at my hips the whole way up, steady and warm, like he's guiding me. Or maybe holding on.

At the top of the landing, I glance at the row of closed doors. "Which one's yours?"

He nods toward the first on the left. "That one."

His hands fall away just before he steps around me, pushing the door open.

His room's surprisingly clean. A little messy, sure—there's a sweatshirt slung over the chair, a water bottle tipped on its side by the bed. But the bed's made, and it actually looks soft and inviting.

I drop my bag by the desk and turn just in time to see him collapse face-first into the mattress.

A smile involuntarily tugs at my lips at the sight of him completely wiped out. But when he starts unbuttoning his jeans, my cheeks flare hot, and I whip my head away.

"Sorry," he murmurs a few seconds later. I sneak a glance back, and his previous smirk is gone, replaced with a faint crease between his brows. "I forgot about tonight."

"It's okay."

He runs a hand down his face, letting out a deep exhale. "I didn't mean to. I just…" His voice drops. "Everything's a mess. I'm not playing, failing classes, coach is pissed. Feels like I'm letting everyone down." He rolls onto his side, his eyes fixed on me. "I just needed to blow off some steam, y'know?"

I nod and sink down onto the edge of the bed. The mattress dips beneath me. "I get it."

He doesn't say anything else. But the way he's looking at me makes my skin prickle.

I want to look away, but I can't stop myself from stealing glances, tracing the shadows under his eyes, the curve of his jaw. He's just… so pretty.

I swallow the lump rising in my throat and start to stand. "I should go—"

"No." His hand clamps over my wrist and his eyes lock on mine. "Stay. Please." My chest twists tight. "I don't want to be alone tonight."

Every part of me knows this is reckless. I should say no and walk out the door.

But my body betrays me, and I nod.

He scoots back, patting the spot beside him. After a moment, I slide in, curling onto my side to face him. I don't know what to do with my hands, so they settle beneath my head as I keep my eyes on him.

His eyes search mine in the dim light, and he shifts closer, his fingers tracing a slow line along my cheek. My breath catches.

"My mom thinks you're pretty," he says softly.

I blink, caught off guard. "She does?"

He hums, his eyes heavy-lidded. "Mmhmm. So do I."

I blink again, my heart skipping at his words. I swallow hard. "You're drunk," I whisper.

"You're gorgeous."

I don't know how to respond. No one's ever said that to me—not like this, not while looking straight at me like they actually mean it.

So I stay quiet, lying there, my heart hammering as I fight the urge to look at his mouth.

His hand moves up my back and I feel his fingers pressing lightly through my shirt as he rubs my back slowly. A shiver runs down my spine.

He pulls back slightly. "What's wrong?"

"Nothing," I say, shaking my head. "Just… feels nice."

He smiles softly. "Yeah?"

I nod, feeling a little breathless, lifting my eyes to meet his. "Will you do it again?"

His grin widens as he leans in, brushing his nose against mine. "You're so cute."

His hand slides lower, his fingers spreading wider across the small of my back, pulling me a little closer.

I never thought I'd be here, in Austin's bed, with his hands on me and his face a few inches away. My breath catches, my skin prickles. I want to memorize this feeling, tuck it away somewhere deep.

He doesn't say anything else, just keeps rubbing up and down along my spine, watching me for a while.

He tilts his head on the pillow. "I'm gonna be your first customer."

My eyes flick up. "What?"

"You said you wanted to open a bookstore café." He pauses. "I'm gonna be the first in line when you do. I'm gonna spend my life savings there, even though I hate reading."

A soft laugh escapes before I can stop it. "I can't believe you remembered that."

He shrugs, lazy and half-asleep. "I might look dumb, but I pay attention."

My throat tightens. "You're not dumb."

His smile softens, a little smaller this time, like he doesn't quite believe it.

"I'm serious, Austin. You're not. You just learn differently. And you've been trying."

He doesn't reply. Just keeps looking at me. His hand drops from my back and lifts slowly, tucking a stray strand of hair behind my ear. I hold my breath as his fingers trail down, feather-light against my jaw.

Everything inside me tightens when his gaze drops to my mouth.

No.

No, he wouldn't. Not me.

He's drunk. He's flirty. That's all this is.

But I still close my eyes. Just for a second. Because it's too much to look at him and not want it to mean something.

The room goes quiet.

His breathing shifts—slower, heavier.

When I open my eyes again, he's already out, his head tilted toward me.

And I'm still lying there, wide awake, my heart pounding, every part of me buzzing from the memory of his voice in the dark and the way he looked at me.

But I don't move. I tell myself I'll stay five more minutes. Just long enough to let my pulse settle. Just long enough to stop memorizing the shape of his mouth.

Five more minutes.

That's all.

But my eyelids grow heavy. The buzzing in my chest fades into something slower, softer. And by the time my thoughts blur into dreams, I forget I ever meant to leave.

When I wake up, everything's warm.

The sheets are twisted around my legs, the room dim except for sunlight slipping through the slats in the curtains. Somewhere downstairs, muffled voices murmur, but I can't make out a word.

It takes a moment to realize where I am. The unfamiliar mattress. My back grazing something solid. Someone.

Austin.

Oh god.

My brain snaps online all at once, and I freeze.

His arm's wrapped around my waist, his hand resting low on my hip, and his palm spread wide. I'm pressed completely against him, my back to chest. All of me against all of him.

And there's definitely something pressed against my butt.

I try to move—just a little, a subtle shift—but the second I do, his fingers flex on my waist, pulling me back the tiniest bit. He sighs, groggy and amused, pressing his face closer to my shoulder.

"Maisie," he murmurs, voice still rough with sleep, "you keep rubbing up on me like that, I'm gonna think it's on purpose."

My whole body locks up. "I didn't mean to—I must've rolled over—"

He laughs, warm and low in my ear, sending a shiver down my spine. "Mmm. Not complaining."

I press my hands to the mattress, weighing how fast I can escape without making this weirder. But then he shifts behind me, slower this time, his nose brushing the curve of my shoulder.

"You smell really good," he murmurs, still drowsy. "Is that like… coconut shampoo or something?"

"I'm gonna need you to stop talking," I mutter, my heart hammering against my ribs.

He laughs again, his hand still resting on my waist. "I'm just saying. You wake up in my bed, wrapped around me, smelling all sweet, and I'm the bad guy for noticing?"

I lift myself off the bed. His hand slips off my waist as I move, and I twist around, glaring over my shoulder.

He's a mess—eyes half-shut, hair sticking out in every direction, pillow lines on his cheek. The blanket's pooled low on his hips. Somehow, that makes him even hotter.

"I didn't mean to stay over. I just… slept."

"You're real squirmy this morning," he says, lips twitching with amusement.

"That's because your—" I gesture toward him, flustered. "Your body was on mine."

He hums, shifting onto his side and propping himself up on one elbow. "I could always help you relax, y'know…"

My brain short-circuits.

He pauses, then, with a slow grin he adds, "Some hands-on tutoring."

My face is on fire. "You're still drunk," I mutter.

Austin tuts, shaking his head. "Hungover, maybe. But not drunk."

He doesn't look away, his lips sleep-swollen, eyes bleary and soft but still so focused and locked on me.

I grab my tote off the desk chair, my fingers fumbling with the strap. My shirt's all creased, my bra definitely crooked, and I can feel mascara smudged somewhere under one eye. *Great. Love that for me.* I rake a hand through my hair, trying to flatten the mess without a mirror, even though I know there's no fixing any of it.

Behind me, Austin flops onto his back with a sigh. "You're not staying?"

I keep my eyes on my bag as I stuff everything inside. "I have tutoring in twenty."

He makes a soft, sleepy protest noise, and I glance back. I hate that my heart stutters a little when I meet his eyes.

He's dangerous like this. Loose and unguarded and warm in a way that makes me want to crawl right back in beside him.

"Come back after?" he asks.

It shouldn't mean anything. It probably doesn't. But the way he says it—like he actually wants me around—makes something twist behind my ribs.

I press my lips together, twisting them into a small smile. "Maybe."

He breaks into a grin, those light hazel eyes twinkling.

I hover at the door for a second, then glance back. "I'm gonna go."

"See ya, Freckles." He stretches, arms over his head. "Best cuddle buddy ever."

I can't stop the smile tugging at my lips as I close the door behind me.

I take a breath, swing my bag over my shoulder, and head down the stairs.

Halfway to the front door, I spot Ryan, Logan, and Nathan, cleaning up in the hallway. Trash bags in hand, stacking empty cups and pizza boxes.

They stop the second they see me.

Logan's eyebrows shoot up, a broom in his hand.

Ryan freezes with a beer can dangling from two fingers.

Nathan doesn't even blink—just looks between me and the stairs like he's connecting all the dots in real time.

I clear my throat. "It's not what it looks like."

"Didn't say a word," Logan says, his mouth twitching with amusement.

My face flames hotter than it should as I duck my head and slip past them without looking back.

I close the front door behind me and grip my bag tighter as I walk toward campus.

A small smile curls on my lips as I remember the way Austin looked at me this morning. The words he said.

I know I shouldn't read too much into it. I can't afford to get my hopes up.

Because if I start believing it means more than it does, I'm the one who'll end up hurt.

I have to be careful.

Even if I want nothing more than to go back into that bed.

NINETEEN

Maisie

I tug my hoodie tighter around me as I cross the quad, my thighs aching with every step.

Practice was hard today. It's getting closer to the Regionals, so Coach is working me harder, expecting more, demanding perfection. And I feel the effects of it in my muscles.

I shift my bag higher on my shoulder and pull out my phone for the fifth time since leaving the rink.

It's been a little over a week since… the whole waking up next to Austin fiasco, and whilst it was awkward as hell when I saw him for tutoring the next day, he acted like it didn't mean a thing. Which it probably didn't. It was just him being his naturally flirty self and me overthinking every little interaction as usual.

I frown when I see there are no new notifications, which scares me a little. He should be done with his exams by now, and if he didn't text me then…

I shake the thought away and scroll back to the message I sent him this morning.

Me: You've got this. I know you do. Good luck today, Austin.

I pocket my phone a second later when I see he still hasn't answered me. I understand, though. I can only imagine how stressed he would have been today for his exams.

Still, I've been thinking about him all day. Wondering how practice went. If he was nervous. If he remembered any of the stuff we went over at the library yesterday. He did well on his practice test. I just hope everything goes well. He deserves this. He's been trying, showing up, working hard.

And I'd never say it out loud, but... I actually like being around him. I think I'm even starting to miss him when he's not around.

I shift my grip on the hot chocolate, holding it with both hands, trying to warm my fingers.

The library doors come into view ahead, and just as I step onto the first stair, my phone buzzes in my pocket.

I pull it out, a small smile tugging at my lips when I see his name on the screen.

Six: Confession.

I blow out a breath, the warm puff of air fogging in front of my face, as I watch the typing bubble.

Six: I almost called you today. I stared at your number for so long before I talked myself out of it. Heard your voice in my head and everything.

My cheeks flush hot, and I'm grateful for the cold air and empty quad so no one can see how much that text messes with my brain. I've thought about what his voice would sound like more times than I want to admit.

I imagine it's a little rough, not too deep, but still enough to make me shiver.

God, I want to hear it so badly.

With a sigh, I slip my phone into my pocket and head toward the library, my boots crunching against the frozen grass.

I push open the doors and head inside. It's warm and quiet as I weave between study tables and disappear into my usual corner behind a tall row of bookshelves.

Dropping my bag to the floor, I pull out my Psych notes, trying to focus, to read, to absorb. But my eyes don't cooperate—they skim, skip, and blur, because my mind keeps drifting back to Austin.

I wonder how it went.

Did he pass?

Did he feel good when he walked out?

Did he smile?

I hope it went well. I really do.

He looked so nervous yesterday, pacing around the library, reciting the answers back to me. He wanted it so bad.

My phone buzzes, jolting me out of the memory.

Austin: where r u?

I blink at the screen, then type back.

Me: West Library. Why?
Austin: be there in 5.

Oh god. Does this mean he didn't pass? I shake the thought away and place my phone down on the table and flip open my notes again, highlighting the same sentence three times, but the words don't register.

Footsteps echo down the row, and I glance up just as Austin rounds the corner.

There's a soft smile playing at his lips, and for a second, I forget how to breathe. He looks so happy. Like his whole face is glowing from the inside out.

Without meaning to, I smile back. It blooms on my face before I can stop it.

"Hey," I say, lifting onto my feet. "How'd it go?"

He doesn't answer.

Just grins harder—so wide his dimple shows—and shakes his head once. He moves toward me and before I can say anything else, his hands are on my face.

And he kisses me.

My heart stutters and nearly stops the second I register what's happening. His lips press against mine, and I'm too stunned to do anything but feel it—the heat, the curve of him fitting perfectly into me, the sharp little gasp that slips from me and melts somewhere between us.

It's quick. Barely a second.

But it lights something deep in my chest I can't explain.

My hands freeze at my sides. My whole body is still, except for the tremor in my knees and the rush pounding in my ears.

And just as quickly as it happened, it's over.

He pulls back fast, blinking like he's trying to figure out what just happened.

His hands drop away and he takes a step back. "Shit," he breathes. "Fuck, I didn't—I didn't mean to do that."

I swallow, nodding. "It's alright."

His fingers run through his hair, tearing his eyes away from mine. "I should, uh—I have… practice."

"Yeah," I say, forcing a smile. "Of course. Go."

He backs away, then turns and heads toward the building.

I stand there, staring after him, my fingers brushing my lips, wondering if the kiss actually happened.

It did.

I felt it. His lips on mine.

Soft. Warm. Real.

And now he's gone.

I draw in a slow breath, trying to quiet my spiraling thoughts. Maybe he was just caught up in the moment. Maybe he's riding the high of getting back on the ice again, or maybe I just happened to be there, and he mistook adrenaline for… something else.

It didn't mean anything.

Even if it felt like everything.

TWENTY

Austin

Fuck. What did I do?

The thought's been on a loop in my head since last week. Since I touched her face and tipped her head back, getting lost in those ocean-blue eyes. Since I kissed Maisie in the damn library like a complete idiot, and then ran off like an even bigger one.

I've spent the last seven days pretending I'm fine. Like I didn't completely ruin something good. Like I haven't replayed that kiss a hundred times and regretted every second that came after.

I haven't texted her. Haven't seen her.

Not on purpose, anyway.

I skipped tutoring on Friday. Told myself it was because I was slammed with practice now that Coach cleared me to skate again. But that's bullshit. I'm avoiding her.

Every time I go to type something, I stare at the blinking cursor for ten full seconds, then chuck my phone across the room.

Because I don't know what to say.

Because I don't know what it meant.

Because she deserves better than *fuck, I panicked* and *my bad* and *please don't hate me, you're the only thing that makes me feel like I'm not completely losing my mind.*

Because I don't want to make things awkward when I don't even know what the fuck that kiss *was*.

All I know is I miss her.

I lean forward, scrubbing my hands down my face, trying to shake it off, but all I see is her. Standing in the library. Those bright blue eyes on mine. Lips pink and parted when I cupped her face. The sound she made when I kissed her.

Christ.

Ryan skates up beside me and nudges my shoulder. "You good?" he asks.

I nod, my eyes fixed on the scratched glass behind the boards. "Yeah."

"Are you sure?" Logan asks, peeling off his gloves. "Because you haven't smiled once today. It's not like you, Rhodes."

"Give him a break," Nathan says. "He just got cleared to practice again. Probably still adjusting."

I shoot Nathan a grateful look.

He shrugs in response and leans over to re-tape his stick.

Because yeah. I *am* adjusting.

I'm back.

Back on the ice. Back at practice. Cleared to play again once Coach gives the official go-ahead.

After weeks of suspension and tutoring and trying not to crawl out of my skin, I finally feel like myself again.

Or… close to it.

If I could just get her out of my head.

I spend the next fifteen minutes on solo drills, pushing hard, ignoring the burn in my legs and the sweat dripping down into my eyes. Coach is barking orders—he clearly missed yelling at me. But I don't mind. It feels good to move. To breathe. To chase something.

For a while, it even works.

Until I hear the doors open behind the glass.

I glance up, watching people trickling in. Mostly figure skaters, a few staff. But my eyes find her immediately.

Maisie.

Walking into the rink with her head down and earbuds in, connected to her iPod. My heart stutters and I slow my pace without meaning to.

She looks up, and for a second, our eyes lock. Just a single second. Feels like eternity, though. A million-and-one questions fly between us, before she looks away.

Isabella waves her over, and Maisie heads toward her, smiling as she approaches her. That crinkly-eye, scrunched-nose, full-face kind of smile.

Fuck, I miss her.

It's insane how much I miss her.

Like a week without her has sucked all the color out of everything. Food tastes dull. Music's quieter. My chest feels too tight half the time. And I keep checking my phone for messages I know aren't there.

Because *I'm* the one who disappeared. *I* made it this way.

She's the reason I passed that test. The reason I'm back on the ice. The reason I didn't completely lose it.

And I haven't even thanked her.

Because I'm a fucking coward.

Great job, Austin.

I let my stick drop to the ice and skate over to the bench. Pretend I'm thirsty. Truth is, I just want a better angle to look at her without it being obvious.

Maisie doesn't even glance my way.

Good. I don't deserve her attention.

Isabella wraps her in a hug and says something else that makes her laugh. A *real* one. Bright and loud, her face lighting up.

It's the same smile I haven't seen in a week.

And I want it back.

I want to walk over there. Say something. *Anything.*

But my feet stay glued to the floor, because I don't know how to fix what I broke. And I'm scared shitless of what happens when I try.

Coach shouts for a line change, and I stay out too long just to burn it off. Whatever *it* is. Guilt. Regret. The ache that's been sitting in my chest since last Tuesday. I told myself kissing her was a fluke, that I was just caught up in the moment, but even now, a full week later, I can still feel the softness of her lips. Still remember the warmth of her cheek under my palm when I grabbed her face like I needed to touch her.

And I did. I still do.

But I can't. I can't want both. I can't be thinking about Maisie like this and still feel what I feel when I talk to—

Coach blows his whistle signaling the end of practice, and I shake off my thoughts, skating off behind the others.

My eyes flick back toward Maisie again. I watch as she waves goodbye to Isabella and walks toward the locker room. Her eyes meet mine for another second and my heart jumps, before she looks away and follows the other girls inside.

I should head to the locker room. Should rip my gear off and get this practice over with. But I'm still standing there, my chest heaving and my eyes locked on the door she just walked through like maybe—just maybe—she'll turn around.

She doesn't.

The door swings shut behind her, and I'm left staring at nothing.

I hear the Zamboni in the distance, and glance over my shoulder watching as the surface is smoothed over again and again.

I wish I could do that with my brain.

Smooth out all the static and just *know* what I want.

Cherry.

Maisie.

Fuck.

I rub my glove across my mouth, like that'll erase the memory. Like it'll stop me from wanting her.

But it doesn't. Not even close.

So I drop my stick, drag a hand through my hair, and skate off into the locker room, trying really fucking hard to stop thinking about that kiss.

And failing.

TWENTY-ONE

Maisie

It's barely four in the afternoon, and I'm already in pajamas. Curled up in bed, tucked between a mess of pillows and my stuffed toys, with a movie I've seen a hundred times playing on my laptop, and a half-eaten sleeve of Oreos beside me.

And I'm alone. As usual.

Austin passed his test.

Not that he told me himself. I found out the same way everyone else did—through a grainy mirror selfie from the rink locker room, with his helmet tucked under one arm, and that cocky grin plastered across his face.

The caption said, "Back on the ice," followed by a fist-bump emoji.

He passed.

And I mean, that's… great.

It's what he wanted.

What *we* wanted.

I should feel happy. I *am* happy. He tried this time. Really tried. He stayed awake through our study sessions, actually listened when I explained the same concept five times in a row. He worked for it. And it paid off.

He got what he needed. And now, I guess he doesn't need me anymore.

I shift under the blanket, hugging my stuffed pink bunny tighter to my chest.

I haven't been able to spiral in peace either, not with Six still radio silent.

I reach for my phone again, even though I already know what I'll see.

No messages from Austin.

None from Six.

Just one from Bailey, asking for advice on a dress for her winter formal, which I quickly type out a response to.

Me: Love it. You'll look amazing.

I hit send and scroll back through Six's thread anyway, and reread the last few messages. Was it something I said? Something I did? Did he get tired of waiting to meet me because I'm such a coward?

I drop the phone onto my chest and stare up at the ceiling, blinking against the burn in my eyes.

I got my hopes up.

I let myself believe that maybe Austin liked me. That maybe there was something there. That the kiss meant something.

And maybe I let myself believe that Six cared, too. That whoever he is behind that screen, he liked talking to me. Looked forward to it.

My throat tightens, and I press my face into the crook of my arm.

I should know better by now. I *do* know better.

But it still hurts knowing that maybe I'm just destined to be the girl no one chooses.

I'm about to close my laptop and do some homework when my phone buzzes.

Austin: hey.

One word. Three letters.

And somehow, it still knocks the air right out of my chest.

I sit up too quickly, my blanket sliding off my legs as I grab the phone, rereading the message.

It's the first I've heard from him in days.

Not since that afternoon in the library.

Not since he passed his test.

Not since that kiss.

Me: Hey.

Austin: got a spare slot 2 tutor me?

I squint at the screen before typing out a reply.

Me: You passed. Why do you need tutoring?

Austin: yeah, well, I want to make sure I keep passing.

Austin: plus, I kinda miss my friend.

Friend. Of course.

It's fine. I never expected anything more. I didn't *ask* for more.

I just thought… I don't know. I thought that look in his eyes, or the way he smiled when he saw me that day, meant something, like maybe he saw me the way I was hoping he would.

Me: I think I can open up a slot.

Austin: right now? come over.

I stare at the message.

Everything in me tugs in two directions at once.

Because I know better. I'm starting to get stupid, ridiculous feelings for Austin, and I know I'll probably leave his house tonight feeling worse than I did before.

But I also remember how it felt to kiss him. The way my heart stuttered, how everything else disappeared for a second.

And how quiet this room's been without him in it. How much I've missed him.

I'm tired of pretending I don't, of protecting myself from something that's already taken hold. So, I grab a hoodie off the back of my chair, pull my scrunchie out, fluff my hair, and I leave before I can talk myself out of it.

It's cold outside. My hoodie doesn't do much against the wind slicing across campus, but I don't slow down.

By the time I'm standing in front of Austin's house, my fingers are frozen—but everything else feels warm. My body's been buzzing since the second I left my dorm. Nerves, probably.

The front door opens before I even knock.

Austin stands there in a hoodie and joggers, barefoot, his hair a little messy like he's run his hand through it too many times. His eyes land on mine—tired, a little surprised. Like he didn't think I'd actually show up.

"Hey," he says, stepping back to let me in.

Austin closes the door behind me as soon as I step in.

His roommates are all in the living room and they all glance up when I walk in.

"Hey. Maisie, right?" Logan says, tilting his head. "You did a hell of a job with Rhodes. We had no faith in him."

Austin shoots him a look. "Thanks, man. Really appreciate the support."

Logan just laughs. "Hey, I'm just being honest."

Nathan tips his chin toward me. "Nice to see you again," he says, offering me a smile.

I smile back. "You too."

Austin nudges me gently with his elbow and dips his head toward the hallway. "Come on."

I follow him down it, my eyes dragging over the space. The muffled sounds of the TV and the guys' voices fade as we head up the stairs. My sneakers creak on the wood floor, and I can't help glancing around. Last time I was here, the place was packed. Loud. Sticky. Everything smelled like beer.

Now it's clean and quiet and kind of cozy.

Austin pushes open the door to his room and I follow him inside.

It's dim inside, just the glow of a lamp in the corner. His bed's made, but a little rumpled like he sat on it earlier and didn't bother fixing it. His guitar leans against the wall, catching my eye.

I nod toward it. "You play?"

He shrugs, setting down his phone. "Here and there. Mostly when I'm avoiding studying."

I blink, stepping closer. "I didn't know that about you."

He gives me this half-smile, that crooked grin that makes my chest squeeze in a way I don't like admitting out loud. "There's a lot you don't know about me, Maisie."

I raise a brow. "That's surprising considering how much you talk about yourself."

He lets out a breathy chuckle, his shoulders shaking a little. "You always know how to humble me, Freckles."

My heart does that annoying thing where it skips. I cross my arms loosely, trying to look unaffected, like he didn't just call me that nickname I haven't heard in days.

I nod toward the guitar again. "Will you… play something?"

His eyebrows lift, and the smirk fades just a little.

"You don't have to," I add quickly, already regretting it. "Forget I asked."

"No," he cuts me off. He swallows harshly, his eyes locked on mine. "I want to."

Austin crosses the room and settles on the edge of his bed, pulling the guitar into his lap. His fingers skim over the strings, tuning them, then he strums a few soft chords.

I sit on the opposite side of the bed, unable to look away from the way his brows pull together in concentration, the way his jaw flexes as he focuses.

The notes grow more familiar by the second, until I freeze.

Wait.

Is this—

Set Fire to the Rain.

I blink.

I'd know that melody anywhere. My chest tightens, something warm blooming behind my ribs.

When the last note fades, he looks up at me, his fingers still resting on the neck of the guitar. He rubs the back of his neck, and for the first time since I've known him, he looks kind of shy.

I swallow, my chest tightening with each second his eyes are on mine. "You're really good," I say, clearing my throat.

That flicker of nerves crosses his face again, but it's gone just as fast. "Yeah?"

I nod. "Why that song?" I ask him.

He gives a half-shrug. "Saw your skating video. You used that song, right?"

I blink.

"Couldn't stop thinking about it," he adds, adjusting one of the tuning pegs without looking at me. "The way you moved. The way it sounded with you."

My throat tightens.

"I figured if I could hear it again—if I could play it—I'd get it out of my head." He glances up then, his eyes meeting mine across the bed. "Didn't work."

The quiet stretches between us. The guitar's still in his lap, but neither of us moves. I'm still watching him. He's watching me. And I wonder if he's thinking about it—the kiss. The way his hands framed my face, the way he looked at me right before. And the regret riddled on his face right after.

Because I can't stop thinking about it.

He sets the guitar down beside him and then he glances at me, his brows tugging together. "Maisie. About what happened in the library…"

My stomach flips.

He runs a hand through his hair, shaking his head. "I'm sorry. I shouldn't have done that." He exhales sharply. "I was so fucked up over this other girl and—"

Other girl. He likes someone else. Of course he does.

"It's just—" He swallows hard. "I don't know what I was thinking."

My stomach twists into knots, heat flooding my cheeks. I want to look away, to disappear, but I can't.

What did I expect? That Austin Rhodes would fall for me? That I was anything more than his tutor or the girl he needed to pass a class? That I was something special?

No. I'm the rule. Not the exception.

I quickly wonder what she looks like. Do I know her? Is she pretty? She's probably drop-dead gorgeous for someone like Austin to be into her. Did he picture her when he kissed me? Did he think about her touch, her smile, while his lips were on mine? The thought burns like acid in my chest, tightening into a painful lump in my throat.

"It's okay," I say, because I don't think I can hear him say the rest.

But he shakes his head. "No, it's not okay. I just… I never wanted to hurt you or lead you on."

"You didn't," I cut in. "It's fine. You were happy and I just happened to be there. It didn't mean anything."

He pauses, watching me. "That's not what I meant."

"I get it, Austin," I tell him. "A guy like you doesn't kiss a girl like me unless he's confused. I know that."

He flinches, his brows knitting together. "Maisie—"

"It's fine. Really."

I keep talking. It's easier than letting him say anything else. If I keep going, maybe I won't have to hear the words I already know are coming.

"You were happy about the grade and you got caught up. I get it. I mean…" I force out a short laugh. "I didn't exactly expect my first kiss to go like that, but—"

He jerks back like I slapped him. "Wait… What?"

My mouth snaps shut.

Oh no.

I feel the blood drain from my face, then rush back all at once, burning across my cheeks, down my neck, flooding me with heat and panic.

He's staring at me, eyes wide, completely stunned. "That was... that was your first kiss?"

Shit.

I try to look away, but the weight of his gaze is like a spotlight. I feel small. Stupid. Like I just revealed something I shouldn't have. Like I gave him one more reason to look at me differently.

"Yeah."

He blinks, like he still doesn't believe it. "Your first?"

"Mhm."

God, this is so embarrassing. Why did I say that? Why couldn't I just lie, or change the subject, or bite my tongue for once in my life?

He shakes his head slowly. "How?"

I stare at my hands, digging my thumbnail into my palm until it stings.

Because I've never been the girl someone wanted to kiss. That's how. Because no one's ever looked at me that way.

I let out a breath, lifting my shoulder in a shrug. "I don't know. Just... happened. Or didn't, I should say."

I glance up and I can see it on his face—the guilt, the surprise, the way he's putting it all together.

And I hate it.

I hate the way he's looking at me now, like I'm some kind of delicate thing he accidentally dropped.

Like he regrets all of it.

He rubs both hands over his face, dragging them down slowly. "*Fuck*. Maisie, I'm so fucking sorry."

"It's okay," I repeat, swallowing the rock lodged in my throat.

"No, it's not," he says sharply, dropping his hands. "If you've been holding out this long, it's because it meant something to you. Because you pictured it going a certain way. Or with someone else. Someone better. And I just—" He breaks off, jaw clenched. "I'm such a fucking idiot."

"Don't say that," I murmur, and before I can second-guess it, I reach out and place my hand over his.

His skin is warm. Calloused. Solid beneath mine. He stills, like I've startled him, like maybe he wasn't expecting me to touch him at all.

His fingers tense beneath mine, but he doesn't pull away. Neither do I.

I don't even breathe. My pulse stutters, and I'm so aware of him—his hand under mine, his scent, the tiny space between us that suddenly feels too small and too big all at once.

His eyes meet mine, dark and warm and swimming with guilt. They're so pretty and so soft it almost hurts to look at him.

He blinks once. Then again, his tongue flicking out to wet his bottom lip. My eyes catch the motion like a hook, holding there for a beat too long.

Then his gaze drops to my mouth.

"How did you picture it?" he asks.

I blink. "What?"

"Your first kiss," he says, his eyes lifting to mine. "How did you picture it?"

My stomach twists. I wasn't expecting him to ask that, or to care.

I shift a little on the bed, the blanket tugging under my legs, and I let out a small breath. "I don't know," I say, even though I do. Of course I do. I've thought about it more times than I care to admit. "I guess… maybe after a date. He'd walk me home. It would be quiet. Sweet. He'd ask first. I'd say yes. Maybe my foot would pop a little."

A smirk tugs at the corner of his mouth. "Your foot would pop?"

My brows tug together, feeling the heat creep onto my face. "It's a thing."

He chuckles, and I hate that it makes my heart ache. Because I want to keep hearing that sound.

The flush on my face deepens and I glance down at our hands again.

"You know what? Never mind," I mutter, pulling my hand back slowly. "It's stupid. It doesn't matter anymore."

He runs a hand through his hair again, his laugh fading. His gaze drops to my mouth again, longer this time. A muscle in his jaw ticks. I watch the way he swallows, like he's holding something back.

"Let me make it right."

My heart stutters. "What?"

His eyes lift to mine. "Let me take you out. Give you the real foot-popping kiss you imagined."

I blink again, because I'm not sure I heard him right.

Did he really just say that?

My breath gets stuck somewhere in my chest, and I can't quite seem to get it out. My brain is scrambling to make sense of his words, but it's like they don't compute. Like they don't belong in a world where Austin Rhodes says stuff like that to me.

He can't be serious.

"Austin." I shake my head, already trying to backtrack. "You don't have to do that just because you feel bad."

Because that's what this is, isn't it? Guilt. Pity. A knee-jerk reaction to something he never meant to happen. A moment he regrets.

"I'm not doing it because I feel bad," he says, his voice low and raspy, making my skin break out into goosebumps. "I'm doing it because I want to."

My stomach flips, fluttering like crazy.

He moves closer. Barely. But enough that his knee brushes mine. Just the lightest touch. So light I could pretend it didn't happen if I wanted to. But I don't want to.

He places his hand on mine and moves his thumb. Just once. A slow, gentle sweep across the back of my hand.

He doesn't even seem to realize he's doing it—until he glances down. And then he does it again. Slow. Soft. Over and over.

I don't want to move. Don't want to breathe wrong and shatter whatever is happening.

My heart is pounding like crazy. I can't look away from him, and I don't know how to say what's building inside me. That part of me wants to trust this. Wants to believe him.

Even if it's not real, I want to know what it's like. Just once. To go on a date. To feel wanted. To pretend, just for one night, that someone like Austin could want me.

But the other part—the louder one—won't stop whispering that I'm reading it wrong. That I always read it wrong.

Still, I nod. "Okay," I whisper.

His smile blooms, his perfect teeth flashing. Those dimples pop and it's so unfair how good he looks when he smiles like that.

"Yeah?" he murmurs, his thumb still brushing my hand.

"Yeah."

He lets out a soft laugh, his eyes crinkling at the corners. Then he leans in just a little closer. "I'm gonna give you the best damn foot-popping kiss in history."

I try to roll my eyes, but it's useless. The corners of my mouth curl up against my will.

Because for the first time in a long time, I want to believe it.

Even though I know I shouldn't.

TWENTY-TWO

Maisie

I change my outfit four times before I admit I'm spiraling.

There's a mountain of discarded clothes in the corner of my bed—sweaters, tank tops, dresses I haven't worn since high school—piled up in a heap that's growing by the minute.

Too casual.

Too formal.

Too much boob.

Not enough boob.

I pull on a cropped sweater, hoping the sleeves will distract from everything else, but the moment I catch my reflection, I yank it off. It clings to my stomach in a way that makes my skin crawl.

I try a sundress next. Soft cotton, pale yellow, sort of cute. But in the mirror I look like I'm trying to sneak into a middle school dance. I tug at the hem, frown, then sigh and peel it off again.

Jeans. Black top. Safe. Fine. Sort of sexy? I can't tell anymore. I stare at my reflection and try to see what he'll see.

Ugh.

God. What am I doing? It's not even a real date. He's just doing this to clear his guilt, because he kissed me when he shouldn't have. Because he's interested in someone else, and I just happened to be there.

Because I told him—awkwardly, painfully—that he was my first kiss. And he looked at me like I'd told him I'd never seen a fork before.

And now he's picking me up in less than an hour, and I'm still standing in my underwear, my hair in a half-dry bun, mascara on only one eye, staring at my closet in panic, hating every single stitch of clothing that lands on my body.

I could just cancel.

Or fake a stomach flu.

Or crawl under the bed and die quietly with what little dignity I have left.

My stomach churns as I dig my thumbs into the waistband of my sweatpants and sigh.

Then I grab my phone, and text the only two girls I vaguely know.

Maisie: Hey. Weird question. If you had to pick something to wear on a date with a guy, what would you wear?

The second I hit send, I regret it. My finger hovers over the unsend button, my brain screaming at me to abort.

But before I can react, Isabella replies.

Isabella: What dorm are you in? We're on our way.

My stomach drops.

Maisie: No, it's fine I didn't mean for you to come over, I was just asking for some advice.

I let out a breath when they don't reply, and quickly tug my sweatshirt on.

There's a knock on my dorm door less than five minutes later. I head to the door, and when I open it, Aurora marches into my dorm without a second glance. Isabella follows behind her, carrying a small tote bag.

I blink at them. "I didn't think you'd actually come."

I'm not used to girls showing up.

I didn't know how much I wanted it.

"You asked. We delivered." Aurora flops down onto my bed, eyeing the crime scene of clothes beside her. "Let's see the damage."

"Damage?" I echo.

She points at the heap of discarded outfits on my bed. "That."

Isabella walks over to my open closet and hums under her breath. "Okay, so, do you want to be casual, or cute, or a mixture of both?"

I lift my hair off my neck, suddenly too hot. "I don't know? He didn't say where we're going."

"Vague men," Aurora mutters, shaking her head. "Hate them."

"Who's the guy?" Isabella asks without looking back, already pulling out a dress I forgot I owned.

My hands tug at the sleeves of my sweatshirt. "It's… Austin."

They both freeze.

Aurora straightens. "I'm sorry. Austin?"

Isabella turns, holding the hanger mid-air. "*Austin* Austin?"

I nod.

"As in Rhodes?" Aurora asks. "Center for the hockey team, tall, loud, annoying, dimples?"

"That's the one," I mutter.

Isabella blinks. "I didn't know he went on dates."

"He doesn't." I pause. "It's not… It's not a date. Not really."

They wait.

I suck in a breath. "He kissed me."

Their eyes widen in shock, mimicking what I feel.

"It was a misunderstanding," I'm quick to add.

Isabella's eyebrows lift. "A misunderstanding?" she repeats.

I nod, sitting down on my bed, pulling Waddles into my lap. "He didn't mean to kiss me," I explain. "He was just happy about passing his test, and…" I trail off, blowing out a breath, because I don't even know how to explain it myself. "He just feels bad, and wants to make it up to me."

There's a beat of silence.

Aurora leans forward, brows pulled together. "Wait. He kissed you, and now he wants to take you out to apologize for the kiss?"

"Yep."

I don't mention that it was my first kiss. The look on Austin's face afterward was enough. I don't need them feeling sorry for me, too.

"Has he kissed you before that?" Aurora asks. "Or, like… flirted with you?"

I shift on the bed, picking at a loose thread on my sleeve. I think about the way he smiled at me that night we watched the movie in my dorm, how his arm slid around mine like it was no big deal. The way he leaned in at the rink, bracing his arms on either side of me, how his gaze always seemed to dip to my lips.

But maybe none of that meant anything. Maybe I imagined all of it.

He likes someone else.

I shake my head. "No. This was… just an accident."

Isabella bites back a smile. "And now he's picking you up for a date to make up for it."

"Yep."

They exchange a glance I don't know what to make of, and then Aurora stands up and heads straight for the closet. "Alright," she says. "We're picking out a killer outfit."

I stare at her. "You don't have to—"

"It's not a big deal," she says, already sliding hangers across the rod. "I love fashion."

"Thank you," I say, exhaling. "For helping me."

"You asked the group chat," she says with a shrug. "That's basically a blood oath."

I let out a laugh as Isabella pulls a pink cardigan from the rack, something soft and oversized, with little pearl buttons and a delicate cable-knit pattern along the sleeves. She holds it up by the shoulders and gives it a small shake.

"What about this one?"

I look at it for a second. It's cute. Too cute, maybe. The kind of thing I'd wear to class. But would it be right for this? Whatever this is?

My fingers curl around the edge of my blanket. "I don't know," I say with a shake of my head. "I've never been on a date."

Isabella turns halfway, her eyes softening. A small smile tugs at the corner of her lips. "You'll be fine. I was a mess on my first date with Ryan, too."

My brows lift. "Really?"

Aurora rolls her eyes, shaking her head. "God, she was a disaster. I had to physically restrain her from freaking the hell out."

Isabella shoots her a look over her shoulder. "And then you threatened him."

Aurora just shrugs, unapologetic. "I stand by that."

I let out a laugh. I never thought I'd have this. Girls who show up and dig through my closet and tease each other in front of me like I'm one of them, like I always have been.

For the longest time, there was only Six.

Just this little bubble of connection, hidden in my phone. Late-night texts and jokes that felt like secrets. The only person I ever really let in.

My fingers twist in the edge of the blanket as something presses at my throat. And before I can think better of it, I blurt it out.

"There's this... other guy."

The room goes still. Their heads turn toward me in sync, both sets of eyes blinking like they're not sure they heard right.

There's something about Six that feels different. Safe in a way I can't explain. Like I've kept him in this small, quiet part of my life where nothing has to be messy or real. Just texts. Just me, and whoever he is, behind that name.

And saying it out loud makes it feel like something else. Like I'm holding it up to the light and asking it to be real.

Aurora smirks, one eyebrow quirking up. "Little Maisie's got game, huh?"

I roll my eyes, but there's a small laugh that slips out anyway. "No, I definitely don't. I don't even know him. It's just... this guy I've been messaging for a few weeks. He goes by Six. That's literally all I know."

Isabella's voice softens. "And you like him?"

I bite down on the inside of my cheek. My heart gives a traitorous little flutter. "Yeah," I admit quietly. "But I'm too scared to meet him."

Isabella lifts a brow, her expression shifting. "And Austin?" she asks. "You like him too?"

I let out a breath and shake my head, more at myself than anything. "Yeah. I do." My chest aches just saying it. "I just… I know this doesn't mean anything to him. This date, it's just to clear his conscience or whatever. To make him feel better about kissing me when he didn't mean to." I swallow, my fingers curling in my lap.

Isabella turns to face me. "I've known Austin for a while," she says, "and he doesn't do anything he doesn't want to do."

I shift on the bed. I want to believe her, I really do. But there's this knot in my stomach that won't allow me to. "I just don't want to get my hopes up, you know? I know what kind of girls he's usually seen with." I glance up, biting the inside of my cheek. "And I look nothing like them."

Aurora shifts the clothes on my bed and faces me. "Okay, listen. I hate most girls. I hate how fake they are, and how boy obsessed they are, and how everything has to boil down to competition with other women. But I don't hate you. I actually like you. Which means you've already won me over. And if you can win me, you can win him."

My mouth twitches into a half smile. "That's… sweet?"

"It's practically a love confession coming from her," Isabella tells me. "Trust me."

"You're welcome," Aurora says with a smirk. "Okay. Enough feelings. Time to turn you into a smoke show."

Aurora orders me to stand up, which I do—because she's slightly terrifying—and they tug me to my vanity. Isabella pulls out some lip gloss, and Aurora is already plugging in my curling iron.

I feel something shift in my chest as the girls hover over me, helping me get ready for a date with Austin. Feeling like maybe for once in my life, I'm not just the background character in everyone else's story.

I can be the main character in mine.

TWENTY-THREE

Austin

I've played in packed arenas with a hundred people chanting my name and coaches breathing down my neck. I've been in fistfights mid-game and taken slapshots to the ribs. But none of that compares to the way my stomach's twisting right now.

I grip the steering wheel tighter, and glance sideways at the girl sitting next to me. She's not saying anything, just fiddling with the hem of her dress—this soft, flowy, blue thing that clings to the curve of her waist and shows off the swell of her chest like it's specifically designed to fucking torture me. Her hands are on her lap, and I catch a peek of her thick thighs pressing into the seat, smooth and soft and driving me absolutely insane in the best way possible.

I can't stop staring. Every time she glances at me, I feel it in my chest.

She looks like everything I've ever wanted but never knew how to ask for.

"Okay," I say, clearing my throat because, fuck, it feels weird saying this to anyone but Cherry. "Confession."

She glances at me, curious.

"This is my first date," I admit.

Her eyes go wide. "You've never been on a date?"

I shake my head. "Never really wanted to. There's never been a girl I was dying to see outside of my bedroom."

She laughs. I swear I feel it crawl up my spine and settle into my chest. "So I'm your first?"

"No." I catch her eyes and my lips twitch. "You're my only."

Maisie flushes, tucking hair behind her ear like she's trying to disappear. The dash lights flicker on her cheekbones, and for a second I'm stuck just staring—not wanting to look away.

I flick on my blinker and turn in, tires crunching over gravel as I pull into the drive-in lot just off campus. A few cars are scattered across the rows, most with their windows down, some with people sitting on their roofs or stretched out in truck beds.

I kill my headlights and ease into a spot near the middle. String lights line the fences and snack stand, and there's that familiar smell of popcorn and something fried drifting through the air.

I shift into park and lean back, drumming my fingers on the wheel. We're probably a little too early. I've never been early a day in my life, but I don't want her to miss the movie.

She looks over at me, her eyebrows lifting in surprise. "We're at a drive-in?"

I shoot her a smile before I hop out of the truck, jog around to her side, and open the door, holding out my hand. "C'mon."

She blinks up at me. "You're really committing to this, huh?"

A grin spreads across my face. "I'm a gentleman. Now, give me your hand."

Her fingers slip into mine as I help her out of the truck. Jesus, I can smell that soft vanilla scent of hers, and the freckles dusting across her nose catch the light just right.

She looks like summer. Like soft blue skies, and warm cheeks and something I probably don't deserve.

"Maisie," I say, quiet, trying not to fuck this up.

She meets my eyes.

"You're—" I pause, blowing out a breath. Screw it. "You look so fucking beautiful."

Her mouth parts, and she goes pink, like she didn't expect that. She smiles softly, drifting her eyes over my body. "You look pretty good, too."

"I know," I tease with a grin. "I always do."

She scoffs, shaking her head, then walks over to the back of the truck and drops the tailgate. Her eyes widen when she sees what I set up.

I laid out every blanket I could steal from the house. Thick ones, soft ones, even stole Nathan's freaking weighted one because I heard it's calming or something—heavy as fuck by the way. I shoved a cooler in the corner with a couple of sodas, a bag of popcorn, and basically every kind of candy I could find at the gas station.

She lets out this breath, like maybe she's impressed or just trying not to laugh. "You went all out."

I shrug, rubbing my neck again. "I wanted to make it special for you."

When she glances at me, that weird ache hits my chest again. The one that only happens whenever she looks at me.

I help her up into the bed of the truck. She settles in against the pillows, and I tuck the blankets around her, checking twice that she's comfortable.

The screen lights up as the projector kicks in.

She blinks, her eyebrows shooting up. "Wait. Is that—"

I nod. "You've Got Mail."

She turns to look at me, those soft eyes that somehow kill me every damn time. "That's my favorite movie."

"Yeah," I chuckle, feeling the stupid grin creep onto my face. "I know."

"You remembered that?"

I shrug, suddenly way too aware of how fast my heart's pounding. I scratch the back of my neck. "I listen when you talk, Maisie."

She looks at me for a second, this soft, quiet look that makes my chest tighten. Like she's actually *seeing* me. And fuck, I'm sitting here on a first date with a girl, and suddenly I'm nervous as hell. I don't get nervous. I always know what to say, what to do, how to flirt.

But I'm at a complete loss when it comes to this girl.

"I've never watched this one," I admit, grabbing a handful of popcorn and stuffing it into my mouth.

She snaps her head toward me, shocked. "What? How?"

I shrug again. "I dunno. I think I tend to go for the more recent stuff."

"Then you're in for a treat," she says with a smile. "The old ones are always the best."

"High praise," I say with a teasing smirk.

She nods. "You better pay attention."

"I'll try," I say, but honestly, I'm barely watching the screen. I'm watching her.

The way her hair catches the light of the glowing screen. The curve of her cheek when she smiles. The soft sounds she makes when she laughs at a line.

I hold the bag of popcorn out to her, but she pauses, eyes flicking from the snacks to me, brows knitting just a little.

I remember that day at the diner when she barely ate, even when I slid the mozzarella sticks her way. She was clearly hungry, but it was like eating in front of me made her freeze up or something.

Which is fucking ridiculous. Everyone eats. She shouldn't feel weird about that. Ever.

And if I ever found out someone said something to her, there's not a goddamn person on this planet that could stop me from plummeting them into the ground.

"I got like six other snacks if you want something else," I offer.

She smiles, and I swear I see something loosen in her shoulders. "I'm more of an Oreo girl."

My smile widens, and I open the bag, reaching for those. "Lucky for you, I panicked in the snack aisle and bought half the store."

She laughs, rips open the pack, and grabs one.

"I used to watch this movie with my sister," she says, her eyes glued to the screen. "We'd quote it line for line." She lets out a sigh. "This part always makes me cry."

I glance down at her. "Why?"

She shrugs. "It's just… sad, I guess. Two people in the same city, walking past each other every day and not knowing what they're missing."

Yeah.

I think about all the times I must've walked past her and didn't even know she existed. And now she's here, curled up beside me, and I don't know how I ever went this long without her.

Halfway through, she shifts. Her head rests lightly against my chest. My arm slides around her waist without me even thinking about it. She lets out the tiniest sigh, nestling in closer, and I just sit there, blinking at the screen, my heart pounding like a jackhammer.

My heart is beating so loud, I'm surprised she doesn't comment on it.

This feels good. This feels right.

I don't remember the last time I felt like this.

I shift closer to her, and I feel her body stiffen just a little.

"You okay?" I murmur, glancing down at her.

"Yeah," she says, lifting her eyes to look up at me. *Fuck, those eyes.* "I just… like this."

I tighten my arm around her just a little. She reaches out and places her hand over mine. Her thumb rubs over my knuckles, and I want to pull her into my chest and keep her there. Forever. She has no idea what that little touch is doing to me. None.

I stare at the screen and pretend I'm following the movie, but the only thing I'm thinking about is the girl pressed into my side.

By the time the credits roll, she's half-asleep on my shoulder, her hand curled lightly over my stomach. I don't move. Don't want to.

I want to stay like this.

Right here, with her tucked into me.

"That was so good," I say, even though I barely watched half of it.

She tilts her head, eyes still sleepy but bright. "You liked it?"

"I liked the company more," I tease with a smile.

She chuckles, rolls those eyes and I feel my stomach churn at the thought of saying goodbye to her tonight.

I force myself to shift, gently nudging her. "C'mon. Let's get you back."

She sits up slowly, blinking up at me. "Yeah. Okay."

I help her down from the truck, my fingers brushing her waist just a second longer than necessary. She doesn't pull away.

While I pack up the pillows and toss the blankets in the back, she waits near the passenger door, arms folded against the wind. Her hair whips around her face, and I swear it takes everything in me not to just kiss her right then and there.

The drive back is quiet, her head leaned against the window, my fingers drumming absently on the steering wheel, looking for something to do.

When I pull up in front of her dorm, I kill the engine and glance over.

"I'll walk you up."

She smiles. "Okay."

The hallway's empty, our footsteps the only sound. Her door's halfway down the hall, and for once, I don't have anything cocky or stupid to say.

She stops at her room and turns to face me.

"Thank you for the date," she says, and her voice is so damn sincere it knocks something loose in my chest.

I reach out, brushing a piece of hair behind her ear, my fingers skimming her cheek. "Best one I've ever been on."

She laughs, shaking her head. "It's the only one you've ever been on."

"Still the best."

She smiles, and my heart is thudding in my chest, in my throat, in the way my thumb brushes along her cheek.

"There's one more thing," I murmur, taking a step closer. "To make this the perfect date."

She looks up at me, those soft, blue eyes all wide and shining, and damn… she looks like a porcelain doll. Gorgeous, delicate, impossible not to stare at, and I'm scared I'll break her just by looking too long.

"Yeah? What's that?"

My thumb traces the corner of her mouth. "This."

I lift her chin gently, my stomach fluttering at the sound of her breath catching in her throat.

I'm freaking out. Not that I'd ever admit that out loud. But my heart's pounding, and I feel like it's *my* first kiss.

"Can I kiss you?" I whisper.

She nods. Barely. Just the smallest tilt of her chin.

I stare at her a second longer, memorizing everything about her. Her freckles. The shape of her mouth. The little dip in her chin. My thumb strokes across her cheek, and then I lean in—closer, closer—giving her every chance to stop me.

She doesn't.

She leans into me.

And I kiss her.

Slow. Soft. Fucking perfect.

I take my sweet ass time, because this girl deserves it. She deserves the best damn kiss in the whole entire world.

Her lips are soft and warm and sweet—so damn sweet—and she tastes like that cherry Chapstick she always wears. I could drown in it.

She gasps slightly, her lips parting, and it feels like permission. I tilt her jaw and kiss her deeper, licking into her mouth, and groan when I feel her gasp, pressing her hands against my chest.

Christ.

This kiss.

This girl.

I don't know how long we stay like that—minutes, hours, lifetimes—but when I finally pull back, her lips are pink and swollen, her breathing fast. Mine's not any better. I don't ever remember having a kiss that felt like that before.

I rest my forehead against hers, my thumb brushing gently over her bottom lip. She's flushed, wide-eyed, absolutely wrecked in the best way, and all because of me.

I can't believe she's real. Can't believe I went on with my life for years, without noticing her, without being in her presence. Because now it feels physically impossible not to be around her.

"Was it everything you pictured?" I ask, my voice still rough.

She exhales. "Better."

My lips twitch into a smirk. "Did your foot pop?"

She rolls her eyes and shoves my shoulder. "You ruined it."

"Nuh uh." I shake my head, grinning like an idiot. "Nothing could ruin that kiss, Freckles."

Her blush deepens as she bites her lip and murmurs, "Goodnight, Austin."

She slips inside and closes the door before I can say anything else.

I just stand there for a second, staring at the closed door, hoping it might open again. My pulse is still hammering, and my chest tight in a way that feels good. Really fucking good.

I run a hand through my hair, blowing out a breath.

I should be thinking about Cherry. Hell, I was spiraling over all this just a few days ago, conflicted as fuck.

But all I can think about is Maisie.

I don't even know if she wants something with me, or if this meant as much to her as it did to me.

But I know what *I* want.

I want her.

More than a tutor.

More than a friend.

And I'm gonna win her over.

No matter what it takes.

TWENTY-FOUR

Austin

I've never been to a figure skating competition before, and I sure as hell didn't expect to be walking into one on a Saturday afternoon with the entire hockey team dragging their sorry asses behind me like we're headed into a group dental appointment.

The second we step through the arena doors, Logan groans. He yanks his hoodie over his head. "Are we seriously doing this?" he mutters, his eyes glued to the rink. "We're watching a figure skating competition?"

I slow my steps just enough to shoot him a look over my shoulder. "Any of you say another word and you're getting a kick to the teeth."

Cole arches a brow. "Chill. We're here, aren't we?"

"Yeah," I mutter, turning back around and shoving my hands into the pockets of my jacket. "To support Maisie. So zip it."

There's a beat of silence, and I know that silence. I feel the look they all exchange behind my back. Teammates or not, they're vultures when they smell something.

"Is there something going on with you and your tutor?" Ryan's voice, dripping with amusement. I don't even have to look at him to know he has a smug smirk on his face right now.

I keep walking, keeping my eyes trained ahead.

Normally I'd toss something back. Push the joke further. Brag, maybe. I've done it before—told a story about a girl just to make the guys laugh.

But with Maisie?

Fuck no.

Even the *idea* of turning her into some locker room punchline feels wrong.

I don't want to explain that I'm not hooking up with Maisie, that I'm not doing anything with her—at least not in the way they're imagining. I just kissed her.

And I haven't stopped thinking about it since.

That kiss is burned into my brain. Every second of it. The way she looked up at me. The way she leaned in. The way her lips tasted.

That kiss was mine.

For once, I don't want to share. I don't want to joke about it or toss it around for laughs. I just want to keep it, hold it somewhere private. Something that no one else can touch.

My jaw ticks. "Mind your business."

Ryan lets out a low scoff, clearly amused. "Excuse me? Coming from the guy who wouldn't stop harassing me last year to tell him who I was texting?"

A grin tugs at my mouth before I can stop it. "And I was right about who it was," I shoot back.

He rolls his eyes. "Yeah, and now it's your turn in the hot seat."

I just shake my head and keep walking, quickening my pace as we start up the stairs toward the bleachers.

I don't want to talk about this with them. Hell, I don't even know what's going on with Maisie, let alone how to explain it.

She's my tutor, but she's also the girl I can't stop thinking about. The one whose laugh plays on a loop in the back of my mind when I'm trying to sleep. The one who walked into my life like she wasn't going to take up space—and then quietly took all of it anyway.

And now I'm here. At a goddamn figure skating competition. On a Saturday. With my teammates glaring daggers into the ice and acting like their balls are shrinking just by being inside the rink.

All for her. I'd sit through a thousand toe loops and sparkly costumes if it means I get to be around her.

The stands aren't packed, but there's a decent crowd. Parents. Couples. People holding warm drinks and chatting quietly.

We find seats halfway up, smack in the middle of the bleachers. The second I sit, my knee starts bouncing.

My eyes go straight to the ice.

Scanning. Waiting.

And then I see her.

Maisie steps out from behind the partition, her coach beside her, and the rest of the arena blurs out. My mouth goes dry. I rub a hand over it, like that's going to help me breathe again.

Holy. Shit.

She's wearing this soft pink dress that sparkles as she walks. The skirt moves when she walks, just enough to tease the curve of her hips, and the neckline dips into this soft V that rests across the top of her chest in a way that makes my heart jackhammer against my ribs.

Her thighs—thick, strong, fucking gorgeous—peek out from under the hem as she steps forward. Her calves are wrapped in clean white skates. Every step is confident. Controlled. Like she belongs out there.

And I can't fucking breathe.

Pretty sure I stop blinking.

I don't even realize I've stood up until Logan leans over and mutters, "Dude. Sit your ass down."

I ignore him.

I'm already moving, pushing past knees and bags and elbows, weaving my way down the steps toward the edge of the rink. The closer I get, the tighter everything inside me feels. My throat, my chest, my fists tucked into my jacket pocket.

Maisie's crouched near the gate, lacing up her skates.

She glances up, probably expecting her coach or a judge or a clipboard, and then her eyes catch mine, and she freezes.

Her mouth parts slightly, her fingers still wrapped around the lace of her skate.

"You came?" she says, voice soft, almost unsure. The top of her hair's pulled back with a white bow, and her cheeks are already flushed pink. Could be nerves. Could be me. *Hope it's me*.

"Wouldn't miss it," I say, my voice rougher than I meant it to be.

I swallow hard and glance down and then back up, trying not to stare at her legs or the way her dress sparkles under the lights. Trying—and failing—not to look completely gone over this girl.

Because I am.

And there's no hiding it.

Her lips part like she's about to say something else, but then her gaze shifts over my shoulder. "You brought your teammates?"

I scratch the back of my neck, wincing. "Don't hold that against me. They insisted."

A shout echoes from a few rows back. "We did not!" Logan yells.

I shoot him a glare, but he just grins like the little shit he is.

Maisie's chuckling when I turn back around.

God, she's so pretty when she smiles. Soft and secretive and a little shy. Like she doesn't even know she's the most beautiful thing in this whole arena.

Her eyes drop to my chest, her lashes fluttering. She looks like she doesn't know what to do with her hands, and the pink on her cheeks spreads down her neck in this slow, gorgeous wave.

I lean in slightly and reach out without thinking. My hand curves against the side of her face, my thumb skimming gently across her cheek.

"You're so fucking cute when you blush."

I want to kiss her again.

Right here, rink-side, under these god-awful fluorescent lights.

"Maisie, you've got five minutes." My hand drops from her face and we both turn at the sound of her coach's voice.

Maisie nods quickly, then glances back at me. "Wish me luck?"

I shake my head. "Don't need to. You've got this."

She gives me this tiny, nervous smile, and then heads for the bench. I watch her go, unable to look away.

A few seconds later, Isabella and Aurora walk into the rink, and weave through the bleachers, sliding into the row behind the guys.

Maisie glances up as they call her name, grinning wide, then looks down at her skates.

"Okay," she says, blowing out a breath. "Don't let me down, you two." She taps her fingertips against the tops of her skates. It's quiet, barely audible, but I catch every word. My brows shoot up in surprise, and my lips curve into a grin before I can stop them.

My fucking soulmate.

I drag myself back to my seat, eager to watch her kill it out there.

The lights shift, and a low hum rolls through the speakers as the first note of her music cuts in.

Then she steps onto the ice.

And the entire goddamn arena goes still.

Even the guys shut up. Logan doesn't say a word. Ryan leans forward. No one breathes.

Maisie glides into the center like she was made for it—like the ice isn't just beneath her, but a part of her. Like it listens when she moves. Like it answers only to her.

And right now, it does.

Every eye follows her. Every breath in the place holds.

She moves slowly at first, arms lifting with the rise of the music, fingers carving something soft into the cold air. There's this quiet confidence in her body, this ease that makes it impossible to look anywhere else.

Then she turns and picks up speed. The wind pulls at her hair, her skirt fluttering as she gathers momentum, and launches into a jump so smooth it barely looks real.

She spins in the air before landing it effortlessly, her arms wide, chest lifted, like she was never not meant to fly.

I'm frozen. Jaw hanging. Completely fucking gone.

I've seen talent. I've played alongside guys who were born with a stick in their hands. Athletes who could make a puck do things that shouldn't be possible.

But this is something else entirely.

This is more than a sport or technique. It's art.

And I'm watching her heart speak in a language I'll never quite understand, but somehow still feel.

That pink dress catches the lights with every turn, glinting like stars. Her thighs flex, her back curves, and her skates carve the ice like she's painting on it.

I think half the guys in here just fell in love with her.

Too fucking bad.

She's mine.

And yeah, I only kissed her once—twice if you count the library—and I haven't touched her since. But it doesn't matter.

Because the second she looks up at me and her eyes soften and her mouth tips into the smallest, most beautiful smile I've ever seen, I know there's not a single other person in this world that can make me feel like she does.

The final note hits, and the crowd goes wild. People leap to their feet, clapping, cheering.

She glides toward the edge, slowing down, her breaths fast and shallow as she coasts to a stop at the barrier. Her eyes scan the crowd, and then land on me.

And when she sees me, she smiles. And my whole fucking chest caves in.

I stand up without thinking, my heart pounding as I make my way down the steps toward the rink.

She steps off the ice just as I reach the barrier, still catching her breath.

"You were amazing," I say.

Her smile widens, but before I can say anything else, Isabella and Aurora explode toward her, full squeals and flailing arms, nearly knocking her sideways as they wrap her in a hug.

I take a step back, jealousy bubbling sharp and fast in my throat.

It's just… I want it to be me. I want to be the one she collapses into, the one holding her while she laughs like that. I want her glow to be for me—because of me. I want her looking at me like I'm the reason she's still buzzing from the ice.

They're all over her—fixing her hair, adjusting her jacket, whispering about the routine, her dress, how perfect she looked out there.

And they're not wrong.

She was perfect.

She *is*.

And I just stand there.

Hovering.

Waiting.

My hands twitch at my sides, and I hate how badly I want her attention, how desperate I feel for her to look at me, just for a second, and let me in.

Finally, I clear my throat and step forward. "Mind if I cut in?"

Aurora raises a brow, amused. "We were just leaving." She throws Maisie a wink as they both disappear toward the hallway.

I watch them go, then finally step closer to Maisie.

She's still got that post-performance shine, her lips parted, cheeks glowing, eyes wide and warm and a little dazed.

I don't think I've ever seen anyone look more beautiful in my life.

"Maisie," I say softly, blowing out a breath. "You were…" I trail off, searching for words. Can't find them, not the right ones, anyway. Nothing I come up with feels big enough. "I'm so fucking proud of you."

Her eyes flick up to mine, surprised. Like she wasn't expecting that. Like maybe no one's ever said it to her and actually meant it.

I lean in slightly, tilting my head so I can really look at her. Take her in. "You were incredible. I knew you skated, but holy shit, Maisie. I didn't know you could do that."

A shy smile forms on her lips. "Thanks," she murmurs.

"I didn't breathe for three minutes," I tell her. "Forgot how lungs work. Might still be struggling, honestly."

She lets out a quiet laugh. "You're dramatic," she says, rolling her eyes.

I step a little closer. "You're talented," I say, not backing down. "And you looked so beautiful out there."

Her cheeks flush deeper, a light pink spreading from her ears down her neck. My favorite fucking color.

"Thanks. It was… a lot. I was nervous."

I shake my head. "Couldn't tell. You looked like you were born on that ice."

I reach into my jacket and pull out the plush hockey puck I picked up before the performance, and hold it out to her.

Her eyes flick down, then lift back to mine, her eyebrow raising a little.

"I heard people usually toss stuff like this onto the ice after a routine," I say, shrugging. "But I wanted to give it to you directly. 'Cause, well… yeah."

Maisie's fingers brush over the stitching. She smiles, tilting her head. "You know I'm not a hockey fan, right?"

I laugh. "Don't break my heart, Freckles. Hockey's the best damn sport in the world."

"Mmm." She chuckles, taking the puck from my hand. "I'm just kidding. Thank you, Austin. Seriously, I…" She trails off, shaking her head like she's trying to clear it. "I didn't think anyone would be here. And you—"

"I'll always be here for you, Mais," I say, stepping in closer. My voice goes quiet without meaning to, eyes flicking down to her mouth—the same one I kissed not even a week ago. The same one I still think about way too often.

"So," she says, raising her brows, that teasing glint slipping into her voice. "Does this mean I have to come to one of your games now?"

I chuckle, reach up, and tuck a loose strand of hair behind her ear. My fingers brush her skin for half a second too long. "Hell yes, it does."

She smirks, that little spark lighting up in her eyes. "We'll see."

I bump her shoulder lightly. "We both know you'll say yes."

Maisie rolls her eyes but doesn't deny it. She turns toward the locker room, but not before glancing back at me. One last look. One last soft smile that curls at the corners of her mouth and punches straight through my chest.

And then she's gone.

But my eyes stay on the spot she left, already counting down the seconds until I get to see her again.

TWENTY-FIVE

Austin

I haven't played in a month.

Thought I'd be rusty and slow as fuck. Figured my legs would feel heavy, my timing would be off, my rhythm shot to hell. But the second my blades touch the ice, it all just… clicks.

Like my body remembers. Like it's been waiting.

My legs know what to do. My hands remember how to handle the stick. My body locks into place, like it never left. It's like the last few weeks didn't happen. Like I didn't screw everything up. Like I wasn't benched for weeks and forced to sit on the sidelines while everyone else kept going.

I didn't think I'd play again this season. I honest-to-god thought Coach would sideline me permanently. Let me rot in my own mistakes.

But here I am.

The student section is on their feet and Coach is yelling and the puck is ours and—holy shit, we're winning.

I shouldn't be surprised. The guys played just fine without me.

The moment I take a pass from Logan, twist around the defenseman, and bury the puck top shelf, it's like every part of me exhales.

I'm back.

And I'm fucking starving for it.

The crowd is loud tonight, louder than I remember, but I don't scan the stands until the first whistle blows and I'm skating back to the bench.

And that's when I see Maisie sitting in the front row.

I asked her to come, and she told me she would, but seeing her here for real is making my stomach flutter.

She's here.

For me.

Our eyes meet and I flash a grin.

Ryan thumps his stick against my shoulder. "Let's go, lover boy."

I shove him with my elbow, moving toward the faceoff circle. I line up, dropping low, my eyes locked on the puck.

The second it hits the ice, we're flying.

It's fast. Faster than I expected. But I feel good. Better than good. I don't realize how much I missed this until I'm slamming my body into the boards for a loose puck and the crowd roars behind me.

I scoop it free, twist on my blades, and send a clean pass to Logan. He barely holds it a beat before snapping it across the crease to Ryan, who hammers it home.

Goal.

Just like that.

My first assist of the night, and I'm grinning so hard it hurts.

My jersey sticks to my chest, sweat dripping down my back, but I don't care. I can't stop grinning. Nothing, *nothing* in the world feels better than this.

I glance up at the stands, and see Maisie standing, with a wide smile as she claps and cheers, her eyes locked on me.

Okay… maybe I lied. There is something better.

The game flies by in a blur of hits, shots, and shouts. The final buzzer sounds with the scoreboard glowing 5–2, and I don't think I've smiled this hard in weeks.

We won.

Logan skates over, bumping my shoulder with his. "Nice work out there, Rhodes. Good to have you back."

I flash him a crooked grin, my chest still heaving. *It's good to be back.*

I don't wait around. The second my skates hit the tunnel, I'm already tugging my gloves off, ready to find her.

She's waiting near the exit, tucked beside Isabella and Aurora, the three of them huddled against the wall. Her eyes find mine instantly and her lips curl into the softest smile. It hits me right in the damn chest.

I slow to a stop in front of her, still fully geared up, sweat cooling under my pads, my breath hitching in my throat for a whole different reason now.

God, she's so pretty, standing there in a denim jacket, and a white flowy dress, and those sky blue eyes I dream about.

The rink's noise fades a little as I catch my breath, sweat dripping down my neck.

"Hey," I say, smiling when I spot her watching me.

"Hey," she echoes, looking up at me through those thick lashes. "You were incredible out there."

I smirk, leaning in just a little. "Yeah?"

She nods, her lips twitching at the corners. "Not that I understand much about hockey, but watching you out there was fun."

A laugh escapes before I can stop it. "You came all the way out here just to tell me that?"

Maisie shrugs. "Thought you might need the ego boost."

"From you? Always."

She bites her lip, trying not to smile. "Though honestly, you probably don't need it. You always seem to know how to get what you want."

I step a little closer, my voice dropping to a murmur. "That's because I'm a playmaker, baby. I know how to make moves when it counts."

She pauses, her lips parting at the nickname that slipped from my tongue. Her eyes lock on mine, intrigue swimming in them. "What kind of moves?"

I close the gap between us, feeling my heart hammer in my chest. "The kind that get me exactly what I want."

Her cheeks flush, but she holds my gaze.

I want to tell her straight up that she's exactly what I want. But I hold back. Not wanting to scare her off.

"You coming out after?" I ask, running a hand through my damp hair.

She quirks a brow. "After?"

"We're going to a bar to celebrate," I tell her, taking a slow step forward and lowering my voice just a little. "I kinda want to see you there."

Maisie's lips part, but Isabella's already grabbing her wrist. "We were planning on it, don't worry," she says, dragging her backward toward the exit.

Maisie casts one last look over her shoulder, that soft smile still lingering on her face. "Guess I'll see you there, Rhodes."

My name on her lips does something to me.

I stand there too long, just watching her disappear into the crowd.

Logan scoffs beside me and slaps a hand on my helmet. "Dude," he says, with a teasing smirk. "You are so fucking gone for her."

I don't even try to deny it.

Yeah… I really am.

<hr>

The bar's packed. Loud and buzzing with leftover energy from the game. Everyone's celebrating—shouting, laughing, drinking.

We've claimed a booth in the back. I've got a beer in one hand, my other arm slung casually over the back of the booth unable to stop looking at the door.

She should be here by now… right?

Ryan slides in next to me, his eyebrow raised and an amused look on his face. "You gonna keep staring at the door all night or actually enjoy the fact that you crushed it tonight?"

I roll my eyes and mutter, "Shut up." But I don't stop looking.

And then, right on cue, the door swings open.

The girls step inside. Isabella, Aurora—and Maisie, right between them.

Her hair's down now, falling in soft waves around her shoulders, and she's ditched the denim jacket and dress from earlier. She's wearing a fitted top and jeans that hug every curve like they were made for her.

Full curves, soft stomach, and thick thighs I can't stop thinking about. Those bright blue eyes shine under the lights and my eyes drift to her lips.

She hasn't seen me yet.

Good.

Gives me a second to just… look.

"Jesus Christ," Cole mutters. "You're gonna burn a hole through her fucking jeans."

I shoot him a glare. "Don't fucking look at her."

He raises a brow at me. "Relax," he says dryly. "I have no interest in your girl."

I open my mouth to say she's not my girl.

But the words don't come.

Because she is.

She's mine. My Maisie.

Logan chuckles. "You should just tell the girl you like her," he says, reaching for a bowl of peanuts. "Or better yet, write her a love poem. 'Dear Maisie, I'm a reformed slut, done with the wits. Pretty please let me touch your—'"

"Logan," Nathan cuts in, raising his brow.

"What?" Logan grins, tossing a peanut in his mouth. "I'm rooting for the himbo. Let him have his fairy-tale ending."

I shake my head and sip my drink, trying to focus on anything else, but then Isabella slides into the booth, parking herself right on Ryan's lap.

"Congrats on the win," I hear her say.

Ryan hums something back, but I don't look at them. Can't.

Because Maisie's still standing across the room, laughing at something Aurora says, and those perfect blue eyes are shining like summer lives inside her.

How is she real?

How in the hell did I not notice her before this year?

Ryan scoffs under his breath. "I don't think he's listening, baby. He's kinda distracted right now."

Isabella twists around on his lap to glance at me, then laughs. "You know I'm rooting for you bud, but… I think you've got some competition."

That gets my attention.

My eyes snap to hers. "What?"

She shrugs. "She's been talking to someone."

My stomach drops.

I blink at her, trying to make sense of what the hell she's telling me. "What do you mean she's been talking to someone?"

"She's got a crush on some other guy," she tells me, making my stomach sink to my ass. "She told Aurora and me when we were helping her get ready for your date."

Ryan chokes on his drink. "Wait. *You* went on a date?"

Nathan leans in from across the table, brows raised. "An actual date?"

But I'm not listening to either of them. My brain's stuck on rewind, replaying Isabella's words over and over, each repetition punching deeper than the last.

Maisie's been talking to someone.

I feel it like a bruise blooming behind my ribs. That hollow, slow-spreading ache.

The memory rushes back—her face going pink that day in the lecture hall when I asked if she had a crush. Her dodging the question. Me teasing her about it. I didn't really care about it at the time.

But now?

Now I care.

A lot.

And now I feel like a goddamn idiot for sitting here thinking about her smile, and practically drooling over her, when she's probably been thinking about some other guy the whole time.

I sit back slowly, my fingers tightening around my glass. "Do you know who it is?"

Isabella shrugs again, completely oblivious to the way my chest is fucking caving in. "Some guy she talks to online. She said she doesn't even know his real name."

My stomach turns.

"She said he goes by a nickname."

My throat goes dry.

I can feel the table around me. The noise. The guys still talking. But everything's muffled now. Like I'm hearing it from the bottom of a swimming pool.

"What's the nickname?"

Isabella scrunches her nose, thinking. "I don't know… something weird. I think she said it was… Six?"

The word slices clean through me.

My chest locks up, my breath catching somewhere high in my throat.

Did she just say—

"Wait." My voice sounds distant to my own ears. "What did you say?"

Isabella blinks, clearly confused by my reaction. "Six? That's what she called him."

And suddenly I'm not sitting in a booth surrounded by my teammates anymore.

I'm in my room, sitting in the dark with my phone lighting up my face. I'm reading her messages. Smiling every time she types back. I'm sitting on the bleachers, my heart pounding every time I see her name pop up, wondering who the hell this girl could be.

And it was Maisie.

Maisie is Cherry.

My Cherry.

I let out a laugh before I can stop it and set my drink down with a shaky clink. "Holy fuck."

Ryan turns. "What?"

I barely register the sound of his voice.

Because *of course* it's her.

It was always her.

It couldn't be anyone else.

Every message. Every late-night conversation. Every ridiculous nickname and unfiltered confession. Her sister. The Oreos. The cherry Chapstick.

My brain's racing to catch up with my body, which already knows. I should've seen it. I should've fucking known.

I glance across the bar like I need proof. Like my brain needs to physically see her to believe it. And when I find her— still sitting at the booth with Aurora, fingers wrapped around a glass, laughing at something I can't hear—my whole damn chest cracks wide open.

That's her.

That's the girl who's been wrecking me for months. The one who made me laugh like a teenager and think about things I'd never said out loud. The one who always knew exactly what to say to make me feel less alone without even trying.

I really am an idiot.

She was right in front of me this whole time, and I had absolutely no idea.

I run a hand through my hair and exhale hard through my nose. I'm still reeling, still trying to make the dots connect. But I don't give myself time to spiral. I push up from the booth before I can second-guess it.

"Where are you going?" Ryan asks, confused.

I don't answer him. Just mutter, "I'll be back," and weave through the crowd on autopilot.

She doesn't see me at first, but when I step into her space, she turns and her lips part slightly when her eyes find mine.

"Hey," she says softly, her voice barely audible over the music.

"Hey." I stop just in front of her, close enough to reach for her if I wanted to. And I do. Christ, I do. "Glad you came."

She smiles, a small one that tugs at something behind my ribs. "Congrats on the win."

"Thanks." I shoot her a grin. "You're my good luck charm."

She lets out a quiet laugh, shaking her head. "I've been to one game, Austin. That doesn't exactly qualify me for charm status."

"Trust me," I say, my voice dipping lower as my eyes stay locked on hers. "It does."

She goes still, just for a second. Her lashes lower, then lift again, slower this time, like she's trying to steady herself.

I step in closer. The space between us narrows, and I can feel the heat coming off her skin. I can smell her—the familiar sweet vanilla scent and that same cherry lip balm I swear I'd recognize anywhere.

"Dance with me," I murmur.

Her brows lift. "What?"

I don't explain. Don't give her room to overthink it, to come up with reasons not to. I just reach for her hand, slipping my fingers between hers, and give the gentlest tug toward the edge of the crowd where people are slow-swaying.

Her hand tenses in mine. A little twitch, like she's not sure. But she doesn't pull away.

I guide her into the open space, and when I press my other hand to the small of her back, I feel her stiffen slightly, but then she exhales, and her body eases into mine.

Her cheeks are flushed, eyes flicking down to where our bodies almost touch.

I reach up slowly, brushing my knuckles along her cheek, soft as I can. Her skin is warm under my touch. I tilt her chin gently until her eyes lift to mine, wide and unsure and so fucking pretty it hurts.

"You're so fucking beautiful, Mais."

Her expression flickers. She draws in a sharp breath and shakes her head. "Don't say that."

I tilt my head, my eyes locked on hers. "Why not?"

"Because you don't mean it," she says, and fuck, it guts me.

"I mean every word." I assure her as I lean in, close enough to feel her breath. "I haven't stopped thinking about these big blue eyes since the day I knocked you in the head."

She swallows hard, her throat bobbing slightly, and I watch her lashes sweep down, hiding herself from me. I hate that she doesn't believe it. That no one's ever made her believe it.

"You don't like me," she says quietly, like she's still trying to convince herself. "You're just—"

"Don't." I step closer, resting my forehead against hers. My hand slides to the back of her neck, holding her gently. "Please don't tell me how I feel."

Her lashes flutter and her breath hitches as she looks up at me again—shy and pink-cheeked and so goddamn breakable I want to wrap her up in my arms and never let go.

Behind us, "The Only Exception" by Paramore drifts through the speakers, and the lyrics might as well be carved into my chest.

Because she's my exception.

The one girl I let past the walls.

The only one I want.

"Stay over tonight," I murmur, my thumb tracing slow circles along her cheekbone.

Her breath hitches. "What?"

"Come back with me. Stay over. My place."

She doesn't answer right away, just lifts her hand and curls her fingers around the back of my neck—light, like she's still not sure she's allowed to touch me like this. Like she doesn't realize I'd let her touch me however she wants.

"Why?" she whispers.

"Because I want you there."

Her teeth sink into her bottom lip, and I can see her mind racing—doubt flashing behind her eyes, all those quiet fears creeping in again.

I slide my hand down, catching hers, fingers warm and steady as I thread them through mine.

"You don't have to," I say. "I just thought we could stay up and watch a movie, maybe. I even bought some Oreos for you and then you could stay over and—" I blow out a breath. "You don't owe me anything. I just—"

"Okay," she cuts me off.

I blink. "Yeah?"

She nods again, her fingers brushing the back of my neck as we dance to the slow song in the packed bar.

I let out a shaky breath, and the smile that spreads across my face feels like the first deep breath I've taken in days. Maybe longer. I pull her into me, wrapping my arms around her waist, her cheek brushing my chest.

She fits there. Like she's meant to be right next to me.

And with her in my arms, her breath soft against my shirt, that song still playing in the background like it's narrating my whole goddamn life, I realize something I probably should've known a long time ago.

I'm not chasing something anymore.

I already found it.

TWENTY-SIX

Maisie

This is definitely not my dorm bed.

For starters, it's bigger and softer than mine. And then there's the fact that someone's arm is wrapped around my waist, and Austin's bare chest presses against my back, the warmth of him seeping through the thin fabric of my shirt.

And then it hits me all at once.

Austin. Last night. The game. The bar. The way he looked at me, like I was the only person in the room when he asked me to stay over. The way he smiled when I said yes, like he'd been waiting for it.

Now I'm here. In his bed. Under his covers. Tucked against him like I belong here.

His arm is still wrapped around my waist, like he fell asleep holding me close and never let go, one of my legs is tangled between his, and his breath hits my neck softly, making me break out into a shiver.

I stay perfectly still. Not because I'm scared of waking him—though I am—but because I don't want to break this feeling.

My heart's pounding against my chest, loud enough I'm sure he can feel it.

Is he awake?

Part of me wants to turn around. See if his eyes are open. Ask what this means. Make sure I didn't just dream it all.

But the other part—the louder part—is afraid to find out. Afraid if I move, it'll all disappear. Afraid if I look too close, I'll ruin it.

My heart races out of my chest as panic starts to rise, because—

What if this doesn't mean anything to him?

What if I'm just another girl who crashed here after a night out. What if he doesn't even remember asking me to stay? What if the way he looked at me last night was just a side effect of adrenaline and alcohol and the high from winning his first game back?

I shift slightly, trying to steady my breath without making it obvious I'm unraveling inside. But the second I move, his arm tightens, pulling me in closer. And I have my answer. He's definitely awake.

His fingers flex against my waist, like he's memorizing every curve.

"Hey." His voice is low and scratchy, sending a shiver straight down my spine.

I blink, turning over to face him. His eyes are heavy with sleep, one barely open, framed by dark lashes. There's a faint red crease on his cheek from the pillow, and his hair is messy, but looks so soft, making me want to reach out and run my fingers through it. His lips curl into that lazy half-smile that steals my breath away.

"Hey," I whisper back, quieter than I meant to.

He shifts onto his side, never breaking eye contact. His fingers trace a path from my waist up to my ribs. "How's your head?" he murmurs.

I swallow, the knot in my throat tightening. "Fine. Yours?"

His smile deepens. "I've had worse," he says. "This is a pretty solid way to wake up."

Heat floods my cheeks. I can't look away. I don't even want to try.

His eyes flick down for the briefest second, but I feel it like a full-body ache.

Then he shifts closer, just enough that his warmth wraps around me again, and I swear the whole world quiets down to the steady rhythm of his breath against my skin.

His fingers brush my jaw, trailing up until they cup my cheek. His thumb drags lightly across my skin, and it's so gentle I want to cry.

He's looking at me like he wants to say something but doesn't know how.

Like he's nervous.

Austin… *Nervous*.

My heart stutters as his eyes flick to my mouth, then back to my eyes. "Is this okay?" he whispers, making my breath catch in my throat.

He's so close. His hand is warm against my cheek, his forehead almost resting against mine, and my body is buzzing with something that feels like hope and fear all tangled together.

I want to say yes.

God, I do.

So badly it aches, so badly it terrifies me.

But the words get caught somewhere deep in my throat. Because suddenly I'm thinking of everything I'm not sure I can handle.

"What about the other girl?" I ask him, hating how quiet my voice is.

His brows knit, a flicker of confusion passing across his face. "What?"

My gaze drops to the hollow of his throat, the line of his collarbone, the soft stretch of skin there. Somewhere safe. Somewhere that doesn't feel like looking him in the eye while I hand him my fear on a silver platter.

"The one you like," I say. "Or were talking to. Or thinking about. I just—if I'm… if this is…" I shake my head, the words jamming up. "I don't want to be a second choice to you. I can't be the girl you settle for because someone else didn't want you."

My voice cracks.

"I don't even understand how that's possible, honestly. That someone wouldn't want you. But if there's someone else—"

I trail off, my breath catching, because saying it hurts more than I thought it would. But Austin doesn't pull away.

He stays right there, his fingers still warm against my jaw, and those light hazel eyes locked on mine.

"There's no other girl, Maisie." There isn't a hint of hesitation in his voice. "There's only you."

I blink up at him because I don't know what to do with those words.

They don't feel real, not when I've spent so long telling myself I don't get to be the girl who gets chosen.

But Austin says it like it's a fact. Like it's always been true.

My throat tightens, my chest pulling in on itself, and I swear I'm going to cry—right here, in his bed, wrapped in his warmth, wearing his shirt, while he says the things I never thought anyone would say to me.

I swallow hard and give the smallest nod I can manage.

He doesn't rush. Instead, he just watches me—his eyes searching mine for permission.

Then, slowly, he leans in. His lips meet mine with a softness that makes my breath catch, warm and patient, like he's been waiting for this moment forever. Like he's thought about it, wanted it, wanted *me*.

His hand slides up to the back of my neck, his fingers tangling gently in my hair. He tilts my chin up just enough, adjusting the angle to deepen the kiss.

I clutch his shirt in my fists, holding on because I don't know where else to put everything I'm feeling.

Then his mouth parts, coaxing mine open. I hesitate for half a second, then follow, and when his tongue grazes mine, I gasp softly against his mouth.

Oh god.

It's barely a touch—just the softest brush of his tongue against mine—but heat blooms low in my belly.

I didn't know kissing could feel like this.

Like I'm unraveling from the inside out. Like he's mapping my mouth with every slow, devastating pass of his lips.

I kiss him back, unsure of what I'm doing. But he makes it easy—guiding me with the tilt of his lips, the warm press of his hand at the back of my neck, the quiet hum of his breath when I get it right.

He makes me feel wanted. My whole body feels light, like I'm floating. Like I could lean forward and disappear into him completely and not even care where I end up.

I've only been kissed three times in my entire life, and they've all been by him.

And somehow, every time feels like the first, and the best, and maybe even the last, if I'm not careful. But I don't want careful. Not with him.

My fingers move up of their own accord, tracing the lines of his chest beneath his shirt, the ridges of muscle, the solid warmth of him, the steady beat of his heart against my palm.

He lets out a low, breathy sound that shoots straight through me, setting fire to every nerve. Then he shifts, and slides one leg between mine.

Heat radiates off him, and suddenly I'm very aware of how little I'm wearing—just his oversized t-shirt and a pair of cotton underwear that feel entirely too thin against the heat of his thigh.

And he hasn't even done anything yet.

Just *this*—his mouth on mine, his breath in my lungs, his skin pressed against mine—it's undoing me completely.

His hand slides down, ghosting over my hip before curling around my waist, his fingers slipping just beneath the hem of the shirt as he pulls back slightly.

"Still okay?"

I swallow hard, and the words come tumbling out before I can stop them. "I haven't… I haven't done anything before."

He pauses, his lips curling up into a small smile. "I figured." There's no judgment in his eyes. "We don't have to do anything, Maisie," he says. "I'm gonna go slow with you. Whatever you want. You take the lead here."

My throat tightens and I nod. "I… I want to."

He leans in, kissing me again. His hand moves, stroking up the side of my ribs, sliding over the fabric of my shirt, and then cupping my breast through the soft cotton.

He doesn't rush. Doesn't push. Just palms me slowly, his thumb brushing back and forth in a way that makes my head spin and my breath catch.

A soft sound slips out from me, surprised and completely involuntary.

He groans low in his throat and presses his mouth to my neck, his teeth grazing my skin lightly. "You're gonna kill me," he murmurs against my skin.

I can't help the chuckle that bubbles up. I arch into him, craving more of him. "Sorry," I whisper.

He grins against my neck, then kisses the spot just under my jaw. "Don't be. Never be."

And then he's kissing me again, but this time it's different. There's a hunger that wasn't there before, like whatever restraint he had is starting to slip. Like now that I've said yes, he's letting himself want me fully.

His hand slides down, fingers ghosting just under the hem of the t-shirt I'm wearing—his t-shirt—and everything inside me sparks to life.

I shiver, nerves dancing across my skin as his touch finds bare flesh. His fingers curve around my waist, his thumb brushing over the soft swell of my stomach.

For a split second I freeze, that familiar self-conscious flickering within me, but he just keeps kissing me.

Then he dips his head, his lips trailing over my jaw, down my neck, across my collarbone, each kiss slow and soft, setting my skin on fire. His hand slides under my shirt, grazing my skin, climbing higher and higher, exploring, learning how I breathe, what makes me shiver.

When his thumb brushes over my nipple, I can't hold back the small, desperate whimper that slips out.

His breath hitches. "Fuck," he mutters. "You're so—Maisie, you're…"

He doesn't finish the sentence. Just kisses my skin, his mouth soft and hot as he sucks gently at the curve of my throat.

I reach up, threading my fingers into his hair. He groans softly when I tug just a little, and presses his hips forward.

Heat pools low between my legs and my breath stutters.

He pulls back just a little, searching my face. "You okay?" he asks, his voice hoarse and rough and so sexy I can't take it.

I nod, probably a little too fast. "I just…" I try to breathe, trying to get the words out. "I don't know what I'm doing."

He gives me the softest smile. "You don't have to know. Just tell me what you want, yeah?"

"Okay."

His lips brush mine again as his hand moves down, skimming my inner thigh, enough to make my breath hitch.

"Maisie," he says, pausing to look at me, "I need you to tell me if you want me to stop."

"I don't," I assure him, locking eyes with his. "I want this. I want you. I feel comfortable with you."

He watches me for a few seconds, before he lets out a low groan, and his hand finally slips between my legs, cupping me over my panties.

Oh god.

I let out a sound I've never made before, a needy, rough moan, and he swears under his breath as he pulls the cotton aside, and runs his fingers along my pussy.

"You're so fucking wet," he grunts, kissing my shoulder as his fingers start to move.

I can't even think. His touch is soft at first, but when I press into it, hungry for more, he grows bolder, dragging his fingers over me again and again until I'm shaking all over.

He keeps his eyes on me, watching my face, every twitch, every shudder, memorizing exactly how I fall apart under his touch.

"Tell me what you want," he murmurs.

"I don't know," I breathe, my voice shaky, "but… keep doing that."

That slow, knowing smile curls over his lips as he keeps doing exactly that. His fingers trace lazy circles, coaxing every inch of me to respond.

"So fucking pretty."

My hips start to move on their own, grinding against his hand, trembling as my body screams for more.

"You like the way I touch you?"

I moan in response. Every touch, every soft, demanding word from him sets something wild free inside me. I'm dizzy and desperate all at once, completely lost in the way he's making me feel.

The pressure builds fast, and I can't stop it. I can't slow it down. It's all too much—his voice, his hands, the way he's touching me like he already knows what I need before I do.

"That's it," he whispers, his fingers moving in slow circles that make my thighs tremble. "You're doing so fucking good for me, baby. You gonna come for me?"

I nod frantically, my breath catching in my throat, but it's not enough. I need more—I need him—I need—

It hits me like a wave, breaking me open from the inside out. I cry out as pleasure tears through me in hot, pulsing waves.

My thighs clamp around his hand and my nails dig into his back.

"Austin," I gasp.

He doesn't stop. Doesn't let up. Just keeps his fingers on my clit while pressing kisses on my skin.

"Fuck, that's it," he murmurs. "So fucking beautiful when you come. Ride it out, baby."

I can't speak. Can't think. I'm trembling in his arms, barely holding it together as he kisses my cheek, my jaw, my temple, every inch of my skin.

"Goddamn," he murmurs. "You have no idea how fucking hot watching you come is."

He kisses me as the rush rolls through me again and again, until I'm breathless. Boneless. My skin tingling all over.

When I finally blink up at him, he's already watching me with a messy, hungry grin that makes my heart stutter in my chest.

"You good?" he asks again.

I hum into the curve of his chest, soaking in the steady thump of his heartbeat. "Mmhmm. That was…" I can't even finish my sentence, because I don't have a word for what that was. Nothing in the twenty-one years I have been on this planet have even remotely felt like *that*.

He leans in, his nose brushing mine. "Yeah. It really was."

He kisses me again for what feels like forever. I hum into his mouth, placing my hands on his chest. I could easily lay here and kiss him for the rest of my life.

Austin pulls back slightly, tilting my chin just enough so I'm forced to meet his eyes. "Are you sure you're good?" His lips twitch into a faint, teasing grin. "You look kinda dazed."

I blink at him, the words slipping out before I can stop them. "I *am* dazed. Do people usually survive that?"

His laugh spills out, and it's impossible not to smile back. He's just so damn pretty when he laughs. His whole face softens, his eyes crinkle, and those dimples of his that I love sink even deeper into his cheeks.

"I have no idea. It's never felt like that to me before," he admits with a warm smile.

I press my forehead to his shoulder, trying to hide the heat crawling up my cheeks.

"You were drinking last night," I mumble. "I wasn't sure if you'd remember what you said to me when I woke up this morning."

He goes still for a beat. Then he pulls back just enough to see me, slipping his fingers under my chin and lifting it gently until our eyes meet. "I wasn't drunk," he tells me. "I know damn well what I told you. And I meant every word."

We hold each other's eyes in silence, neither of us moving as the morning sun spills through his window, wondering what happens next.

Finally, he breaks the quiet with a slow, cocky smirk. "You're still wearing my shirt."

I breathe out a laugh, heat creeping up my neck. "Would you prefer it if I was naked?"

His smirk deepens instantly. "Well…"

I narrow my eyes, shooting him a look, but he just chuckles.

"It looks good on you," he says as his eyes fall to the length of my body, still lying here in his bed. His lips twitch, the smugness returning. "It'd look even better on my bedroom floor."

I roll my eyes, but my mouth twitches before I can stop it. "God. You are such a walking cliché."

"And yet, here you are. In my bed."

"Against my better judgment."

"Lies," he murmurs, nipping lightly at my jaw. "You're obsessed with me, Freckles."

I try to shove him, but he's quicker—rolling on top of me in one smooth move, braced on his forearms, that lazy grin spread across his lips. "Say it," he teases. "Say you're obsessed with me."

I narrow my eyes. "I will not."

"Say it and I'll make you breakfast."

I raise a brow. "Do you even know how to cook?"

"Nope." He doesn't even try to deny it. "But I'll order you whatever you want if you say it."

I laugh under my breath. "Fine," I concede. "I'm mildly fond of you."

He hums, leaning in until his mouth brushes mine in a soft kiss. "Close enough."

I don't think I'll ever get used to kissing Austin Rhodes. I close my eyes and feel every brush of his tongue and his soft lips against mine.

I'm scared I'll wake up and this will all be a dream. I'm scared it'll all blow up in my face.

But right now, here in his bed, wrapped in his shirt, and his lips on mine…

I think I'd be okay with taking the risk.

TWENTY-SEVEN

Maisie

The rink feels different in the afternoons.

There's no shouting, no hockey blades tearing up the ice. Just the soft hum of music from someone's phone, the occasional burst of laughter from the locker room.

Most of the girls barely look up when I step inside the locker room. A few glance my way, then drop their eyes just as fast. No one says anything. No one really ever does.

I'm used to being invisible.

But today, I don't even mind.

I'm still thinking about the other day. About Austin. About the way his hands settled on my hips, his voice low in my ear, and his lips pressed against mine.

The memory has been looping in my head for days now, slipping in at the most inconvenient times and leaving me flustered.

Since then, he's been practically begging me to come over every single night. I tried to resist—honestly, I did—but last night I gave in. Which is why I'm a little later than usual for practice… because staying in Austin Rhodes' bed, warm and tangled up in his sheets, sounded a whole lot better than coming to the freezing cold rink.

I sit down on the bench in the far corner, but my attention is snagged when my phone buzzes.

Once. Then again. And again.

I glance down, expecting maybe a message from Bailey, but when I see Austin's name lighting up the screen, a slow smile spreads across my face. He still messages me on social media, for some reason. I guess it's because we never actually got around to exchanging numbers.

Austin: you left 10 minutes ago and I want you back already.

Austin: come back.

Austin: right now.

Austin: I'll give you my hoodie. my wallet.

Austin: there's like 10 bucks in there but they're yours.

Austin: we can watch whatever movie you want.

Austin: we can eat cookies.

Austin: we can bake cookies.

Austin: you looked so fucking beautiful today.

Austin: you always do.

Austin: come back.

Austin: please.

A laugh bubbles out of me before I can stop it. I press a hand over my face and shake my head, grinning like crazy. He's ridiculous. And sweet. And... *god*, I don't even know how to deal with this version of him.

A couple girls glance my way, mildly curious, but I duck my head and focus on my phone.

Me: Do you even have the ingredients to bake cookies?

Austin: omw to buy them right now.

My bottom lip catches between my teeth, and I don't even try to stop the smile this time. It stretches wide and helpless across my face.

Me: Fine. After practice I'll be right over.

I send it before I can talk myself out of it. Before the doubts can creep in.

But my finger hovers over the screen for a second longer than it should. Because before I lock my phone, I swipe out of the app and open my texts.

Six.

His name taunts me and before I can talk myself out of it, I tap his name, seeing our previous texts. Even though I've read them all a hundred times, I scroll anyway. My eyes trace every word, every reply. And then, I start typing.

Me: I don't know how to say this, but I think I need to stop texting you. You've meant more to me than you'll probably ever know. You made me feel seen when I didn't think anyone could. But I've fallen for someone. And it doesn't feel fair to keep holding on to this. Thank you for everything. Truly. You helped me more than you know. But this has to be goodbye.

I don't let myself reread it. I just hit send, and then turn off my phone and stare straight ahead, letting out a deep breath.

I tug my hoodie off and fold it beside me on the bench, then start my usual off-ice warm-ups. Normally, I'd do this back at my dorm or the gym before coming to the rink, but coming straight from Austin's place this morning, I didn't have much time.

I warm up for a while, jogging down the hallway, high knees, butt kicks—which feel ridiculous but are very effective. I grab the wall and swing my legs, trying to loosen my hips without looking too awkward. Arm circles, hip rolls, and a few rotations.

I move onto a couple of off-ice jumps, double loop and axel, careful not to twist anything the wrong way. Then heel raises, toe walks, ankle circles, and rolling my foot over a golf ball to ease the tight spots I always seem to get.

By the time I finish stretching, my muscles are humming, ready to get on the ice.

I tug my hoodie over my head, fold it beside me on the bench, and finish lacing my skates. I roll my ankles a few times, stretch out my legs, then push to my feet and make my way toward the rink.

A few of the girls are already scattered across the rink—two running programs at the far end, one looping through footwork drills near the center.

I step onto the ice and skate toward my usual spot in the corner. I start easy with some edges and figure eights, giving my body a chance to settle into the movement. My legs ache and stretch, slowly loosening, settling into the rhythm.

I move onto crossovers next. Forward, then backward, leaning hard into each turn, letting my weight shift, my muscles waking up and humming with heat.

Coach watches from the boards, clipboard in hand. "Keep your hips over your foot on those crossovers. Don't let yourself fall forward."

I nod and bite back a sigh because, honestly, that's easier said than done when my legs are already starting to scream.

"Spin sequence," she calls out next. "Camel, sit, then combination."

Spins are always a little tricky for me. I kick up into the camel spin, feeling my free leg extend behind me, making sure my free leg extends straight behind me, toe pointed out—not down—and I dip my left arm before sweeping it back up, slicing through the air.

But I end up too far forward on my toe pick, and lose balance, wobbling just enough to fall out.

"Reset and try again," Coach says. "Your chest rises a lot when you come up. Keep your right hip back and when you stand on your spinning leg, make sure it's open."

I nod, taking a deep breath, and try again, focusing on keeping my chest low and hips back. The entry feels smoother this time. I spin, round and round, counting each rotation in my head. Ten clean, solid turns before I finally wobble.

"Better," Coach nods, a rare smile breaking through. "You're finding your edge again. Sit spin next. Focus on getting low, keep that free leg parallel to the ice. Don't let your hips dip."

I bend into it, trying to sink low enough without shaking. My muscles burn, but I keep my gaze fixed on a spot in the rink, anchoring myself. The spin builds, solid enough to keep going for fifteen rotations before I slow down.

Coach nods. "Good. You're getting stronger."

I kick up into the camel, smooth the transition into the sit, and then pull my free leg in for the final upright spin. It's tricky, switching positions without losing momentum, but I push through, and nail a solid twenty rotations before stopping.

My chest heaves and a grin spreads across my face. "That felt… pretty good."

She arches a brow, nodding. "That's what I want to hear. Keep it up."

She moves farther down the rink, eyes locked on Brianna as she runs through her drills, and I shift my focus on practicing my jump combinations next. Triple toe loop into a double salchow—the bane of my existence. Every time I try them, they leave me with a bruised hip and a bruised ego, but skipping practice isn't an option if I want to avoid embarrassing myself at Nationals.

I crouch low, coil, and launch into the triple toe. The air rushes past my face as I spin, and I stick the landing. Relief washes over me for half a second before I push into the double salchow. My landing wobbles hard and my chest tightens, frustration prickling up my spine. But no time to sulk. I shake it off, reset, and line up again.

When I'm finally done with practice, I slip into the locker room, and sink onto the bench, a smile curling up despite the ache as I peel off my skates, rubbing the tightness from my calves. I roll my ankles in slow circles, reach for my toes, feeling the familiar, deep stretch tug through my hamstrings and hips.

A few of the girls gather in a circle, whispering about the latest music choices for Nationals, and I can't help but listen.

"Seriously? *Swan Lake* again?" one of them groans. "It's such a cliché."

I smirk to myself as I unlace my boots. My own program music definitely isn't classical or expected. Coach raised a brow when I picked it—told me it didn't have the right tone—but I fought to keep it. Something about it just felt like me.

I peel off my tights and tug on my sweats, my legs throbbing in that deep, heavy way they only do after a good practice.

But despite the burn, and the sweat cooling at the back of my neck, I tuck my skates into my bag with a small smile.

Because I know exactly where I'm going after I leave this rink.

— ♥ —

His door's already cracked open when I get there.

I knock once anyway, then push the door open and peek inside.

Austin's standing in the middle of his kitchen, wearing grey sweatpants that hang low on his hips and a white t-shirt that clings like it grew there, one hand holding a whisk, the other a mixing bowl. His face is twisted in pure concentration as he stares down at what I can only assume is a baking attempt gone very wrong.

When he looks up and sees me, his whole face lights up into a goofy grin, like I just made his day, and my heart does that stupid wobble thing. "Hey, baby."

I swallow hard at the nickname, chuckling as I take in the spilled flour on the counter. "You're actually baking?"

He glances at the bowl, then back at me, his eyes narrowing. "Define baking."

I drop my bag by the door and walk over, eyeing the flour-dusted countertop and a very questionable bag of chocolate chips. "Did you follow a recipe?"

He wipes a streak of flour from his forehead and lets out a dramatic sigh. "I followed my heart."

I snort. "So, no."

"I measured," he says, lifting the whisk like it's a mic. "Emotionally."

I lean against the counter beside him, shaking my head. "That's not how it works."

"Cookie dough's cookie dough." He shrugs and holds the bowl toward me. "Try it."

I dip a finger into the bowl, taste the dough, and squint up at him. "Did you put sugar in this?"

"Yeah," he says, brows furrowing. "Wait. I think. I mean… that canister was open so I just kinda—"

I lift a brow, my lips twitching in amusement. "Are you sure it was sugar or baking powder?"

His brows tug together and he blows out a breath. "Okay but in my defense," he says, taking a cautious step back, "they're both white powders, and I have absolutely no clue what the hell I'm doing. But you're smiling and that's all I really wanted, so technically, I win."

"You're ridiculous," I say, rolling my eyes.

He grins, that lopsided smile, and boops my nose. "And you're adorable."

I roll my eyes again, but I'm smiling when he sets the bowl down and pulls me close. His arms slide around my waist like it's second nature.

He smiles, leaning down to kiss my temple. "Hi," he murmurs, breath brushing against my skin.

"Hi," I whisper back, my voice embarrassingly soft.

He laughs, low, scratchy. "You came back."

"You bribed me with cookies."

Austin grins. "I would've bribed you with the moon if you asked."

I narrow my eyes at him, trying not to smile. "Who knew Austin Rhodes was such a sap?"

He shrugs, his eyes locked on mine. "Only for you."

God. The way he says it, makes something flutter low in my stomach.

I don't trust my voice, so I reach for one of the cookies from the tray instead. It's kind of lumpy and weirdly shaped, but still warm, and I turn it over in my hand.

He leans back, wiping his hands on a dish towel. "I know you like baking," he says. "But dorm kitchens suck, so if you ever wanna use a real oven… mine's always open." His eyes flash. "As is my bedroom door."

I snort, shaking my head. "So generous."

Austin just winks, completely shameless. But then something flickers in my brain.

"Wait." I tilt my head at him. "How do you know I like baking?"

His whole body stills for a half-second. He clears his throat and runs a hand through his hair, suddenly very focused on straightening the already-straight dish towel hanging on the oven handle. "I think… you told me. Probably during tutoring or something."

My eyebrows scrunch together. "I don't think I remember that."

He shrugs again. "Maybe it came up. I don't know. Doesn't matter." He flashes another grin, but it doesn't quite reach his eyes this time. "Either way, you've got a standing invitation to use my oven. And Nathan's stand mixer. He won't mind. He's a saint."

I laugh, and step into his space without thinking, leaning my head against his chest. His hands settle low on my back, fingers flexing slightly, and I feel him breathe me in.

Then his thumbs start moving—slow, lazy little circles against the fabric of my shirt—and I swear I could melt on the spot.

When I look up again, he's already watching me. His fingers come up to tuck a loose piece of hair behind my ear, and my breath catches. It's that look. The one that makes me feel like I don't have to be anyone but myself. Like I'm enough, just like this.

His gaze drops to my mouth, then back up. He leans in, slowly, and our lips meet in a kiss that's so soft and so perfect, I feel my knees threaten to give out.

He pulls me closer, his hands tightening on my waist. One hand slides down, trailing lower until it cups my ass, giving it a firm squeeze.

I break the kiss on a gasp. "You just touched my ass."

He grins. "Mhmm. Wanna touch more."

I glance up at him, my eyes widening. "Like what?"

"Every single part of you," he whispers, his lips tugging into a smirk.

The heat in my face spreads down my neck. My brain, unhelpfully, conjures the thought of what it'll feel like to be completely naked with him. To have Austin touch me like that.

My breath catches. He must notice, because his brows pull together slightly. He leans back just enough to search my face, one hand still resting on my cheek, his thumb brushing gently over my skin.

"You okay?" he murmurs.

I nod. "Yeah. Just…" I pause, trying to untangle the knot in my chest. "Still wrapping my head around this."

He tilts his head. "This?"

"You," I say quietly. "This whole thing." My gaze drifts to where his hand rests at my waist. "I keep expecting you to remember the kind of girls you usually date."

He goes quiet.

And instantly, I regret saying it.

God, I hate how fragile my voice sounds. How small it feels to admit that out loud.

But he doesn't pull away. Instead, he brings his hand to my cheek, and tilts my chin up with the lightest pressure until I'm forced to meet his eyes.

"Maisie," he says, quietly. "I've never dated *anyone* before you."

I blink.

"You're the only girl I've taken on a real date," he continues, holding my gaze. "The only one I've actually wanted to spend time with."

My throat tightens, and something deep in my chest squeezes. Hard.

"And," he adds, lips twitching slightly, "you're the only girl I've baked for. Not well, obviously," he admits with a chuckle. "But I tried."

I can't speak. I can't do anything but look at him.

"I like you," he says, running the pad of his thumb over my bottom lip. "And I know I joke around a lot, and flirt and tease, but I mean it. I've never liked anyone how I like you."

I step in closer and rest my forehead against his chest, closing my eyes. "I don't know what I'm doing," I whisper.

His hand lifts to cradle the back of my head, fingers threading gently into my hair. "That's okay," he murmurs. "Neither do I."

I pull back slightly to glance up at him. "You're really sure about me?"

Because if he changes his mind, if he one day comes to realize that this—that I'm—not what he wants… I don't know if I'll be able to handle it.

He meets my gaze without flinching. "I'm sure about nothing but you." His fingers trail along my jaw, cupping my face. "What about you? Are you sure about me?" he asks, quiet.

I nod. "I am," I assure him, feeling my lips pull into a smirk. "Even if you suck at baking."

He lets out a laugh, burying his lips in my hair as he presses a kiss to the top of my head. "You want some Oreos instead?"

I hum, smiling. "Do you have peanut butter?"

He freezes a bit, his smile widening. "What a weird combination."

"Don't knock it until you try it," I tell him.

He chuckles, his hand flexing on my hips. "What my baby wants, my baby gets," he says, his eyes twinkling. "The only dessert I really want is you, anyway."

He wags his brows at me, and I roll my eyes just before he cups my face and leans down to press his lips against mine.

And I smile against his mouth, because this is starting to feel real. And I'm finally starting to let myself believe that I can trust it. That it's mine.

That *he's* mine.

TWENTY-EIGHT
Maisie

If someone had told me six months ago that I'd be spending a Friday night in a dorm room with two girls who were actually friends of mine, I would've laughed in their face and gone back to my room, alone like usual.

I've never had anything like this before. A real girls' night. Friends who text me. Friends who actually want me around.

I've spent so long on the outside, watching everyone else laugh like they belonged. I used to think that was just how it'd always be for me, like maybe I just wasn't built to fit in anywhere.

But here I am.

Isabella's sitting on the floor trying to paint her nails, which—considering we're two glasses in and packed into a dorm room with zero ventilation—is going about as well as you'd expect.

"You're seriously doing French tips?" Aurora lifts an eyebrow. "What are you, someone's stepmom?"

Isabella barely glances up. "French tips are timeless, thank you very much."

"Boring, more like," Aurora mutters. "They look like the acrylics I got in seventh grade."

I bite back a laugh and take another sip of wine. It's kind of sour and definitely not good, but I'm not exactly picky right now.

Isabella peels off one of her under-eye patches, flicks it into the trash, then looks at me with that glint in her eye. "So… how's it going with Austin?" she asks, wagging her brows.

My cheeks go hot. I stare down at my cup. "It's good."

Aurora gives me a look. "Like, walking funny good or…"

"Oh my God," I groan, but I can't stop the laugh that slips out.

Isabella grins. "Look at you. Blushing like crazy. It sure took you guys long enough."

Aurora rolls onto her side, propping her head up with her hand. "I knew that whole 'kissing as an apology' thing was bullshit."

I shake my head, but I'm smiling. I can't help it. I smile like a maniac any time I even *think* of Austin.

"Have you told him about Six yet?" Isabella asks, making my smile disappear.

My chest tightens. "Uh… no," I admit. "Not really."

Aurora's head whips around. "Wait. Seriously? He still doesn't know?"

I shake my head, chewing the inside of my cheek. "I mean… I told him I had a crush on someone when we first started hanging out. But I never said who."

Isabella raises her eyebrows. "Do you think that's a good idea? Keeping it from him?"

"I'm not keeping it from him," I say quickly. "It's just… complicated. We never even met in person. And it's not like anything really happened."

Aurora's expression softens. "But he mattered to you."

I nod, my fingers twisting the edge of the blanket in my lap. "Yeah. He did."

My phone buzzes, and I know it's Austin before I even glance down.

Austin: how's girls night? you miss me yet?

Me: It's good. Aurora brought Reese's. You've officially been replaced.

Austin: baby, please don't make me get jealous over candy.

Baby.

My cheeks warm and my stomach flutters like crazy at the nickname.

Me: You'd probably pick Reese's too if you had the choice.

Austin: nope. Reese's don't stand a chance. I'd pick you every time. you're sweeter, hotter, and way more addictive.

I press my lips together, trying to swallow the smile tugging at the corner of my mouth.

Isabella looks up from her phone, arching a brow at me. "It's Austin, isn't it?"

Aurora's already watching me with a knowing smirk. "You're blushing," she says, wagging her wine glass at me. "God, you're so obvious."

I shrug, not even bothering to deny it. "Yeah. It's Austin."

Isabella grins. "You guys are disgustingly cute."

I laugh under my breath, shaking my head. "I just… I like him," I admit, even though it's clearly obvious. "A lot."

It's scary how easy things feel with him. How fast it's gone from us being friends to… something else. Something real. And real always makes me nervous.

I press a hand to my stomach, trying to settle the fluttery ache that's been there all day. It should feel good. And it does. But then something shifts—like a switch flipping—and my smile falters as a tight, unwelcome knot twists in my gut.

Because I'm happy. Really, genuinely happy. And that's the part that scares me.

My brain's already bracing for the fallout. For the moment it gets taken away.

Because I've never had something like this before. And some part of me still thinks I don't get to keep it.

"Hey," Aurora says quietly. "What just happened? You looked all dreamy a second ago."

I blink, glancing down at my drink. "I don't know. I guess… I just keep waiting for something to go wrong."

Isabella shifts closer on the rug, watching me carefully. "Maisie…"

I bite my lip. "We haven't—" I stop. The words get stuck. Then I exhale and force them out. "We haven't done anything yet."

Isabella doesn't say anything at first, but I feel her watching me.

Aurora frowns. "Wait. You guys haven't…?"

I shake my head. "Not all the way. We've messed around a little, but… I've never actually had sex. With anyone."

Isabella's brows lift slightly. "Oh."

"I know," I mutter, heat prickling under my skin. "It's just…" I inhale, steadying myself. "Sometimes I feel like I'm on this completely different timeline than everyone else. Like I'm trying to catch up but I don't even know where the starting line is."

"You don't have to be embarrassed, Mais," Isabella says.

"I'm not embarrassed," I mutter, half-laughing and not even sure why. "I just don't want to disappoint him. He's so—he's Austin. He's confident and hot and definitely more experienced than I am and I'm just—" I blow out a breath. "What if he gets bored? Or thinks I'm too inexperienced? Or starts wondering why he's with someone who doesn't know what the hell she's doing—"

"Maisie, stop," Isabella cuts in. "First of all," she says, tossing a gummy worm at me, "you're not boring."

"Literally the opposite," Aurora adds.

"And second of all, the right person doesn't care if you've done stuff. They care if you're safe, if you're happy. They wait, because waiting means getting to keep you longer."

"She's right," Aurora says, setting her glass down and leaning forward. "Being inexperienced isn't a flaw. It's just where you're at. And if Austin's the kind of guy who makes you feel safe, he won't give a shit. If all he wanted was an easy hook-up, he could find that. But he doesn't want that. He wants *you*, Maisie."

My throat tightens.

I nod, slow, pressing my lips together.

"I'd only been with one guy before Ryan," Isabella says, lifting her shoulder in a shrug. "And even then, it took me a while to feel ready with him. The right person doesn't pressure you."

I nod, my fingers curling around the stem of my glass. I want to believe that. I really do. But it's hard not to spiral.

"I know it's scary," she adds, her voice softening. "But honestly? That boy looks at you like you hung the damn stars."

Aurora hums, smirking. "Also? You're a total catch, Mais. He should be counting his lucky stars you even think about letting him see you naked."

I laugh, the tension cracking just a little.

"Besides, it'll be different with you," Isabella adds. "There are feelings involved. It's so much better when it's with someone you actually care about."

There's a beat of silence. And then Aurora groans, tipping her head back. "God, I miss sex."

Isabella snorts. "Didn't you just talk to Chase yesterday?"

"Yeah," Aurora huffs. "And he lives three hours away. FaceTime can only do so much. That's why I love my vibrator. It gets the job done and lets me nap in peace."

I let out a laugh. My heart is so full it aches a little. I never thought I'd be able to have friendships like this. I'm so glad I found them.

"I don't know what I thought this year would be like," I admit. "But it wasn't this. I never would have expected you guys."

Isabella reaches over and squeezes my hand. "You've got us now."

I smile into my glass, warmth blooming behind my ribs.

Aurora lifts her glass, smirking. "Here's to not having it all figured out."

Isabella rolls her eyes but smiles. "And to good friends."

"And to vibrators," Aurora says with a grin.

We all laugh again, and for the first time in my life, I feel like I belong somewhere.

TWENTY-NINE

Austin

I'm not even ten minutes into practice, and I already feel like shit.

Not physically. Physically I feel great. I've got a full night's sleep behind me, my legs are firing, and my passes are sharp. But inside? My stomach's twisted and weird, and it's not from the skate drills Coach just made us run. It's because there are two things I've been thinking about nonstop since I woke up this morning.

One: I still haven't told Maisie I know she's Cherry.

And two: I keep replaying the way she looks at me.

I've never had a girl look at me like that before. Sure, they give me the sex eyes, lick their lips imagining what I look like naked. But Maisie… she looks at me like she trusts me. Like maybe I'm more than just the guy who knows how to flirt, kiss, and unhook a bra one-handed.

Which, for the record, I absolutely do know how to do. But that's not the point.

The point is, I think I'm in trouble. Deep trouble.

My legs are burning, sweat dripping down my back, but all I can think about is Maisie. Maisie in my bed, curled into my chest. Maisie blushing when I kissed her shoulder. Maisie, trusting me enough to let me touch her, to feel her soft skin and her racing heart under my hands, and still—still—I couldn't say it.

That I know she's Cherry.

I should've told her last night. Or this morning. Or the second I realized.

But I didn't. I just held her and pressed kisses into her neck and told myself I'd figure it out later.

Only now it's later and I still have no fucking idea what I'm doing.

I whip a pass across the ice to Cole, who fumbles it like a jackass.

"Jesus, Cole," I bark. "You catching passes with your chin?"

He flips me off without looking. "Maybe if you didn't throw it like a psychopath, I'd catch it."

"You calling me strong?" I grin, skating backward.

"Calling you annoying," he fires back.

I click my tongue. "Same thing."

Logan skates past and smacks my stick with his. "Keep flirting, maybe he'll take you to dinner."

I smirk. "Dinners aren't his thing. More like silence and glares."

Laughter echoes down the ice, Coach's whistle slicing through it a second later.

"Enough with the jokes!" Coach yells. "Back to the drill. Austin, stop chirping and lead the line."

I raise a hand and shoot him a wink. "You got it, Coach."

"Don't wink at me, Rhodes."

I shoot him another one because I like to bust his balls, but even with the laughter and fun I'm having being back on the ice, my thoughts keep drifting.

Because here's the thing. If I tell her now, she'll think I was using her. That I took her secrets and confessions and used them to get close to her. To get in her pants or whatever else she might concoct in that brain of hers.

And yeah, I want her. I want her bad. But not because I read her private thoughts. I want her because she's Maisie. Because she's stubborn and brilliant and rolls her eyes at my jokes but secretly likes them. Because she makes me feel like something more than the guy who screws up his grades and gets suspended.

And I want her to believe that.

Coach blows the whistle again, and we're off. Sprint drills, shooting drills, 3-on-2 plays. I'm sweating and breathing hard but it feels good to move, to focus, to be back on the ice with the guys.

Practice wraps an hour later and I peel off my helmet, sweat soaking my hair, my jersey stuck to my chest. The guys are filing off toward the locker room when I see Maisie, lingering by the wall.

I skid to a stop, caught off guard. She doesn't have practice today so what the hell is she doing here.

Screw it. I don't care. I'm just happy to see her. I break out into a grin at the sight of her standing with her arms crossed, and her dark brown hair twisted into a bun.

I stash my skate guards and head her way.

"What are you doing here?" I ask her, running a hand through my soaked hair.

She shrugs. "Just wanted to watch you practice."

A smile tugs at my lips, wide as fuck. "You were watching me, huh?" I tease.

She rolls her eyes, pushing at my chest. "Sue me for trying to support my boyfriend."

Everything in me short-circuits.

My heart actually skips.

Boyfriend.

Never been called that before. Never been anyone's boyfriend.

Maisie freezes. Her eyes go wide, mouth parting like she can't believe the words just came out of her.

"Oh my god," she breathes. "I—I don't know why I said that. I didn't mean—obviously we're not—"

"Yes we are."

Her brows shoot up. "What?"

I step closer, careful not to crowd her. "When I kissed you the morning after the game, I didn't do it on a whim, Maisie. I kissed you because I meant it, because I knew what it would mean for us if I did."

She looks stunned, but I keep going, because fuck it. I'm all in now.

"I'm not just messing around here, Maisie. I know what I want." My voice softens. "And I want you."

She blinks hard. Her hand flutters like she doesn't know what to do with it before she tugs at the end of her sleeve, eyes darting everywhere but my face. "I should go," she says, voice quiet. "I've got studying to do and—"

"Let me get changed. I'll walk you back."

Her gaze lifts again, cautious. "You don't have to do that."

"I know." I cup her face gently, letting my thumb brush her cheek. "I want to."

Her face softens and her lips pull into a cute smile. I can't help it; I lean in and kiss her. Just a quick kiss, but when I pull back, she's looking up at me like I just tilted her entire world.

God, she's cute.

One day I'm going to tattoo those eyes on my body, I swear.

I force myself to back away before I say something dumb, like *marry me* or *drop out and come on the road with me forever*. I've officially lost all self-control when it comes to this girl.

I head to the locker room, moving fast. I pull off my gear, hit the showers, get dressed in record time. The guys chirp me the whole way, because of course they do.

"She's got you whipped already," Logan says, smirking.

"Don't care," I mutter, pulling my hoodie over my head.

And I mean it. I've never meant anything more.

By the time I step outside, she's still there, waiting for me.

Her head lifts as I approach, and her whole face lights up. It hits me square in the chest.

"You ready?" I ask.

She nods and I hold out my hand, threading my fingers through hers.

We walk back to her dorm like that, her hand firmly in mine, and our shoulders brushing every so often. I make sure I'm on the outside of the sidewalk—don't know when I started doing that, just feels right. It's cold as fuck, but I barely notice. Everything feels warm with her beside me.

When we finally get to her dorm, she stops and turns to face me. "Thanks for walking me," she says softly.

"I should be the one thanking you, baby." I lean in, kissing her again, because I'm already craving the feel of her mouth on mine again. When I pull back, I press my forehead against hers.

"It's rare that I have someone I care about watching my games."

She scoffs under her breath. "Right. Tell that to the sea of girls with 'Rhodes' plastered across their backs."

I smile, catching her chin gently and tilt her face up to mine. "You didn't hear me."

Her brows knit, confused.

"I said someone I care about. Couldn't care less about the rest of them." I pause. "You though—" My thumb brushes across her cheekbone. "It was really fucking cool having you out there for me."

She holds my gaze, her eyes flickering away for a moment before settling back on me. Her lips part slightly, as if she's about to say something, then closes them again. She swallows, hesitating just a second longer before finally whispering, "Do you… want to come in?"

My heart flatlines for a second.

Do I want to come in?

Hell yes, I want to come in. But—

I run a hand through my hair, trying to gather whatever's left of my self-control.

"Maisie," I say, my voice rough, "you know I do. But I told you I'd go slow. And I meant it. I don't want to fuck that up just because—"

My words trail off when she places her hands flat against my chest, running them up until she wraps them around my neck. "But what if I don't want you to go slow?"

It punches the air right out of me.

I freeze, blinking at her. And when she lifts onto her tip-toes and presses a soft kiss against my lips, I groan, pulling her closer as I step inside her dorm.

The door clicks shut behind us as she kicks off her shoes. I do the same, following her across the room.

We fall onto the mattress in a tangle of limbs. She's under me, her hands sliding up my chest, warm and eager and a little shaky, and it's *killing me*. My blood's rushing so loud I can barely hear myself think.

My fingers find her waist, slipping beneath the hem of her shirt. Her skin's so fucking soft and hot under my hands. She shivers at my touch, and my stomach tightens because I want to give her everything I have, every bit of me.

I hover over her, my breath ragged, trying to keep it together. "You're so fucking beautiful," I whisper.

Her hands slip under my shirt, her fingertips grazing my bare skin, and I let out a shaky breath, pressing closer. My own hands explore the curve of her side, the gentle dip of her back. Her body arches toward me, and when I trail my lips just below her ribs, she gasps.

I pull back slightly, my hand resting at the hem of her shirt. "Can I take this off?" I ask. "I want to see you."

There's a flicker of hesitation, a pause that makes my chest tighten. Then she nods, lifting her arms a little.

I ease the fabric up slowly, inch by inch. I'm not rushing this. Not with her. I want to savor every single second.

But just as the shirt clears her chest, she jerks, her hand snapping out to shove mine away. "Wait—no."

I freeze instantly. Her shirt's halfway off, caught awkwardly, and I pull it back down without saying anything, my heart thudding in my chest.

I shift back, giving her space. "I'm sorry. I thought—"

"No, I just—" She's already tugging the fabric down, arms crossed over her chest. "I don't know why I freaked out. I'm sorry."

"Don't," I say, sitting up. "Don't apologize. You didn't do anything wrong."

She won't look at me. Her jaw's tight, and her eyes are shining in a way that makes my stomach twist. "We've done stuff before," she says quietly, like she's trying to explain it to *herself.* "I don't know… I just… I thought I was okay, but then—"

"Then you weren't," I finish softly. "You're not ready and that's okay. I can wait as long as you need."

Her lips press into a thin line. She shakes her head, frustrated. "I don't want to mess this up."

My chest aches. "You're not," I say. "Maisie—hey, look at me."

She does, locking those clear blue eyes with mine.

"I'm not here because I'm trying to get laid. I'm here because I like you and want to spend time with you. And if your body's saying no, I'm listening. Every time. No matter what we've done before."

Her throat bobs like she's swallowing back something sharp. "I don't want you to think I'm teasing you or that I changed my mind or—"

"Baby." I scoot closer, careful not to touch her until she lets me. "You're allowed to change your mind. You're allowed to have boundaries even if you were kissing me five seconds ago. You don't owe me anything."

"I just…" She fiddles with the hem of her shirt. "I don't want you to be frustrated," she whispers. "Or get bored of waiting and—" She shakes her head. "I've heard the rumors, Austin. I know what you were like before—"

"Before what?" I cut her off. "Before *you*?"

She blinks up at me, unsure.

I reach up, tracing my thumb along her cheek. "That's the point, Maisie. That was all before I opened my eyes and saw you. Before I knew you. Before I wanted no one and nothing but you."

She exhales shakily.

"Trust me, baby. I'm good with waiting. Months. Years. However long it takes for you to feel comfortable and open up to me. Don't think about my past because all of that is irrelevant. The only thing that matters to me is how you feel. I'm not in any rush. I'd lie in this bed with you a hundred times and never ask for more than this if that's what you want."

She sniffles, tears glinting in her glossy eyes, and her lashes stick together. "Why are you like this?"

"Like what, baby?" I ask her, wiping the tears under her eyes.

"Too good to be true."

"Definitely not too good to be true," I say with a shake of my head, brushing my thumb over her knuckles. "I'm just trying not to fuck this up. Because you matter to me."

She doesn't say anything to that. Just shifts forward and presses her forehead into my shoulder.

After a while, she whispers, "Will you stay? I don't want you to leave."

My whole body softens. "Yeah, Mais," I whisper, pressing my lips to the top of her head. "I'll stay."

She changes into comfier clothes and makes me face the wall while she does it—pure agony—and when she finally climbs into bed, she curls into me without a word, her cheek pressed right against my chest.

She puts on some old movie I don't recognize. She mouths the lines, and I barely register the plot because I'm too busy watching her.

Eventually, her breathing slows, her lashes rest against her cheek, and she falls asleep right there, tangled up in my arms.

A smile tugs at my lips as I close my eyes, feeling her heartbeat steadying against mine.

I'd wait forever for her without a second thought.

THIRTY

Austin

I don't usually get nervous before games.

But today, I keep glancing up at the stands.

I've already untaped and re-taped my stick twice. My fingers are twitching nonstop—tugging at the hem of my jersey, cracking my knuckles, fidgeting with the pads I've worn the same way for three years.

Because today, my mom and sister are coming.

And Maisie's here too.

Which is fine. Totally fine. I'm not freaking out or anything.

Okay, I am. It's just… I've never really had anyone to bring around before. Never introduced a girl to my family.

So yeah, I'm nervous as hell.

Before I even pull on my helmet, I crouch down by my skates like I always do. I press two fingers to my lips, then tap them to the side of each skate.

"Don't let me down boys," I murmur.

I drag my hands through my hair, stand up, and blow out a breath.

When I push open the locker room door and walk out onto the bench, the sound hits me instantly. The arena's already packed. People are banging on the glass. It's loud. Hot. Tense. Everything I love about hockey.

I'm still buzzing when I skate toward center ice, adrenaline pounding in my veins.

Ryan smacks me on the helmet as he settles into position.

I glance up, scanning the stands, finding her in seconds.

Maisie's leaning forward against the railing, the crowd packed tight around her, but she's the only thing I see. Her hair's tucked into the collar of her puffer jacket, and she's squinting through the glass, scanning the ice.

Searching for me.

And when her gaze finally locks onto mine, she smiles. Slow. Soft. My heart thuds like I've taken a puck to the chest. That smile of hers floors me. Every single time.

I skate a little closer, grinning up at her. I tap my stick against the boards and blow her a kiss, because I'm an idiot and I don't know what else to do with all this—whatever the hell it is that's been building, shifting, twisting in my chest since the second I met her.

One corner of her mouth tips up. She rolls her eyes and shakes her head, but she's still smiling as she lifts the cup and takes a sip out of her drink.

God, I'm a goner.

"Jesus, get a room," Logan mutters as he coasts by.

"You're just jealous 'cause your last hookup ghosted you," I shoot back with a grin.

Logan tuts, shaking his head. "Correction. I ghosted him."

I let out a scoff. "Yeah, somehow I don't believe you."

Logan holds a hand to his chest. "Unbelievable. No faith in your boy."

Nathan doesn't say anything from behind his goalie mask as he stretches near the crease.

"Alright, focus," Ryan yells as he skates to center ice, voice sharp over the buzz of the crowd. "We can take these guys. Coach said if we win, wings are on him."

"Tell him I want extra fries," I call, coasting up beside him.

"You'll get celery sticks and you'll fucking thank me for it," Coach shouts from behind the bench.

I laugh, but my stomach's buzzing. Not hunger or nerves, just pure fucking adrenaline on steroids. There's something about tonight. Maybe it's the home crowd, maybe it's that I saw Maisie, maybe it's the fact that my mom and sister are somewhere up in those stands, watching.

Cole doesn't say a word. Just cracks his neck and chews his gum like he's ready to body slam someone through the glass.

Ryan glances around the line-up. Nods once.

We line up. Puck drop.

Game fucking on.

Nathan makes a sick glove save early on—snatches the puck right out of the air. Logan picks up the rebound, swings it to Ryan, and I'm already moving, skating like my life depends on it. Ryan sends a clean pass up center. I take it and cut left, fast, ducking past one defender, then two.

Then I fake right and shoot.

Goal.

Top shelf, baby.

We're up 1–0 before the five-minute mark.

"Let's fucking go." I skate toward the guys and fist-bump Logan.

Second period, we're still holding the lead. Cole nails a breakaway, stone-cold expression the whole way down the ice, and slaps one into the back of the net. We're on fire tonight. Tight passes. Clean shifts. Our D is solid, and Nathan's a wall back there. They've only managed to score once tonight, and if we keep it up, we'll get the win.

I get another goal midway through the third and the place erupts in cheers.

I wanna look so bad, wanna sneak a peek to the stands and see if they're out there cheering for me.

I don't let myself look yet. Not until the final buzzer blares and the crowd fucking explodes as we win 4-1.

I rip my helmet off and skate in to tackle Ryan in a hug. Logan jumps on both of us, crushing me in the process. Cole just stands there watching us, the corner of his lips lifting an inch before he skates off.

Nathan gives me a shoulder bump once we're back on our feet, smiling under his mask.

My heart is racing with adrenaline and I finally allow myself to glance up and look for them.

I spot Mom and Scarlett first.

They're near the top of the stands, bundled in scarves and puffer coats, holding up a massive glittery-ass sign that reads RHODES RAGE in all caps, with sparkles. I let out a breathless laugh, skating in lazy circles during our cool-down, wondering where the hell I'm going to store that thing—because of course I'm keeping it.

And then my eyes find my girl, halfway down the bleacher steps, weaving through the crowd. She's looking down, focused on not tripping over someone's feet, and then she glances up.

Her eyes lock on mine. Just for a second.

And my heart thuds against my chest.

I hear you, buddy. *I know*.

I tear off my gloves the second we hit the tunnel, still high off the win, sweaty, and half-grinning like an idiot. My ribs are sore. My legs are shot. But none of it matters. Not when she's standing at the bottom of the stairs, waiting for me.

"You were amazing," she says the moment I reach her.

I can't spend a minute away from her, clearly, because the minute she's in front of me, I grab her face in my hands and lean down to kiss her. "You came," I breathe against her lips.

"Of course I came," she replies breathlessly, blinking up at me. "I will always come for you."

I can't help it. My lips tip up in a smirk and I wag my brows at her. "Oh yeah?"

She smacks my chest lightly, rolling her eyes. "Don't make this weird."

I laugh, running a hand through my hair which is drenched. "It's already weird. Because my mom and sister are here, and they really want to meet you."

Her face goes pale. "Wait. What? Why didn't you warn me?"

"Because if I told you, you'd freak out, and if you freaked out, you wouldn't come, and then I'd have to explain to my mom why the girl I'm obsessed with doesn't actually exist."

She blinks slightly, her pretty lips lifting into a shy smile. "You're obsessed with me?" she asks, as if she heard me wrong.

"Painfully," I assure her, lace my fingers through hers. "Come on, it'll be fine. They're normal." I pause, squinting at her. "Ish."

"Austin," Maisie hisses, her eyes flicking down to her outfit. "I'm not dressed to meet your mom."

My eyes drift down—black hoodie, jeans, knockout body that makes my mouth water. "You look beautiful," I tell her.

She shakes her head, a cute flush coating her cheeks. "You're biased."

"Exactly. I'm the only opinion that matters." I grab her hand, lift it, and kiss the back of it. "You're good, baby. I promise."

"I'm scared," she admits, swallowing hard. "I don't want her to hate me."

"She won't." I tug her a little closer. "My mom doesn't hate anyone. Least of all her son's first girlfriend."

Maisie blushes, smiling at that word. It was a shock when she first called me her boyfriend, but nothing has ever felt so right either.

I rip my eyes away from her when I see my sister standing under the stairs. Mom's standing beside her, bundled up in her coat, waving us over. We head toward them, and Maisie's grip on my hand tightens just a little.

"There's my boy," Mom says, pulling me in for a hug. "That was one hell of a game."

"You say that every time," I murmur with a chuckle.

"And I'm never wrong." She pulls back, smiling, then her eyes shift to Maisie. "And you must be Maisie," Mom says, already stepping in for a hug.

Maisie blinks. "Yeah—uh, yes. I'm Maisie. It's really nice to meet you."

Mom wraps her arms around her, giving her a squeeze before pulling back. "I've heard all about you. I'm Erin. And this—" she gestures to Scarlett, who's standing next to mom with the glittery sign still in her hands— "this is Scarlett."

"Hi, Scarlett." Maisie smiles. "Love the sign."

My sister arches a brow. "Austin told us you weren't his girlfriend," she says, eyeing me up. "Is that still true?"

I groan. "Scarlett."

She shrugs. "Just saying. You said it very clearly. Multiple times."

I slide my arm around Maisie's waist, glancing down at the best thing that's ever happened to me. "Well, clearly I was an idiot."

"I knew it," she says, pointing an accusatory finger at me.

"You knew nothing," I say, pulling her into a side hug. She yells at me for being sweaty and gross, which only makes me hug her tighter.

Mom's watching the two of us, then her eyes shift back to Maisie.

"My son can be a lot," she says. "But he's got a good heart. I'm glad he found someone who sees it."

Maisie shifts her weight. Tucks a piece of hair behind her ear. "I'm glad he saw me," she says quietly, glancing up at me.

I squeeze her hand.

My chest is still buzzing from the game, from the adrenaline and the noise and the win. But nothing hits harder than this moment right here.

"Have you played anything new?" my sister asks.

I shrug, running a hand through my damp hair. "Yeah. A few things." I glance at Maisie without meaning to. "Got inspired."

Maisie lets out a soft laugh. "He plays constantly," she tells my sister. "He even woke me up in the middle of the night the other day to play me a song."

Scarlett's head jerks toward her. "Wait. You've *heard* him play?"

Maisie pauses, glancing at me like she's not sure if she's allowed to say more. "Um. Yeah… a few times."

Scarlett turns to me, her eyes widened. "You never play for anyone. Like, ever."

Maisie stares at me for confirmation, her lips parted in shock.

I scratch the back of my neck. "It wasn't a big deal."

Scarlett shakes her head slowly, then looks back at Maisie with a grin. "He's lying. It's a huge deal."

My mom nods in agreement. "He wouldn't even play for his grandma's birthday."

Christ. They do *not* know how to play cool, do they?

Scarlett looks back at me, her lips twitching in a cocky smirk. "You must really love her."

Okay, someone please muzzle her.

Maisie's eyes flick to mine. Her lips part, like she's about to say something, but luckily for both of us, she doesn't.

I clear my throat, yanking at the collar of my jersey. "Okay. Let's move on before I strangle my sister," I joke, avoiding Maisie's eyes.

We hang out near the stands for a while. Mom's chatting with Maisie about her classes, Scarlett's going on about making junior varsity volleyball—which I groan at.

"I cannot believe my own blood would betray me with a sport that doesn't involve blades or a puck," I say, slinging an arm over her shoulder.

She rolls her eyes. "Sorry I don't want to skate around smashing into people like a caveman," she says, ducking out from under it. "And I'm not playing a sport where I might lose teeth."

"Losing teeth builds character," I mutter, mostly to Maisie, who just chuckles and rolls those eyes that knocked me on my ass from day one.

I'm very aware that I'm smiling like a damn idiot, but I can't stop. Not when I look at the three of them—my mom, my sister, and the girl who's somehow tangled herself into everything I care about—and my chest feels tight in the best possible way. I just want to pause this moment and live in it forever.

At some point, Mom touches my arm, pulling me a few feet away.

"She brings out a version of you I haven't seen in a while," she says, pursing her lips. "I like her."

I let out a laugh. "That's good, considering she's my girlfriend."

Mom studies me for a second. Then her lips tug into a small smile. "You've got that look," she says.

My brows knit together. "What look?"

"You love her," she adds quietly.

I don't answer.

But I don't deny it, either.

She hums and strolls off to show Maisie my embarrassing baby pics.

Did I say my family was normal? Yeah, I take it back.

They're loud and embarrassing as hell... but I wouldn't trade them for the world.

THIRTY-ONE

Maisie

I don't know what I expected from a hockey afterparty.

I mean, technically, I've been to one of Austin's parties before—by accident—and it was wild. But tonight, it's louder, even bigger and more insane.

Someone's already mid-keg stand in the front hall while a group of guys chant. There's a broken chair in the middle of the living room, and the music is vibrating my actual spine.

Aurora's already halfway across the room, weaving through the crowd in boots that could easily double as weapons.

Isabella slows her steps beside me, looping her arm through mine. "Are you okay?"

I nod, adjusting the strap of my top. "I just forgot how loud and cramped parties are."

She chuckles, and squeezes my arm. "Come on. Alcohol usually helps."

The house is packed wall-to-wall with bodies. I tug at the hem of my top. My jeans that felt cute ten minutes ago now feel too tight. My top keeps riding up every time I move. And I *definitely* shouldn't have worn my hair down. It's already sticking to the back of my neck like glue.

We push into the kitchen, which somehow manages to be louder and hotter than the rest of the house.

Aurora halts in front of us the second she spots Cole.

He's leaning against the counter, his jaw ticking as his eyes flick toward us. Or toward her, more accurately.

She doesn't bother hiding her scowl. "Don't you have a sewer to crawl back into?"

Cole's jaw tenses as he chews his gum. "Didn't realize they let Viper off her leash tonight."

Aurora flips her hair. "Careful, Reaper. Keep looking at me like that, and I'll bury you in the backyard."

He pops his gum with enough force it sounds like a threat. "Keep talking and I'll catch a felony."

Aurora gives Cole a sugar-sweet smile, full of venom. "Good. I'd love to see you behind bars," she says, before brushing past him, knocking her shoulder against his.

I blink, turning my attention to Isabella. "Did they just threaten to kill each other?"

She chuckles "You'll get used to it. What do you want?" she asks, gesturing toward the drink table. "Jungle juice? Punch?"

"I don't mind," I say, even though I don't really feel like drinking.

She fills up my cup with something orange and hands it to me, and I take a sip.

My gaze is torn when a group of people all cheer, though I can't see where it's coming from since the house is packed with bodies, reeking of beer and weed.

And somewhere in this mess is Austin—my boyfriend.

That word still throws me. Boyfriend.

I glance around the crowd of people and spot him before he sees me.

He's across the room with Logan, both of them laughing and drinking. At least he looks like he's having a good time. My eyes drift when I see a girl standing close to him, one hand on his arm. She's smiling, leaning in closer to him. My stomach sours at the sight, but a few seconds later, Austin shakes his head and takes a step back.

"She was two seconds away from climbing him," Aurora says, arching a brow as she sips her drink.

"He moved away," Isabella points out.

"Still. That girl had a mission," Aurora says. "I saw her lick her lips like he was dessert."

"Let her try," Isabella says. "It won't work."

The nerves in my stomach settle from their words. But before I can say anything, I notice Austin climbing onto the coffee table in the middle of the living room, Logan helping him up.

"Oh no," I mutter, already mortified. What the hell is he doing?

"Everyone," Austin shouts, raising his cup in the air. "Listen up!"

The music cuts off and everyone turns their attention to Austin. Some people laugh. Others yell '*Take your shirt off!*'

Austin shoots them a wink. "Appreciate the energy. But I'm here for an announcement. Just in case anyone missed the memo," he says, placing a hand over his chest, "your boy is taken. Locked down. Off. The. Market."

He scans the crowd and then smiles when his eyes lock on mine and points directly at me.

I want to sink into the floor.

"That's my girl," he says. "Right there."

I attempt to hide behind my cup as all eyes turn toward me. My face is on fire.

"So unless your name is Maisie Wilson, do not flirt with me. Do not touch my arm. And definitely do not ask me to do a body shot off your belly button. I'm a committed man now."

Logan helps him down, and Austin throws an arm around him. "Now this guy?" He jerks a thumb at Logan. "This guy's single, and fucking ready to mingle. Go nuts."

The music kicks back in a few seconds later. The crowd cheers and the party rolls on like nothing happened, but I'm pink from head to toe.

He's ridiculous, but I can't stop smiling, knowing he willingly climbed on a table just to tell everyone I'm his.

But because the universe can't let me enjoy anything for more than three minutes, I hear two girls near the hallway, talking too loudly to be subtle.

"Didn't you hook up with Austin Rhodes last year?"

"Mmhmm," the other says, sipping from her drink. "Twice. He was wild."

I go still, my ears perking up.

The first girl laughs. "God, you're so lucky. He's so hot."

"He used to throw me around like a ragdoll."

The other one snorts. "Think he's like that with her?"

She laughs in response. My stomach sinks. "Are you kidding? She looks like she doesn't even open her legs for him."

Aurora freezes when she finally hears them.

"I mean," one continues, "she's got a pretty face, but come on. He's Austin Rhodes. He'll get bored. What does he even see in her?"

"That's probably why he's shouting it from the coffee table," the other adds. "Trying to convince himself."

Something sharp lodges in my throat. I grip my cup tight in my hand. My face burns for a whole new reason.

Aurora turns and steps toward them. "You done listing your sex résumé? Congrats, you got laid. No one fucking cares."

They whip around, startled.

"It's a party," one of the girls replies. "We're just talking."

"No," Aurora says flatly. "You're running your mouth about someone's girlfriend."

The girl rolls her eyes and they stalk off, muttering under their breath.

Isabella's hand finds my arm. "You okay?"

"Yeah," I lie.

Aurora glances at me, her brows knitted, and Isabella wears a similar expression. They don't really look like they believe it, but they don't push either.

I move toward the drinks, dump what's left of my cup, and refill it with whatever's closest. My hands shake as I lift the cup to my mouth. The burn of vodka hits hard, but it's not enough to drown out the words still playing on loop.

What does he even see in her?

He used to throw me around.

He used to want girls like them.

And now he's with me.

My chest tightens. I thought I was over this. Over the body image stuff. Over the voice in my head telling me I'm not enough.

But it's back. Yelling, filling every single one of my thoughts.

I tell myself not to let it in.

Not to let their words carve into me.

But they do.

Because deep down, some part of me agrees with them. Some part of me still wonders if Austin will wake up one day, look at me, and think—*what the hell was I doing with her?*

I don't want to think like that. I want to believe in the way he looks at me. In how proud he is to call me his.

But it's hard. Right now, it's really, really hard.

I lean harder into the counter and refill my cup, trying not to fall apart. Not here. Not tonight. Not when I'm supposed to be happy.

So I drink, trying to push all of those thoughts out of my head.

THIRTY-TWO

Austin

The house is packed, obviously. Midnight Wolves win, and suddenly everyone thinks it's their personal victory too. Happens every time.

I used to love this shit—loud music, enough booze to drown a small village. Now? All I want is for everyone to clear the hell out so I can hang out with my girlfriend.

Never thought that'd be me. The guy who hangs with his girlfriend at a party. The guy who even *has* a girlfriend. But yeah, that's me. In a committed relationship with a girl I'm completely and utterly obsessed with.

I didn't see it coming. It shocks me how much she's already changed everything without even trying. How she makes me want to be better—for her. Just having her around makes me want to throw all my old rules out the window and write brand-new ones.

Ryan and Nathan disappeared into the kitchen like twenty minutes ago, and I lost the rest of the guys, but I don't really care, because they're not who I'm looking for.

I do a slow lap of the living room, scanning the crowd, until I catch a flash of soft brown hair and light blue eyes across the room.

Maisie's perched on the arm of the couch with Aurora and Isabella beside her. Her cheeks are flushed, more than usual, sipping from her red solo cup.

Even from across the room, I spot those freckles I'm crazy about—little dots scattered over her cheekbones. Twenty-six on the left side, thirty-two on the right. Or was it the other way around? Fuck, I don't know. I lost count half a dozen times when she slept in my arms the other night, but I kept going anyway, tracing each one with my eyes. I kept staring at her, because it felt like I couldn't not.

I don't even realize I've started moving until I'm already in front of her and she's looking up at me like I've just appeared out of thin air.

Those big blue eyes I adore lock onto mine. "Hi," she says with a dopey smile.

"Hey, baby," I say, grinning as I brush some hair behind her ear. "You having fun?"

She nods with a hum. "I had… two shots. And half a White Claw. Mango, I think."

I blink, letting out a laugh. "That explains the red cheeks."

She blinks back at me, all slow and dazed, and then reaches out to poke my chest. "You're so *tall*," she says. "Has anyone ever told you that?"

My lips twitch at her adorable drunken state. "Once or twice."

"You're so handsome," she adds, with a sigh. "I mean, like, obnoxiously handsome. I should be mad about it."

That makes me laugh. I loop an arm around her waist when she leans a little too far sideways. She fits there so easily, completely relaxed against me.

"Alright, sweetheart. Maybe we call it quits on the drinks tonight, huh?"

She tilts her head back and rests it on my chest for balance. "Don't call me sweetheart," she says, a line forming between her brows. "Makes me feel things."

Her fingers curl into the hem of my hoodie like she's anchoring herself. She smells like vanilla lotion and fruity alcohol.

I duck my head, inhaling the sweet scent of that vanilla stuff she always puts on after a shower, and the fruity alcohol on her breath.

"Want to go catch some air?" I ask, pressing my lips against her cheek.

She shakes her head. "I wanna go to your room."

I arch a brow. "My room?"

She nods. "I need to lie down. Your bed is nice and soft and smells like you. I like it there," she adds with this dreamy little sigh.

I chuckle. She's so damn cute. "Okay. Let's go."

I guide her down the hall, one hand pressed to the small of her back, the other hovering in case she tips over.

"Did I mention you smell good?" she asks as I push open my door.

"You might've," I say, flipping on the lamp by my desk.

"You smell like heaven," she says, dreamily, which makes me chuckle.

I help her sit on my bed and reach into my nightstand, grabbing a pack of Oreos for her, hoping it'll soak up some of the alcohol—always keep one there just for her. There's even a jar of peanut butter nearby. I hold out a water bottle, expecting her to take a sip. Instead, she lets the bottle hit the mattress and grabs a fistful of my hoodie, yanking me toward her.

And before I can react, she's kissing me.

My brain short-circuits when her mouth meets mine, and instinct takes over as I kiss her back, my hands braced on either side of her thighs. It's hot, fast and a little messy and I can't think straight.

Her fingers sneak under my hoodie, tugging at the hem of my shirt, and then she starts to pull it up, trying to undress me.

"Wait—" I murmur against her lips, catching her wrists. "Maisie, hold up."

She locks eyes with me and licks her lips. "I want to have sex."

Her words hit me like a bucket of ice water. Not because I don't want to—God, I want to—but because she's clearly very drunk and not thinking straight.

I pull back fast, shaking my head. "Maisie…"

She sways a little as she kneels on my bed, placing her hands on my chest. "I want to," she says again. "I want to. Please."

Fuck.

I close my eyes for half a second, because it kills me to say no. I want this girl so bad, and every part of me wants to climb into that bed and touch every inch of her. But not like this. Not when she's drunk out of her mind and will wake up tomorrow with no memory of what happened.

I cup her jaw, brushing my thumb under her cheek. "You're drunk, baby," I say, meeting her eyes. "And as much as I want this—Jesus, you have no idea how much—I'm not doing it like this. I'm not taking advantage of you when you're drunk."

Her face twists. "You're not taking advantage. I said I want to."

"I know you did. I believe you." I kiss her forehead. "But I want you to be sober when I finally slide inside you."

"I'm not drunk, Austin," she insists, even though the words come out slurred. "Here, I'll prove it."

She leans in and kisses me again. And because I've fallen way too fucking hard for this girl, I kiss her back, even though I know I shouldn't. Fuck, I love kissing her. I used to truly take kissing for granted. I didn't care much for it, never really thought about it. It was always just a step toward hooking up. But I could sit here and kiss her for fucking hours.

"Please," she breathes against my mouth. "Please, Austin."

The sound of my name on her lips undoes something in me. I close my eyes and exhale, my heart thudding so loud I can barely think straight.

I pull back just enough to see her face. "Maisie," I say quietly. "Why now?"

She blinks a couple of times, and her shoulders fall as she sinks back on her heels, the fight bleeding out of her. And then, just like that, her expression crumples, like paper in a fist.

"Because I'm scared," she whispers.

My brows tug together. "Scared of what, gorgeous?"

She blows out a shaky breath. "I'm scared that if I wait—if I'm sober—I'll talk myself out of it. I'll get too in my head. I'll think about every bad thing I've ever believed about myself. I'm scared you'll see me and change your mind. So it has to be now, while I still have some courage left."

My stomach drops.

She looks down, shaking her head. "Every other girl you've been with… they don't look like me. They don't have stretch marks. Or stomachs that fold when they sit down. Or thighs with cellulite that—" she swallows "—touch. And I keep thinking… what if I get naked and you realize I'm not what you want?"

Fuck.

It *kills* me hearing her say that.

Without thinking, I reach for her. My hands cradle her face, brushing my thumbs along her damp cheeks. Her skin's warm, flushed, and I can feel her shaky breath hit my chin.

"Maisie," I whisper. "Look at me."

Her lashes flutter, hesitant, and then she does.

Big, blue, break-my-heart eyes. Shining with tears she's trying to blink away.

And God, I love her.

I've never said it out loud, but I fucking know it without an ounce of hesitation. It's been there for a while now. Curling deeper every time she smiles at me like I'm something good.

"Every single woman in the world could be naked in my bed right now," I say, keeping my eyes on hers. "And the only one I'd want is you."

Her bottom lip wobbles, and she bites down on it like she's trying to hold something in. She opens her mouth, then shuts it again.

"I'm just… I haven't done anything before, Austin," she says. "Every first I'm doing with you… you've already done with someone else." She looks away for a second, then back at me. "I know that's not your fault, but I just… I want you to want *me* the way you wanted *her*."

I stare at her, stunned for a second.

Her?

What *her*?

Because I can't even think of anyone else when she's in the room. I haven't thought about anyone but her since the moment

I met her—before that, even. It's always been her for me. It will *always* be her.

My hands slide down to her waist, pulling her into me. "Maisie." I shake my head. "There is no her. There's no girl before you that meant a damn thing compared to this."

I wait for her to say something, but she doesn't. She just looks at me like she's trying to believe it.

"I want you in ways I've never wanted anyone. And it's not just because you're beautiful—though you are, insanely so— it's because you're you. It's your laugh. Your smartass comments. Your brain. Your heart. It's the way you talk to me. The way you see me, even when I'm being a complete idiot."

Her breath stutters. "Austin…"

"I mean it." I brush my thumb across her cheek. "I've never wanted someone like this before," I whisper. "You're it, Maisie. You're the only one I want. You're the best thing that's ever happened to me, baby."

She shakes her head. "You don't know what you're saying."

"I do." There's no doubt in my voice—none. "I've never been more sure of anything."

"Surer," she corrects softly with a sniffle.

I chuckle and lean in, press a kiss to her forehead. Then one to the tip of her nose. And finally, her lips. She sighs against me, and I kiss her like she's the only thing that matters.

Because she is.

Eventually, I help her out of her clothes, swap her top for my hoodie—*her* hoodie now, really—and tug the blanket up over us. I grab the trash can just in case. She's not blackout, but she's definitely never been this drunk before. And it kills me that this was the only way she felt brave enough to be with me.

She curls into me like she's always belonged there. Warm. Small. Soft in all the ways that make me want to protect her with everything I've got.

"Next time I try to seduce you while drunk," she mumbles, voice muffled against my chest, "you have to promise to stop me again."

"Deal," I say, laughing quietly. "But just know it's gonna kill me every time."

She hums, smiling against my chest. "You like me."

I dip my head and press a kiss to the top of her hair. "I do."

"A lot."

"An embarrassing amount," I admit with a smile, brushing her hair off her face.

She giggles. Makes my heart pound against my chest. "Good," she whispers, already half-asleep.

Her eyes flutter shut, and I just lie there in the dark, her body tucked tight against mine, and her breath warm on my skin.

I don't say anything else. Don't need to.

Because my chest is full, and my thoughts are loud, and all I can think is some things are worth waiting for.

And I'd wait a lifetime just to meet her all over again.

♥

Maisie stirs beside me sometime after eight, groaning softly as she burrows deeper under the covers, like if she just tries hard enough, she can disappear entirely.

I smile into the pillow. "You alive, Freckles?"

She lets out a longer groan, muffled by the blanket. "Barely."

I roll onto my side to face her, and immediately my chest squeezes. Hair tangled. Mascara smudged under her eyes. My hoodie falling off one bare shoulder, exposing a strip of soft skin that makes my brain short-circuit. The sight of her first thing in the morning shouldn't do things to me—but it does. It absolutely, irreversibly does.

Her legs are tangled in the blanket, one knee draped over mine, and I get a perfect view of the curve of her hip and the cotton panties she's wearing—the ones I saw when I helped her out of her jeans last night.

And now she's half on top of me, stretching like a sleepy cat. I'm already hard. Because of course I am. I've basically been semi-hard since she got into my bed and curled into me last night.

Not my fault. I'm only human.

I shift carefully, trying not to wake her, but her lashes flutter open. Big and blue and still a little puffy from sleep.

She squints up at me, her expression adorably groggy. "Did I try to have sex with you last night?"

I could be a gentleman and lie, pretend none of it happened. But… "You did," I say with a chuckle.

She groans and hides her face in my bare chest. "Kill me. Please. Right now."

I laugh, dragging a hand down her back. "You also called me obnoxiously handsome and said I smelled like heaven. So you know. Bonus points."

"I hate myself."

"I don't." I tilt her chin up, force her to meet my gaze. "I loved every second of it."

Her blush spreads instantly—flaming red across her cheeks, down her throat. I swear I can *see* the heat racing across her skin.

She looks away. "I just… I was nervous. I didn't want you to change your mind."

I sit up slowly, bracing my weight on one elbow so I can reach her, sliding a hand into her hair. My palm cups the back of her neck. "Maisie, baby. I couldn't stop wanting you if I tried."

Her lips part. Her eyes flick to my mouth for a beat, then back up to mine, and I swear I feel it all the way down my spine. Her gaze drops again—this time lower. She bites her lip. Her hand drifts across my chest, tentative and slow. Her fingers brush over my skin, tracing along the top of my abs, and I almost forget how to breathe.

She blushes, and I can tell she's holding back something.

"What?" I ask softly.

She swallows. "I was thinking…" she starts. "If you wanted… maybe I could learn something new."

My pulse jumps. "Something new?" I ask.

Maisie's gaze drops lower. Slowly. Like she's working up the nerve to follow through with whatever thought just landed in her brain. Her fingers trail lightly over my chest, but I feel it like she's dragging fire across my skin.

"Like… maybe you could teach me?" she murmurs.

Then her palm drifts downward, smoothing over the line of muscle just above my waistband.

And I—

Yeah. I nearly fucking die.

Fuck me.

My entire body locks up. I can feel the heat rush through me.

Don't blow your load. Don't blow your load. Do not fucking blow your load from having her hand on your fucking chest.

My cock twitches, straining against my boxers, and I have to take a full breath before I answer because she looks so nervous and I don't want to scare her.

"You sure?" I ask, keeping my voice as even as I can manage.

She nods immediately, sitting up a little straighter. "I've never done it before, but I want to learn—with you."

I stare at her. Squint slightly. "Are you still drunk?"

Maisie blinks. "No. Just… horny."

I groan and drag a hand down my face. "Jesus Christ. You're gonna kill me."

She laughs, keeping her hand on my stomach. Still exploring. Still driving me absolutely insane.

I peek out from under my arm. "You sure you want to? There's no pressure. We don't have to—"

"I want to," she says softly. Her eyes meet mine. "You make me feel safe."

And just like that, my heart flips over.

That one sentence hits me harder than anything else. Because this girl—this stubborn, beautiful, brilliant girl—*trusts* me.

I reach for her hand and lace our fingers together, lifting it to my mouth to press a kiss to the back of it.

"You're such a good tutor, baby," I murmur. "But now it's your turn to be the student." I glance at her, heat simmering low in my stomach. "You gonna let me teach you how to suck my cock?"

She nods, her breath catching as her cheeks turn the most delicious shade of pink.

I lean in and kiss her again, my tongue brushing hers just enough to tease, to taste her. Then I guide her hand down between us, curling her fingers around me through the thin cotton of my boxers.

Her eyes go wide. "Oh."

"Yeah," I say, barely holding back a groan. "That's what you do to me."

She shifts closer, adjusting her grip. Testing the weight of me in her hand like she's trying to figure me out.

I shift, just slightly, and let out a breath through my nose, trying to keep myself from combusting. My boxers are clinging to me now, tight and damp with how hard I am, and every time her hand moves, it's a new level of torture.

So I do the only thing I can think to do.

I hook my fingers into the waistband of my boxers and push them down.

Her hand freezes and her breath catches when she sees me. Her mouth falls open just slightly, and for a second, she just… stares.

My cock is right there in front of her, flushed and thick and leaking at the tip. I'm fully hard now, resting against my lower stomach. I know what I look like naked. I've had girls brag about my size. But her reaction is the best thing that's ever happened to my ego.

Maisie swallows, her cheeks burning. Her gaze flicks up to mine, then back down like she's not sure if she's allowed to look.

"You're… um." She blushes even harder. "You're really big."

Jesus fucking Christ.

My cock twitches at her words.

Do not come. She just fucking looked at you.

A laugh rips out of me. "Baby, if you keep looking at me like that, I'm gonna embarrass myself."

She shifts a little closer, watching intently as she moves her hand. Her grip is awkward at first, uneven, but I don't care. The second her palm drags over the sensitive underside of my cock, I have to grip the blanket just to stay grounded.

I wrap my hand over hers, guiding the rhythm. "Start slow," I murmur. "Use your hand first. Wrap it around the base."

Maisie sinks her teeth into her bottom lip and her fingers twitch around me, resuming that slow, tentative stroke, and this time, I *do* groan. Louder.

"Just like that," I manage. "God, that feels good."

"Yeah?" she asks.

I groan in response, my head tipping back against the pillow, eyes fluttering shut. I force them open again because I want to watch this. Want to remember every second of it.

"Now just… spit in your hand a little," I murmur, breathless. "Get it nice and wet."

She glances up at me, hesitant.

"Don't overthink it," I tell her. "It's just us, baby."

She nods, leans forward a little, and spits delicately into her palm. She brings her hand back to me, her fingers wrapping around my cock again, and this time it's slick. Her grip glides easier now, smoother, and my entire body tenses at the first slow stroke.

Her hand moves again, more confident now, more curious, and I swear, I black out for a second.

"Fuck, that's good," I mutter, dropping my head to the pillow. My hips twitch against the mattress. "Jesus. You're a fast learner."

She smiles shyly, and I can tell she likes the praise, likes knowing she's making me come undone with nothing but her hand and wide eyes locked on mine.

"Can I try with my mouth?"

I choke.

Literally. I cough like a dumbass, because apparently that's my body's reaction to hearing the hottest sentence ever come out of her mouth.

"Mais," I manage, already half-gone.

Her eyes flick up. "Can I?"

I just nod. Because that's all I can do. Words? Language? Never fucking heard of them.

Maisie leans over, moving her hair out of the way as she moves down, and then she places the softest kiss right at the tip.

I hiss in a breath.

Then she does it again. And again. Lower now.

Her lips barely graze me and I'm already straining like a goddamn lunatic. Every part of me is wired tight. One wrong move and I'll lose it in the lamest way possible.

She kisses along the base, her hand wrapped around me like I showed her, thumb brushing just under the head.

"Slow," I murmur. "Use your tongue—just a little. You don't have to take everything."

She listens. Follows every instruction. Girl's about to ace the class.

Then she licks me like a fucking ice cream cone. She tastes and teases me until I can't fucking take it anymore. I grunt, tipping my head back and before I can react, she finally takes the tip into her mouth, sucking on it.

"Fuck," I groan. "You're doing so good."

She hums, like she likes hearing that, and the vibration sends a shiver down my spine.

"God, you're such a good student," I mutter, brushing her hair off her cheek as she pulls back for air. "A fucking overachiever."

She takes more of me in, and I can't stop watching her. Her soft lips stretched around me, her cheeks hollowing a little, her hand still pumping slowly in rhythm.

"Look at me," I breathe, and when she does—*fuck*—I nearly lose it. Big blue eyes, blown wide, her lashes fluttering. There's something so pure about her, and yet here she is, mouth full of my cock, learning how to wreck me.

"You're gonna make me come if you keep looking at me like that."

She pulls off for a second and her lips are wet. "Isn't that the point?"

I groan, hand sliding into her hair. "Dirty, little tutor. Already trying to outdo me."

She leans in again, this time more confident. She sucks harder, deeper. Her tongue circles the head every time she pulls back, and I know I'm close.

I grip the sheets. Try to hold back. But it's too good. "Maisie, fuck, I'm gonna come."

She doesn't stop. She keeps going, keeping her eyes locked on mine, so pretty and focused, like she wants to watch it happen.

And when I let go—when it finally hits—I come so hard I forget where I am. My whole body jerks. My hips lift off the bed. A groan rips out of me loud enough to echo, her mouth warm and perfect around me as I spill down her throat.

She stays with me through it. Keeps her mouth on me. Lets me ride it out.

When I finally stop shaking, she pulls off with a breath and licks the corner of her mouth.

"Was that okay?" she asks quietly.

I pull her up into my arms immediately, and kiss her hard. "You have no idea."

She curls back into my chest, still flushed, still smiling. I wrap both arms around her and press a kiss to her forehead, holding her close.

"You were fucking amazing," I murmur.

"You're kinda easy to please," she says with a teasing smile.

"Hey." I shoot her a grin. "You just blew my mind. Don't sass me."

She chuckles, softening as she leans into me. "I like learning with you."

I kiss the tip of her nose. "Anytime, baby. Class is always in session."

THIRTY-THREE

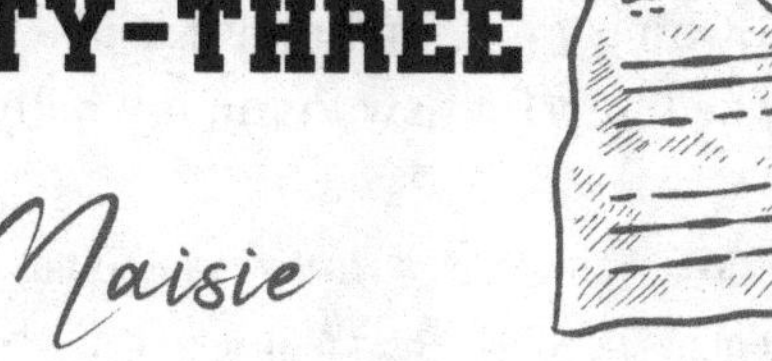

Maisie

I've read the same paragraph five times. I'm not even processing the words anymore. Not because I don't get it. I do, I've got the concepts down, I already outlined the chapter last night, but my brain is done—tapped out. My eyes are dry, my wrist aches, and I've been sitting cross-legged on my bed for so long my legs are tingling.

I check the time. 8:42 PM.

My phone lights up a few seconds later and I glance down, smiling when I see Austin's text.

Austin: what are you doing?

Just seeing his name makes me smile. I roll onto my side and text him back.

Me: Studying and trying not to die.

Austin: come over. I'll revive you with my lips.

Me: Wow. Poetry.

Austin: I contain multitudes babe.

Austin: also pizza.

Me: Tempting, but I'm trying to be responsible.

Austin: boooooring. come be irresponsible with me. we can make bad choices together.

I roll my eyes, but my stomach flips anyway. I'm literally drowning in notes, and all it takes is a few texts from him to make butterflies swarm in my belly.

Me: Some of us actually want to pass our exams. Not all of us can get people to do what we want just by being hot.

Austin: baby, you underestimate the power you have over me. You could tell me to jump off a cliff by batting those blue eyes and I would do it without a second thought.

Austin: also, is that you admitting I'm hot? bc if so, I'm framing this text.

Me: You're annoying.

Austin: come over.

Austin: pleeeeease.

Austin: we can study together.

Austin: or like ignore studying completely.

Austin: your choice.

I stare at his last message, chewing on my bottom lip. I shouldn't. I have a quiz tomorrow and two chapters left to write. But also… I really want to see him. I tell myself it's just for an hour. Just a break. Just to clear my head.

Me: Ok fine. I'll be there in five minutes

Austin: that's my girl.

I shove my notes into a pile, tuck my highlighters into my pencil case, and zip everything up. I slip my phone into my pocket, put my earbuds in, grab my keys, and head out.

The walk to his house is short, but by the time I'm halfway there, I've second-guessed myself at least three times. Should I have changed out of this hoodie and worn something better? I probably look exhausted. I *am* exhausted, and definitely don't look my best. But I just want to see him.

I tug my earbuds out when I reach his house, and the front door swings open before I even knock.

Austin steps out and grins the second he sees me, lazy and warm and so damn pretty it makes my knees weak.

Before I can say a word, he hooks an arm around my waist and kisses me.

His mouth moves over mine slowly, his tongue running along my bottom lip until I open up for him. It's a slow, confident kiss that makes my head spin. I kiss him back, sliding my arms around his neck, my fingers brushing the back of his hair where it's still damp from a shower.

God, I've missed him.

When he pulls away, he rests his forehead against mine. "Hi."

"Hi," I whisper back, slightly dazed.

"You're wearing my hoodie again," he says with a smirk, tugging the strings of the hoodie.

"I'm cold." Though right now I'm burning up with his hands on me.

"Uh uh," he says, shaking his head. "You're obsessed with me."

I roll my eyes but before I can say anything, he kisses me again, this time slower, and I feel it all the way down to my toes.

When he pulls away again, I think I actually whimper.

He hooks his fingers through mine and pulls me inside. The door swings shut behind us with a thud that probably echoes through the entire house.

We barely make it a few steps into the living room before someone calls out.

"Hey, Mais," Nathan says around a mouthful of noodles.

I open my mouth to say hi back, but—

"Get your own girlfriend, Hayes," Austin cuts in.

Nathan raises a brow. "Relax. I was greeting her, not proposing."

Austin turns to me like Nathan doesn't exist. "Wanna go upstairs?"

"Please do," Nathan mutters, shoveling another bite of noodles into his mouth.

I snort under my breath, but let Austin pull me toward the stairs anyway, his grip still locked around mine like he's not risking letting go.

He doesn't say anything as we head up. Doesn't look back. Just leads me straight to his room.

He kicks the door shut and flops onto the bed and I let myself sink onto the edge of his bed.

"You okay?" he asks.

"Just tired," I say with a shrug.

"Wanna talk about it?"

I shake my head. "Not really."

He doesn't push. Just shifts closer and nudges my arm with his knee. "Cool. Then let's not. Wanna cuddle and ignore the world for a while?"

I blink at him.

He shrugs. "We could also make out. Whatever works."

I roll my eyes, but the moment he wraps his arm around me, I melt into him like I don't have four papers due and a thousand unread emails in my inbox. My cheek finds his chest, and I close my eyes as he presses a soft kiss to the top of my head.

This is dangerous. How easy it is to relax here. How good it feels to be held without needing to say anything.

"You've been pushing yourself too hard," he murmurs.

I sigh, my fingers curling in the hem of his T-shirt. "I have things to do."

He shifts under me until I'm looking up at him. His brows pinch, his eyes serious. "You can take a break, baby. You're like… the smartest person I know. You don't need to go this hard all the time."

I want to believe him.

I *do*.

But my self-worth is so tightly wrapped around how well I do in school, how good I am at being good, it's hard to let that go. Being the smart one, the responsible one—that's who I *am*.

"I'm taking one now, aren't I?" I say quietly.

He chuckles, low and warm. "You're the only person I know who has to schedule being a girlfriend."

My gaze flicks up. I bite my lip—mostly to stop the smile trying to tug at my mouth.

He notices.

Of course he notices.

His eyes drop to my lips, and then his thumb is there, dragging slowly across them like he's trying to memorize the shape.

"What's up, baby?" he asks, voice all soft edges now.

"You called me your girlfriend."

His lips twitch into a smirk. "You *are* my girlfriend."

My face heats instantly. "You never actually asked."

He stares at me for a beat, then laughs, his head falling back against the pillow. "Oh my God, you're right. What a scandal. Should I draft a formal letter? Deliver it via pigeon?"

I give him a look. "You're insufferable."

He shoots me a look. "Maisie."

"Yeah?"

"I like you." He cups my face with both hands. "Like a lot. Will you be my girlfriend or do I need to get down on one knee and make it weird?"

He starts to lift himself, but I laugh and grab his hoodie. "Please don't."

"Good," he says, flopping back beside me with a groan. "Because my knee cracks every time I bend it."

"You're twenty-one."

"I'm fragile."

He rolls toward me again, nosing into the crook of my neck like he's been starved for this. His arm slides around my waist, tugs me closer.

"God, I missed you."

I can't help but smile. "You saw me yesterday."

"Exactly. It's been way too long."

His thumb strokes the dip of my waist through my sweatshirt. And even though we're fully clothed, my body knows exactly what his is doing. *Exactly* where he is. I feel every brush of his fingertips like a spark down my spine.

My hand moves without thinking. I drag my fingers across his chest, right where the fabric of his hoodie dips at the collar, revealing the edge of warm skin and muscle. He shifts slightly, sucking in a breath, like even that small touch gets to him.

One of his arms curls behind my back, pulling me in. The other hand slides up, brushing along my jaw before cupping my cheek again.

Then his mouth finds mine, and I feel it all the way down my spine.

He groans into my mouth, and pulls back just enough to look at me. "Fuck," he mutters. "You taste like cherries."

I blink. "It's my lip balm."

He smirks, shaking his head as his thumb traces along my jaw. "That's fine by me. Cherry reigns supreme."

I freeze.

He doesn't notice at first. His hand is still stroking over my hip, his mouth back at my neck, kissing a line just below my ear. But my brain has already spiraled into overdrive.

Because those words?

They aren't just words.

They're *his* words. *Six's*.

Stupid, jokey words that shouldn't mean anything. But they *do*. Because I remember the first time he said it, how my stomach swirled and how much I smiled.

I remember the way he used to say stupid things like that, turning nonsense into inside jokes. The way he made me laugh when I was having the worst week. How it felt easy with him, safe, even though I didn't know his real name or face or anything beyond his words.

And now Austin's here.

Warm. Real. Tangled up with me on his bed. And I'm thinking about someone else.

I suck in a quiet breath. He murmurs something against my skin—something I don't even catch—and all I can feel is the panic starting to creep up my throat.

This isn't fair to him.

I pull back a little, enough that he notices the shift. His arms don't fall away, but they tense. His eyes search mine.

"Austin?"

He stills completely.

His brow creases, like he already knows something's coming. "Yeah?"

I hesitate, biting down on the inside of my cheek until I taste blood.

"I have to tell you something."

He lets out a breathy laugh that's nowhere near amused. "Oh. Okay. Cool. These words are never terrifying or anything." He lifts his eyebrows, half-sitting up now. "Please don't tell me I already fucked up the boyfriend thing. I'll do anything. Swear to God. I'll even learn to bake."

That makes me smile, even though it shouldn't.

I reach for his hand, lacing our fingers together even though I know what I'm about to say might screw everything up. But I have to say it.

Because I like him.

Too much.

And he deserves to know the truth.

"You've done nothing wrong."

I reach up, brushing my fingers through his stupid, messy hair, pushing it back from his forehead. He's still got that half-smirk like he's expecting me to tease him again—but it drops when he sees my face.

"I just… I want to tell you about something," I murmur. "Or someone."

His expression sobers a little. "Okay."

"I'm telling you because I trust you, and I don't want to hide anything from you."

Austin nods slowly, his hand sliding down to rest on my thigh. He doesn't speak, just waits.

"Remember when I said I had a crush before?" I ask quietly, my gaze on his collarbone because looking him in the eyes right now might make me chicken out. "It wasn't someone from class. Or school. It was this guy I was texting."

Austin's hand stills. Completely. I feel his gaze flicker across my face.

"I didn't even know his name," I continue. "We met completely by accident. I sent a text to the wrong number. He replied. And we just… kept talking."

Austin keeps his eyes on me, and I just wish I knew what he was thinking.

"We talked for weeks," I say, my voice wobbling a little. "I don't even know how it happened. It just did," I admit with a shrug. "It was so easy. He made me laugh and he made me feel… seen, I guess."

I finally look up.

"And then I met you," I say, my heart thudding against my chest. "And I really, *really* liked you. Even though you annoyed the hell out of me sometimes."

His mouth twitches. "Only sometimes?"

I narrow my eyes. "I'm trying to tell you something here."

"Sorry, baby. Continue." His thumb starts moving again, slow circles on the inside of my knee.

"I told him we couldn't talk anymore a few weeks ago," I admit. "Once I started to have feelings for you, it didn't feel right. But he was still my friend. The only one I had for a while. And I guess…" I pause, my throat tightening. "I guess I still miss him sometimes. That's all."

There's a long pause. He's looking at me again, not saying anything, and I hate how unsure I suddenly feel.

But then he leans in. His hand comes up to cup my cheek, and he brushes his thumb over my cheekbone. "I'm sure he misses you too," he murmurs. "He'd be an idiot not to."

I was so worried to tell him about Six. I'd been dreading this conversation for days. Rehearsing it. Bracing myself for the way he'd maybe pull back, or tense up, or act weird.

But of course he's understanding.

But he didn't.

And the pressure in my chest builds—louder now, heavier. Like my heart's trying to tell me something I'm not ready to hear.

I blink up at him. He's so close, still holding my face, his thumb moving so gently across my cheek it makes my breath catch.

So I lift up and press my lips to his.

He kisses me back immediately, groaning low in his throat, and the sound shoots straight down my spine.

His hand slides into my hair, the other one gripping low on my waist as he shifts and rolls on top of me.

His knee presses between my thighs, right against the seam of my leggings, and I arch up without thinking, chasing the friction, chasing him.

I moan into his mouth when it hits just right, my fingers clinging to the hem of his T-shirt, and he groans again.

The kiss turns messier. Hotter. Tongue and teeth and breathless noise. His hips rock down, just once, and I gasp.

He slides his hand up my side, slipping beneath my hoodie, dragging the fabric higher and higher until cool air hits my bare skin. My breath stutters, catching in my throat.

His thumb moves slow, rubbing circles over the thin fabric of my bra, and I gasp into his mouth.

But then he pulls back. Groaning, breathing hard, shaking his head. "Fuck," he mutters, resting his forehead against mine. "This isn't why I called you over."

I grab a fistful of his hoodie and tug him back toward me. "It's okay," I whisper. "I want you to."

He blinks. Shakes his head a little like he's still not sure if he's dreaming. "You sure?"

I nod, then take his hand—still resting high on my ribs— and guide it back up. Over my breast again. "Please."

He groans loudly. "Don't beg me," he murmurs, his hips pressing down against mine. His head dips to my neck, mouth brushing over my throat. "You don't know what the fuck that does to me. Looking at me with those big eyes of yours, begging... *Jesus*, Maisie."

My cheeks are on fire. I've never done this before. Never been this bold. Never begged anyone for anything. But with him?

It's easy.

It's terrifyingly easy.

His hand moves again, slower this time. Almost like he's savoring it. His thumb grazes the lace edge of my bra, then slides higher, right over my nipple.

The hoodie's bunched at my ribs now, and I don't care. I want it off. I want all of it off.

I need him to touch me. I need to feel his body against mine. I need *him*.

I curl my fingers into his back, dragging him closer, until I can feel every line of muscle pressed into me and look into his eyes.

"I want you inside me."

THIRTY-FOUR

Austin

*F*uck.

Did she really just say that?

I glance down at her, watching for any sign that this is a dream, but all I see in her eyes is pure want.

"Please, Austin," she says again, confirming that, yep—I didn't make it up. "I want this. I want you."

Her voice doesn't crack or tremble. It melts, soft and breathy. My fingers are still in her hair, frozen like the rest of me, and my heart's hammering against my chest.

Maisie looks up, her eyes flickering with something that resembles a mixture of nerves and desire. She's breathing faster, harder. I don't think she even knows it.

"Maisie…" Her name scrapes out of my throat like gravel.

I'm trying to keep it cool, like I'm not short-circuiting inside, but fuck. This isn't how I saw tonight going. I thought we'd have a movie night, maybe make out a little, and I'd keep my dick in my pants and my hands above her waist like a gentleman. Not… this.

"We don't have to rush," I say, holding her gaze, hoping she hears how serious I am. "I'm fine with just kissing. Or cuddling. Or—*fuck*, Maisie—whatever you want."

She swallows hard and her fingers twist into my hoodie, searching my eyes. "Don't you want me?" she whispers, furrowing her brows.

Fuck me, the way she says it, barely audible, like it scares her to ask. Her teeth catch her bottom lip, and I swear I see a flicker of fear that I might say no.

I run a hand through my hair and exhale hard, trying not to just yank her against me and kiss the living daylights out of her. "You have no *idea* how much."

That earns me a soft smile. Her breath tickles my cheek when she speaks again. "Then have me," she breathes against my mouth.

The moment our lips meet, all my hesitations fall apart, because she's not doing this because she thinks I want it. She wants this. She wants me.

And I want this girl. I want her so damn bad I ache with it.

I pull back to look at her again, trying to memorize her exactly as she is right now. Hair mussed. Lips kiss-swollen. Cheeks burning.

"You really want it to be me?" My voice comes out lower than I expect as I try to swallow the nerves crawling up my throat.

Her eyes soften—those ridiculously gorgeous eyes—and she nods. Her hand comes up, warm against my jaw, her thumb brushing over my skin.

"I couldn't imagine someone better."

And just like that, I'm done for. Because *holy shit*—out of every guy she could've picked, she wants me. I don't know whether to kiss her or ask if she's sure one more time just so I can hear her say it again.

I drag my knuckles down her cheek, then lower, to the hem of her hoodie. I hook my fingers in and pull it up inch by inch, slow enough to give her time to change her mind. She doesn't. Her arms lift. Her shirt comes off, and underneath she's in a white bra that probably wasn't meant to be sexy but looks like sin against her skin.

"Jesus," I breathe, kissing the strip of skin just above her waistband. Her stomach is soft under my mouth, and she exhales sharply when I trail my lips along the curve of her hip. My hands explore, gliding under the fabric of her bra to cup her breasts gently. They fit perfectly in my palms, warm and full and firm.

I find the clasp and undo it gently, easing the straps off her shoulders. She watches me the whole time.

The bra drops, and suddenly I'm staring at her. Bare. Vulnerable. Fucking stunning.

I shake my head, the words swallowed up by the sight of her bare beneath me. "I want you so fucking bad," I start, my voice shaky. "But I'll go as slow as you need," I assure her. "Tell me if you want me to stop." My voice is rough with how much I crave her. "At any time. You say the word, and I'm done."

She nods, breathing hard. "I trust you."

I groan as I lean back down, kissing down her chest, dragging my tongue in slow circles over one nipple while my thumb teases the other. She gasps, her fingers tightening in my hair, and arches into me, her mouth falling open in a breathy moan. "Ahh. Austin…"

My name on her lips, like that? Jesus.

I wrap my arms around her and pull her close. Her skin is like silk, trembling slightly.

"You're so fucking gorgeous," I whisper as I kiss her again, guiding her gently down onto the bed.

Don't rush. I remind myself. *Don't fuck this up. She's everything.*

I run my fingers along the edge, and her breath catches.

I pause for a second, wondering if she wants to stop, but she signals for me to keep going. I peel her leggings down slowly, revealing white cotton panties stretched snug across curves that make my mouth water.

She buries her face in her hands, and lets out a soft groan. It's the most goddamn adorable thing I've ever seen.

"Don't hide from me," I tell her, slowly peeling her hands away so she's looking at me. "You're beautiful, Mais. I've never seen anything so beautiful before in my life."

Her lashes flutter as she looks up. "I'm nervous," she admits.

My lips curve into a slow smile, and I rub my thumb along the edge of her thigh. "Open your legs for me, baby."

She flushes deeper, and my cock throbs. Her breath shudders out, but she spreads her legs for me slowly.

I lean back for a second, just to take her in. The soft swell of her stomach, the curve of her thighs, the way her cheeks are pink and her chest is rising fast. Every inch of her makes me fucking ache.

My hands slide over her hips, running over the soft skin of her stomach, feeling the faint ridges under my palms.

She goes stiff. "Don't," she whispers, her eyes darting away. "Don't look at those. They're… ugly."

I freeze, because… what the hell? My chest actually aches hearing that. "Ugly?" I shake my head, leaning down before she can argue. "Maisie…" I kiss one, then another. "These are so fucking beautiful."

She lets out a shaky breath, like she doesn't buy it.

I glance up at her. "God, baby… you have no idea what you do to me." Another kiss, lower this time. "I love every inch of you. Every single one."

Her breath hitches, and I feel her start to relax under me, her eyes softening.

I smile against her skin because she's letting me in and I press another kiss to her belly. "You're perfect to me," I whisper against her skin.

I settle between her thighs, kissing the inside of one, then the other, tracing lazy paths with my mouth. She shivers underneath me, and I lick my lips, my tongue tracing slow lines up her skin, inching closer to where I want to be.

I press a kiss to the softest spot, right at her center, through the cotton and she lets out the sweetest gasp.

I groan against her soaked panties, and hook my fingers under them, sliding them down, slow as hell, revealing her pussy glistening with arousal. She's so wet she's shining and I'm dying for a taste.

I tug her panties off and press a soft kiss to her pussy which she gasps at.

"What… what are you doing?" she asks, breathlessly.

"Getting you ready for me," I murmur, licking slowly up her slit. "I need you wet and relaxed if you're going to take my cock inside this pretty pussy."

She moans, her fingers tangling in my hair, pulling me closer, and I lose myself in the sounds she makes.

"You gonna let me make you feel good?" I hum against her, flicking the tip of my tongue right over her sensitive clit. "Hmm?"

"Yes," she moans, tipping her head back as I devour her pussy.

"Goddamn," I grunt against her skin. "You taste so sweet." I wrap my lips around her clit sucking as I push my finger inside her slick warmth, feeling her flutter tight around me.

She trembles, rocking her hips, and I dive deeper, soaking in every moan, every shiver.

I lift my head when she moans loudly, my eyes dark with need. "Tell me if it's too much."

She shakes her head, letting out a soft whimper that makes my cock twitch in my sweatpants. "Don't stop."

Grinning, I run my fingers along her slit. "God, you're so wet for me."

She bites her lip but a moan escapes her anyway. Her hips jerk, her thick, gorgeous thighs clench around my head, and I groan into her. My tongue circles her clit and I lap at her until her fingers claw at my scalp.

She's shaking, moaning, and I have no doubt my teammates can hear her, but I'd rather cut my left nut off than tell her to be quiet right now. I fucking love her moans. I love how needy she is for me.

"Austin. Oh god."

I slide a second finger inside her, feeling her walls pulse tight and slick around me. She cries out, tipping her head back.

Fuck me. Those noises will be the death of me.

"You're doing so good, Maisie," I whisper, licking her again, curling my fingers inside her just right. "Taste so sweet. So fucking pretty…"

Her legs are trembling around me, and she's panting, her moans coming out in short, choppy breaths. "I—I think I'm gonna—"

"Let go," I murmur against her, sucking her clit into my mouth. "Come for me, baby."

She explodes with a choked cry, her legs clamping around my head as she comes hard, trembling and gasping my name.

I kiss her thigh as she rides it out, then her stomach, and crawl back up, cradling her face in my hands.

Her eyes are dazed and her lips are slightly parted. She's so goddamn beautiful.

"Still good?" I ask, brushing hair from her face.

She nods, licking her pink lips. "I want more," she whispers.

I quickly strip off my shirt and yank my sweats and boxers down, my cock aching so hard I feel like I'm about to burst. I fumble through the nightstand for the box of condoms I haven't touched in months, tear one open, and roll it on with shaking hands.

She lies beneath me, her legs splayed wide on my bed, revealing her dripping wet pussy I'm dying to be inside. My chest is tight with how much I fucking want to make this good for her.

I stroke her cheek, leaning over her. "You okay, baby?"

She nods, but it's shaky. "Yeah," she whispers. "Just… a little nervous."

"I know." I kiss her forehead, then her nose, then linger at her lips. "You tell me everything, okay? If something doesn't feel good, if you wanna stop. Anything."

"I will," she says, her voice so soft it trembles. She swallows, her eyes fluttering closed, then opens them again. "Just… go slow?"

I nod. "I'll be slow. As slow as you need."

I reach between us, guiding myself to her entrance, the tip of my cock pressing against her heat.

I nudge forward just barely, teasing both her and myself, watching the way her breath catches.

"Just the tip," I whisper, my voice breaking as I start to push inside her.

She gasps, her hands flying to my arms, clutching hard as I slide in that first inch.

"A-Austin—" she whimpers, brows drawn tight, her legs tensing.

I stop right there, breathing hard, shaking from holding myself back. "You're doing so good," I whisper, kissing her mouth, her throat, her chest. "Breathe for me."

She inhales, then lets it out slowly, and I press in a little more. Her walls clamp around me so tight, so warm and slick I have to grit my teeth not to lose it.

She moans softly. "You're big."

"I'll go slow," I assure her.

I ease another inch inside and she gasps at the fullness. "More," she breathes, lifting her hips. "A little more…"

God help me.

I push deeper, slow, careful, trying to keep it together—but she's too wet, too perfect, her thighs quivering around my waist as I sink farther into heaven.

"Jesus," I groan, hands shaking as I brace above her. "I— *fuck*, baby."

Her fingers lace behind my neck, pulling me down, her mouth pressed against mine. "Austin."

I'm barely inside her, maybe halfway, and I already feel like I'm gonna lose it. My control's hanging by a thread—frayed, burning.

I breathe hard, my forehead dropping to hers. "You're so tight," I rasp. "Feel so good."

I ease in another inch, feeling every tight pull of her body, every flutter as she opens around me. She gasps, her pussy clenching around me, and I pause again, forcing myself not to shove all the way in.

"Oh, Christ," I grit out, eyes squeezed shut. "I'm sorry, baby… I can't stop. Tell me to pull out and I'll do it—I swear—"

She shakes her head immediately, her hands flying to my face, cupping my face. "No. Don't. I don't want you to stop."

And just like that, I lose the battle. Slowly—agonizingly slowly—I push the rest of the way in, groaning as her body takes me inch by inch.

She cries out, her breath hitching, her legs shaking as I fill her completely until I bottom out.

"Holy fuck," I groan, my chest pressed to hers. "You feel fucking perfect." I glance down at her, breathless from how fucking good she feels. "Are you okay?"

She nods, eyes glazed over. "It's… full. But I'm okay."

I kiss her slowly, both of us trembling. I don't move yet. I just hold her there, letting her feel me inside her, letting her body adjust to the stretch.

Her fingers slide up my back, then she moves her hips, urging me deeper inside her. "You can move now," she breathes. "You feel good."

I pull out just an inch, then press back in, slow and steady, watching her mouth open in a loud moan.

"Fuck," I groan, gripping the sheets beside her head. "You feel like heaven, Maisie."

Her body is still tense but slowly softening underneath mine as the pain gives way to pleasure.

She clings to me, wrapping her arms around my neck, her legs around my waist, drawing me in.

"You're doing so good," I whisper against her lips. "You're perfect. So fucking perfect."

I move a little deeper, a little faster, her hips rocking into mine as her gasps turn into moans, her shy little sounds spurring me on.

"Ahhh. You feel so good, Austin."

"Yeah?" I murmur, kissing her throat. "You like that?"

"Mmhmm," she whimpers, clutching me tighter. "More…"

And I give her more. Still slow, still careful, but with more pressure, more rhythm, letting her feel it, letting her ride it.

I'm deep inside her, buried to the hilt, and everything in me is straining not to fall apart. Her walls grip me tight, warm and slick and pulsing like her whole body is wrapped around mine, and I've never felt anything like it. Never even imagined anything could feel this good.

Every slow thrust pulls a soft moan from her lips, and fuck—those sounds. Sweet and high, like she's trying to hold them back but can't. Her thighs hug my waist, trembling, and her fingers are tangled in my hair, tugging when I rock into her just right.

I kiss her neck, tasting sweat and skin.

"Austin," she whimpers, her breath stuttering.

"Yeah, baby?" I murmur, lifting my head to look at her.

"I—I think I'm close," she whispers, pinning her bottom lip between her teeth.

Fuck.

My hips falter for half a second, then drive back in slow and deep, and I feel her flutter around me. "I can feel you," I groan. "Jesus, Mais… you're squeezing me so fucking tight."

Her body's straining under mine, her breath catching every time I bottom out inside her. My brain's barely functioning, but I want to be the reason she comes. I want her to fall apart with me still inside her, kissing her through it, holding her like she's the only fucking thing in the world that matters.

"Let go, baby," I murmur against her lips, fucking her slow and deep. "I want to feel you coming around my cock."

Her back arches off the bed, hips jerking up into mine, mouth falling open on a sharp cry as she comes hard around me, her pussy clenching around my cock so hard I nearly lose it.

"Oh fuck—Maisie—" I groan, losing control, my hips snapping once, twice more before it hits me too.

I come with a rough gasp, my forehead pressed to hers as I empty into the condom, my whole body jerking with the release. My muscles lock, then melt, pleasure hitting me so deep it feels like my chest could cave in.

"Holy fuck," I whisper against her lips, still inside her, still reeling from the mind-blowing orgasm.

She breathes hard, nuzzling her face into my neck, her breath hot on my skin. "That was—"

"Incredible," I finish for her, pressing my lips to hers. I brush her hair away from her face, staring into those eyes I'm so deeply in love with. "Thank you for trusting me."

She looks up at me, the corners of her mouth twitching into a smile, like she can't believe it just happened. "I'm happy it was you."

Fuck me, so am I.

I lean in and kiss her slow, my hands smoothing over her sides, wanting to show her how much this meant to me, how much *she* means to me.

I don't pull out yet. I don't want to. I just stay inside her, letting our heartbeats slow together, my body wrapped around hers like I never want to be anywhere else.

Because I don't.

Not after that.

Not ever again.

THIRTY-FIVE

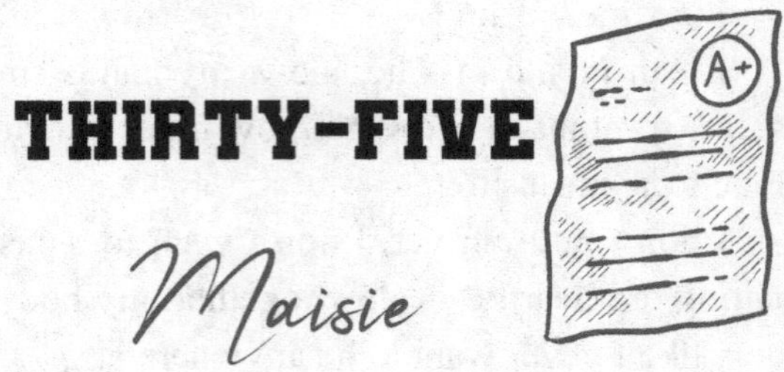

Maisie

I wake up to the feel of sunlight on my cheek and the weight of his arm slung heavy over my waist.

His chest pressed to my back, one of his legs tangled with mine like he couldn't bear to stop touching me, even in sleep. I turn my head just enough to look at him. His face is soft and peaceful in a way it never is when he's awake. His mouth is parted slightly, his lashes brushing his cheek, and I can't help but smile.

And I'm still floating over what happened last night, wrapped in the hazy glow of everything he whispered, everything we did, everything I felt. I didn't think I could have something like that.

I let my eyes fall closed again and smile softly into the pillow, feeling… full. Like a piece of me I didn't even know was missing has finally clicked into place.

I feel him stir and glance up at him. "Mm," he mumbles, his voice rough with sleep. "You're still here."

I arch a brow and chuckle. "Good morning to you too."

Austin nuzzles into my hair. "Didn't mean it like that. Just… happy."

His hand squeezes my waist and he shifts closer, pressing his body firmly against mine. I can feel the unmistakable weight of him against my lower stomach.

He groans softly and kisses my shoulder. "Sorry," he mumbles. "Morning wood. Science. I can't control it."

I laugh, still half-asleep and completely drunk on him. "It's okay."

He kisses my shoulder again, softer this time. "You sore?"

"A little," I admit, voice barely a whisper.

He pulls back just enough to meet my eyes. "Too much?"

"No," I say quickly. "Just… new."

He studies me for a long moment, eyes gentle. His thumb strokes slow circles over my side. "You're okay, though?"

I nod, throat tight. "Yeah."

"Okay." He leans down and kisses me, slow and warm. "If you want me to shut up about it, I will. I just… I care about you."

"I know," I reply, unable to stop smiling.

He tugs me onto my back and props himself over me with one arm, the sheet slipping dangerously low on his hips. "Can I kiss you some more?"

I nod, my heart doing somersaults as he leans down and presses his lips to mine.

His mouth moves lazily over mine. I curl my fingers in the back of his neck, letting myself melt into the bed, into him, into this feeling I never thought I'd get to have.

His hand slides up under the sheet, skating over my hip, my waist, the dip just under my ribcage. My skin tingles everywhere he touches.

He groans against my mouth. "You're gonna kill me, Maisie."

"You said that last night," I tease.

"I meant it then too." He kisses the corner of my mouth, then the line of my jaw. "I need a shower or I'm gonna do something very stupid."

"Is it stupid if I want it too?" I ask him, tugging my bottom lip between my teeth.

He groans, his eyes locked on mine. "Don't say that unless you mean it."

I smile a little. "I mean it."

He kisses me again, lingering, then rolls off the bed and heads for the bathroom. "Don't move," he says over his shoulder. "I'm taking you out after this."

My heart stumbles and I sit up, pulling the sheet over my naked chest. "What?"

"A date, Maisie." He glances back at me and smirks. "Try to keep up, baby. I'm doing this boyfriend thing right."

He flashes me a wink before disappearing into the bathroom, and I hear the shower start a second later. I flop back onto the bed, my cheeks aching from smiling so much.

A date.

Just a few months ago, I had absolutely no one, just an anonymous number on my phone, a stranger who somehow got me through the nights I felt completely alone.

And now…

Now I have two best friends who show up for me without me having to ask. I have a group chat that actually makes me laugh. I have people who *want* me around.

I have him.

My eyes flick toward my phone on the nightstand. I reach for it, scrolling out of habit, and see a text from Isabella.

Isabella: Want to grab coffee before practice?

I smile a little as I type back, but my thumb hesitates before I close out. Because right above our chat, I see his name.

Six.

I haven't clicked it in weeks. But now my finger hovers—and then taps.

The thread opens, and there they are. All the old messages. The late-night jokes, the gentle check-ins, the way he always knew how to talk me down when I was spiraling. My chest tightens.

He never replied to that last text I sent.

Which makes sense. I asked him not to.

It was the right thing. The healthy thing. But staring at the empty screen now, all I can think about is how *not* empty it used to feel.

He saw me. Long before anyone else did.

And yeah, maybe we were just words on a screen. But those words kept me company when nothing else did. They gave me something to look forward to. They helped me hang on.

I swallow hard, pressing the phone to my chest for a second before locking it.

I don't regret choosing Austin. Not for a second.

But a small part of me still misses the boy who helped me feel a little less invisible.

So I type out a message.

Me: I don't know if you'll ever read this, but I wanted to say thank you for every message. Every confession. You helped me more than you know. I miss talking to you, but I understand why you haven't replied. I just wanted to tell you that… I met someone. His name is Austin, and I'm really happy. I think you'd like him.

Send.

The second my thumb taps the screen, something shifts. I exhale slowly, like I've just let go of something I didn't realize I'd been holding onto.

I set the phone down beside me on the bed and sink back into Austin's pillows. My cheeks ache from smiling.

And then, out of the corner of my eye, something glows, and I glance over.

Austin's phone lights up on his nightstand, and I almost don't think anything of it.

Until I see the preview.

And my whole body stills.

It's my message. The one I sent not even thirty seconds ago. Still glowing on *his* screen.

My heart stops.

No.

No no no no—

I sit up, heart hammering in my chest.

That can't be right. That *can't* be right.

I sit up too fast, sheet clutched to my chest, heart thudding. Maybe it's a glitch. A shared contact name. Something— *anything*—that isn't what I think it is.

But when I get up and walk across the room, I see it again. I just stand there and stare at the screen like it might blink away and tell me I imagined it.

It's not—

It can't be—

But it is.

Cherry.

Right there. Clear as day.

There's no mistake.

The contact name. My words. The timestamp.

And just like that, everything tilts sideways.

The world. My stomach. My brain.

Because this entire time—every message, every night, every stupid inside joke—I thought it was someone else. Some faceless stranger who somehow got me when no one else did.

But it wasn't a stranger.

It was *Austin*.

Austin is Six.

And he knew.

He knew *exactly* who I was the whole time.

THIRTY-SIX

Austin

I'm whistling.

Like actually whistling.

In the shower. With shampoo in my hair and soap in my eyes and not a single goddamn care in the world.

It's embarrassing, honestly. But I don't even care. I'm so happy. Never been happier in my life.

I rinse the shampoo out of my hair, letting the water fall down on my shoulders. Everything aches in the best possible way. My back, my legs, my fucking jaw. I smile into the spray, trying not to think about how she sounded when she whispered my name. Or how she looked naked in my bed. Or the way she touched me like she was learning me from scratch, and liking every part she discovered.

My brain's a highlight reel and every second of it is her.

Her thighs tightening around my hips. Her lips parting when I kissed the inside of her knee. The quiet little *please* that slipped out of her mouth.

I lean forward, pressing my forehead against the shower wall, grinning.

For a guy who's fucked up a lot of things, I want this to be the one thing I do right.

I turn off the water, towel off, and run my fingers through my hair. All I can think about is crawling back into bed, curling my arms around her, and kissing every inch of her.

I wrap the towel around my waist and step into my room with a grin.

Except she's not there.

The bed's still messy, my sheets rumpled, her shape pressed into the pillow, but she's gone.

"Mais?" I call out, rubbing the back of my neck with the towel.

Nothing.

Okay. Maybe she went to the kitchen. Or to our downstairs bathroom.

Except… her sweater's not here either.

Neither is her bra. Or her leggings. No shoes by the door. Her phone's gone from the nightstand.

My stomach tightens, an ache blooming low and slow in my chest.

I grab my own phone off the desk, my hands already clammy, and that's when I see it.

One new message.

Cherry.

My heart stutters. I open it and as I read, every muscle in my body locks.

I drop down onto my bed, my towel slipping, water still dripping from my hair.

Fuck.

She knows.

She figured it out.

She sent me that message thinking she was talking to Six and watched it light up on my phone. Saw her own words flash on my screen and put the pieces together.

And now she's gone, because she thinks I lied to her. Used her. Played her or whatever twisted story she's telling herself.

Because I didn't tell her. I just let her keep talking, keep opening up, keep trusting me, even after she sat right in front of me and told me about Six.

She told me everything about *him*—about *me*—and I didn't say a goddamn word.

I scramble to get dressed, my stomach sinking like a stone. The jeans from last night, a hoodie thrown over, my fingers fumbling to type even though my vision's blurred.

Me: I'm so fucking sorry. Please talk to me.

No read receipt.

Me: I didn't mean to keep it from you. I was going to tell you. I swear. I just—

I stop. My fingers hover over the screen.

What the hell do I even say?

That I got scared? That I fell for her twice—once through a screen, and then again in person—and I didn't know how to make those versions line up?

None of it feels like enough.

But I need to fix this somehow before it's too late.

I grab my keys, yank on some sneakers, and race down the stairs.

Ryan lifts his head from his cereal bowl when he sees me. "Hey, where are you—"

I don't even stop to answer him before bolting out the door.

I won't let her walk away thinking any of this wasn't real.

Not when it's the realest damn thing I've ever had.

———❤———

At first, I think she's not going to open the door. She'll tell me to go to hell, that she doesn't want to see me, and I'll sit on the dirty carpet flooring outside her dorm, because I don't want to be anywhere that she isn't. Because I want to talk this out. Because I want her.

But when she doesn't reply, I breathe out a sigh and knock again. "Come on, Maisie. Please. Just… let me talk to you."

A few seconds later, the door swings open and my heart fucking stops.

She's standing there in an oversized hoodie—mine, I think—with the sleeves shoved up her forearms like she was fidgeting. Her hair's twisted up in a messy bun, loose strands falling over her face. And her eyes—Jesus. Red and puffy. Like she's been crying for hours. Like maybe she hasn't stopped.

It hits me straight in the chest. Hard enough to knock the breath out of me.

Because I did that.

I made her look like this.

And the worst part? I didn't even mean to. Didn't know I could.

She just stares at me. Like she's trying to decide if she wants to slam the door in my face.

"What are you doing here?" she asks finally.

Not angry. Not cold. Just… tired. Like she's hanging on by a thread and praying I don't cut it.

I clear my throat, trying to slow my pulse down. It's still racing from running over here. From the way my stomach bottomed out when her name popped up on my phone and I realized exactly what she saw. What she knows now.

"You know why I'm here." My voice sounds like it got dragged through gravel.

She crosses her arms over her chest. "You're Six."

The words slice clean through me.

I nod. Can't even pretend otherwise. I've imagined this moment a hundred times. The first time I'd meet Cherry, finally see her face, hear her say my name. I just never imagined it would hurt this much.

"And you're Cherry," I say quietly.

She flinches, eyes squeezing shut, like the words hurt more than she expected. Maybe they do. Maybe hearing it aloud makes everything so much more real.

I take a cautious step forward.

She steps back.

Fuck.

"You let me tell you about yourself," she says, voice fragile, eyes glued to the floor.

I nod, swallowing the lump in my throat.

"You let me miss you," she adds, still avoiding my gaze. "And you just… said nothing."

My fingers twitch at my sides, desperate to do something.

"I didn't know how," I admit, my voice rough, like it's scraping its way out.

"That's not an excuse."

"I know."

Because what the hell else can I say?

She's not wrong.

And there's no excuse good enough to make this okay.

Silence spreads between us and my eyes lift to a few loose strands of hair, curling around her face, and all I want—so fucking bad—is to reach out and tuck them behind her ear. Just touch her. Let her know I'm here. I'm not leaving.

But I don't move.

Because right now, she looks like if I get too close, she'll break.

She shakes her head and takes another step back.

"Talk to me, Freckles," I whisper, the nickname slipping out before I can stop it. "Please."

"How…" she starts, then falters. Blinks rapidly, swallows hard. "How do I know this is real?"

Her question hits me like a punch.

"What?"

She finally looks up, just for a moment, just enough to steal my breath away.

"How do I know you didn't fall for Cherry… and then settle for me when you found out it was me?" she whispers.

Her voice is small, shattered, like those words are ripping themselves free.

"How do I know this isn't just some obligation? Because you felt sorry for me. Because you knew things about me I never told anyone else."

I blink, stunned into silence as a sharp ache spreads through my chest because there it is—the thing she's always been afraid of, even when she smiled, kissed me back, and let me in. It's not just about me keeping a secret; it's the fear that she's not enough, that no one could truly want her if they saw the real her. That the only way I could love her was if I loved the idea of her first.

I step forward again. "Maisie," I call out, but she won't meet my eyes.

"Hey," I say gently, "look at me."

Slowly, she lifts her head, and fuck, she looks heartbreakingly fragile—pink, tear-rimmed eyes and blotchy cheeks—and yet, she's still the most beautiful thing I've ever seen.

My chest tightens like it's being crushed, and I wonder how she can't see what she means to me, how she can't know what she does to me.

"I didn't know," I whisper. "Not until after the championship."

Her brows furrow in confusion, so I explain.

"Isabella told me you liked someone else at the afterparty, and honestly, I saw red. I was jealous as hell, Maisie. I didn't even understand why at first. It just felt like someone had kicked a hole right through my chest."

She keeps staring, frozen.

"And then she told me the name," I say quietly. "My name."

Maisie's arms drop to her sides, fingers twitching like she's trying to figure out what to do with them. Her whole body goes still, except her eyes, wide and glossy, fragile like they're about to shatter.

"I fell for you twice," I tell her, stepping closer, close enough that I could reach for her if she let me. "Once when you were just an anonymous name on a screen. The person who made me laugh when everything felt like shit, who saw me when no one else did."

I swallow hard. "And the second time…" My voice catches. "The second time was in the library. When you rolled your eyes at me, showed up to help me study, even though I was a dumbass who didn't deserve it."

She shakes her head, voice soft and raw. "You're not dumb."

A tear slips down her cheek, and without thinking, I reach out, pressing my lips against it, kissing it away.

"I should've told you the moment I figured it out," I say, cupping her face gently. "I know that. But I was scared. Scared I'd lose you. That I'd fuck it all up before I even had a chance to be yours."

I shake my head, desperate to get it all out. "But Maisie… finding out it was you? That you were Cherry? That was the best moment of my life."

She makes a soft, broken sound, and it punches straight through me.

"I was already falling for both of you. And then I realized… it was always you. Every message, every night I couldn't wait to talk, every secret, every late-night rant—it was all you."

She stares at me like she's afraid to believe it, like if she blinks, I'll disappear.

"Falling?" she repeats, voice barely above a whisper.

I smile, my heart pounding. "Yeah, baby. I'm so in love with you."

Her breath catches, lips trembling.

"I'm in love with you, Maisie Wilson," I say with absolute certainty. "Not Cherry. Not some perfect version behind a screen. Just you. The girl who makes spreadsheets for fun and still blushes when I tell her she's beautiful, the girl who skates like she was born for it, who gave me her time, her patience, her trust—even when I didn't deserve it."

My throat tightens, but I don't look away.

"I loved you before I even knew you were my Cherry. And I loved you even more after."

She blinks rapidly, her body trembling like she's holding too much inside and doesn't know where to put it.

"You're in love with me?" she whispers, barely daring to say it.

I grin, because I can't help myself. "That's all you caught?"

She lets out a broken laugh, and I lean in, pressing a soft kiss to her lips. Then another. I don't want to stop touching her. I won't.

"I love you," I say again. "I love you so much it physically hurts, Maisie."

Her eyes flutter closed. Then she leans in, our foreheads resting together, her breath shaky against my skin. "I love you too," she whispers.

I swear, nothing in my life has ever felt better than hearing those words come from her.

I know, without a doubt, I will never stop falling for her.

Not now. Not ever.

She steps back slowly, tugging my hand toward her bed. She turns, blinking up at me with those glassy blue eyes, and then leans in again, lips meeting mine.

"I meant it," I murmur against her lips. "Every word."

She nods, chin trembling. Her hands slip under the hem of my hoodie. She pulls, and I don't hesitate—I peel it off and toss it aside. She's on me again, lips, hands, body pressed tight like she's scared I'll vanish if she stops touching me.

"Hey," I murmur, pulling back just enough to catch her gaze. "We don't have to rush. I'm not going anywhere."

Her breath stutters. "I know. I just…"

She trails off, no need to say more. Because I feel it too—the ache to close the space between us, to feel everything again—us. And damn, I want that just as badly.

I guide her backward until the backs of her knees bump the edge of her bed. She sits without breaking eye contact, breathing a little faster now.

I drop to my knees in front of her, my hands sliding up the outsides of her thighs, feeling the faintest tremble in her legs.

She watches me as I reach for the hem of her shorts and slide them down her legs. She lifts her hips without being asked. Then I peel her top off next, revealing the soft curve of her stomach, the dip of her waist, and the prettiest tits I have ever seen in my life.

And I just stop and stare.

She's so fucking gorgeous it almost hurts to look at her. I get it now, why men used to carve women out of stone. It wasn't about art. It was about trying to hold onto something you knew you'd never deserve. Because when something is this beautiful, all you can do is try to preserve it. Witness it. Worship it. I could look at her forever and still never have enough.

Maisie blushes under the attention, her hands twitching like she wants to cover herself. But I shake my head and lean in, kissing the inside of her thigh. Then the other. Then the spot just below her belly button.

"You're beautiful," I murmur, and her breath hitches. I kiss my way up her body, starting at her soft belly, kissing every single one of her gorgeous stretch marks. "You're perfect," I whisper, trailing my lips over the slope of her ribs, up the underside of her breast, then pressing a soft kiss over her heart. "You're everything I ever wanted."

I lay her back on the bed, my hand cupping her cheek, and when I press my mouth to hers, it's soft and deep and full of everything I don't know how to say.

She wraps her arms around my shoulders, pulling me down with her, and I feel her shift under me, reaching for something in her nightstand.

She presses the foil packet into my hand without a word.

I pause just long enough to tear it open, my hands shaking a little as I roll it on.

And then I slide inside her in one slow thrust, and everything else falls away.

Her breath catches. Her eyes flutter closed. My forehead drops to hers and we both just breathe for a second. Just feel.

I've had plenty of sex before—more than I should probably admit. It was always fun. A little reckless. A hobby, if I'm being honest.

But this?

This isn't a hobby.

This is *holy*.

THIRTY-SEVEN

Maisie

He curses low and rough against my lips as he pulls out. His hand slides up to cup the back of my neck, his fingers threading through my hair as he kisses me softly through the orgasm. He groans softly as his hand bumps against a stuffed duck nestled in the sheets.

He pushes it aside, still catching his breath. "Sorry for the things you just saw, Mr. Quackers," he mutters, shaking his head.

I laugh quietly, reaching over to tuck the duck back beside me. "We totally traumatized him."

He leans in, brushing his lips against mine with a smirk. "Yeah, poor guy's gonna need therapy after this."

He rolls onto his side beside me, tugging me with him, our limbs tangled beneath the blanket. His arm wraps around my waist like a reflex, pulling me into his chest.

"I still can't believe it was you," I say, my thumb brushing over the pulse in his wrist.

His eyes flutter open. "You think I can believe it?"

I lift my head a little to meet his gaze. "But you knew," I whisper.

"Not at first. Only after Isabella told me the name of the guy you were talking to."

My heart stops for a second. "Your name."

He nods, squeezing my hand gently. "My name."

He brings our hands to his lips, kissing each knuckle slowly. One. Two. Three soft kisses.

"So," he murmurs, a crooked smile tugging at his mouth, "now that I know it's you… why Cherry?"

I groan and hide my face in the crook of his neck. "It's stupid."

He chuckles. "Try me."

"I panicked," I admit. "You asked me for my name, and I didn't know what to tell you. And I looked around my dorm and my eyes landed on my cherry Chapstick."

He chuckles, his chest shaking against mine.

"Shut up," I mumble, trying to bury myself under the blanket.

He drags it back down and shoots me a grin. "I love it. It's very you. Sweet, delicious, and the sexiest fruit ever."

I shoot him a look. "Don't act like yours was better. Six?"

"Mine was fucking excellent," he declares, puffing out his chest. "Six-string-guitar, baby."

I blink up at him. "Wow. I didn't even make the connection."

He chuckles, nudging his nose against mine. "I thought you were smarter than that, Freckles."

I roll my eyes. "You were the last person I thought it could be."

His laughter dies down as his hand slides up to cup my cheek. "Were you disappointed?" he asks. "To find out it was me."

I look at him for a long second and then shake my head. "No."

His eyes soften and his shoulders drop in relief.

"Six was—you—were there for me when no one else was. When I felt lonely, and had no one… I had you. But then I started to fall for you, and Six at the same time that…" I shake my head. "I started to feel guilty when things got serious between us, because I didn't want to let go of that connection we had, even if it was just through a screen."

His thumb brushes over my cheekbone and I glance up at him. "Finding out it was you was confusing and unexpected." He stiffens slightly at that. "But also the best moment of my life, because the two people I had fallen for were right here in front of me, and I didn't have to choose. I could have both." I lift my hand and place it on his chest, right over his heart. "I could have you."

He rubs his thumb over my cheek, leans in and kisses me. "I felt so fucking guilty," he whispers against my lips. "Because I wanted both of you. I wanted Cherry's words. And I wanted you. I didn't know they were the same person." He pulls back just enough to look me in the eyes. "I didn't know you were right fucking here." He cups my face, his fingers brushing just beneath my jaw. "You were right here," he repeats, like he still can't believe it.

He sighs, dragging his hand through his hair. "How the hell did I not notice you before?" he murmurs, mostly to himself.

I tug the blanket higher. "No one did. I was invisible."

He frowns, like it physically pains him to hear that.

"I should've noticed you," he says, a pained expression in his eyes. "I should've seen you. I should've dropped to my knees the second you walked into class Freshman year and begged you to love me."

My stomach flutters from his words.

He brushes a strand of hair off my cheek, his thumb lingering there. "You came out of the blue," he says, shaking his head. "I never could have seen you coming. You're the last thing I ever expected and the best." He smiles and the way he's looking at me makes the breath in my chest disappear. "You're everything I didn't know I wanted."

I blink fast, fighting the burn behind my eyes.

"Thank you," he says, and he says it like it's the most serious thing in the world, "for agreeing to tutor me."

I smile, feeling my lower lip wobble. "Thank you for loving me."

His smile widens. "Easiest thing I've done in my life."

We lie there for a minute, just holding each other, our legs tangled under the sheet, his hand resting over my ribs.

"Do you want to grab some breakfast?" he asks eventually.

"I wish," I say. "I have to go to the rink soon."

He groans. "Sectionals prep?"

"Yeah," I sigh. "Coach made me swap the footwork sequence again."

He pulls back a little, his thumb brushing over my hipbone. "Is your mom coming tomorrow?" he asks.

I freeze.

There's a heartbeat of silence. I could lie. I could say *maybe* or *I think so* or *she's trying*, but I don't. Something about the way he's watching me makes the truth crawl right out.

"No," I say. "She's not."

Austin's expression shifts, brows pulling together like he's trying to figure out how to fix it.

"I invite her every year," I say, keeping my eyes fixed on the edge of the blanket between us. I run my finger along the hem, over and over, needing something to hold onto. "Every single year. And she always has a reason not to come. She says she's busy, or the timing's bad, or she can't get away from work."

Austin shifts beside me. I feel the movement, but I don't look. I'm not ready for whatever's in his eyes.

"She hasn't been to any of them," I say quietly. "Not since I was a kid."

His mouth pulls into a soft frown, his thumb brushing my wrist where he's still holding my hand. "Maisie…"

"I'm fine," I say quickly. "I'm used to it."

But I'm not. Not really.

Because I still try. Every year. I still send the invites. I still text the details. I still check flights and hotel prices, just in case she changes her mind. I still make sure the venue isn't too far. I still stress about whether she'll hate the dress code, or think the music's too loud or the rink's too cold.

I try to make it easy for her to come. I still hope she'll show up.

But she never does.

I blink hard and my throat burns. I hate that it still gets to me.

Austin reaches for me, tugging me into his chest like he's done it a hundred times before. His arms wrap around me, one hand curling protectively at the back of my neck.

"I'm sorry, baby," he murmurs against my hair. "That fucking sucks."

I nod. A tear slips out anyway, and I'm glad he's holding me so tight I don't have to look at him.

"It's not a big deal," I mumble.

"It is a big deal," he says firmly.

He leans back just enough to tilt my chin up with his fingers, his eyes fierce and full of something that makes my chest ache.

"You're a fucking star on that ice, Maisie. And she's missing it."

That breaks something in me. My laugh cracks halfway through. "Stop saying nice things or I'm gonna cry."

He doesn't stop. Instead, he pulls me closer, wraps both arms around me again, and presses his face to my shoulder.

"I'll be there," he says, pressing his lips to my skin. "Front row. Screaming your name. Probably embarrassing the shit out of you."

I bury my face in his neck, smiling against the warmth of his skin. "You're gonna get kicked out."

"Worth it," he says, and I can feel his grin against my temple. "I'll be the loudest guy in the rink," he adds. "Recording everything. Blowing up the group chat. Hyping the hell out of you."

I pull back enough to give him a look. "Austin."

"What?" he says, looking way too pleased with himself. "It's important to show I'm there to support my girlfriend."

I breathe out a laugh. "You're deranged."

He just smirks. "And yet, you love me."

"Yeah," I say, my lips curving into a smile as I look into his soft hazel eyes. "I really do."

His whole face softens. He breaks out into a grin and his hand slips into my hair, and then he kisses me again, like he's saying it back without words.

And I swear I could drown in the way he touches me.

And I wouldn't even mind.

THIRTY-EIGHT

Austin

My heart hasn't stopped pounding since we parked. I'm trying to play it cool—really, I am—but I've stood up three times in the last five minutes just to sit back down again. Logan has already threatened to tape me to the bleachers if I don't chill out.

"Rhodes," he says, balancing a comically large coffee in one hand and elbowing me with the other. "You're gonna burn a hole through the rink with that stare."

"Can't help it," I mutter, fingers tapping out an anxious rhythm on my jeans. "She's skating today."

"Yeah, no shit," Ryan adds, seated beside me, his hoodie sleeves pulled over his hands. "We're all aware. You've said it—what—thirty-seven times?"

"Thirty-eight," Nathan deadpans from behind us.

Cole just folds his arms and stares ahead, his gum clicking between his teeth. "If you pass out, don't expect me to carry you."

"Not necessary," I say, brushing them off. But honestly, I'm not sure I'm fooling anyone.

We've taken up half a section. A small army of hockey players, girlfriends, and friends, all here to scream our lungs out for the girl who somehow made me fall in love without even trying.

The announcer's voice booms through the arena, calling the skaters for their warm-ups. I watch as competitors lace up their skates, stretch at the boards, and nervously tap their blades on the ice.

"She's up next," Aurora says over her shoulder, smirking. "Ready to embarrass yourself in front of everyone?"

I barely hear her. My eyes are already locked on the rink, searching for Maisie.

I freeze when I finally spot her, stepping out onto the rink like she's always belonged there. The world gets a little quieter. A little slower. Her dress is an ombre pink, hugging her waist before flaring at the hips. It moves like liquid every time she shifts.

She skates toward center ice, glancing at the crowd like she's searching for something—someone.

Me.

I stand again, cup my hands around my mouth, and yell, "You got this, Maisie!"

Her head snaps in my direction, our eyes lock, and she breaks out into a smile.

I feel it in my chest. Like sunlight cracking through clouds.

The announcer's voice cuts through the air, calling her name.

She holds my gaze a heartbeat longer, then settles into her starting pose as the music begins.

And I stop breathing.

I lean forward, my heart in my throat, watching her start the routine she's talked about, studied, practiced—each movement slow and precise, rising perfectly with the first notes of "Rewrite the Stars."

I'm so focused on her, I almost miss the woman who steps into my peripheral vision.

She takes a seat beside me, placing her expensive looking purse onto her lap. Brown hair twisted neatly, a sleek coat. Older. Reserved. Watching Maisie intently, as if trying to memorize every movement.

I glance sideways. She notices, catching my eye.

"You know her?" she asks, nodding toward the rink.

I swallow hard. "Yeah. That's my girlfriend."

Her expression shifts—something flickering across her face so fast I barely catch it.

"I'm her mom."

My stomach drops straight through the bleachers.

Oh fuck.

This is her. The mom who never shows up. The one Maisie said hasn't seen her skate since she was a kid. The one she didn't invite this time because she couldn't handle being let down again.

"You're—?" I blink. "You're Maisie's mom?"

She nods slowly, still watching the rink. "I wasn't planning to come. But someone sent me a message. They told me I'd regret it if I didn't. That she's magic out there."

My throat tightens. "That was me," I say quietly. "I sent it."

She turns to look at me fully now, her brows lifting. "Is there a reason why?"

I glance back at the ice where Maisie's on the ice. She lifts her arms, then her whole body curves into motion, elegant, confident, like she's telling a story I've never heard but suddenly know by heart.

"Because I love her," I say. "And she deserves to be seen."

Her mom looks at me for a long second, and then turns her attention back to the rink.

Maisie skates like she's dancing with the music itself. Like her body knows the beat better than the speakers. Every jump lands with perfect control, every spin seems to hang in the air a little longer than it should.

I hear a collective inhale from the crowd.

She's perfect. I don't have another word for it. Every spin, every step, every little flick of her wrist feels like it's dipped in gold. I can see her breathing through the transitions, feel the emotion pouring out of her as the music swells.

When the final sequence hits, she takes a deep breath, throws her arms up, and nails a clean triple toe loop. The crowd stands, cheering as she comes to a stop.

I lift out of my seat, clapping, and whistling, and making all the goddamn noise I told her I would. "That's my girl!" I yell.

Her mom sniffles beside me, wiping under one eye.

"She always loved to skate," she murmurs. "She'd practice outside. On the sidewalk. On the tile in our kitchen with socks. I used to think it was just a phase." She pauses. "I should've come before."

I don't say anything. I don't know what to say. There's a pressure building in my chest, tight and aching. Not because of her. But because of Maisie. Because I know how much this moment will mean to her.

Maisie lifts her arms slowly, and gives a small, graceful bow toward the crowd. Her eyes flicker across the stands, searching, and then land on her mom.

Her mom's expression softens, her lips trembling.

The announcer's voice cuts through the noise, reading out the scores. Technical elements, program components. High numbers that confirm what we all saw. She nailed it, just like I knew she would.

Maisie's shoulders relax, a shy smile tugging at her lips. She steps off the ice, heading toward the boards where her coach waits, clapping quietly.

Her mom catches my eye for a brief second, but doesn't say anything. She doesn't need to. I know exactly what she's thinking. She's grateful I made her come see her daughter perform.

I catch her mom's eye one last time and nod. Maisie deserves this. She deserves to have someone here who sees her.

I'm just glad she finally does.

THIRTY-NINE

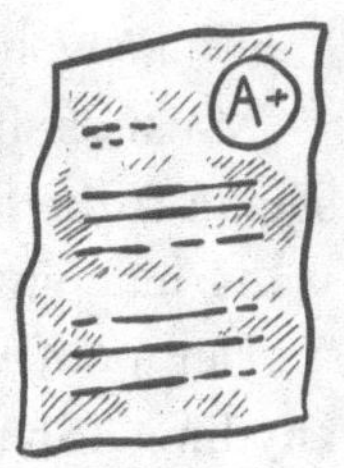

Maisie

The moment I step off the ice, the world feels like it's spinning.

Not from the routine—I've done it a thousand times. But from the rush of adrenaline, the heat under my skin, and the pounding of my heart that still hasn't settled.

My mind is reeling, thinking about the face I saw in the stands—the face I thought I'd never see up there.

My mom's here. She actually showed up.

For a moment, my mind wobbles. Like maybe I imagined it, the way I used to when I was little, squinting into the bleachers, desperate to find her among strangers. Maybe I made her up to survive the silence she left behind. But no, she was there. Right there. Next to my boyfriend.

Coach pulls me aside, claps me on the shoulder, and nods. "You did it, Maisie. That triple loop was sharp. One of your strongest skates."

I nod, breathless, still clutching the towel she handed me. My dress clings to my back, the sequins glinting under the overhead lights. I slide onto the bench near the kiss-and-cry, my body buzzing, and my eyes fixed on the scoreboard as numbers begin to roll in.

Personal best.

The crowd erupts again, but it all fades into background noise.

As the next skater steps onto the ice, I catch movement out of the corner of my eye and notice my mom, slowly making her way down the bleachers.

She pauses at the barrier, just a few feet away, and for a second, I forget how to breathe.

Everything about her is perfect—her outfit, her posture, her hair slicked into a twist without a strand out of place. But her eyes…

Her eyes are red-rimmed. Glassy. Like she's been crying.

"Maisie," she says, her voice thin.

I stare at her, my heart lodged somewhere in my throat. "You really came."

She nods, blinking fast like she's trying not to fall apart. "You were…" Her voice catches. "You were beautiful out there."

I shift awkwardly, not sure where to put my hands. "It was… okay."

"No." Her voice is firm, but soft. "It was more than okay. I—" She swallows hard, voice breaking. "I'm sorry it took me this long to see it for myself."

I stare at the wall behind her, pretending not to feel the weight in my chest.

"There's no excuse for missing all the ones that already passed. I just… I wish I had been there."

I can't meet her eyes. "I invited you every time."

"I know."

"I emailed you links. I found competitions near your work. I told you I'd pay for your gas."

"I know, sweetie."

My gaze finally lifts to hers. Her hands are trembling where they clutch her purse, knuckles white.

"Why now?" I ask her, wondering why she suddenly decided to show up.

She presses her lips together, letting out a sigh. "I got a message from a boy named Austin."

My breath catches.

"He told me you'd never ask me to come again, but that you deserved someone there. That you've been working so hard. That you shine on the ice. And that you'd never say it, but you still hoped I'd show up."

I press my hand to my chest, my heart pounding beneath my palm. "He told you that?"

She nods slowly. "It wasn't a long message. But it was enough to make me feel ashamed for not being there sooner."

My mouth opens, but the words don't come.

Austin.

He made this happen. He reached out to her.

"Oh my God," I whisper.

I take a shaky breath, scanning the hallway until my eyes land on him.

He's leaning against the vending machines. When our eyes meet, he straightens up and his lips widen into a smile.

"He's very handsome," my mom says, nodding in his direction.

I laugh softly, turning back to her. "He knows it."

She laughs under her breath. "And he clearly adores you. I watched him the entire time you were out there. He didn't blink once."

I smile, the sound of her voice easing the tight knot in my chest. I step forward and wrap my arms around her. Her hand finds the back of my head, fingers threading gently through my hair, and I close my eyes, just letting myself lean into it for a second.

"I'm really proud of you, sweetie," she whispers.

My throat tightens, my eyes stinging, but I nod as I pull back.

She's looking past me now, and when I glance over my shoulder, I see him.

Austin, standing a few feet away, watching us. His eyes are on me like always, like I'm the only thing he sees in a crowded room.

I turn and walk toward him, and he doesn't wait. He meets me halfway.

"Hey," he says, with a huge smile on his face. "You were amazing."

"You emailed my mom?"

His smile vanishes as his eyes widen and he holds his hands up. "Uh… I plead the fifth."

I breathe out a quiet laugh. Then I lift up on my toes, slide one hand behind his neck, and kiss him.

His arms wrap around my waist instantly, pulling me in like he needs me close.

"You didn't have to do that," I whisper against his lips.

"I wanted to," he murmurs. "You deserve to have people show up for you."

He brings his hands to my cheeks, thumbs brushing softly over my skin. His gaze is warm and full of so much pride it nearly undoes me. "I'm proud of you, Mais. So fucking proud."

I blink rapidly, trying to hide the flush creeping up my neck. "Stop it."

"I'm serious," he insists. "That last spin? I almost fainted."

I bury my face in his shoulder, laughing softly. "You're so dramatic."

"You were glowing out there," he says. "Like your body just knew what to do. I couldn't look away."

My cheeks go even hotter, but I don't move. I just breathe him in, hiding in the space where I feel safest.

"I love when you get like this," he teases. "All flustered and pink. It's my favorite look on you."

I pull back and narrow my eyes at him. "I hate you."

"No, you don't," he grins. "You love me. And I love you. And I'm gonna keep screaming your name from the stands until they throw me out."

I let out a laugh, my heart feeling so full I can't contain it. "You're annoying."

"Yeah, well." He boops my nose. "You're dating me, so what does that say about you?"

I roll my eyes. "I have terrible taste."

"Rude," he mutters with a frown.

I laugh, and slip my hand into his. His fingers curl around mine like they've always belonged there, tugging me close until I'm pressed to his side, warm and steady and home.

Then he goes quiet for a second. "So, uh… do I have to talk to your mom now?"

I can't help but laugh, lifting an eyebrow. "Are you scared of my mom?"

He shrugs, blowing out a breath "She's got courtroom energy. I feel like if I say the wrong thing she'll get me arrested."

"C'mon," I say with a laugh. "You'll be fine."

His hand flexes in mine and we walk toward where my mom is standing.

Austin's eyes widen, and he lifts his hand in greeting. "Hi," he says. "I'm Austin."

"I know," she replies. "We talked before."

"Right." He blows out a breath, running a hand through his hair. "Well… I just thought I'd introduce myself properly."

"Thank you for writing to me," she says after a moment. "You were right. I needed to see her. And I'm very glad I did."

Austin breathes out, relieved.

"I'm really happy she has you," she adds. "You seem like a wonderful boy."

He glances down at me, his eyes shining when he smiles. "She's the best thing that's ever happened to me."

My chest tightens, and I have to blink fast to hold it together.

He leans in, pressing a kiss to my forehead, then the tip of my nose, and finally my lips. I lean into him, kissing him back, because it feels like home. Like this is exactly where I'm supposed to be.

Because this is what I always dreamed it might feel like, to be held like this. To be wanted. To be seen. Not just by him—but by her too.

And it feels better than I ever thought it could be.

FORTY

I don't even remember the drive home.

No clue how we got from the rink to my driveway. Couldn't tell you what street we turned on, what music was playing, if I even stopped at red lights.

All I know is Maisie Wilson—girl of my fucking dreams— is sitting in my passenger seat in her leggings and a puffy jacket. Her lipstick's faded, just a hint of color left on her mouth, and I've got a white-knuckle grip on the steering wheel because if I look at her too long, I might crash the damn car.

We pull up outside the house and I kill the engine. For a second I just stare at her. She blinks back at me, her cheeks the cutest shade of pink. But before she can say anything, I climb out, jog around to her side, and open the door for her.

I keep her hand in mine as we head up the drive. The porch light's already off, since it's past midnight, and everything's quiet.

I unlock the front door and push it open, letting her go first. She slips past me, and I follow close behind, reaching back to pull the door shut with a soft thud.

I toss my keys somewhere on the counter—don't even look. They clatter and land on something that's probably not meant to be used as a key dish, but I don't care.

I step behind her, press a hand to her lower back, and lean in close.

"C'mon," I say quietly. "Upstairs."

I guide her down the hall and up the stairs and push open my bedroom door, letting her step inside first before closing the door behind us.

She's the prettiest thing I've ever seen.

I just stand there like an idiot, watching her like I don't already know every inch of her face. And then I cross the space between us, slow, and hook my thumb under her chin, tilting her face toward mine.

"You were fucking incredible tonight, baby," I say.

She lets out a tiny breathy laugh. "You already said that."

"Yeah, well." I shrug. "I meant it then. Still mean it now."

Her lips twitch like she's fighting a smile, and she tugs the sleeves of the hoodie down again, trying to disappear into it.

"You're really bad at taking compliments, you know that?" I tilt my head at her. "You deflect every time."

"I'm not deflecting," she mumbles. "I just… I'm still kind of recovering from seeing my mom, I guess." Her eyes flick up to mine—bright, nervous, blue as hell—and it knocks the wind out of me. "Thank you," she adds. "For everything."

"Anytime, baby." I slide my hand to her cheek, thumb stroking her skin. I love holding her like this. Her face fits in my palm like it was made for it.

Maisie gives a quiet little chuckle. "She liked you, by the way," she says.

My eyebrows lift. "Yeah?"

"She called you sweet," she says, scrunching her nose. "She doesn't know how annoying you are sometimes," she teases.

"Charming, baby," I say, nudging her gently with my nose. "The word you're looking for is *charming*."

She rolls her eyes, but her smile stretches. "She also said I was lucky. For having someone like you."

That stops me.

Her voice is quiet now. Honest. No teasing in sight.

I brush my thumb along her jaw, tilting her face back to mine.

"You are," I say, unable to help myself. "I'm a fucking catch."

She scoffs, but she's smiling, and it's the kind of smile that makes my knees feel a little weak.

I grin, my hands finding her hips. Her fingers bunch into the front of my t-shirt, and she pulls me closer, just slightly, like she's not totally sure she's allowed to want this.

"You tired?" I murmur, brushing my thumb along the dip of her waist.

She shakes her head. "Not even a little." Her voice is breathy, her pink lip caught between her teeth, and it about ends me.

"Thank fuck," I mutter, before leaning in and brushing my mouth against hers.

I step forward, guiding her back slowly. Her knees bump the edge of my bed and she sinks down onto it without me asking.

I reach for the jacket and t-shirt, tugging it off slowly, letting my knuckles brush the soft skin of her stomach. She lifts her arms, her eyes on mine, trusting me. I pull it over her head and toss it aside, my mouth watering when I see pink lace.

Fucking pink lace.

Her bra's delicate, the straps sliding just barely off her shoulders, and I have to close my eyes for a second just to breathe through it.

"Jesus, Maisie," I mutter, stepping between her legs.

She laughs softly, like she knows exactly what she's doing to me.

I slide one hand around her back, fingers finding the clasp. It comes undone easily—thank god—and her bra falls away, slipping down her arms.

My mouth finds her neck, kissing slowly down her jaw, collarbone, the top of her chest, until she's gasping quietly, her fingers tangling in the hem of my shirt.

I kiss her again, cupping her face with both hands. Her mouth moves against mine, eager and hot and so fucking talented. My tutor is a quick study when it comes to kissing.

Her hands slide under my t-shirt, her fingers skating across my back like she can't stop touching me.

I shift, sinking down onto my knees, and hook my thumbs into the waistband of her leggings. Her breath stutters, but she lifts her hips, letting me peel them down slowly. Over her hips, her thighs, past her knees. I slide her underwear off with them in one smooth motion, then drop them to the floor.

I lean in and press a kiss to the inside of her knee. Then a little higher. And higher.

"Baby," I murmur against her skin, "tell me what you want."

Her lips part on a moan when I kiss a few inches away from where she needs me. "You."

I groan, dipping my head to kiss the inside of her thigh again. "You already have me."

I ease a finger inside her pussy and her hips buck, needy and sweet. My tongue works her clit as I work her open, until she's begging me under her breath.

I lift onto my feet and tug my shirt over my head. Then I unbuckle my belt, drag my jeans down, and kick them off. Her eyes drop automatically, her breath catching again.

I pull open the drawer by my bed, grab a condom, and tear the foil open with my teeth. Her eyes widen slightly like she's never seen anything hotter, and, honestly, that reaction might ruin me.

I roll it on, and guide her back onto the bed. Her body melts into the pillows and I follow her down, bracing myself on my forearm as I line my cock at her entrance. I kiss her again as her hands slide up my chest, curling around the back of my neck.

Her lips part, her breath catching in her throat as I push in— slow, so slow—inch by inch until I'm fully buried inside her. My jaw clenches, muscles locked tight, because it's all I can do not to come right fucking then.

"Jesus, Maisie," I breathe, my forehead dropping to hers.

It's heaven. Pure heaven.

She's warm and wet and perfect, and being inside her feels like nothing else.

I start to move in deep, steady thrusts, and she gasps, her breath stuttering out in little whimpers. Her hands grip my back, legs wrapping around me, anchoring me to her like she never wants to let go. Which is good. Because I'm not going anywhere.

I kiss her shoulder, her jaw, the corner of her mouth, and whisper into her skin, "You're perfect. So fucking perfect."

She shivers at my words. Her grip tightens, and I feel the little stutter in her rhythm, the way her whole body reacts to every slow push of my hips. I can't stop looking at her—her flushed cheeks, those wide blue eyes going soft, the way her mouth parts with every roll of my hips.

She moans louder, and that's exactly when someone pounds on the wall.

"For fuck's sake, Austin!" Nathan yells through the drywall. "Some of us are trying to sleep!"

Maisie gasps, slapping both hands over her face.

I bury my face in her neck, laughing. "Guess they heard that."

"Oh my god," she groans. "Can we pretend that didn't happen?"

"Nope," I grin, nipping at her earlobe, dragging my hands down her waist. "But we can make it worth the noise complaint."

She tries to glare at me, but I flip us over, easing her on top of me in one smooth motion, and just like that, the attitude's gone.

She blinks down at me, wide-eyed and unsure, her thighs trembling a little where they straddle my hips. Her hands hover like she doesn't know where to put them, and I can feel her hesitation building, written all over her flushed cheeks and bitten lip.

"I don't really know what I'm doing," she admits, tugging her bottom lip between her teeth.

"Don't overthink it," I murmur. "Just do what feels good."

Her eyes search mine, and I give her a soft smile. One hand still on her waist, the other brushing the back of her thigh, I help guide her down until we're pressed together again and her mouth parts on a gasp.

"You okay?" I ask.

She nods, shifting her hips, rolling them forward, testing it out. A soft moan slips out of her.

"Fuck yeah," I groan, my head falling back, jaw tight. "Does that feel good, baby?"

She moans again, breathier this time, and nods. "Yeah," she whispers.

"Good. Keep going. Just like that."

I slide my hands down to her hips, guiding her as she does it again. Slow, dragging friction that makes my spine arch off the bed. She bites her lip, trying to stifle the sounds, but her eyes flutter shut, and I can feel how wet and tight she is around me.

"Put your hands on me," I say, my voice rough. I don't even know how I'm speaking right now because I'm numb with pleasure. I tap my chest twice. "Right here."

She plants her palms flat on my chest, bracing herself. Then she lifts up slightly and sinks back down.

My mouth parts on a groan. "Ah, fuck."

My hands slide to her full ass, helping her move as she rocks against me again—harder this time—and she gasps, her back arching.

"Fuck, look at you," I moan, dragging her hips down harder, grinding up into her. "That's it. Ride me, baby. Take what you need."

Her movements get more confident, more fluid. Her fingers dig into my chest, nails scraping lightly over my skin as she lifts off my cock and slams back down.

I can't take my eyes off her. Her flushed skin, the way her tits bounce with every thrust, the way her mouth keeps parting like she's too overwhelmed to speak.

She gasps when I thrust up to meet her, her whole body jolting.

"You like that?" I ask with a cocky smirk. "You want me deeper?"

She nods frantically, her hair falling into her face. I push it back, my fingers curling around the back of her neck as she moves again.

"You're fucking gorgeous," I whisper, watching her fall apart on top of me. "Every fucking inch of you. I want to see you come just like this."

Her thighs are trembling around my hips, her fingers clawing at my chest as she bounces on me harder, messier. Her eyes flutter. Her mouth falls open, and I know she's close.

Her body shudders, her thighs tightening around my hips as she moans through it, falling apart right there on top of me. It's the hottest fucking thing I've ever seen.

I don't even give her time to come down.

I grab her waist, flip us in one smooth motion, and press her back into the mattress, her hair fanned across the pillow. She blinks up at me, dazed and breathless, her skin flushed and fucking gorgeous.

"Too much?" I murmur, brushing my nose against hers.

She shakes her head. "No. I want more."

Fuck.

I settle between her thighs again and push back in with a groan, burying myself deep, the stretch still tight, still perfect.

She wraps her legs around me, heels digging into my back, and I start to move, letting her feel every inch. Her fingers twist in my hair as I thrust again, harder this time.

She squeezes her eyes closed and lets out a moan. "Austin… you feel so good."

I swear I lose my damn mind.

"You fit me like you were made for me," I groan, my lips brushing her ear. "Every part of you is perfect. Mine."

She tilts her hips and I slam deeper, hitting just the right spot. She gasps, her nails clawing down my back.

She lets out a desperate whimper, the sound crawling up my spine. "Austin—please—"

I don't even know what she's begging for anymore. Doesn't matter. I give her everything I've got. My hands grip her hips, my body flush against hers, and our mouths crash together between broken gasps and half-formed words.

She breaks the kiss, her head falling back against the pillow with a gasp.

"Austin—" she moans, voice high and desperate.

"I've got you," I murmur, grinding my hips deeper, holding her through it.

Her back arches and she clenches around me, coming hard with a choked cry, shaking beneath me. Her lashes flutter, mouth parted, eyes squeezed shut like she's falling apart at the seams.

"Fuck," I groan, watching her lose it. "That's it, baby. Let go."

She shudders again, her pussy squeezing around me—and that's all it takes.

Her orgasm tips me straight over the edge.

I groan her name against her lips, thrusting deep one last time before I come, everything inside me unraveling at once. My entire body tightens, my hips stutter, and I ride it out slow, still buried in her.

She clings to me, her arms tight around my shoulders, and her breath shaky against my neck.

Neither of us moves for a long moment as the pleasure courses through us. Eventually, we catch our breath and collapse onto the bed.

I wrap an arm around her and pull her toward me. I kiss her temple. Then her cheek. Then the tip of her nose where her freckles are the most pronounced, because I can't help it.

She laughs, fluttering her eyes closed. "You're clingy after sex."

"Yeah, I am," I admit, brushing my lips over hers again. "Can't help it. I can't seem to get enough of you… and I don't want to." I press another kiss to her forehead, my hand tracing slow circles down her spine. "I love you," I whisper.

Her eyes blink open, blue and soft and sleepy. She smiles so softly it makes my chest ache. "I love you too," she says quietly.

I tug the blanket over us and tuck her against my chest. "Good," I murmur, pressing a kiss to the top of her head. "Because I'm not letting you go."

She curls closer, and as her breathing evens out, I stare at the ceiling, completely wrecked in the best way.

I close my eyes with a smile on my face, knowing that I could do this forever.

Just me and her.

My Cherry.

My Freckles.

My girl.

FORTY-ONE

Maisie

"Could you not breathe in my direction?"

Cole doesn't even bother looking up from his beer. "Hard to do when your perfume's choking the oxygen out of the room."

Aurora narrows her eyes at him. "I hope your skate blade snaps and takes out your ankle, Reaper."

He finally looks up, keeping his expression flat. "Charming as always, Viper."

"Don't call me that."

"Then stop hissing at me."

"Bite me."

"Not even with someone else's mouth."

Ryan groans into his beer. "Jesus Christ, can you two chill for one night?"

Cole pushes his chair back, his jaw tight as he heads toward the bar.

Aurora stands a few seconds later. "I need a bathroom break before I actually poison someone."

Logan slides in beside Austin, flashing his usual cocky grin as he slams his beer down on the table. "Five bucks they make out before the next round."

"She's got a boyfriend," Isabella reminds us with narrowed eyes.

Nathan leans back against the booth, his eyes flicking to Logan with a dry smile. "Five bucks Aurora murders him first."

Austin snorts beside me, burying his face in my neck. "They're gonna get us all banned."

I laugh, running my fingers through his hair. His thigh's warm against mine, his arm slung over the back of the booth, and his fingertips are brushing my bare shoulder where my dress slipped.

I lean into him, feeling the steady beat of his heart through his chest.

I never thought I'd be part of something like this. And I definitely never thought someone like him would want someone like me. I never thought I'd be in love. But here I am, with a group of friends and a boyfriend that loves me.

Across the booth, I spot Ryan and Isabella tangled up like they're in their own world. She's curled into his lap, lazy and soft, doodling tiny hearts on his hand with her fingertip. He looks down at her like she's the only thing in the room. Like nothing else even exists.

That used to make me ache.

Now it just makes me warm.

Because Austin's watching me the same way.

He tugs my hand into his lap, tracing his thumb over the back of it. I think he's going to lace our fingers together or make some stupid joke about my nails.

But he lifts my hand instead, brings it to his mouth, and presses a kiss to the base of my ring finger.

"A ring would look so pretty here," he murmurs with a smile.

I stare at him, stunned. "Calm down," I laugh. "We just started dating."

"I know." He kisses it again. "I just know what I want. I'm gonna put a ring on this finger someday, Freckles."

My heart thuds against my chest. I try to laugh it off. "Okay, you're officially drunk."

He holds my eyes, shaking his head. "I'm serious."

I swallow, my cheeks still burning, and turn toward him, half-hoping someone will change the subject before my brain explodes.

Logan groans loudly, running a hand through his hair. "Anyone want a beer? I'm heading to the bar. Definitely need something stronger if I'm gonna survive this love fest."

Nathan looks up from his phone, lifting an eyebrow. "You've had three already."

Logan smirks, a mischievous glint in his eye. "You watching me, Hayes? That's cute." He flashes a grin and saunters off toward the bar.

Nathan's cheeks flush just the slightest bit, caught off guard. I notice it out of the corner of my eye, but I look away fast—not my business.

Austin's hand settles lightly under my chin. He tilts my face up, eyes searching mine.

"You okay, baby?" he asks.

I nod, feeling my lips curl into a smile. "Yeah," I say. "I'm just… happy. I never had this before."

He furrows his brows. "What?"

I shrug, my heart still thumping. "This. Friends. A group." I swallow hard, keeping my eyes locked on his. "A person."

He doesn't laugh or make a joke like I expect. Instead, his lips brush against my temple. "You've got all of it now." His eyes soften and a beautiful smile spreads across his face.

"You've got me." He scoffs out a laugh, shaking his head. "Thank fuck I failed that anatomy test."

I let out a laugh. "You're literally the first person to ever say that."

He turns toward me, arching a brow. "I mean it. If I hadn't bombed that class, I wouldn't have gotten suspended. Wouldn't have needed a tutor. Wouldn't have met you."

My eyes drop to our hands, tangled together on the table, his big, warm fingers wrapped over mine. "I think we would've met anyway," I say. "Especially since we were already speaking online as Cherry and Six."

He tilts his head. "You know what? You're right. We were meant to meet someday. It was fate."

I shoot him a look, pressing my lips together to keep from laughing. "Austin Rhodes believes in fate?"

"Only when it comes to you."

I laugh, shaking my head. I never thought Austin Rhodes would say things like this to me. "I was terrified to meet you in person," I admit. "I thought maybe you'd built me up into someone else, and if we finally met in person, you'd take one look at me and our conversations would stop."

His hand cups my chin and he turns my face to his, eyes locked on mine. "Hey. Don't say that."

I swallow hard, whispering, "I just… I know I'm not—"

"You're gorgeous," he interrupts, voice low but sure. "You're smart as hell. You're the only reason I didn't flunk out of school and the only reason your bedroom wall needs plastering."

I groan, burying my face in his neck, the memory flashing through me of the headboard slamming against the wall when he lost control. "I still haven't recovered."

He chuckles against my skin. "I have. And also, I'd like to schedule a repeat performance, maybe next weekend?"

I smack his arm playfully. He catches my hand, brings it up, and kisses my knuckles gently. It's such a small thing, but it sends this warm rush straight to my chest.

He leans in close, his breath brushing my ear. "I love you, Cherry."

I smile, remembering all the nights I stared at a glowing screen, wondering who he really was. Wondering if we'd ever meet. I used to reread his messages and try to imagine his voice, try to picture the stranger on the other side.

And now he's here. Real. Mine.

"I love you too, Six."

EPILOGUE

Austin

I check my pocket again.

Ring's still there.

That makes five times in the last ten minutes in case anyone's counting.

It's currently humming like a grenade in my suit pocket. A sparkly, terrifying, life-altering grenade.

I'm pacing the living room while my girl takes an entire lifetime to get ready.

"Babe," I yell toward the bedroom, dragging a hand through my hair. "How long are you gonna take? We're gonna be late, and I swear to God if I miss the crab cakes—"

"Then you'll survive," Maisie calls back.

"You look hot in anything," I tell her. "Or nothing. Especially nothing."

Kevin—our rescue dog—lifts his head from his little blanket cave and glares at me.

"You could at least pretend to be supportive," I mutter.

He groans and rolls back over.

I rip my eyes away, glancing toward the bedroom door that's still shut. Maisie's been in there for fucking forever. Getting ready. For dinner. For a normal night out. That's what she thinks this is. But she has no idea what she's stepping into.

This is torture. Not just waiting on her—I mean, yeah, that too—but sitting here with this box in my pocket like I'm not two inches away from combusting.

I pat my pocket once, then twice, then drag my hand down my face and groan like a man on the brink.

Because I *am* on the brink.

Of proposing. Of combusting. Of texting the guys again even though Cole told me he'd block me if I did.

I grab my phone off the coffee table and open the group chat.

Me: how long does it take for a girl to put on eyeliner? I'm gonna puke.

Cole: And they say romance is dead.

Ryan: You don't need to worry. She's going to say yes.

Logan: And then realize she's stuck with you forever. Poor girl.

Nathan: She's the best thing that ever happened to you. Don't screw it up.

Cole: Too late.

Ryan: You're fine. Breathe and drink some water.

Cole: And don't cry. Jesus Christ.

Me: I'm not crying, but like… hypothetically if I did. It's fine right?

Nathan: Yes.

Cole: No.

Logan: I'm crying for you rn and it hasn't even happened yet.

I lock my phone and let it fall on the couch beside me.

I glance at the time. WE're officially thirteen minutes behind schedule. And still no sign of my girl.

"Freckles," I call out toward the bedroom, "I swear to god, if I get any hotter in this blazer, I'm gonna die in it and haunt this apartment forever."

She just laughs from the other side of the door. Little shit. My lips tip up into a smirk anyway.

A little over five years ago, I flunked anatomy, got kicked off the team, and met her. I thought she hated me. And maybe she did, a little, but everything changed between us in a short amount of time. I think about the first time I kissed her. The first time she said I love you. The first time she called this place home.

I used to think love was a weakness, fragile… scary. I was so terrified of opening up to another person that way. But then Maisie looked at me, and everything in my chest cracked open.

I don't have words for the way she changed me. I just know that every cell in my body bends toward her.

I breathe for her.

I skate for her.

I *exist* for her.

And now I want forever. I want her name next to mine. I want to call her my wife and see her wear this ring and never, ever take it off.

The bedroom door clicks open.

"Sorry, sorry," she calls. "I couldn't find my—"

I look up. And my heart stops.

"Holy *fuck*," I whisper.

Maisie pauses in the doorway, cheeks pink, lips curled in a shy smile. She's wearing a dark red dress that hugs her curves and dips at the collarbone, soft satin that flows when she walks, and she has her hair pinned up, with a few loose strands falling around her face.

"You say that every time," she teases, smoothing her dress as she steps into the room.

"Because you take my breath away every time," I say, already standing, closing the distance between us in three quick strides.

I stand there for a minute. Just… looking. Like it's the first time and the hundredth time all at once.

She lifts her gaze to meet mine. "Why are you looking at me like that? Should I be worried?"

Fuck. Play it cool, Austin. I let out a laugh, shaking my head. "Nah. Just admiring my girl."

I wrap my arms around her waist and pull her in, kissing the side of her neck.

"We're gonna miss your reservation," she says, her voice a little raspy.

"I'll rebook. Priorities." I lean down and press my mouth to hers. "You're my priority."

She melts into my arms the second my lips meet hers, and my hands slide down to her hips. How long will it take to take this dress off her?

"Mmm," she murmurs against my lips. "Is this part of the plan?"

"Every plan involves kissing you," I say, my lips brushing her cheek. "Even the retirement one."

She loops her arms around my neck, pulling me close. I swear she knows something. She might not know about the hole that's burning in my pocket, but she's aware of *something.* Especially since I practically demanded Aurora and Isabella take Maisie out to get her nails done for tonight. I wanted my girl to be prepared.

"How was practice?" she asks, a little skeptical.

"Good," I reply with a shrug. "Coach yelled at me for trying to chirp the new guy, but… come on. It's tradition."

I still can't believe I get to play for The New York Storm with Ryan. Being on the same team as him felt like a pipe dream when we graduated, and yet here we are.

I'm on a nationally ranked team, and I live in a beautiful house with the love of my goddamn life, who owns her own bookstore café.

She's still looking at me and I can't breathe. My eyes lock onto hers, remembering the first time I ever saw them and how they took my breath away.

"I'm so fucking happy I knocked you in the head all those years ago," I say, blowing out a breath.

She laughs, her eyes crinkling and her cheeks going pink, and I swear, if I wasn't already planning to propose tonight, I'd drop to one knee *right now*.

But not yet.

Not until I've said something halfway coherent. Not until I've told her that I want to be her person forever—through training seasons and off seasons, good days and hell days, and every single day until I'm old and grumpy.

I can't wait to see wrinkles around those blue eyes, to come home to her every single night and kiss those pretty pink lips. To have kids with her, to argue with her, to have make up sex with her. I want it all. Every single part of it. With her.

Maisie grabs her clutch and turns toward the door. "You ready to go?"

I check my pocket one last time.

Ring's still there.

God, I hope I don't mess this up.

I exhale. "Yeah," I say, slipping my fingers through hers. "Let's go."

She thinks we're heading to some fancy dinner with white tablecloths and overpriced crab cakes.

Instead, I'm taking her back to the rink. The same one where I met her, where I skated with her, where everything between us really started.

Ryan set up the champagne and Isabella made me rehearse what I was gonna say so I didn't sound like an idiot.

Nathan got me the keys—perks of having a dad who runs the team—and Logan gave me a pep talk about making it romantic but not too cheesy.

Aurora helped string fairy lights across the boards and Cole set up a camera so we'll have the whole thing recorded—every stumble, every kiss, every second of me making the best play of my life.

When we walk out onto that ice tonight, it'll be just her and me.

And when the music plays, and she realizes what's happening, I'll drop to one knee in the middle of center ice and ask the only question that's ever really mattered.

And if all goes right, I'll skate off that rink tonight with a fiancée.

No pressure.

The End

Acknowledgements

When I started writing this book, I had no idea just how much I would come to love them. These characters completely took over my brain and their story was just so incredibly fun to write.

Austin and Maisie had me giggling like a five year old over the smallest interactions. I had never been so… blushy (definitely not a word, but let's roll with it) over a book before—especially not one I had written.

But these two just made my heart utter mush and I adore them so so so so much!

Maisie's POV was especially close to my heart. Writing her character felt like putting every single one of my thoughts and feelings onto the paper, and honestly… it's a little scary because it feels like putting myself out there for the whole world to read and judge and critique.

But I just hope that her story and character makes you feel seen, too. If Maisie could find her voice, her confidence, and her love, then I hope it reminds you that you can as well.

Thank you so much for picking up this book and I really hope you enjoyed reading it. I hope you stick around for the rest of the Colton U gang because they're so fun!

Thank you to my incredible editor, Sophie, for taking my messy manuscript and making it readable.

Thank you to my Patreon members for being so supportive of me and cheering me on every time I share a little snippet of the book. Sometimes the imposter syndrome bug bites me in the ass, and it's just really nice knowing I have readers who enjoy my books. Thank you so much for sticking with me!

And finally if you enjoyed this book, then please leave a review and I hope you stick around for the rest of the series.

About the Author

Stephanie Alves is an avid reader and writer of smutty, contemporary romance books. She was born in England, but was raised by her loud Portuguese parents. She can speak both languages fluently, though she tends to mix both languages when speaking. She loves to write romantic comedies with happy endings, witty banter and sizzling chemistry that will make you blush. When she's not writing, she can be found either reading, or watching rom coms with her two adorable dogs cuddled up beside her.

You can find her here:
Instagram.com/Stephanie.alves_author
Stephaniealvesauthor.com